11

Kylie Brant

Also by Kylie Brant:

Chasing Evil
Touching Evil
Facing Evil

Cover art by Middle Child Marketing, LLC

ISBN:
978-0-9906607-9-8

*For Nate, our soon-to-be only favorite son-in-law.
We're so excited to have you in the family.
Welcome to the craziness :)*

Acknowledgements:

This plot careened across the world and then ping-ponged across the United States. And it seemed with each new locale I had a fresh set of research to do. My great appreciation goes to Virginia Lockett for the fascinating details about Da Nang. I wasn't able to use everything, but you gave me enough information to convince me I need to make a trip there!

For Chris Herndon, for being a constant for all things corpse-related, thanks so much! No blowflies this time around, alas. But there's always the next book.

Thanks also go to Jessica Bae Welter, sister-in-law extraordinaire, for facilitating the answers regarding Vietnamese language. You are ever so much more useful than your husband ☺.

And I'd be remiss not to thank Jill and Jordan, helpless victims to my crazed deadline process. Next time will be different, guys. (I hope.)

PROLOGUE

"Once again, you disappoint, Eleven."

The slight push he gave sent her body swaying from the length of chain like a pendulum. She hung upside down, sheathed in a clear thick plastic tarp that was held in place with bungee cords. Her ankles were suspended from a metal beam that ran the length of the building. Discipline was harsh and frequent. She braced herself for what was to come. Knew the agony would outweigh her anticipation of it.

"Who helped you?"

The lie was immediate. "Nobody."

The first blow landed, a fist to her belly. Oxygen rushed out of her like steam from a boiling teakettle. "Try again."

She was unable to draw a breath. Just shook her head in mute protest.

"Refusing to answer is just another form of disobedience." The next punch caught her in the left kidney. But his voice sounded more amused than angry. He relished the punishments. They were meted out in varying intensity for the smallest infractions.

Finally able to speak, she gasped out, "Just… exploring…"

"With. Who?" The question was punctuated with a series of slaps. Her face. Breasts. Butt.

"Alone."

"Should your punishment focus on your lies or your disobedience, I wonder?"

From her position, he was visible only from the knees down. She could feel the blood shifting slowly toward her upper body. In minutes numbness would start to creep into her shoulders and arms.

Although she'd be expected to bargain the length and severity of her penalty, her words were meant to spare another. "I'm not lying."

The others were silent. But she knew they huddled at the front of their cells watching, because he'd ordered them to. Punishments were group affairs. Lessons to be seared into psyches, designed to break spirits. To reduce them to their basest states. Cowering primitive beings whose every action was designed to avoid pain.

"Disobedience it is, then. Whose turn to choose the weapon? Four?"

"The whip!" The woman's voice was gleeful. "No, no, the antenna!"

"Four, you've chosen wisely."

He bent then, reaching out to turn her body until he could peer into her face. "Eleven, thank Four for her input." As always her captor wore a mask that covered his head. This one was adorned with a curved black beak and a rainbow of turquoise feathers. A beautiful frame for a soulless monster.

"Eleven!"

Nausea threatened. It wasn't that the humiliation was worse than the abuse. Nothing was worse than the pain. But each time she obeyed him, in even the smallest way, she felt a tiny shred of humanity stripped away. Soon there'd be nothing left of her. She'd be hulled out, an empty shell.

"Thank you, Four." *You blood-sucking bitch.*

He straightened, and her muscles tensed as she heard the slight whistle the weapon made in the air before contact. Then agony exploded. Her back bowed, and a primal howl escaped her.

"Begin your lessons."

The second blow landed, and pain radiated beneath the skin, dancing across nerve endings. Skipping along synapses. "You are my lord and master."

The third blow had her body swinging. "I am… nothing. I exist…only…to serve you."

The blows were coming faster now. Biting back the screams served only to enrage him so she let them echo and re-echo in the cavernous enclosure.

"Who are you?" The metal whipped across her back, her stomach, her thighs. "Whom do you belong to?"

"I am Eleven. I am yours."

There was a roar of blood rushing to her head, ringing in her ears. The words were little more than whispered croaks. The blows rained upon her and unconsciousness crept along the hem of her suffering. She reached for it. Yearned to cloak herself in its veil of nothingness.

But before the tidal wave of blackness consumed her, a last tiny spark of defiance flashed through her mind.

Mia. My name is Mia.

1

Five years later

The light tap at his door had Jude Bishop hissing out a disgusted breath. "Yes, Shannon?"

He swiveled his chair from his computer toward the entrance of his office as it opened and the regal blonde stepped inside. As usual, after one quick furtive glance at his face she averted her gaze, waiting until the door snicked shut behind her before speaking. "There's a man here to see you. He doesn't have an appointment, but he's insistent that you'll meet with him."

Jude waited in silence for a count of twenty as his firm's newest employee looked at everything in the office besides him. He mentally damned his long-time secretary's daughter for picking this month to give birth. "Does he have a name?"

"Adam Raiker. I thought maybe I should call security." Her ice blue gaze landed on him for an instant before immediately flitting away. "He looks like a rough character."

Humor warred with annoyance. "If by rough you mean dangerous, then I'd agree. Send him in."

Alarm widened her eyes. "Oh, but he's…" One hand gestured toward her face.

His earlier flicker of amusement faded. "Disfigured? Then he and I can be bookends, can't we? Send him in." When she turned, one hand on the doorknob, he added, "Oh, and Shannon. See Kacee about a different job in the firm. Something more in keeping with your… sensibilities."

Her erect posture eased just a bit in what he suspected was relief. But she made no comment as she

4

opened the door and spoke in her cultured voice, "Mr. Bishop will see you now, Mr. Raiker."

Jude rose and started across the room. As the other man filled the doorway, then stepped through it, the corner of his mouth lifted. "You scared my secretary."

Raiker cocked a brow and shut the door behind him. "If she scares that easily, how she'd come to be working for you?"

"I imagine she's been asking herself that daily." Jude took the man's outstretched hand, genuine pleasure filling him. "Been a while, Adam."

The other man set his briefcase down and leaned on his cane, engulfing Jude's hand in a tight grip. "Too long. A year and a half? A little longer, I think. New York. The Brownlow case."

Jude wasn't fooled. If pressed, Raiker would be able to recite the day and time they'd last met. The hell the man had been through on his final case for the FBI was written on his visage, but his mind was unmarred. "When it went to trial, yeah. You destroyed the scumbag's defense. It was a thing of beauty."

"We all had a part."

Jude waved the man to the leather chairs arranged in front of the marble fireplace and followed him to a seat.

Raiker looked around, his laser blue gaze missing nothing. "New office. High rent building. Business must be good."

"No complaints." He felt a twinge of humor. "At least not from me." Without asking, he walked to an ornately carved rosewood table that held several decanters. Poured two fingers of Scotch into a couple glasses and returned to hand one to Raiker.

There was a bond between them that ran deeper than friendship. One that existed despite the other man's disapproval of some of Jude's methods. As the head of the renowned Mindhunters agency, Raiker worked cases at the invitation of law enforcement entities. As such his services always operated squarely within the law.

Jude wasn't without scruples. He picked his clients very carefully. His work often paralleled that of law enforcement. At other times he operated in the shadows. Where niceties like legalities were considered suggestions, rather than hard and fast rules.

The other man let his cane rest against his chair, and brought the glass to his lips. Drank. His brows rose. "You have better taste in Scotch these days, too."

"I learned from the best." Jude sipped companionably and studied his friend. He was Jude's senior by less than a decade, but the scar that traced down Raiker's face, the one across his throat and the black eye patch he wore were visual reminders that they were unmatched in experience.

Or... He fingered the web of scars on his left cheek absently. Perhaps not totally unmatched. They'd both once been at the mercy of a monster.

Raiker drank again, lowered his glass. "Tell me what you know about Russell Deleon."

Jude was too used to the man's abrupt transitions to be thrown by this one. "Deleon. Forbes had him breaking the billionaire bracket this year. Outwardly charming, but ruthless. Has his finger in a lot of pies, all of them legal from what I've heard. Although," he lifted a shoulder and drank again. "What's legal for Wall Street folks would get most others a lengthy sentence."

"And his daughter?"

Thoughts of that particular client still rankled. "You had to remind me. She'd be…twenty-seven, twenty-eight by now. And likely still a train wreck, although I haven't seen her for years."

The other man settled more comfortably into the leather chair, the heavily cut glass nestled in one hand. "Refresh my memory."

Jude snorted. His friend's memory was like a stone tablet. Once an experience had been etched on it, it was there for eternity. His gaze landed on the patchwork of scars covering the back of Adam's hand clutched around the glass. In Raiker's case, perfect recall wouldn't necessarily be a blessing.

"Russell Deleon made the initial contact. Or," he corrected himself, "the family lawyer did. Creighton Upton. Said Mia Deleon was suffering from anxiety. Depression. Wanted security until she was feeling better."

Adam's expression was unreadable. "They didn't offer any details beyond that?"

He gave a negligible lift of his shoulder. "I filled in the blanks myself." He never accepted a job without knowing who—and what—he was dealing with. And handling Mia Deleon had been like balancing a basket of explosives. He paused to drink, more deeply now. Remembering the Deleon case could do that to him. "She'd been a party girl. High society. If not empty-headed, then determined to appear that way. Always in the press. Regular arrests for drunk and disorderly, wild parties, high speed chases… I imagine her behavior contributed to several ulcers for her father." The man's pretty pampered princess of a daughter had been a willful out-of-control brat.

"And then she disappeared."

Nodding, Jude tapped an index finger against his glass. "For three years her father didn't hear from her. But there were regular withdrawals from her account. Transactions on her cards. Reported sightings in Vegas. The occasional yacht party. Until her father cut her off. About a year after he did, she came home."

"And landed herself in the middle of a media frenzy once again."

"A way of life for her." Jude drained his glass. A natural reaction to memories of the woman. "Came back with her head shaved, dressed in rags spouting a wild story about being abducted and held captive with several other women. Only problem was she couldn't narrow down the area where she might have been held. Or even the state." He rose and crossed to the decanter again. Adam was right. It was damn fine Scotch.

He tipped more into the other man's glass before filling his own. Replaced the container. "Difficult to separate the facts from the crap printed in the rags devoted to reporting on the rich and famous. Didn't spend much time trying, to tell you the truth. There was a manhunt for this criminal that she claimed was responsible. It fizzled, because every damn lead she gave them went nowhere. Then came the private investigators, hired with Daddy's money, most likely. As far as I know they found nothing to support her claims."

"And then she became your client."

He gave an imperceptible wince. "She did. It was after her that I devised a more stringent screening of the person requiring security prior to accepting a new job."

Raiker's grin was not without sympathy. "Made your life hell, did she?"

"She ran through six bodyguards." Jude emphasized the words with accompanying fingers. "Male. Female.

Caucasian. Non-Caucasian. It didn't matter. After a period of time she'd request someone different."

The other man's expression was contemplative. "What was her behavior like at the time?"

Of course Raiker would ask that. The man had been the Bureau's top profiler. Right up to the time that he'd been captured and tortured by the child killer he'd been trailing. Adam had intimate knowledge into the workings of the criminal mind.

Jude had personal experience in the area, himself. "I met the woman several times. Whenever a new security detail was changed, actually. As well as a final occasion." He hadn't been surprised when she'd disappeared again. He'd made it possible. "She was...erratic. Alternately demanding and paranoid. Emotionally unwell, I'd guess. According to my people, she'd spend hours, even days locked in her bedroom. No security measures we took seemed to be enough. She was highly anxious." A memory slipped in. Of Mia, one leg drawn up on her chair. Arms clutched around her knee as she stared at him expressionlessly. Her face would have been beautiful if there was a flicker of life in it. But it'd been blank. Empty. She hadn't shied away from looking at his disfigurement as so many others did. Jude had always had the impression that she didn't see him at all.

He drank, uneasy at the mental image. "How she struck me? Spooky."

Raiker leaned forward, face intense. "Your best guess. What really happened in the time she was gone?" He made an impatient gesture with his hand. "I know you didn't come on board until later. But you met with her. Several times. What's your take? Party girl who came home with a story once her rich daddy shut off the money spigot? A sensationalist intent on landing herself back in the news? Or…something else?"

Gently swirling the amber liquid in his glass, Jude considered the questions for a minute. "All three maybe. But…" He remembered her skittish behavior. Her difficulty with decision-making. The alternating paranoia and defiance. "I think something happened to her." The undamaged side of his mouth quirked up. "How's that for definitive? Maybe she disappeared on her own. But when she came back, she wasn't the same person, at least from what I could put together from news stories. She rarely went out and when she did she was surrounded by a security detail. Which in itself, of course, attracted attention, I guess."

His words brought a gleam to Raiker's eye. "You just described the behavior of a person who might have sustained some sort of trauma."

"Or someone with a mental illness." Jude's response was dry. In truth, to this day he wasn't certain which described Mia Deleon. "My turn for questions. Why your interest? After all this time?"

In answer, Raiker set his glass on the Oriental rug beside his chair and reached for his leather briefcase. Snapped it open and took out a file folder, handing it to Jude.

He flipped it open. Stared dispassionately at the photo inside. "It's always dead bodies with you."

"Not always." The other man's voice was amused. "My agency consults on the occasional kidnapping and serial rapist."

Damn occasionally, Jude knew. Still, he studied the photograph carefully. A thought stabbed through him then, and his gaze rose to his friend's. "This isn't Mia, is it?"

Adam shook his head. "This woman has been dead about four years. Very well preserved, though. That tarp worked to mummify her."

"I'll have to take your word for it." The corpse looked leathery, with suspect slashes of dried yellowish ooze mottling the body. Yet he was oddly relieved to discover it wasn't Mia Deleon. Despite the professional stress she'd caused him, he preferred to believe she'd finally found some peace.

"Look at the next picture."

Obeying, Jude saw a photo of a skull, with only bits of skin intact. He glanced up. "Other people invite friends to view slide shows from their vacation. Disney World. The Grand Canyon."

Raiker's teeth flashed. "You wouldn't want to see a slideshow of where I've been." And Jude was reminded again of all the man had endured. Nodding toward the photo, Raiker said, "See that area circled on the skull?"

Jude peered closer. "I see the circle. No idea what it's supposed to signify."

"Caitlin Fleming is working the case. One of my forensic anthropologists. Someone left that young woman in a mineshaft in Wyoming. A pair of trespassing spelunkers discovered her. Two things in Caitlin's report caught my attention. One was that no hair was on or near the body. Given the state of decomposition there should have been clumps, or at least strands still clinging to the remaining scalp. Barring that, some should have been found in the tarp. Or at least in the vicinity."

"Okay." He'd take the other man's word for it. Raiker was the one with the world- renowned forensics agency.

"Caitlin found a mark on a scrap of scalp. She's narrowed it down to ink. The kind used by tattoo artists."

Jude stilled. And at last the reason for his friend's visit became apparent. "That was part of Mia Deleon's account when she returned home. That her captor kept her head shaved. Tattooed with a number."

"Eleven." Satisfied, Raiker sat back in his chair and reached for his glass again. "Caitlin's findings with this corpse reminded me of Deleon's story."

Jude handed the photos back to the man. Watched him slip them back in the briefcase. "Then you should have recalled that nothing ever came of following up on that story, despite some pretty intensive investigating. Upton told me that Mia's father tried to have her committed once she'd returned. Twice." He sipped, watching Adam over the rim of his glass. "She's not exactly a reliable source."

"Still." The inexorable tone was familiar. "I want to speak with her myself. I've had no luck. Either she's off the grid or she's left the country, although not under her own name." He paused a beat. "I figured since you have some expertise in that area, you could help me find her."

Security wasn't the only service at which Jude's agency excelled. He also had a reputation for discovery. People, things, information. The flip side of that skill was an acquired expertise in helping them disappear.

"I could." Jude sipped, deliberately holding the man's gaze. "But I don't divulge that kind of information about my clients."

"I'm not asking you for client secrets." Impatience threaded the words. "I want you to contact her. Tell her we met. Ask if she'll talk to me about this case. That's all."

Jude frowned. "False modesty aside, once I find her I can't promise she'd consider your request. Unpredictability is her MO."

"Just a phone call," the man pressed. "I can be very persuasive." He nodded toward the photos in the closed brief case. "The family of the woman in those photos deserves closure. Even if I end up agreeing that Deleon is a nutcase, at least I've eliminated the possibility that the two are connected."

Jude thought of the unidentified woman in the mineshaft. And he had to agree with his friend. Everyone required answers. Even the dead.

"I'll see what I can do."

It seemed to be enough for the other man, and they both finished their drinks in a companionable silence. Perhaps because Raiker knew with Jude on the job, it wasn't a matter of *if* Mia Deleon would be found.

It was when.

* * * *

The woman known as Samantha Simmons pedaled down the Da Nang streets, winding through a snarl of street vendors packing up their wares and narrowly missing a collision with a brightly colored four-wheeled taxi. The driver's spate of furious Vietnamese warred with the shrieks of the egrets wheeling against the sky. Palm trees flashed by as she rode further out of the urban area toward her high-rise apartment building near the beach. For once the charm of the coastline dotted with palm trees was lost on her. Her mind had only room for one thought.

Dr. Halston was dead.

The words hammered through her until her insides throbbed with the bleak truth. He hadn't been too busy to continue their now occasional correspondence. He hadn't grown ill, despite the fact he'd been over eighty. The reason he hadn't responded to her last two messages was because he couldn't.

...killed in a home invasion...

Her dry eyes burned, blind to the scenery flashing by. Her knees pumped powerfully on the bike, an outlet for the violent emotion churning through her. It had taken her nearly a month to get curious enough to look for other possible explanations for Halston's unusual silence. A simple Google search to discover it.

...friends and family are invited to gather to commemorate his life...

Samantha had been neither. She bent over the handlebars, letting the hot sticky air whip through her hair. She'd been an anonymous cry for help in the vastness of cyberspace. Halston was dead. But because of him she still lived. Had perhaps even found a sliver of contentment.

She'd never be able to articulate how much she owed to a man she'd never met. Or how bereft she felt now that even that tenuous lifeline had been clipped.

Whizzing by her building, Samantha then coasted for several more blocks before turning and heading toward home on the road that ran in back of it. It was a mistake to form attachments. She accepted that as one of the few absolutes of her existence. So this rush of emotion was surprising. Unfamiliar. And utterly devastating.

Braking to a stop in front of her favorite cà phê, she walked the bike to lean it against the fence separating the property from the sidewalk. Crossing the small cobblestoned patio area, she sat down at one of the scattered wooden tables. The breathtaking view of the Sơn Trà mountain and peninsula to the north failed to soothe her as it normally did. Her tee shirt was damp with perspiration. The grass umbrella gave little relief from the brutal heat, which hovered in the nineties, with humidity to match. Her apartment had air-conditioning, but thoughts of her empty home were unappealing. Hoa, her roommate, was a flight attendant. Gone for days at a time, she wasn't due in until later this afternoon.

A narrow street and small courtyard were all that separated Samantha from her building. Trees obscured her view of the lower level, but counting up three floors she could clearly make out her small terrace. The potted palm. The small metal table and chairs that sat on the outdoor woven mat.

"Sam-an-tha." Quyen, the owner came out of the cà phê to greet her with a big smile. "You are hot?" You need cà phê đá? I bring quick." The woman bustled off.

The traditional Vietnamese iced coffee with cream was usually a favorite. But Samantha could feel no pleasure in what had come to be an almost daily custom. She felt disconnected in an odd way that had nothing to do with the years she'd spent living in foreign countries, or her solitary lifestyle.

Shrugging out of her navy backpack, she placed it carefully beneath the table between her feet. A gaggle of young Vietnamese schoolgirls, riding three and four abreast, went by on bicycles in their blindingly white uniforms. Samantha watched them until they were out of sight. She'd once been that young. A lifetime ago. She'd been that careless, exactly that unobservant of safety precautions. The image of the girl she'd been was clear, but the memory felt as though it belonged to someone else.

Quyen returned with a tray from which she took two glasses, one filled with ice and topped with a metal phin, the coffee brewer. The other held the condensed milk to be added. She set both on the table. "You pay now? We close soon. Open later." Belatedly, Samantha realized the significance of the schoolgirls returning home. Everything came to a halt in the country between eleven and one-thirty for lunch and naptime. She took her wallet from her backpack and counted out the correct dong notes to hand to Quyen.

"Hoa returns soon?" the woman asked chattily.

"Later today, I think." Samantha removed the phin, and poured a thick stream of the milk to the beverage. "But she never stays long."

The other woman made change then wiped her brow. "You drink. Go home. Nap."

Samantha said nothing. The Vietnamese custom of the midday break was one she'd never embraced. Sleep wasn't a condition she welcomed. Slumber lowered inner defenses, allowed memories to rush in. More often than not she woke sweating and shaking, terror trapped in her chest. A scream on her lips.

"You nap. I'll enjoy my coffee."

Quyen shook her head, obviously puzzled by the idiosyncrasies of foreigners, but after a few more minutes of small talk, she bustled away to enter the shop. Locked the door.

Samantha busied herself with pouring the coffee, following it with a stream of sweet milk. She couldn't get Halston's death out of her mind. Couldn't prevent a feeling of loss for a man she'd never met.

Traffic thinned to the occasional vehicle. Taxis— either scooters or cars—remained open for business, but it was a slow time. The occasional shopkeeper might skip the traditional break time in order to prepare for the next influx of customers, but as a rule the city rested. Even most police and government officials would be at home during the searing noon heat.

A man on a motorbike approached at a leisurely pace on the street. The pale skin beneath his helmet caught her attention. Tourist, was her first thought. Or a visitor like her who didn't practice the customary daily rest. His head turned, his gaze lingering on her for a fraction of a second too long. Paranoia, honed by hyper-vigilance reared.

He wasn't a threat. She took a deep breath. Released it slowly. She was safe. The mental assurances had become automatic under Dr. Halston's tutelage. It was normal to notice another pale-skinned foreigner among the Vietnamese. But her gaze was wary as she watched him pass. Non-citizens were prohibited from driving, but that didn't stop many visitors to the country. The government was loath to disrupt their newfound tourism, so turned a blind eye to such infractions. Samantha had never chanced it. Her false ID had been good enough to get her into the country, but there was no reason to invite increased scrutiny.

She had only a moment to study the stranger as he went by. The helmet covered his face, but foreigners stood out in Da Nang. Samantha had tried fading into the anonymity of the largest cities in the US. But felt safer living outside its borders. At times living halfway around the world could almost make her believe she'd run far enough.

The man passed and her gaze traveled beyond the street and across the narrow courtyard to her building. A flash of movement at her terrace door caught her eye. There and gone so fast she thought at first that she'd imagined it. But in the next moment the terrace door burst open. A woman rushed to the balcony.

Hoa. Samantha started to raise her arm to wave. But a scream split the air. Someone followed Hoa out the door. The stewardess turned. The two locked together, as if moving in a silent choreographed dance.

"Oh my God!" Terrified she jumped up, not noticing when her sudden movement had the coffee sloshing over the rim of her cup. The stranger forced Hoa backwards. Another scream sounded. As if in slow motion, Samantha watched her struggling roommate forced over the railing. And fall to the ground three stories below, out of sight.

Time freeze-framed. Then the stranger on the balcony looked in all directions. Caught sight of Samantha. Stared hard.

Under that gaze the blood congealed in Samantha's veins. A chill carved a path down her spine, leaving ice in its wake. She opened her mouth. Couldn't utter a sound. Could only gaze at that face. The fall of blond hair wasn't familiar, but the features...

An instant later the stranger disappeared back into the apartment. The action released Samantha from the numbness that gripped her. She turned, clumsily stumbled across the patio to the door of the shop. Pounded on it with both fists. "Quyen! Quyen! Help! Please help!" Her voice was broken. Craning her head around she threw a glance over her shoulder, half-expecting to see the intruder heading across the small courtyard toward her. There was nothing. No traffic. No pedestrians.

No witnesses.

She resumed pounding, a persistent rhythm that had her fists and arms aching. Finally Quyen could be seen through the door's window, a frown of concern on her face. "Call the police! Someone hurt Hoa. Call an ambulance!"

The other woman seemed to take forever to unlock the door and pull it open. "Sa-man-tha. What is wrong? Hoa hurt?"

The words tumbled from Samantha's lips, forgetting for a moment the woman's limited English. "Someone pushed her over the balcony. Hurry! Call the police and a doctor."

The sound of an approaching motor had panic streaking up her spine. Turning, Samantha raced back to the table, reached beneath it for the backpack and shrugged into it, all while running toward her bike. She wasn't thinking now. Fear had catapulted her back to that sticky morass of terror that could still suck her in. Suck her under. Transform her from a rational adult to a quaking terrorized mass of primitive emotion.

She hopped on the bike, glancing up as a motor neared. A car. She began to pedal, hugging the curb as her legs pumped faster, waiting for the vehicle to pass.

It drew beside her. Her nerve endings quivered as seconds ticked by and it didn't pass. She threw a glance into the vehicle and her legs stopped movement. She stared hard at the driver. Blinked.

It was impossible. Had to be. Because inside the car was the person who'd thrown Hoa off that balcony. She didn't recognize the hair, but she knew that face. It belonged to someone she'd thought never to see again.

It was the woman she'd once known only as Four.

2

She turned sharply and jumped the bike over the curb. The car followed her onto the sidewalk, the driver attempting to pin her against a building. Samantha screeched to a stop just short of the vehicle's bumper and it grazed the stucco of the shop beside her. Caught between the wall and the car, she used her feet to back the bike up until she could turn and take off in the opposite direction.

Her heart beat a frantic tattoo in her chest, the rhythm of it ringing in her ears. Dimly logic reared. How could the woman be here, now? And if she was here...*he* must be close by.

The thought threatened to paralyze her limbs, leaving her helpless. *Prey.* The word flashed across her mind, strengthening her will. She'd spent years ensuring that she'd never be vulnerable again. Risking a glance over her shoulder, she saw the driver attempting to turn around in the nearly empty street, almost hitting a scooter in the other lane. Samantha's knees pumped faster. She had the advantage here with her familiarity of the neighborhood. That would have been more helpful if she didn't know all the shops would be closed. Locked.

The sound of the motor was drawing closer. She turned sharply, shooting down an alleyway too narrow for the car to follow. The pack was heavy on her back, weighing her down. But it had everything in it she needed. She wouldn't have to return to the apartment to pick up her things...

Hoa. Samantha shot out of the alleyway and across the two-lane street. The memory of her roommate being injured or killed because of her could summon crippling remorse at a time she could least afford it. So she shoved all thought aside and concentrated only on survival.

It was a condition she was all too familiar with.

Sirens sounded in the distance. She could only hope that meant help was headed to her apartment building. The screech of tires behind her was much closer. And much more critical.

Samantha wheeled into another narrow passageway, this one barely wide enough for her bike. At one point she had to get off and hoist it in her arms, shimmying by a large Dumpster. The bricked exterior of the building caught at her thin tee shirt, abrading the skin beneath. Her progress was slow. She got to the mouth of the passageway and saw the car fast approaching, already pulling up on the sidewalk to block her exit.

Trapped. The blood coursed through her veins in a torrent. Fear transported her back in time. She wasn't in Da Nang anymore. She was in her cell in that large shadowy building, at the mercy of a monster. And the woman chasing her now had been nearly as bad. What had she become after spending five more years in captivity?

Samantha lifted the bike again, this time throwing it at the car. It bounced on the hood and the blonde behind the wheel put up an arm, as if to shield her face. Samantha took the opportunity to turn and run, retracing her steps through the narrow alleyway, her breath coming in jagged little gasps. The suffocating heat and humidity squeezed her lungs in sweaty fists. Adrenaline spurred her on.

She burst out onto the sidewalk and dashed across the street and, after a moment's hesitation, took the alley again. Reason was making a belated appearance. She wasn't going to be able to outrun the woman, so she needed to outsmart her. Samantha knew the city. She had to believe her pursuer did not.

Although, she realized darkly, her hand going to rub at the stitch in her side, the other woman knew the culture well enough to realize when she would be most likely to get away with her crime. In the full light of day, while the city slept.

Taxis were one business that didn't close down midday. An occasional yellow cab could still be seen on the streets. Other drivers operated scooters and suffered the brutal heat in the hopes of a fare. A line of them dotted the curb across the street, many of the drivers stretched out atop their motorbike, waiting for customers. Samantha peered around the edge of the building at the alley entrance and eyed the row of vehicles. The blue car could be seen pulling around the corner to the left. In half a block it would reach her.

Samantha drew back into the alley, the warm brick of the building pressed against her back as she sidled to a doorway and ducked out of sight. She waited, breath strangled in her chest for the car to pass by the entrance. Ten seconds. Twenty. It wasn't until a minute ticked by that she realized she was holding her breath and released it in a long stream.

The driver would have to park or go by. And if she parked...Samantha's hand crept to the knife she kept strapped beneath her tee shirt. She stood a far greater chance of survival if the battle was hand-to-hand. Since escaping her prison, she'd learned a few things. And she had no qualms about using her newly acquired skills on the woman behind the wheel.

Finally the fender of the small blue car could be seen. Then the hood appeared. Samantha melted back against the doorway, counting silently. After thirty seconds she chanced a peek around the corner of the doorjamb, in time to see the sun glinting off the back bumper. Her muscles eased a fraction. Enough to allow her to think for a moment. To plan.

Was Hoa dead? A brutal hammer of remorse pounded through her. Dead or wounded, the woman had suffered because of Samantha. Grief gripped her throat, hazing logic. They hadn't been close. Samantha's inner defenses wouldn't allow that. But the woman had befriended her, offered her a place to live, sharing expenses in a mutually beneficial relationship.

A familiar cloak of desolation settled over her as she considered options. Hopefully when Quyen spoke to the police, the timing of Samantha's appearance at the shop would remove her as a suspect. But she was realistic enough to know that the fact she was a foreigner, in the country with phony identification would cast the spotlight of suspicion on her. The US Embassy wouldn't be able to protect her once that came to light. Samantha inched out of her hiding place. Her only chance was making it to the airport. She had other ID, but it was likely her face would be splashed over the news within a few hours. The longer she waited, the fewer her options.

She was about to step out into the sunlight when she noticed two of the taxi drivers straightening on their vehicles, casting glances across the street. Caution reared.

Risking a peek around the corner of the building, she caught a glimpse of a blue car parked at the curb, a lone occupant behind the wheel. A taxi driver rose to a sitting position on his scooter, directing his companions' attention across the street toward Samantha as he released a spate of Vietnamese. The driver turned her head, even as Samantha ducked back into the alley, turned and ran. There was a screech of tires. Throwing a frantic glance over her shoulder, she saw the car in reverse, slamming to a stop across the alley's entrance.

With a burst of speed Samantha raced to the opposite opening. Only to stumble to a halt when a motorbike roared over the sidewalk to block it.

Panicked, her head swiveled to the opening behind her. The woman's car door was opening. She was getting out of the vehicle. Facing forward, she looked at the scooter. Its driver was male. Light skinned. Her memory flashed to the man that had driven past her at the café. The one who had seemed to be staring in her direction. Maybe it hadn't been paranoia at all.

Her fingers crept under the hem of her tee shirt to the sheath strapped around her ribs. Of course Four wouldn't be here alone. Who else would accompany the woman, other than the monster that had once enslaved them both? She withdrew the knife, and raced toward the man.

The alley might end up being her tomb, but she wouldn't be the only one to die here.

"Mia!" The man's voice was familiar. Sharp with annoyance and command. "Put the knife away and get on. Now!"

She stumbled to a halt, momentarily shocked. The driver lifted the visor on his helmet. And although she hadn't seen him for years, she immediately recognized the scarred visage, the short-cropped brown hair and the penetrating moss green gaze. "It's Bishop. Now move!"

Without further thought she raced the last few steps toward the vehicle, while replacing the knife in its sheath. "Stop, Eleven!" The woman's voice was heard behind her, closer than she would have thought. "You must..."

Bishop reached out a hand when she neared him and practically dragged her onto the scooter. Then flipping his visor down he roared off.

He wove a zigzagging path through the neighborhood. Down alleyways, up streets, doing U-turns to double back and crisscross the area until Samantha lost track of where they were. She kept a sharp eye out for the blue car but after fifteen minutes her chest eased. They may have outrun Four. For the moment.

Bishop picked that instant to yell, "Hang on." She tightened her grip around his waist as he jumped a curb and pulled up onto the sidewalk behind a line of taxi motorbikes. He parked, then, shoving his visor up, turned to face her. "Talk fast. Why was that woman chasing you? Who was she?"

Mia shook her head, keeping a wary eye on the drivers resting on their scooters in the searing sun. Most natives of the country didn't speak English well, but there were always a few who did. "You went by when I was at the café."

His face was a mask of impatience. "And?"

"Shortly after you did, that woman threw my roommate off the balcony of our apartment, directly across the street."

His expression blanked. "Were there witnesses?"

She shook her head. "I'm not sure. I think help arrived, but I can't return there. I have to get out of the country before she finds me."

"Do you know her?"

Her body gave an involuntary shudder. "She was one of the women kept with me. Five years ago. She had special privileges. He…trusted her. More than any of the rest of us."

Bishop studied her enigmatically. One of the man's most disturbing traits was that she'd never known what he was thinking. Another was that she could never look at his scarred left cheek without wanting to press her palm against it. Her fingers curled reflexively, an unconscious effort to keep from doing so.

"Do you have a change of clothes with you?" He unstrapped the helmet. Lifted it off and handed it to her.

"No." Mia put the helmet on and shoved the ends of her hair up inside it.

Without another word he started the scooter again and took off. She clutched at his waist, recalling that he'd always been a man of few words. Impossible to read. Nerves tap-danced up her spine until she realized he was heading toward the docks. Not toward the city and the police station.

Her lungs eased a bit. Of course it would be difficult for Jude Bishop to turn her over to the Da Nang police when it was he who had provided her with the false ID she'd used to enter the country. She'd learned the hard way that she could trust no one. She had only herself to rely on.

But in this moment, with panic still shimmering under the surface, she distrusted this man less than most.

* * * *

Fifteen minutes later he pulled to a stop along a crumbling curb and turned off the engine. He dismounted, but when she would have followed suit he stayed her with a hand to her shoulder. Flipping up the visor on the helmet she wore he bent close to speak in a low tone. "I'm going to find us a room. We'll need a place for at least a few hours while I figure this thing out. Don't take off the helmet. It's your only disguise. "

She grabbed his wrist when he would have walked away. "No one can rent you a room without reporting your stay to the police."

One corner of his mouth curled. "Don't worry. There are always people who don't cooperate with the police and their regulations. I just need to find one." Extending one index finger, he tipped down the visor and walked away, his stride swift.

Unease skittered down her spine. She'd been to the wharf area many times. It was well traveled by tourists and locals alike. Restaurants and shops crowded the trendier streets near the bay, but they were blocks away from that neighborhood in a shabby section dotted with deteriorating apartment houses, dive bars and brothels. Mia swallowed, looking from side to side. The helmet hampered her vision. Her skin prickled. She wouldn't be able to see behind her.

The realization had her leaping from the scooter with more haste than gracefulness. She squatted down next to it, as if to check the rear tire and surveyed the street behind her. There was no blue car in the vicinity. No blonde driver, who—at any rate—would have stood out like a neon sign among the dark haired Asians ambling along the sidewalks. There were more trucks than cars lumbering down the streets. The vise in her chest eased a fraction. In this locale, under these circumstances, Four would stand out even more than Mia did. Still, she willed Bishop to return soon. She'd lost track of him when he'd melted into a group of men lounging against a building half a block away.

Perspiration dampened her scalp beneath the helmet. The heavy covering was suffocating. But Jude was right. It was the best disguise she had available; even if some of the men nearby were casting her odd looks for keeping it on.

She moved to the opposite side of the scooter, kneeling before the front wheel in a feigned inspection. The activity on the street continued around her without a break in rhythm. An illegal dice game on the corner had drawn a crowd, and there was steady foot traffic in and out of bars and tattoo parlors. Scantily clad women enticed passersby with sultry poses and thinly veiled invitations. She knew this area came under closer scrutiny from law enforcement in the night hours, but there was no sign of a police presence now.

Still, the minutes crawled by until she caught sight of Jude again.

He attracted more stares than she did from the people on the sidewalks. He topped most of the locals' height by six or seven inches. His pale skin would draw attention; the deep scars on his left cheek would hold it. Crowds parted for him as he strode toward her. Mia rose and remounted the scooter. He got on without a word and started it, pulling slowly into the street.

They drove close enough to the wharf to catch the smell of the fresh catches filling the bottom of a couple small fishing boats before Jude turned left to travel three more blocks. He halted before a two story building in a state of advanced disrepair, got off and went inside without a word. This time Mia stayed on the scooter. There were fewer people on the street in this neighborhood, and only a couple bars. The buildings huddled close to the curbs. Next to the doorway Jude had disappeared into a man sat slumped against the wall, head on his chest. After she stared for several minutes without him moving, she began to wonder if he was asleep, drunk or dead. The few people who shuffled by never gave him a glance. They seemed far more interested in Mia.

Her hand crept under the hem of her tee shirt, withdrawing the knife she had strapped there. She kept it hidden as two men approached, making a wide circle around her. They would be as interested in the vehicle as they were in her. They'd get neither.

One man looked back at the building Jude had disappeared into. Emboldened, he drew close enough to run his fingers over the handlebar closest to him. "Pretty, pretty." He spoke in Vietnamese as he leered at Mia's chest. His hand moved to her thigh. "Đẹp."

She withdrew the knife in a flash and drew it across the back of the man's hand in one smooth slice. He leaped back, howling, his free hand clapped around his wound, blood seeping between his fingers.

Jude picked that moment to exit the building, and was on the stranger in a few long strides. "Cút đe! Tao sẽ giết may!" He grasped the man's shoulders with both hands, spun him around, and sent a hard right punch to his mid-section. The smaller man folded, gasping for air. Jude gave him a shove to send him on his way and turned toward Mia. "Are you hurt?"

His words were muffled by the helmet she wore but she could read his lips. Shaking her head, she fumbled for the hem of her shirt, replaced the knife beneath it. He reached her, opened the helmet's visor to look at her face. Whatever he read in her expression must have reassured him. "Come with me." She got off the motorbike, faintly shocked when he took the handlebars and walked it back to the building. Up the two steps to the entrance, and then inside and down a long dark hallway lined with doors. At the fifth one on the right he stopped and fit a key into the lock. Swinging the door open he waved for Mia to precede him and followed her in with the scooter.

The door had an old-fashioned slide lock rather than a dead bolt. Mia secured it as Jude wheeled the vehicle inside and stabilized it with the kickstand. He did a quick search of the small space, moving in swift economical movements to check under the narrow swayed bed and inside the minuscule bathroom. After examining the lock on the single window in the room, he drew the shade and turned back to her as she was removing the helmet.

Mia set it on the floor and bent over, raking her fingers through her damp hair. She was a hot sweaty mess and wanted nothing more than a shower. Something told her it would be a while before she got one. She straightened, shoving her hair back from her face and stopped in mid-action when she caught him staring at her with that mesmerizing green gaze.

"What?"

"Nothing." He walked to one corner of the bed and sat down gingerly. The mattress sagged beneath his weight. "Your hair is longer."

"It matches the picture for the Samantha Simmons ID." She'd worn wigs for two of the photos, Mia recalled. One ID matched her hairstyle at the time, another had her as a redhead and the third was very close to the length her hair was now. She'd used all three passports to move in and out of countries anonymously.

"Tell me again what happened." The command in his voice was familiar. His employees had responded to it. She had not. Rather than seating herself on the bed beside him, Mia moved to take up position near the window. A quick peek under the torn blind showed it faced another building, as shabby as this one.

She repeated the story she'd told him earlier, ending with, "The Vietnamese government insists that anyone renting a room or an apartment be reported so they can be placed on a list. That's how they keep track of visitors to their country. I met Hoa my first week here, through Quyen, the owner of the coffee shop you saw me at. After we met a few times she invited me to live with her, to share the rent. She's an international airline stewardess and is rarely home."

He eyed her impassively. "Which means she is in and out of the country all the time. Interacting with strangers every day. Did she ever mention having a problem with a passenger? Do you have any reason to suspect she might be involved in…" He hesitated for an instant. "…illegal activity?"

Turning to face him, she said flatly, "Those options might be feasible if I hadn't recognized the woman who assaulted her. Hoa wasn't the target today. I was."

"Because you know the stranger."

It was her turn to pause. "Not in the way you mean." When the man who called himself their master was absent, there had been cameras running. Every movement, every sound they made was recorded. Talking amongst each other was prohibited. Using a given name would result in a brutal beating that would take weeks to recover from. "I don't know her by name, only by face. He called her Four. She was almost as sadistic as he was."

"Would he be with her?"

Giving word to her fear had gooseflesh breaking out on her arms. "I think so, yes. I can't imagine him allowing any of the women in his captivity this kind of freedom."

Jude stared at her in silence for a long minute. She sometimes went days without talking to another person face to face. It had never bothered her. But the long quiet seconds under his gaze had all her nerves tightening. "Okay." He got up and without another word started for the door.

"Wait!" Because her voice held a thread of panic, she worked to steady it before continuing. "Where are you going?"

"To check on some things. Find a way out of the country. You're going to stay here and wait for me."

The self-assured tone set her teeth on edge. "I'll go with you."

He turned toward her with exaggerated patience. "She's looking for two of us now, Mia. She'll recognize you, but probably not me." He reached into his back pocket and took out a dark ball cap he'd had stuffed inside and put it on, the bill pulled low over his face. "When I leave, move the scooter to block the door. That will slow down anyone who tries to break in, and give you time to get out the window." He unlocked the door and stepped out into the hallway, pulling the door shut behind him.

She resecured the lock, her mind whirling frantically. The last hour and a half was like something out of a nightmare, with a jumble of disjointed pieces that didn't make sense. How could he be here, now? Four's purpose for coming had been all too evident. But...Jude Bishop?

She went to the motorbike and wheeled it to block the door, as he'd ordered. Commands came a little too naturally to him. She remembered the research she'd done on him years ago when her father's lawyer had recommended Bishop's firm for security. He was ex-military of some type. Maybe that's where he'd gotten in the habit of snapping out orders and expecting them to be followed unquestioningly.

Because there were few other choices in the room, she sat on the bed. It was all almost too much to take in. First discovering Dr. Halston's death, and then seeing Hoa… When memory of her roommate threatened to make her nerves quiver, she clamped them tight. Forced herself to think about the incongruity of Jude's appearance.

Coincidences always made her paranoia worse, and Halston had advised her on ways to work through it. Look for links. Construct viable and unviable scenarios. Weigh them carefully. Usually Mia found the exercise calming.

But in this case the quiet time spent thinking filled her with ice. Because there was no escaping the fact that despite all her precautions, somehow Four had found her.

And the only person who could know the names Mia traveled under was Jude Bishop.

* * * *

The open area on the dock was a prime location to use the satellite cell he traveled with. Open water all around him. No buildings to block the signal.

And an opportunity to observe the boats punctuating the horizon. To think about how to approach an owner. Jude took his time with his calls, content to watch the activity around him, taking mental notes.

First he sent Raiker a text. Two words, no more. *Found her.* At this point he had little else to share. Tracking down Mia Deleon hadn't been an issue. The scenario he'd discovered her in was. Like everything else about the woman's life it was messy and murky and he still couldn't separate her version from reality. Although he'd seen enough to be certain the Caucasian woman in the blue car had been bent on injuring her.

He just couldn't be sure why. Not yet. He dialed Kacee; used the intervening time to take the sunglasses out of his pocket, slip them on. The sun was scorching, but he'd been in hotter places. Lying completely still. Waiting. Watching. Compared to the searing sands of Afghanistan, the Da Nang wharf was a walk in the park.

"Did you locate the POI?" Kacee's voice was brisk on the other end when she came on. Probably dealing with a dozen other things during the call. Her multi-tasking ability made her invaluable at keeping the operational details of his business running.

"Finding the person of interest wasn't the problem. Figuring out what the hell is going on is." Briefly he filled her in on the events of the day.

Kacee was silent for a moment. "Her kidnapping story just got a little more implausible."

Jude grunted. The thought had crossed his mind. "I need information, fast. I have to know what I'm dealing with. Get an interpreter in there and put Hunter on the Da Nang police scanners, or whatever they have here that's comparable. Local radio and TV stations. I need to know if the story about the roommate checks out, and if so, what they think happened. If that doesn't work, put out an Associated Press feeler. The fact that she's a foreigner will make international interest believable." The Samantha Simmons ID was British, if he recalled correctly, via the Cayman Islands. That would misdirect the Vietnamese police interest and buy them some time.

Them. The use of the word made him uncomfortable. He owed a favor to Adam Raiker. He owed nothing to Mia Deleon. He was in this only as long as he could trust her. And right now that wasn't very far.

"I'll want airline tickets bought under Mia's first ID, and my third. You can start researching them now, but I can't give you a departure date yet." Vietnamese banks didn't offer lockboxes, and there were no lockers at bus depots and train stations. He'd be willing to bet that Mia carried everything of value on her person, the same way he did. "Best route would be through Paris. Or London. Then we'll use alternate IDs to get back to the US."

"Destination?"

"DC. For both of us," he added, thinking of his promise to Raiker. If he discovered that Mia had nothing to do with her roommate's fate, he'd help get her out of the country. If she did…she could face the Vietnamese police alone, after he facilitated a call with Adam. Whatever the tactics he sometimes employed, Jude had his own moral code. Steering clients toward high quality phony IDs and hacking government databases were acceptable. Helping a killer avoid justice was not.

"Departure city?"

He had to think about that one for a moment. Hong Kong would be closer, but the Philippines would be a safer bet. "Manila," he told her, then thought of one more thing. "See if Logan can get the incoming airline manifests for Vietnam this last week. Looking for a woman, likely American, mid to late twenties." The driver of the blue car would undoubtedly be using an alias, but even a false name would be useful when tracking her passport. "Call me when you have something."

"You got it."

Jude disconnected, certain he wouldn't have to wait long for results. He employed people he trusted and they maintained that trust by producing outcomes.

A river of sweat snaked down his back. Slipping his phone back in his jeans pocket he turned and retraced his steps, heading to the nearest tavern. He'd order a Vietnamese beer and if he couldn't find someone there who spoke at least a little English, he'd continue to the next bar, and then the next until he found one. Sometimes the most casual of conversations could yield the most interesting details.

He stepped back up on the curb swiftly, narrowly avoiding having his foot run over by a driver on a scooter who'd maybe already imbibed a few too many. Jude wasn't sure the food could be trusted around here, but eventually he'd find something to take back to Mia.

The only question was whether she'd still be where he'd left her. He couldn't assume that the last five years had made her any less unpredictable.

The first bar he tried was the sort of dive that he was all too familiar with. It was a type to be found the world over, with shifty-eyed occupants and questionable sanitation. The beer was warm, the flies thick, and if any of the customers spoke more than a word of English, they were keeping their linguistic skills to themselves. After forcing down half a beer, Jude made a point of looking at his watch and hastily took his leave. No one seemed any more interested in his departure than they had his arrival.

The next one was across the street and boasted a neon Coors sign in front that was half burned out. The inside was almost a twin for the establishment he'd just left, with wobbly wooden tables ringed with equally unsteady chairs. Backless barstools faced a marred counter top overseen by a pudgy woman with a grim expression and guarded eyes.

"English?" Her expression never changed. "Coors Light." She turned and snatched a glass off a rack next to the sink and went to pour him a draft. Turning to set it in front of him, she said, "Five dollars."

"So you do speak English." He peeled a ten-dollar bill from his pocket and handed it to her, gesturing for her to keep the change.

She didn't answer directly. "American?"

"Yes. Vacationing with my wife. She went back to the hotel to get out of the heat." He lifted a shoulder. "It doesn't bother me." The bartender appeared impervious to it, as well. If there was air conditioning in the place, it was turned down low enough to be barely noticeable.

Another customer three seats away raised his mug and said something in Vietnamese. The woman moved away. Jude was content to drink in silence for a few minutes. A barely dressed young female who looked like she was still in her teens got up from a table where she'd been fanning herself desultorily and made her way toward Jude. He waited until she got close enough to catch his eye, and shook his head, stopping her in her tracks.

Or maybe she'd halted midstride only because she'd drawn near enough to see his scars. Either worked, because she did an about face and sauntered over to the man who had just ordered a fresh beer, straddling a stool beside him.

When the woman behind the bar glanced his way, he crooked a finger at her. He still had a half full glass in front of him, but she ambled toward him. No one seemed to want to expend more energy than they had to in this heat.

"Whiskey? Rum?"

"Maybe later." He leaned forward. "My wife likes boats. I'd thought maybe I could surprise her with a midnight cruise. Boating. After dark." His lips quirked. "Romantic."

She looked unimpressed. "Try boats. Hotel will know. Many tours."

"Yeah, that's where she got the idea. But they're expensive. I thought you'd know someone. A fisherman maybe. A guy who'd like to make extra money for a couple hours tonight."

The woman made a derogatory sound. "Big spender? Boats smell like fish. Your wife no like."

"She'll like," he assured her. Slipping another bill out of his pocket he slid it across the bar. The bartender palmed it a smooth movement that spoke of practice. "Do Hong Minh. Or Nguyen Thanh Hung. Lazy man. Drink much. But boat nice. Your wife like."

"What time do the boats dock?"

The woman shrugged, moving away. "All times. Before dark. When time to eat."

Although he'd gotten what he'd come for, he forced himself to take some time to drink more of the beer before leaving. He'd collect several more names before heading back to the room, because he was a cautious man. And one of his cardinal rules was to always have multiple exit plans. Whether or not he'd need them in the end depended on what Kacee had to share with him when she called back.

What she revealed would determine whether Mia would be accompanying him out of the country.

It took another couple hours of making his way through the neighborhood bars, dodging the occasional prostitute and causing a would-be pickpocket a sprained arm and some degree of pain. When he was satisfied he had all he needed, Jude walked over several blocks, back to the more touristy area of the waterfront, with its restaurants and souvenir shops. It was while he was choosing some take out from a small dining establishment that he glanced out the front window.

And saw a small blue car driving much too slowly down the street.

* * * *

Holding the bags of food in one hand, Jude rapped at the door of their rented room. Silence. The knob turned in his hand. Caution rearing, he stepped aside and pushed the door open. There was nothing to stop its swing inside.

The scooter was parked in the corner of the room. Had Mia left? On the heels of that thought, came another. That perhaps she'd opened the door for someone who hadn't given her a choice about leaving. Silently he set the bags on the floor and in a burst of motion, went in low and fast, prepared for anyone who might be waiting for him around the corner. But the room was empty. He glanced under the bed. Nothing. The bathroom door was half open, light spilling from it.

"Mia?" He pushed open the door, took a step inside the small space. The flimsy shower stall's curtain was closed. His hand rose midway in the air to open it, he heard a slight sound behind him and immediately realized his mistake. Cool steel kissed the side of his throat.

"I had a little time to think while you were gone. And I decided that you owe me some answers."

"Not bad." Jude's tone, damn him, held a tinge of amusement. "I wouldn't have guessed you were that fast. You opened the window, and hid inside it, right? Behind the shade?"

"I'm the one with the questions, remember?" Mia increased the pressure against his throat. He wasn't taking her seriously, but he should. There had been a few others in recent years that had underestimated her, to their regret. Right now she was half convinced he'd sold her information to Four and the demon that had enslaved them both. Paranoia was running high, warring with reason.

"I'm not fond of knives." The humor had vanished from his voice. "Normal enough reaction, after someone tried to peel my face off with one." With the speed of a striking snake his hand came up to clamp her wrist, while he pivoted toward her. Anticipating his move she pulled away, kicking his half bent knee while he was turning and danced out of reach.

"Nice move." The compliment was delivered with almost clinical detachment. "You shouldn't attempt to use a knife in close proximity with someone so much taller. It's too easy to be overpowered, and you're limited by your shorter reach."

"Am I?" Her tone was derisive, her gazed fixed on his. "And yet here I am, still armed."

"Only because I'm more interested in eating than in hurting you." He started for the door. Stopped when she deliberately stepped in his way.

"As I said, you have some explaining to do."

He spread his arms. "You want to slice me up? Go ahead. Aim for a major artery. Any other place and you risk the chance that I just take it away and use it on you." A moment ticked by. She didn't move. "No? Then I'm going back into the hall to get the food I left out there. We can eat while we talk."

She let him go because she didn't doubt that he'd return. Either because he didn't take her seriously, or because he was that confident of his own defensive abilities. Probably both. Still wary, Mia lowered the knife to her side but didn't put it away. She wasn't without defensive moves of her own.

He reentered the room, stopping to relock it before striding to the bed, paper bags in his hands. She watched as he removed boxes from the bags, spreading them across the bed before he rummaged for plates, chopsticks, napkins and plastic silverware. "I had to do some fast talking to get her to include plates. Picnic must be a universally understood word." He knelt in front of the bed and nonchalantly filled a plate, as if used to having an armed woman standing near him, only degrees away from doing him harm. Given his personality, maybe it was a common occurrence.

"There's no way Four found me without help." Her stomach growled, a reminder that she hadn't eaten since breakfast. But she made no move toward the food. "I was too careful."

Bishop sat on his haunches, plate balanced in one hand while he expertly wielded chopsticks with the other. "Yet here she is. You must have screwed up. Left a trail."

The accusation had her fingers curling more tightly around the hilt of the knife. "Or you sold my information to her."

He paused, the chopsticks midway to his lips. "Why would I do that?"

Mia jerked a shoulder. "The same reason people do anything. Money. Greed. Sex. Power. Pick one."

"None of the above." He continued eating, working around the different dishes he'd served on the plate. "You got complacent. It happens when people are on the run for too long. You must have let something slip to the wrong person. Made a phone call that could be traced. Left a cyber trail. It doesn't take much for someone with the right motivation and resources to pick up on."

She could have told him that complacency and carelessness set in only when people began feeling safe. Mia doubted she'd ever experience that particular emotion again. "Seems a lot of work when all she'd have to do is go to you. If you didn't sell the information outright—and I'm not convinced you didn't—maybe she hacked your computer files."

He laughed at that, seeming genuinely amused. "Not a chance. And if she had she wouldn't have found the information she was looking for there. You think I leave evidence that I provide services that some narrowly focused on the law might consider illegal?"

It was one of those loose ends that didn't fit. And yet she knew she hadn't left a trace either. Paranoia tended to keep a person hyper-vigilant. "Then the only other possibility is that you sold her the information. That you'd arranged for my disappearance. The names on the false passports. It wouldn't have been difficult to guess that I'd retain security. Or to discover I'd hired your company."

"Technically I was hired by your father."

She smiled thinly. "My father's not that altruistic. He forwarded the billing to me."

Having devoured everything on his plate, he moved to the bed to serve up more. "Just a tip—a security business doesn't last long if word gets out they sell privileged information about their clients. But if I were interested in scoring some big bucks I'd have leaked your info to a paparazzi rag. Their owners have deeper pockets than the ordinary citizen."

Her suspicions began to fray under his logic. "Then why are you here? It's a bit too coincidental that both of you appeared at the same time."

"Coincidental." He had resumed eating. "And fortunate for you. I didn't give your information to anyone, but I *was* asked to find you."

Something flickered inside her. Something she'd thought long buried. "My... father?"

His headshake doused the tiny flicker. Of course. She should have known better. *Had* known better. As far as Russell Deleon III was concerned, he didn't have a daughter. He'd told her as much before she left the US. It hadn't been news. The only times he'd ever remembered her existence was when her outrageous behavior had forced him to deal with her.

"Have you heard of Adam Raiker?"

He looked surprised when she nodded. "He's one of the leading forensic profilers in the States." She didn't bother to say how she recognized the name. Mia had known exactly how crippled she was from her trauma. She'd barely been able to make the most mundane decisions once she'd escaped. Could scarcely function in a crowd. Her physical prison had been behind her, but she'd remained caged in an emotional one. She'd realized that she required professional help to deal with her trauma. So meticulously she'd gathered information on the people with the expertise to help her. And then, when she'd felt secure enough, she'd contacted one of them. Dr. Erich Halston.

The slight smile he gave only lifted one side of his mouth. She wondered if the wounds on his face had caused paralysis on the left. "Raiker would object to part of that descriptor, but close enough. He's working on a case and found a small detail that reminded him of your story. He wants to speak to you about it."

Mia didn't harbor hope. It was too fragile an emotion, and much too devastating when it was squashed. But something very close to the emotion was blossoming in her chest with a strength that strangled the oxygen in her lungs. She sought to rein it in. Bishop would know exactly what to say to her to allay her fears.

He set his plate on the floor and reached into his jeans pocket to withdraw a phone that vibrated in his hand. "Let me guess." Her words were caustic. "Raiker conveniently picked this moment to call."

"Nope. My office." He tossed the cell across the bed to her. "Go ahead and answer it. I'm sure you're already suspecting that the woman chasing you is on the other end, waiting to hear a progress report."

She picked it up. Pressed the Talk button. "Yes."

There was silence for a moment. Then, "Who is this?"

"An...acquaintance of Bishop's."

"Put him on."

The woman's voice was imperious, with an edge Mia recognized. It didn't belong to Four. It was one of Bishop's employees. The one who'd given her a hard time when she'd called with her third request to switch bodyguards. Kacee something.

"Who hired him to look for me?"

"Why don't you ask him?"

"I did." Seemingly unconcerned with the conversation, Jude continued eating. "Now I'm asking you."

"Adam Raiker. He runs the Mindhunters agency. He has a question…"

Mia tossed the phone back to Jude. "She's well-trained."

Setting down his chopsticks, he picked up the cell. "I'm certain she'll be pleased to hear you say so." His side of the conversation didn't prove illuminating. He listened more than talked, glancing once at Mia, but otherwise ignoring her. She crossed to the bed and set the knife on the floor near her foot, then pulled the stained coverlet toward her until she could reach the remaining plastic plate and food. Discovering the call was from his employee didn't prove he wasn't working with Four. It didn't prove anything at all. Which is why she kept her weapon nearby as she filled the plate and began eating mechanically. Food was fuel. And whatever the rest of the day brought, she needed to preserve her energy.

Her plate was nearly emptied by the time he finished talking. Immediately afterwards, he sent a text. Then he looked at her.

"The local police are searching for you now. You're wanted for questioning in your roommate's death."

The news rocked her, the food in her mouth turning to ashes. "She's…Hoa's dead?"

"Snapped her neck in the fall. What's the name of the woman you say you talked to right before Hoa was killed?"

Her throat was tight. It took effort to force the words out. "I only know her first name. Quyen. But the shop is called Nahn Café."

His fingers flew over the keys on the phone as he sent another message. "She can corroborate your story?"

"I…" It was hard to think. To concentrate on anything but the litany hammering through her. *Hoa was dead.* And Mia had led her killer right to their door. "Quyen would at least be able to provide a timeline. She was closing the shop right after she waited on me. She'd know the approximate time I pounded on the door, yelling for her to call for help."

"Assuming she did, the police would be talking to her already. We'll make sure she calls them, tells them about seeing you if she hasn't already. Best case scenario, she already has and they have a witness to establish time of death and they just want you to add what you might know."

He didn't have to continue with the worst-case scenario. She could already imagine it. If they believed she could have returned to the apartment to commit murder and then hurried back to rouse Quyen…or that she'd killed her before going to the coffeehouse… Mia put down the chopsticks, unable to eat more. It would take a very gifted defense attorney to extricate her from the Vietnamese prison system.

"Maybe I should call them. Give my side of the story."

"No offense." He slipped the cell in his pocket before reaching for his plate. "But your tale about Hoa's killer doesn't exactly ring with plausibility. Especially once they check with American authorities, discover nothing came of the investigation surrounding your story five years ago, your credibility here will be zilch. You're a foreigner in the country with a false ID, and a history—in the eyes of many—of providing false information to the police. You have too much to lose and nothing to gain. Don't worry. Kacee is handling it."

He had a way of setting her teeth on edge. "You'll forgive me if that, coupled with your professed skepticism about my past doesn't fill me with confidence."

"I didn't say I didn't believe you. Exactly. I'm reserving judgment for the time being." He tugged on the coverlet to pull the boxes of food closer to him. Selected some more caramelized shrimp. "Kacee found the names of six American women under the age of forty on the Da Nang airline manifest." He reeled off the names from memory. "Any of those ring a bell?"

She shook her head. "I told you, I don't know her real name." And perhaps the woman hadn't known hers. She hadn't used Mia's name when she'd called out to her in the alley before Jude and she had driven off together. "I don't even know if she's really blonde."

"Maybe we'll find out. I sent her picture to Logan, one of my IT specialists. Poking around the Vietnamese Customs database will get us a matching name."

Suspicions billowed up again, smoke from a simmering fire. "And you just happen to have her picture."

He nodded somberly. "I do. Because when I was buying the food, she was driving up and down the streets in the restaurant district. I followed her. She got out a couple times to try to talk to people. I took some photos on my camera phone."

Fear skittered up her spine. The food she'd been eating seemed to clog in her throat. "She followed us?"

"Doubtful." He reached for another box, considered its contents before offering it mutely to her. When she shook her head he emptied it onto his plate. "But she might have considered the avenues out of the country and figured you couldn't chance the airport. The water would be the next logical choice."

Mia stared at him, arrested. "I wouldn't have tried either."

Cocking a brow, he chewed deliberately before asking, "You hoped to hide indefinitely?"

"No, I'd steal a scooter if I could. A bike if I couldn't. Leave town, keeping to the smaller villages. Head to Hanoi, change my appearance, and use another ID to get an airline ticket."

"Well, at least you had a plan." Seeming finally full, he began stuffing the trash into the empty bags. "Probably wouldn't have worked if a Vietnamese version of a BOLO had gone out country-wide."

There was no reason for the criticism to smart. It wasn't like she gave a damn about his opinion. "And you have a fool-proof escape strategy?"

"Nothing's fool-proof." He wadded up the cartons in the sacks and set them on the floor. If there was a trash receptacle in the room, Mia hadn't seen it. "But I've got some names of fishermen. Given the right incentive, one will agree to leave tonight, head for the Philippines."

"Somehow that seems fraught with possible complications."

"Complications are unavoidable. But all things considered, I like my odds." He fiddled with his phone for a few moments, then surprised her by stretching out on the bed, setting the cell beside him. Folding his arms beneath his head on the pillow, he closed his eyes. "The boats won't return for hours yet. Don't forget to close and lock the window."

Mia gaped at him, vaguely insulted. He was sleeping? With an armed pissed off suspicious woman in the room? "You do appear to enjoy living dangerously."

"If you were going to use that knife on me, you'd have done it already." He didn't bother opening his eyes. "And whatever doubts you might have, I'm your best chance of getting out of the country."

The truth in his pronouncement burned. She wasn't without options, but traveling with Bishop might be safer than striking out on her own. She didn't trust him yet—not even close. But his story about Raiker was just as plausible as was her fear he'd sold her out.

"There's plenty of room on the bed." A man shouldn't look that comfortable in a room with a woman still contemplating doing him bodily harm. "You should get some sleep. Now, or later when I go out to find a boat for this evening."

Mia eyed the bed. It wouldn't have passed for a double in the States, and he filled it up. His shoulders were surprisingly broad for someone so lean. And the chances that she'd crawl up there with him were only slightly less likely than the chance she'd ever close her eyes with another person in the room. Time and Dr. Halston had helped her heal. But the doctor had been a psychologist, not a magician. Some wounds were incurable.

She went to the window and locked it, before going to the corner near it and sliding down the wall to sit cross-legged. Leaning her head against the wall, she set the knife on the floor next to her, within easy reach. She'd told Bishop she couldn't imagine Four being released to come here alone. But if their captor were in the vicinity, why would he need the other woman? Mia couldn't identify him. She'd never seen him without a mask. He could pass her on the street and she'd be clueless, whereas she'd recognized Four immediately, even from a distance.

There were no easy answers to the questions bubbling inside her, so she had to put them aside, at least for the time being. It didn't matter what Bishop thought of her. It wasn't like she was unfamiliar with being disbelieved. He could be useful. Authorities would be watching for a lone woman leaving the country, not a couple.

Shifting to a more comfortable position, her gaze rested on Jude. Given the even rise and fall of the man's chest, he'd fallen asleep immediately. But somehow she thought the slightest move on her part would bring him instantly alert. Little had been resolved. He'd countered her suspicions with rational explanations, and she needed to sort through the mental tangle to find coherence.

But right now her thoughts were full of Hoa. A woman who had offered friendship and shelter. And in return Mia had brought death to her door.

* * * *

The next time Jude returned to the room it was locked. "We're set, Mia. Open up," he murmured in a low voice. He could hear the sound of something being moved. The motorbike. Then the bolt slid back. But she didn't open the door. He pushed it open, reached inside to flip on the light before entering cautiously.

This time he found her in the center of the room. Upon seeing him, she tugged up the hem of her tee shirt to reveal a band of ivory skin while she replaced the knife.

"Progress?"

She sent him a questioning glance as she turned to pace the small area.

"You put the knife away." He relocked the door and went to the bed, tossing the sack he held on the bed and setting a six pack of Vietnamese beer on the floor beside it. "I'm touched."

"Don't mistake it for a sign of trust." Reaching one end of the room she turned to stride to the other. "I hate being confined. I'm ready to peel the paint off the wall with my fingernails."

He flicked a glance at the aged walls in question. "Looks like someone beat you to it." He selected a beer, twisted the top off and raised the bottle to his lips. *She'd spend hours, even days locked in her bedroom,* he'd told Raiker. Of course that had been five and a half years ago. And compared to this minuscule hotel room, her bedroom suite would have been the size of a small apartment.

"It'll be a few more hours." He regarded her over the top of the bottle. It wasn't just the pacing. Tension was radiating off her in waves. "After midnight."

"What if the boat's owner doesn't show?"

She was giving voice to his fear. The man he'd finally settled on didn't summon a great deal of faith. But the fact that the boat owner had to appear in order to cash in on the final payment was Jude's ace in the hole. Appealing to the baser side of human nature usually paid off. "I think he will. If not…" He paused for another drink. "Then I'll try again tomorrow night."

The words failed to reassure her. Mia's expression was grim. "The longer we're here the better chance of being caught. Of someone seeing something on the news. Is Hoa's death on TV?"

"Yes." He returned her gaze steadily. "And so is your passport photo."

That stopped her. She drew a deep breath. And then another. "Was there a police presence on the dock when you were down there?"

She was too astute. "No. But there may be tonight. Unless I've managed to divert their attention from you." He slipped his thumbnail under the bottle's label to loosen it. "Kacee called back with a match on Four's passport photo. Shelby Kronberg, from Colorado Springs. Heard of it before?"

At her headshake he continued, "Likely because the Social Security number belongs to a five year old who's been dead for twenty years. I arranged to have that information passed along to local police, along with the pictures I took this afternoon of the woman and the license plate of the car she was driving." He rolled his shoulders. His muscles were tight. "We haven't gotten much from the police records yet. Probably will have to wait until the first written reports are submitted through the department." Hacking the Da Nang police department's server would have been child's play for his IT people. He knew from experience that poking around in the Customs database was much dicier.

"A police interest will slow Four down," murmured Mia. "Maybe send her underground."

"Divide her focus for sure." Whatever the blond had been after today, it had been clear she'd meant Mia harm. For that alone she deserved any unwanted attention the police might bring to her. Jude raised the bottle for another swig. The heat index had eased somewhat toward nightfall, but the humidity near the water had still been stifling. "We have several hours before we have to go to the docks. It'd be best if you tried to sleep."

As an answer she approached him where he leaned against the wall and reached for a beer. Opened it. "What's in the sack?"

"Several sacks stuffed into one, actually. I didn't want to draw attention by buying everything at the same place. A few odds and ends that might come in handy tonight."

She crossed to the bed and went through the bags. Her brows rose when she saw some of his purchases, but she said nothing.

"You can talk to Raiker now. There's plenty of time. It's ten hours earlier in Wyoming, nine in DC. Not sure where he'll be." Setting the carton on the floor, he took out his cell.

"No."

His fingers paused in the act of tapping in a number. "No what? No, there's not plenty of time, or no, you're not going to talk to Raiker?"

Still restless, she went to the window, cracked the shade. Something furtive skittered in the alley outside, but at least it was a four-legged animal rather than two. "I won't talk to Raiker until I'm back in the States. And then I'll do it in person."

His voice was impassive. "You're not exactly in a position to start making demands."

Mia gave a brittle laugh. "Is that what I'm doing? And here I thought I was playing it safe." Turning from the window she looked his way, their gazes clashing. And had the random thought that eyes the color of his were wasted on a man. "You claim to want something from me. Before you receive it you'll get me safely out of the country. Our level of distrust is reciprocal. Call it hedging my bets."

His mouth flattened to a thin line. That he wasn't used to being faced with mutiny was obvious. But she'd been dealt few cards, and she'd bluff the hand she held for all she was worth. If he had sold her information to Four, he could summon the woman at any time. But she was beginning to believe he was at least telling the truth about Adam Raiker. Which gave her a tiny bit of leverage. She'd wield it ruthlessly.

"Five years haven't made you easier to deal with."

"I've been told I'm not particularly malleable."

An artic gust of memory blew across her mind. *You make things hard on yourself when they could be so very easy, Eleven. You exist only to please me. Your every thought, your every breath should be devoted to that end. And I will Break. You. Down. Until you are everything I want. Until you are perfect inside, as well as out.*

Chilled, she brought the bottle to her lips. Drank. Dr. Halston had once mentioned that there was research being done on using amnesiac drugs to ease the fear response to traumatic memories. But it wasn't the response she'd want to erase, but the memories themselves. They lived inside her, jagged slivers of recall that could rise at will, hurtling her back to a time she doubted she'd ever scour from her mind.

"You don't trust me, but I'm supposed to trust that you'll make the call if I get you out of the country?" The sound of disgust he made was unmistakable. He drained the bottle he held and bent to replace it in the carton.

"I'll reimburse you for any expenses you incur," she said stiffly. The condensation collected on the bottle must have transferred to her palms. Nothing else could explain how they'd gone inexplicably damp.

He gave a slow nod. "Don't worry, you'll be billed. But know this— if I discover that you've lied to me about your roommate's death, I'll personally wrap you up like a Christmas gift and hand deliver you to the Da Nang police department's doorstep."

Curiously, something inside her eased at his show of scruples. Was he too scrupulous to have led Four to her? Mia wasn't quite ready to believe it yet. But if she could get on that boat he'd hired, a major problem would be solved in a matter of hours.

She saluted him with her bottle. "Sounds like we understand each other perfectly."

* * * *

The night was balmy, but they each wore one of the dark sweatshirts Jude had bought anyway. Hooded, they looked like a duo bent on committing a B&E. Their intent was no less illegal.

Given the area of town, the occasional bar was still open as they walked to the wharf. More than once a police cruiser rolled slowly, one stopping to break up a scuffle outside a tavern.

Jude was glued to Mia's side. At the appearance of the first cruiser he'd thrown an arm around her shoulders, hauled her uncomfortably close in a half walk half stumble pace. She knew the pose would make them look like a couple making their drunken way home after too long at a nightclub. But his proximity had all her muscles tensing. She avoided physical contact whenever possible. Especially with males.

With effort she withstood the unease scampering through her. Being pressed against Jude Bishop was not her biggest problem right now. Not by a long shot.

As they drew closer to the wharves the noise dimmed. The infrequent activity quieted. Mia turned her head to scan the street behind them. If anyone was interested in their movement they were hidden in shadows. The knowledge wasn't exactly calming. Her heart was tripping a rapid rhythm in her chest. The darkness veiled them, but also provided anyone watching them with the same anonymity.

"We'll be early on purpose." Jude breathed the words. "I wanted to beat the fisherman here to be sure he doesn't arrange for any surprises."

Her steps faltered at the words. Of all the myriad dangers they could possibly be confronted with, she hadn't even considered the boat owner. For once she was —if not exactly grateful—certainly not unhappy Bishop was accompanying her.

If it had been daylight they would have been able to see Cau Thuan Phuoc, the tall suspension bridge that spanned the water where the mouth of the Han River emptied into Da Nang Bay. But the docks they approached were working wharves, lined with fishing vessels that would set out for the South China Sea before dawn. Only an occasional light dotted the rows and rows of piers, making Mia grateful for the heavy half moon that lit their way.

The lines of wooden docks were a maze with a common passway that connected them a hundred yards out. The individual docks radiated from it like fingers, each lined on both sides with boats.

"Watch your step. It's dark as pitch." As if to prove the words he stumbled over a coil of rope lying on the wooden planks in front of them. "The boat we want is about three-quarters ways up."

"Stop! What are you doing here?" A flashlight beam spotlighted them in its glare. Mia froze.

With a warning squeeze to her shoulder Jude turned. "My boat." In an undertone he hissed, "Stay here." And walked casually back to the man who was rapidly approaching them. The beam from the light the stranger held bounced as he moved. Although he wore some type of uniform, he wasn't law enforcement. Security maybe.

The knowledge failed to calm her. A vise was tightening in her chest. Policeman or not, there was no way he'd believe a Caucasian man had a boat docked in the area. He'd alert someone else, perhaps police this time.

There was a scuffle. Something heavy hit the dock. Nerves wound tightly, Mia whirled to see the flashlight the man had once held rolling dizzyingly across the planks until it dropped into the water with a quiet splash. Jude was grappling with the shorter figure. There was the sound of a fist meeting flesh and the stranger slumped into Bishop's grasp. Unceremoniously he dragged the man onto the nearest boat and was lost from sight.

A long breath shuddered out of her. It didn't occur to her to assist him. Jude Bishop was a man who embodied self-reliance. The rope that had been one of his purchases was wrapped around his waist, the duct tape in the pocket of his hoodie. He wouldn't need the wicked-looking knife that had also been one of his purchases. The stranger was already subdued.

She moved slowly further up the pier, in the direction of the boat he'd indicated. Without knowing exactly what time the owner was supposed to meet them, it was impossible to know how soon to expect him. But there was movement in the shadows up ahead. Someone was on the connecting wharf.

Mia swiveled to survey the dock behind her. Bishop still hadn't reappeared. When she faced forward again the stranger had turned and was heading Mia's way.

A nasty tangle of nerves clutched in her belly. The figure was about her own height, wearing a wide-brimmed conical straw hat popular with men and women alike in the city. Gender undetermined. The stranger's pace was non-threatening, something between a stride and a stroll. Mia's hand crept under the tee shirt and hoodie to hover over the knife still strapped there.

Returning to the boat where Jude had disappeared would put her back to the approaching stranger, something Mia was loath to do. She slowed until she was barely moving, keeping her head ducked, her free hand in her pocket.

The figure was nearly upon her. Loose-fitting dark long-sleeved top and jeans. Sneakers. Close enough now that Mia could see the person had arms crossed, both hands tucked in the opposite sleeve. Unease skittered along nerve endings already heightened. Fight or flight. Primitive instincts were especially well honed after her captivity. Her fingers tightened around the hilt of the knife as the person approached her. Passed.

She began to pivot in order to watch the figure's departure. Heard a rush of air. A shoe squeaked on the dock. Mia dodged, but too late. Something short and solid missed her head and made contact with her shoulder, numbing her arm at the precise moment her knife cleared the sheath.

When the stranger's body hit her, Mia went down, landing hard on the planks. The knife skittered from her grasp. She rolled awkwardly to her back, the pack she wore keeping her from a prone position, and bucked beneath her attacker's body. No. Not a stranger at all. Because it was Four's face above her. She pressed the short wooden club she'd concealed up her sleeve against Mia's throat. Pressed hard.

"Our master is anxious to get you back, Eleven. Why, I don't know. You never deserved to be selected." Her face was close, eyes glittering in a way Mia recognized. They'd held that exact look whenever she was about to cause pain.

Mia bent her leg awkwardly to kick hard at the woman's back, one hand going to clutch at the Four's fingers. There was a buzzing in her ears as the outside world faded. Dots danced before her eyes. Four applied more pressure and Mia labored for air. Her free arm stretched, straining as she searched feebly for the knife she'd dropped.

The woman's lips were moving. Mia could no longer hear her. Lungs strangled, her chest was bursting with the need for oxygen. Her struggles grew weaker, as unconsciousness eddied. Then her fingers touched metal. Conscious thought was impossible. Sheer instinct had them closing around the handle of the knife. Bringing it upward with more determination than strength.

Four stiffened, a screech bursting from her lips. The pressure against Mia's throat eased a fraction and she drew a great gulp of air before stabbing the woman again, her body heaving beneath her assailant.

Mia managed to dislodge her, and lay there for a few moments, filling her lungs, regaining a semblance of conscious thought. Only then did she become aware of another voice, further away, calling her name.

Four struggled to her feet, stumbled off. Mia forced herself to her knees, then rose drunkenly to go after her.

"Mia! Stop! Not another step!"

Dimly she was aware of Jude's voice, low enough not to carry, but still fraught with command. She didn't obey. Four would know where *he* was. If there was the slightest chance the woman could be made to talk, Mia had to catch her. Dark fingers of clouds smudged the half moon, casting the area in more shadows. Her focus narrowed to the slim figure staggering away from her along the docks, picking up speed as she turned onto the main connecting wharf. With a burst of adrenaline Mia closed the distance between them. Grabbed a fistful of Four's shirt. Pulled her to a halt.

The other woman turned and tugged mightily, trying to free herself. The fabric slipped from Mia's hand. She let go suddenly, sent off balance by the abrupt release.

Four reached for her as her body teetered. Then her eyes went wide. She made a wild clutch for Mia but she was too far away. Her heel slipped from the edge of the dock. As if in slow motion Mia watched the woman's arms wheel wildly before falling backwards into the water, hitting her head on a nearby boat before becoming completely submerged.

"Mia!"

She heard fury and fear in Jude's voice and he ran with near silence toward her. She got down on her belly, searching the water's surface frantically for a sign of the other woman. The nearest boat bobbed gently from the small disturbance but the water was already smooth. And try as she might, Mia couldn't discern a human shape anywhere in the vicinity.

"Dammit."

She fought when she felt herself being lifted. Was Four dead? If she'd been knocked unconscious she soon would be.

"Are you hurt?"

The feel of two warm male hands doing a quick clinical check for injuries finally diverted her attention. She slapped them away.

"I'm fine. Help me find her. Four. She went in the water there." Mia pointed. "She may be knocked out."

"Good riddance, then." But he peered closely in the direction she'd indicated for several moments. Then his attention returned to her. "C'mon. The commotion might have alerted others. We need to get hidden before anybody else gets here."

"Wait." She dug her heels in, felt a flash of annoyance when he took her arm and began to lead her away inexorably. "If she's not dead…she could tell me where he's at. The Collector. He could finally be caught."

Jude stopped, grabbed her other arm to bring her close to him. "Listen. I'm not doing any diving tonight to rescue a murderous nutjob. If she's dead, great. If not…we'll deal with that later. We've got a lead with her passport. But every second you stall, our chances of getting away tonight diminish. So you decide whether you're coming, conscious or unconscious. Because one way or the other, you *are* coming."

Mia swiveled her head, scanning the waters where the other woman had disappeared. "It's not just me." Her voice was subdued. The waves were dark. Unwilling to give up their secrets. "He still has the others. She's their best chance, too. If I could get her to talk…"

"You have no idea what she does or doesn't know, or what information she'd give up." His voice was calmer. Rational. He let go of one of her arms to bend down and pick up the knife she'd dropped. When he began moving again this time she went with him. "But she's not an option now. Focus on the priority. Getting out of the country."

In some distant part of her brain she knew he made sense. But with every step she took she felt an increasing sense of loss.

Four's loyalty to the monster that had held them captive was absolute. Could she be made to give up facts about his whereabouts? They'd never know now.

And Mia couldn't help but believe that somehow this evening she'd failed every one of those women who still waited, clustered in their cells, hope dying a bit more each day.

4

Mia's fingers tightened around the glass she held as Jude reentered his office, this time accompanied by another man carrying a leather briefcase. Adam Raiker. She recognized him immediately from the research she'd done years ago. He looked no more approachable in person than he had in the photos she'd found of him. The scar across his neck and one cheek captured her attention for a moment, before she caught herself comparing his wounds to Jude's. The articles she'd found had detailed the events that had resulted in Raiker's injuries. She was more curious about how Jude had acquired his.

She wouldn't ask. After the harrowing experience on the docks, they'd both been hyper alert on the boat trip across the South China Sea. The boat owner Jude had hired hadn't seemed all that trustworthy to Mia. And the crewmember that had come along had spent more time focused on her than he had on crewing the boat. But in the end, the captain's professed knowledge of the Coast Guard's patrol patterns aided in their escape. In the two days since they'd been back in the country Jude had arranged for an apartment and security for her. His deft dispassionate professionalism was somehow simultaneously admirable and annoying. The man's tactics might set her teeth on edge, but he got things done. With that she couldn't argue.

"Ms. Deleon." Raiker's voice was gravelly. A result, quite possibly from the scar that rode across his throat. "Thank you for meeting with me. I thought you'd be more comfortable in Bishop's offices."

"Mr. Raiker." Mia inclined her head. She could have told the man that in spite of the time she'd spent in close proximity with Bishop in recent days, she found nothing about him particularly *comfortable*. Although she doubted he'd admit it, she thought he felt the same. Most often they were like two feral animals, circling each other warily. He was opaque, but he'd made it clear enough he didn't believe much of what she said. Which meant she was losing her edge. Because it had been a long time since she'd given a damn what anyone else thought of her. "Jude didn't tell me many details, but it was enough to intrigue me."

"I didn't have a lot of details to give him. I have more now." When Jude headed for the bar he had set up across the room, Raiker said, "Nothing for me. My wife and stepson are waiting in the car. From here we're heading to look at a new school for Royce."

There was a flicker of surprise on Bishop's face before he retraced his steps and sat down at the man's other side. "Something wrong with the one he's in now?"

"He likes it." Raiker set his briefcase on his lap and unsnapped the locks. "I think it could be a bit more security conscious." His attention switched to Mia. "What do you know about my agency?"

A bit taken aback by his abrupt transition, she hesitated. "Not much. You had an impressive career with the FBI and now head a renowned forensics agency."

He gave a curt nod. "I also compiled a team of the top investigators and forensic scientists in the country. In addition to lab services, my agency provides consultation on specific cases at the invitation of law enforcement entities." Reaching into his briefcase he withdrew a file and glanced at her. "Hope you don't have a weak stomach."

She stared back at him. All of the most human tendencies had slowly diminished in captivity. Being regularly brutalized by a sadist had pared down traits shared by normal people. Surprise. Empathy. Disgust. Mia sometimes wondered how much longer it would have taken for her to turn into something like Four. Walking, breathing, talking, but no longer human in a way most would understand. A soulless robot fashioned by a monster.

"I'll be fine." Five and a half years of freedom had rebuilt some softer emotions. But her defenses were fortress strength.

He handed her a folder and she set down her water to take it. As she looked at the photos stoically he explained, "Female. My forensic anthropologist is working on an approximate age. She was left in a mineshaft about four years ago. We found a scrap of scalp that had ink on it...the type used for tattoos."

Mia's gaze flew to Raiker's, before looking at Jude. His face was expressionless. He'd known about that fact before coming after her. She'd bet on it. But he hadn't chosen to share it. She wondered if that stemmed from loyalty to Raiker, or his distrust of her.

"Your tattoo." Raiker's voice had grown quieter. But his brilliant blue gaze never wavered. "Do you still have it?"

A sudden wash of nausea threatened. Fighting it, she swallowed hard. Mia hated that his mark was still on her. Had been tempted more than once to have it removed. But something...some niggling *thing* had prevented her from doing so. Although the police hadn't considered it much of a clue, it was the only tangible proof she had of the demon who'd kidnapped her. Who'd raped and abused her for years.

And it was the only connection she carried of the other women she'd left behind. If she erased it, she'd erased the last link to them. And her abandonment of them would be complete.

"Yes." The word was barely audible. She cleared her throat. "Top of the head, here." She pointed to a spot four inches above her eyebrows in the center of her scalp. *Four inches, centered exactly.* That hated voice remained so clear despite the intervening years. *Precision is important, Eleven. Perfection is all.*

"It's unlikely that a matching sample of the ink will give us any particular clue about the killer's identity. But it's remotely possible a match would help establish a link between this victim and your case."

She stared at him; unable to believe she'd heard him correctly. "You think she…this victim…she's one of The Collector's?"

He exchanged a glance with Bishop. "The Collector?"

Mia considered the photos again. "I thought of him that way. He called us his collection. All perfect specimens on the outside. Beautiful. He said he was perfecting us on the inside. So we'd be worthy of him." A quick tremor racked her. Steeling her spine, she shook it off. Gazed more closely at the pictures in her hands, before looking at Raiker. "What grade is that clear plastic sheeting she's wrapped in?"

Something flickered in his gaze, although his expression remained impassive. But she had a feeling she'd startled him. "Why do you ask?"

She shuffled the pictures, peering at each more closely. The skeletal body inside the tarp told her nothing. But the sheeting… "He used twenty grade." She stopped, thought a moment. "No, that's not the right word. Mil. Twenty mil. It's the thickest clear sheeting available. We'd be wrapped in multiple layers of it for punishment." Jude made a small sound then, but she didn't glance his way. It was easier to pretend he wasn't here.

"He had cuffs." Unconsciously her wrists drifted together. "Fur lined, so as not to leave abrasions, but a metal exterior. If our transgression wasn't too great, we'd be hoisted to a pipe overhead like this. For worse offenses we'd be suspended by our ankles."

"Why the tarp, Mia?"

"He was…an enthusiastic disciplinarian."

Repeat your lessons! Who do you belong to? The words swirled across her mind, leaving ice in their wake. "But he didn't like to leave marks. We were no longer perfect if he left marks. So we were wrapped in layers of sheeting first. It was held in place by…" Her mind blanked. "Those thick elastic stretch cables with hooks."

"Bungee cords," Jude murmured.

She looked down at the photo. Only one showed the body bound in the sheeting, but she could make out a familiar cord holding it in place. Mia shook her head, gathered the pictures in a pile and handed them back to Raiker. "He doesn't kill. At least he never did while I was held. We heard over and over again the time and effort he put into choosing each of us. Successfully snatching us away from our friends and family was part of the thrill for him."

The room was silent for several long moments. A thought occurred then and she asked Raiker, "What kind of shape was the body in when it was found?"

Obviously choosing his words carefully, he answered, "The state of decomposition…"

"No. I mean, was she...broken? Was the body dropped down the shaft? Or...somehow preserved. Like placed there or lowered inside."

"Why do you ask that?" The man's voice was sharp.

She rose, suddenly unable to stay still another second. "Because he idolized perfection. He talked about it all the time. We were chosen because we filled some fantasy he had. The perfect beauties." Bitterness filtered the words. There had been a time when she'd taken her looks for granted. Had even used them to get what she wanted. Chin, eyes, mouth, nose, cheekbones...all put together by some random lottery of genes. An arbitrary collection of features that had somehow drawn a monster to her.

"I don't think I'm following."

She picked up her still full glass and took it to the ornately carved table and set it down with the decanters and glassware. Although she thought she was guarded enough not to get her hopes up, she couldn't help a feeling of disappointment. It likely wasn't him. Almost certainly wasn't.

"I'm just questioning whether a man like that could drop a body—part of his collection, chosen and groomed to his specifications—down a mineshaft without any consideration to what the fall would do to it." As brutal as he'd been, there were never any broken bones, or disciplines resulting in scars. Nothing could mar what he saw as perfection."

"Maybe they ceased to matter once they were dead. Dead is the height of imperfection."

She glanced at Jude as he spoke. "Maybe. I just..." Shrugging, she crossed to stand behind her chair. Clutched the back of it. It wasn't like she was an expert on that monster. He'd regularly shocked her with the heights of his sexual depravity. He'd proven over and over again that there was little he wasn't capable of. And any curbs on his behavior stemmed from what *he* wanted.

"Bishop's probably right. But I'll give you a sample of the ink on my scalp. As soon as you like."

Raiker inclined his head. "I appreciate that, Ms. Deleon."

"Caro will take you home." Jude walked with Mia to the office door. "I'll let you know about the arrangements for the sample."

He opened the door and she saw the woman he'd chosen for her protection detail rise in the outer office. For just the briefest moment her step faltered. "I want to hear what you've found out. About Hoa. About…Four."

"There have been some developments. We'll talk soon."

Hardly satisfied, she walked out with Caro. She was already feeling confined and that didn't bode well for her security. Each of them had kept their word. He'd gotten them safely out of Vietnam and she'd spoken to Raiker. She was willing to admit that it seemed increasingly unlikely that Jude had been the link that had led Four to her.

But his reticence on Hoa's death spoke louder than words that he didn't trust her any more than he ever had.

* * * *

"How soon do you think you can have her at my lab in Manassas?" Jude cocked a brow. Raiker had already replaced the file in his briefcase. Locked it.

"There's a clinic here I know. They're discreet."

"I prefer using my own facilities when possible. That way I can guarantee the validity of the results. I'll send a car for her if need be. Her security would be assured."

Shrugging, Jude said, "That won't be necessary. I can take her."

The other man stood. "Sooner is better than later. The results will be run immediately to compare it to the ink Caitlin found on the corpse."

They fell in step as they walked to the door. "Why the rush? You said yourself that even a match wouldn't give you much."

There was a telling glint in the man's eye. "Maybe not. But Deleon revealed some intriguing details."

Intriguing. Jude wouldn't have used the word. What he'd known of Mia's story revolved around the failure of the police to find a shred of evidence corroborating it. And the common perception—even from her own father —that she'd fabricated it completely.

But her description of her abuse had shaken him more than he wanted to admit. What had been worse was the expression that had slipped over her face in the telling. That blank vacant mask she'd worn five years ago when he'd first taken her on as a client. And even now, not being certain of what was true and what wasn't, he wondered what the verbal exchange had cost her.

They halted before the door. "Which detail… exactly?"

"There were two." Raiker's hand clasped over the top of the cane he carried. "The plastic sheeting around the body? It was twenty mil. And the body itself was completely unmarred. That shaft was one hundred feet down, but there were no broken bones. There was rope found around the corpse. Mia called it correctly. Whoever dumped that body lowered it into the shaft."

When he would have reached for the doorknob, Jude's hand on his arm stopped him. "If that's the case," he said slowly, "I think you need to hear in more detail exactly what went down in Da Nang."

* * * *

"I've rung Jude in. He'll be taking you to the appointment himself."

Mia looked up from the iPad on the table before her. The apartment Bishop had arranged for was fully furnished, the trappings comfortable but anonymous. The ease in which he'd found the place made Mia suspect that it was a holding of his company's, kept specifically for client needs. He'd refused to let her return to her own place until he'd had a chance to check its security, although he'd dispatched someone to fetch a suitcase of her things.

"Be sure and discuss with him the plans you have for an Internet presence." Caro had expressed strong reservations when Mia had arranged for a home delivery from a big box electronics store. "I don't think he'll approve."

"I will." Mia's agreement was only to stop the discussion. She'd actually worked with Caro before. She'd been the fourth—or fifth—in the series of security personnel Mia had worked with five years earlier. If the woman harbored any ill will from being replaced back then, it was well hidden. Perhaps she'd realized that the revolving door of bodyguards had said far more about Mia's state of mind at the time than any shortcomings on her part.

There was no sound at the door. But the older woman checked her vibrating phone, tapped in a message and then waited until she had a responding one.

Seconds later, checking the peephole first, the woman pulled the front door of the apartment open to admit Bishop.

Mia glanced over. In the hours since she'd met with him and Raiker, Jude had changed to black jeans and a button down white shirt. He hadn't been clean-shaven this morning, and the shadow on his jaw had darkened somewhat in the intervening hours. Rising, she grabbed the purse that had been brought with her things and went to meet him.

"Ms. Deleon and I have been discussing the wisdom of her going online."

He arrowed a glance at Mia as she reached his side. "Thanks, Caro. We'll discuss it."

Jude's body shielded hers as they walked to the elevator. It didn't escape Mia's notice that this was the only apartment on this floor of the building, with a private elevator and entrance. Although her home had good security, this place was on a whole different level.

"I have secure computers that you can use if you want to get online," he said as they entered the elevator and waited for the doors to close. "I'll have one delivered. It would be careless to get on the Internet without some safety precautions. A cyber trail can be just as easy to trace as a physical one, and it can be done with guaranteed anonymity."

"I know my way around cyber security." She inched away from him. He seemed to take up more than his share of room in the enclosed space.

He turned toward her, destroying her attempt to gain distance. "Did you use the web overseas? In Da Nang specifically? Because any of your online correspondence could have been intercepted. That might be how the woman…Four…managed to trace you there."

Although she'd very much like to understand how her whereabouts had been traced, Mia remained confident it hadn't been through her use of the Internet. "I know how to use anonymous web proxies. I visited different Internet cafes and coffee shops each time and no more than a couple times monthly. I didn't communicate with anyone from my old life, either by email or phone. I didn't even take a phone overseas with me."

The elevator doors opened almost soundlessly and he exited first, checking the private vestibule before ushering her out. "Five years. How many countries? And you never made a phone call?"

There was a dark late model Suburban pulled up to the curb outside. Jude guided her through the door and into the vehicle with smooth well-practiced moves. She was settled in a plush leather seat, the driver pulling into the street before she answered. "Three countries. Panama. Bermuda. Vietnam. Although I moved around in each of them. And no, I never made a phone call. Not to the States anyway, and never on a phone I owned."

She could feel him regarding her from the seat next to hers. The driver was a stranger, but he must have had the address of where they were headed, because there had been no exchange between him and Jude once they'd entered.

"Did you maintain contact with your father?"

She looked out the window at her side. "My father and I have never really communicated. And we have nothing more to say to each other." Everything she'd always feared about Russell Deleon's true feelings toward her had been realized in their final showdown before she'd left the country.

"So you haven't let him know you're back in the States?"

"It's exhausting trying to carry on a one-sided relationship. No, I haven't spoken with him."

"Good." When she looked back at him he was surveying her soberly. "We have to figure that you communicated in some fashion with the wrong person, leading to your discovery. At least," his voice was dry, "if you've eliminated me from the suspect list."

It would be gratifying to deny it. Mia was all too well aware that the level of distrust Bishop felt for her was unchanged. But in light of the risks he'd taken on her behalf to get her out of the country, and the lack of concern he'd shown for Four after the woman had gone in the water, her earlier suspicions had faded several degrees.

"That's just it." Deliberately she skirted the admission he was seeking. "I didn't falter in my story. I didn't slip up or trust the wrong person, because I don't trust anyone. I haven't figured out yet how Four could have found me, but I will. If you want me to wait and use your computer, have one sent over immediately. Because Four didn't act on her own. She wouldn't have come after me if she hadn't been sent."

"About that…" The vehicle made a turn and Mia could see a flash of the Washington Monument in the distance through Jude's window. "I've got someone monitoring the situation in Da Nang. The papers. The police reports."

"You mean you hacked the police server."

He swiped a hand over his short brown hair then leaned forward to adjust the back seat controls to turn up the air conditioning. When it came to temperature, DC in the summer had a lot in common with Da Nang. "Hacked has such a negative connotation. At any rate, no body has been discovered in the water near the wharf area."

Everything inside her stilled. Mia tried to speak. Found it impossible for a moment. Finally she managed, "So…she survived?"

"That's hard to say." He reached down for a lever that would ease his seat back and settled himself more comfortably. "Her passport hasn't been used to leave the city either. It's possible the woman's body was taken a ways out to sea, and will wash up further down the coast. The police are looking for her after I had her picture anonymously sent to them before we left the country. A neighbor admitted to allowing Four into your building. She convinced the man she was a relative of yours. There was a groundskeeper below when the…when your roommate went over the railing. He said he saw a flash of blond hair above but was unable to identify Four from the photo. The neighbor who allowed her into the building, however did ID her."

Absorbing the news, she said, "So that at least establishes a question about my involvement in Hoa's death." At least a physical involvement. There was still no doubt in Mia's mind that she was indirectly responsible. Four had gone there to confront her. In an unfortunate cosmic twist of fate, she'd found Hoa instead. Hoa. Who hadn't been expected back for hours. A change of schedule had marked her for death as soon as she'd headed home early.

"The apartment was apparently ransacked. The police have no clues." As if to forestall her next comment, he added, "And you have nothing to share with them right now that can be proven. So communicating with them will have to be put off."

Although the argument was logical enough, it still burned. After the heart-racing events in Vietnam and their stomach-lurching sea escape, she'd spent every minute on the plane ride from Manila waiting to be accosted by authorities. In comparison, since returning to the States she felt like she was wrapped in cotton batting. Confined. Constrained. Mia was already restless at the forced inactivity. There were too many questions still unanswered. And if they weren't forthcoming, she was going to dig for them herself.

They rode in silence for nearly an hour. Manassas was at the outer edge of the DC sprawl, and the scenery had grown more rural as they neared it. Their vehicle turned into a heavily wooded campus that was barricaded with a heavy iron gate. Jude leaned forward to pass his ID to the driver to present to the security guard in the small enclosed building at the foot of the drive.

The man turned away for a few minutes. Mia could see a bank of screens inside the enclosure, all showing different vantage points of the front of the property. As he handed the ID back, he said, "All passengers will need to step out of the vehicle, please."

Startled, she shot a glance at Jude, but he was already opening his car door. She got out and was met by a man carrying a metal wand. "Raise your arms, please." Another guard was running the wand over the driver. Slowly, Mia did as she was bid.

The metal wand beeped wildly when it passed over her torso. "Ma'am?" The man's gaze was cautious. "Are you armed?"

"Mia." Jude's voice sounded from the other side of the Suburban. "Give him the knife."

That wouldn't be easily accomplished. She'd chosen to wear a sundress today. Turning her back on the man, she lifted the front of the dress and withdrew the knife. Smoothing the fabric back in place, she turned and handed it to the guard. "I'm going to want this back." She and Jude had bought a duffel bag to check at the Manila airport, because she had flatly refused to leave the weapon behind. Had felt naked the entire plane ride without it.

The guard didn't crack a smile but his expression eased a bit. "Yes, ma'am. When you leave."

"It'll be just another moment, Mr. Bishop." The three guards, two men and a woman who had conducted the physical checks went back into the small building and returned with different instruments. One efficiently passed a long-handled device beneath the vehicle's undercarriage, while another scrambled inside the Suburban to do an interior check. The female guard expertly wielded a wand over the exterior. Minutes later, they were allowed back in the Suburban and the entrance slowly opened.

"Wow." Mia turned to see the gate swing closed behind them. "Raiker takes security pretty seriously."

"He had some trouble a while back. He tightened up procedures in response."

The drive wound through the wooded lot, finally opening to reveal a sprawling complex with several different brick structures. They were stopped once more, the check more cursory this time, as Jude stated their business and they were directed to building four.

Leaving the driver with the Suburban in the lot, Jude and Mia walked to the lab facility and were once again required to present identification. She caught sight of the small handheld video monitor the guard was holding.

Her and Jude's photos were already on it for comparison. "Here you go." He handed them back their IDs and stepped in front of them to press his hand over a palm print scanner for a few moments, before opening the door and allowing them inside.

There was yet another level of security before a female tech led them into what looked like a small examination room. "We have a pathologist on staff," she explained, taking a cell from her pocket and texting a message. "Dr. Frazier. He'll be the one to take the sample." She looked at Jude. "Will you be staying for the procedure, or can I call someone to accompany you to an area where you can wait?"

Plainly neither of them would be left alone for the duration. Jude looked at Mia and she shrugged. "It doesn't matter to me."

"I'll stay."

The tech nodded. "May I get either of you anything?" She looked at Mia. "Or maybe you'll want to wait until after the procedure. Dr. Frazier will be using some numbing agents prior to collecting the sample."

"No." Her answer was automatic. Emphatic. "No drugs."

The woman looked concerned. "Oh, but…there's going to be some discomfort involved. It would be best if…"

The reaction was visceral. Uncontrollable. Mia could feel her palms dampening, her chest going tight. The jackhammering of her heart sounded in her ears. A conditioned response. Knowing it, being able to identify it didn't make it less real. "No." Her voice was hoarse. "I won't do it if there are drugs involved. I won't take anything. No pills. No shots."

"It's okay, Mia." Jude's voice sounded in her ear. "You don't have to do anything you don't want to." She could feel him close to her side, but couldn't look at him. She was too busy trying to breathe through the vise in her chest. To beat back the memories that threatened to spring.

There had been drugs at first. Plenty of them. The last thing she recalled her final night of freedom outside the nightclub was a prick in her arm. And then nothing for hours. Perhaps days after that. And when she'd come to he'd been on top of her. Inside her. And the pain was a constant eddy of agony that shrieked through her system, demanding a release.

"All right. That's fine. I'll let Dr. Frazier know." There was a slight sound as the tech slipped out of the room. A soft murmur of voices could be heard, the words indistinct.

"Close your eyes." His hand at the back of her nape urged her forward to bend at the waist. "Focus. Visualize the room full of flowers. See them?" His words were insistent little jabs that beat back the panic crowding her throat. "All different colors and types. Their aroma. Do you smell them? Deep breath, through your nose. Good. Hold it. Exhale through your mouth." She gasped, her lungs strangled, then drew in a deep breath. "Another."

"I'm all right." Mortification nudged aside the panic. "I'm fine."

"Of course you are." His hand was gone. "Worst part of the whole procedure will be if he has to shave a bit of your hair to get at your scalp."

The statement was casual, meant to put her at ease. She lifted her head at the exact moment the door opened again. A man of indeterminate age with a completely bald head entered the room, pulling on latex gloves. "Ms. Deleon." He stopped for a moment before her. "No Novocain, no numbing agents. Is that right?" The tech that had been in earlier followed him silently into the room.

"Yes."

"Okay. Show Leslie where we should look. Oh, yep." He peered closer after the tech followed Mia's indication and bared a portion of her scalp. "Yeah, I see. Is there more? Okay, there. That'll work."

She sat stoically, eyes straight ahead and they fussed and snipped away hair to bare the spot he'd use for the sample. "This is just a cleanser Leslie is going to put on," the man said. "To sterilize it. It's non-narcotic."

"That's fine." Mia had perfected the technique of going somewhere else in her mind. She tried to summon the trait now.

"This will be sharp." The slice had her stiffening, hissing in a breath. "Hurts, I know." The doctor's voice above her was dispassionate. "You'll have to stay still, though."

"Okay." Dots of pain danced at the edge of her vision. She blinked them away. So little, really, compared to what she'd once endured. What the others were still enduring.

"Almost got it. Okay. Where's the slide?" Her scalp was on fire but she sat perfectly motionless. "This will require a stitch or two. I'll be as quick as I can."

A scrape of a chair sounded. Then her fingers were enclosed in warmth. Her gaze dropped to the hand covering hers, then rose to meet Jude's. He was down on one knee in front of her, his expression somber. "Find a focal point," he murmured. "It will help."

It was good advice. But somehow she couldn't tear her gaze away from him. The voices of the tech and the doctor grew distant. The pain faded.

His nose split his face into two halves, forever unmatched. Hard, chiseled male beauty on one side. On the other, an angry snarl of scars, some deeper than others, that started at his chin. Notched the side of his mouth and veered onto his jaw, blooming on his cheek, stopping short of his eye socket. Like nature had wanted to start over on that side of his face, and had mangled the act.

...someone tried to peel my face off...

His eyes were unreadable. A deep bed of green that promised softness but gave nothing away. She'd been in agony before, and so had he. An unimaginable morass of pain. Once again she had the compulsion to press her hand against that scarred cheek. And in a flash she suddenly realized where the need came from. He wore his injuries on the outside, a silent testament to what he'd experienced. She carried hers within, invisible to the naked eye, but the wounds were just as real. Just as unhealed.

A thought occurred and her eyes widened a fraction. She saw the question in his expression. "This will leave a mark." The words were nearly inaudible. His response was as well.

"Likely."

"Then I won't be perfect anymore."

"Nope."

A slow smile curved her lips and the corner of his mouth kicked up. Somehow, in that instant, the scar she was in the process of getting seemed like a final act of defiance.

* * * *

Jude pushed open the door into the sunlight, habit having him shielding Mia while he scanned his surroundings. He could think of few places safer than where they were right now. He should know; some of the technology and security measures had come from Bishop Security. But not all. Adam Raiker was much too cautious a man to entrust his complex to one company. Jude didn't know for sure how many separate industries had had a hand in this campus's security. It was a safe bet that some of Raiker's own technology was in place to secure the various structures.

"Mr. Bishop." The guard who'd allowed them into building four was at their side as soon as they walked out. "Mr. Raiker has requested that you wait on site until the testing process is complete."

Jude frowned, flipped his glasses open and settled them on his nose. "He didn't mention that to me this morning."

"No, sir." There was a faint note of apology in the other man's voice. "He just called. Something has come up and we're to offer you a late lunch while you wait. We have an excellent cafeteria. He said by the time you finished eating the results should be completed."

"Did he say please? We'll stay if he said please."

Something in Mia's tone had Jude's attention snapping to her. He couldn't see her eyes behind the large-framed sunglasses she wore but he had a feeling if he could they'd be alight with humor.

"Ah…well…" Finally the man gave up. "No, ma'am. But he's very interested in having you stay for a time."

"That's fine." Jude's hand drifted to Mia's elbow. "If you can just point us in the right direction."

"This approaching gentleman will escort you."

Jude shrugged mentally and started toward the guard heading their way. He could work anywhere, and it wouldn't hurt Mia to eat. He'd seen grown men break down under less duress, and despite her stoicism throughout the procedure, her normally creamy features seemed paler than usual. He knew better than to suggest a pain reliever for the headache she had to be experiencing.

"You and Adam Raiker seem to have something in common," she murmured as they followed the security guard across the blacktop. "You both like to give orders."

He slanted a look at her. The sundress she wore was the color of smoke and an exact match for her eyes. Jude imagined that was not by accident. Her appearance today was a far cry from the tee shirt and jeans she'd worn in Da Nang, or even the shorts she'd had on this morning. With her too casually tousled long dark hair, high-heeled sandals and sunglasses she looked like she'd stepped off the page of a glamor magazine. And given the repeated glances their new guard shot her way, the effect wasn't lost on him.

He was beginning to suspect that Mia Deleon wasn't above using her appearance as a shield. People saw what they wanted to see.

But Jude was guessing that very few had ever glimpsed her vulnerability when that shield cracked, the way it had earlier today.

They took their time in the cafeteria, which in true Raiker fashion was much more like a small restaurant. Jude had his driver come in to eat, as well. No use him sitting out in the heat. He used the time to touch base with Kacee about different operatives they had in the field, and to discuss a potential new client. With two death threats hanging over his head, the man had built a fortress and wanted cutting-edge security measures to protect it. Since this was just the type of job guaranteed to bring future jobs his way, Jude was already constructing mental plans about the latest technology they could offer the man.

And if he occasionally looked Mia's way, it was just to assure himself that she'd suffered no ill effects from the procedure earlier. There was no sign of the hint of panic she'd displayed when the tech had mentioned drugs. Given her reaction he knew there was more to her aversion to drugs and needles than a queasy stomach. Much more.

It was close to an hour and a half before he received a brief text from Raiker. Cryptic and abrupt, it was much like speaking to the man in person. As if choreographed, the same guard who had shown them the cafeteria appeared at the door. Jude wondered if the man had been posted outside it the whole time, or if he had received orders right before Jude's message.

"I'm to take you to Mr. Raiker. He arrived a short while ago."

They left the building that held the cafeteria and walked to the structure that contained Raiker's offices, while the driver returned to the car. Jude had been there in the past. But always before he'd had a clue about what the hell he was doing there. His interest was piqued as the guard gave them over to another man stationed outside the door. Their IDs were checked again before the security guard used the palm print sensor for their entry.

"The place is like Fort Knox," muttered Mia as they entered a small waiting area.

"There was a bounty on Adam's head two years ago. A couple of the attempts were a bit close for comfort. He's tightened safety precautions." They waited for a few minutes until the next door opened. But instead of another guard, they were faced with Raiker himself.

"I appreciate your waiting." He nodded at Mia. "I wanted to talk to you after the results were back." He led them down a long corridor and bypassed the security to get into the glassed in offices that housed his personal space. But he didn't take them to his office. Instead they were led to a large conference room dominated by a long polished table and a large screen TV hanging on the wall.

"I want to know about the test results," Mia said bluntly. Rather than taking a seat, she remained standing. "Was the ink a match?"

Jude eyed her carefully. He was beginning to recognize her moods. Forced inactivity brought on restlessness. Which then increased her unpredictability. Funny that he should have learned that now, after spending a few days with her. Five years ago their business relationship had lasted months. At the end of that time he'd known no more about her than he had at the start.

"To cut to the chase, yes." Raiker went to a shelf beneath the TV and picked up a remote. "As I said earlier, in terms of the investigation, the link isn't much help in that we aren't going to be able to trace it. Too common. Far too many distribution channels. But the similarity in composition is intriguing. No chemicals, toxics, lead, or plastics found in some. The main components are water, sodium and aluminum, which places the ink in the organic category, for marketing purposes."

"That's not so unusual these days." Jude kept watch on Mia from the corner of his eye. Pulling out a chair he sat next to hers, hoping she'd do the same. She didn't. Her gaze was riveted on Raiker. "More and more people are requesting non-toxic ink these days. The composition isn't regulated by the FDA."

"What is irregular is that the scientific makeup of both samples is exactly the same."

Her voice was dispassionate. "You're saying the same person might have tattooed both of us?"

"No. All I can say is there's a good possibility you were both branded with the same ink. I'm going to ask you to carry your cooperation a little further. My forensic anthropologist just completed a facial reconstruction for identification purposes. She's submitting the likeness to missing persons' databases as we speak. I wondered if you'd care to take a look."

"Or Adam can send me the pictures for you to look at later. Maybe tomorrow." Jude didn't know where the objection came from. He provided protection services, but he didn't do *protective*. At least not on a personal level. And if there were ever a woman more self-sufficient than Mia Deleon, he'd yet to meet one.

"No." The resolute tone was familiar. "I'll look at them now."

Raiker lifted the remote and clicked a button. A three-dimensional head fashioned of plaster appeared on the screen. Another click had it revolving slowly. Headshot. Left profile. Right. Before it returned to forward position again. "This process isn't exact, of course. Hairline, eyebrows, and lips are the most difficult to get correct."

Jude didn't even pretend to look at the screen. He was watching Mia. Her features were arranged in the expressionless mask he was beginning to recognize. The chair scraped the floor as she pulled it out. Collapsed into it as if her bones would no longer support her body.

Her voice was a whisper. "She should have come with me. Why didn't she come with me?"

"Do you recognize this woman, Miss Deleon?"

"She was one of us. He called her Eight."

5

"I don't know her name." Mia spoke to forestall Raiker's next question. "That was his first rule. No names. No talking. The first month I was taken...I was in isolation. I think he did that with all of them. Chains on the wall. A bare mattress. He called it boot camp. Constant assaults and beatings. Drugs." A violent shudder shook her then. The hallucinogens had heightened the nightmare. One more tool in his quest for mind control. "The time was spent learning his rules. His...needs. But I know now that his intent was really to strip us of our identities. Numbers rather than names. Completely shaven. No clothes. We didn't exist as people anymore. He wanted to make sure we remembered that."

She stopped and considered the sculpture on the screen more critically. They hadn't been allowed to keep eyebrows. But the lips were close to Eight's. Perhaps a bit thinner. "Her eyes...they were brown. It was hard to keep track of time, but I know she came well after I did. Maybe a year. No more than eighteen months."

"Eight came after you? So the numbers...they weren't chronological?"

She shook her head in response to Jude's question. "I don't know what the numbers represented to him. Four was his first. She reminded us of that often. But Eight..." Her gaze returned to the screen. "I always thought...she might have come from Michigan. Or at least visited there."

"Why would you say that?" Raiker's question was sharp.

"We could earn privileges." Hers had been damn infrequent. She hadn't been a model pupil. "Sometimes he let us paint. I saw a picture she'd done. It was a street scene of Mackinac Island." At Jude's blank look she added, "I went on vacation there when I was a senior in high school with a friend's family. I recognized it." She went silent then. A year after graduating she'd been at the mercy of a monster, her future forever detoured. Fate was a miserable bastard.

And it had been even more so for the woman she'd known only as Eight.

Abruptly she pushed her chair back. Stood. "I want to leave now." She was only half conscious of Jude rising as well.

"You've been more than cooperative. I realize this has been difficult." Raiker's voice gentled. "I appreciate your help."

"Maybe you can do more with it than the police could five years ago." It was difficult to keep the bitterness from her voice. "Because if they'd found him back then, Eight wouldn't be dead."

She turned, her eyes burning, but dry. She'd lost her capacity for tears long ago. Mia pulled open the door. Was met by the guard who had accompanied them to the building. Silently she followed him outside and started in the direction of the vehicle they'd arrived in.

Four years. The words burned through her. Eight had been dead a year after Mia had escaped. How had Mia's gamble for freedom impacted the others? She'd often wondered. Had the women been moved? Treated more harshly?

The heat dampened her temples as she strode along. She'd worried that he might have killed them all to avoid police scrutiny. But Dr. Halston hadn't thought so. The victims were too important to him. What was a collector without his collection?

But he'd killed one. And although living as the captive of a monster was its own kind of death, Eight's was much more final.

If Michigan was indeed the woman's home, she'd never see it again.

At her approach, the driver started the vehicle and cruised up to her. Mia got inside and let her head fall back on the headrest. The day seemed interminable. It would be longer still before she'd get to sleep tonight.

Because now those pictures of the corpse Raiker had shown her this morning would all wear Eight's face.

It was several more minutes before Jude joined them. Although he shot her a concerned glance, he was silent other than to give the driver instructions to return to the apartment where she was staying. They collected Mia's knife at the security station at the gate. The drive back to DC was slower than it had been on the way down. The afternoon was getting later, and traffic was thicker, although not yet as snarled as it would be in another hour. They'd traveled nearly forty minutes before he finally spoke.

"Adam said they've also submitted a DNA sample taken from the remains to the missing persons' databases."

"Let me guess." She felt as though she'd been drained of all emotion. "There have been no matches."

"Nothing yet. But not all missing persons reports are submitted to databases. He's going to make sure the sculpture photos get to all law enforcement agencies in the country." When she said nothing he continued, "That's big, Mia. Any detective who's taken a missing person's report across the nation will see this. Someone is going to recognize her."

She lacked the strength even to lift her head, so she merely rolled it on the headrest to look him. "Unless she's like me." The bleakness in her tone couldn't be tempered even if she tried. "And no one missed her after she disappeared."

Something flickered in his eyes. Something she couldn't identify. "I wondered about something you said." He folded his arms, the gesture pulling the shirt across his chest. "About the woman in those photos not coming with you when you escaped."

The last few hours had hollowed her out. She drew her bent knees to the seat, arranged the skirt of her dress and wrapped her arms around them while she shifted her gaze. Talking about her captivity was more difficult with his eyes on her. Maybe because she still felt like he was weighing her every word. Searching for nuances and fabrication.

"There were cameras. Wired for sight and sound. We were punished for anything we might say or do when he came back. He must have monitored us remotely. We were never let out of the building. Never went outside. Once he brought us there, that became our world." She stopped for a moment. Found it more difficult than it should have been to go on. It wasn't her world any longer. She'd beaten the odds. But the past still had a death grip on her. Perhaps it always would.

"The only time I could be sure he couldn't view the cameras, at least immediately, was when he was assaulting one of us. So I knew that would be my only chance. We were locked in our cells if he...when he chose someone else. Except when he selected...a group of us."

She focused on the horizon, the rise and dip of where sky met land. "He took sexual enhancement pills. At least I assume so. And when he was finished with one or more of us he'd send us back to our cells. But first we had to fetch others. We were supposed to go back and lock ourselves in our spaces. To disobey…no one ever did."

"Until you."

"I was terrified. But I was dying inside, a little more every day. I sent the others as he'd ordered. But…I didn't go back to my cell. Eight was with me. I grabbed her hand, tried to pull her along…" She could still feel the way the woman had dug in her heels, her eyes wide and frightened. She'd tugged her wrist out of Mia's grip and scurried back to her cell. But she hadn't given Mia away. She hadn't yelled for help. And now Mia wondered what that act had cost the woman.

"Chances were one in a thousand that those exact circumstances would ever occur again." Her voice was a near whisper. "He'd carried in some…props…for the night ahead. The main door was usually barred, but that night he only locked it. Eight was two cells down. The women on either side of me and directly across were…" Their screams shrieked across her mind, supplied by a haunting snippet of memory. "…with him. I didn't even think. Not really. I grabbed something from my cell and ran." Across the shadowy building to the door he always entered through. She'd gone to the discipline room. Picked the lock with a bit of wire she'd hidden there. Then grabbed one of the slim plastic strips he sometimes used as whips. Worked it into the crease of the doorjamb on the main door and after several attempts managed to slip the lock.

"I saw a YouTube video once." Unconsciously she began to pleat the dress fabric in her fingers. "An animal rescue team unlocked a pen of dogs that had been horribly abused. Some of them growled and snapped at the rescuers. Others cowered in the corner of the pen.

Wouldn't leave the area even when the door was left wide open. I think Eight…it was like that." He made a small sound but she didn't turn toward him. Couldn't. "Fear of the unknown can be crippling. The odds were insurmountable. I climbed a staircase, pushed open a door and found myself in darkness outside. Then I just…ran."

"Ran where?"

She shook her head mutely. She hadn't known. "It was terrifying to walk up that staircase. It was terrifying to be free. No one can understand. I expected him to catch me at any minute. I distrusted every decision. I stayed away from roads, tried to find wooded areas to hide in." She'd lain all day in some weeds watching a farmhouse, Mia recalled. It had seemed empty, but it had taken night to fall before she'd gotten the courage to break into it. It had no phone, although people seemed to be living in it.

"Every house I saw could have been his. I stole some clothes. Traveled only at night. And finally got brave enough to go up to a gas station. I was going to ask for help…but a sheriff's car pulled in. He'd made us think that the law couldn't touch him. I thought he might be law enforcement himself. So instead I jumped in the back of a semi. Rode for hours before finding another one and rode hours more…" She shook her head, finally chancing a look at him. "It didn't occur to me that I needed to figure out where I was, because all I wanted was *away*. Fear…it takes over everything. Shuts down logic. I was operating on sheer animal instinct. You probably can't understand."

"I do." There was a storm brewing in his eyes, but something told her it wasn't directed at her. "I understand what fear can do. What helplessness feels like."

She searched his expression, hardly believing his words. How could he know? How could anyone else really comprehend that kind of terror? Her gaze fixed on his cheek then. *Someone tried to peel my face off...* And she recalled his military service. An experience there maybe. She felt an odd sort of kinship.

"I'll never be helpless again," she murmured hoarsely. She'd die before ever being at someone's mercy.

Some days, it didn't seem like much of a sacrifice.

* * * *

Jude watched her enter the apartment and head directly to the bedroom she was using. The door shut behind her with a quiet note of finality. He stared at it, strangely torn.

"Did you eat before coming back?" Caro turned from resecuring the front door. "I can order something."

"We had a late lunch."

"Well maybe she'll be hungry later." She shot him a curious glance when he made no move to leave. "Anything I need to be caught up on?"

That managed to snag his attention. "What? No. Raiker is checking out some information Mia provided."

"I would think there would be police files he could access." She smothered a yawn with one hand. "Wasn't there some sort of investigation a few years back?"

"Yeah." An investigation that had yielded nothing to support Mia's story. Proof hadn't mattered to him at the time. Her security needs had been his priority. But even as recently as two days ago he'd given her little credibility. About her past, her roommate's murder, the woman after her... Jude was unused to feeling guilt. A suspicious nature was a natural by-product of his experiences, and had saved his life more than once. But it'd take a harder heart than his to listen to her today and remain unmoved. If even a fraction of what she shared was true, she'd been let down continuously once she'd returned five and a half years ago. By the police. By her father. By the investigators she'd hired. Damned by public opinion in the rags that made celebrities their business. Damned in private by those who mattered most to her.

And he had an inkling of what that must feel like.

Involuntarily, his gaze went to her closed bedroom door again. Without conscious volition he crossed to it. Knocked. "Mia." He half expected her not to answer. When she did he opened the door and slipped inside, closing it behind him.

He found her at the window, looking out between the slatted blinds. The glass was bullet proof and the blinds were selected with privacy in mind. She turned as he entered, her face composed in that blank mask he was really coming to hate.

"Have you heard something already?"

"No." She'd mean from Raiker, but Jude wasn't there for the other man. He'd come for himself.

He jammed his fingertips into the pockets of his jeans. Now that he was here he felt oddly uneasy. "I lived with my dad when I was little." The words were unplanned. Unprepared. And offered to few others in his life. "Never knew my mom. It was just the two of us, but we did okay. At least to a little kid it seemed that way. He went to prison when I was five for manufacturing and distributing meth. I still remember when my grandfather came for me in foster care. I'd never known I had a grandfather. But there he was. Big booming voice. Charismatic. He was a minister in his town. Respected. Well-liked. I was lucky. Everyone said so."

She took a single step in his direction. Stopped.

"There were social worker visits." He propped himself against the wall. "More at the beginning, but they began to taper off. I was just so lucky, see. Nice house. A doting grandfather who was thrilled to discover he had a grandson. I'd get a good Christian upbringing. I was one of the few fortunate ones."

He recognized something in the tone he heard himself using. Recalled that it was much like Mia's in her recounting earlier today. And he knew the reason for that purposeful disengagement.

"I was six when he began sexually abusing me." He watched her face for shock. Pity. Finding neither made the rest easier. "I told the social workers each time it happened. But he was so believable." Long concerned talks with the school counselor about his penchant for wild stories. Serious discussions with the police officers that brought him home each time he ran away. *I don't know what gets into the boy. I'm afraid he takes after his father. You know Chris was never quite right.*

"With each subsequent report there was less and less follow up. And after every time I ran off, I just gave his story more credence. When he started raping me, there was no one left who believed me. No one who listened. He'd drag me into his closet and take his fishing knife off the shelf. Hold it up to my face and told me he'd fillet me if I didn't keep my mouth shut about him." Sometimes, in the middle of the night he woke up and swore he could still feel the steel biting into his face.

"He started loaning me out to 'friends.' His mistake was showing me where the knife was. I took it with me one day when I was sent with another man. Sliced him with it before running away. My grandfather found me. He was as furious as I'd ever seen him for *embarrassing* him. He dragged me down to the basement and proceeded to follow through on his threat. A neighbor heard my screams and came running." His mouth twisted. "All through rehabilitation and countless surgeries I was told over and over by doctors, counselors, social workers. 'You have to tell someone, son. Tell someone if you're being hurt.'"

He looked at Mia then. Gut-wrenchingly beautiful on the outside. Unimaginably damaged inside. "I know what it's like to be helpless. At someone's mercy. I know what it's like to have no one believe you. I hate that it happened to you."

His words hung in the air for a moment. She tilted her head a fraction, as if unsure she'd heard correctly. Then she walked slowly toward him. Her heels were in a pile at the foot of the bed and her bare feet were soundless on the carpet. Reaching out a hand, she pressed her palm gently against his ruined cheek, her touch as gentle as butterfly wings. "No one has ever said that to me. No one."

His hand went to her wrist, intending to move it away. At least that's what he told himself. But instead it lingered there, his thumb brushing once over the delicate blue veins beneath cameo skin. The moment spun out. Became fraught with emotion.

An inner alarm shrilled. There was danger here of a kind he always avoided. Some long buried primitive instinct had him stepping back, breaking the contact. Turning on his heel, he went to the door. Pulled it open and shut it quietly behind him.

And tried not to feel like he was running away from something he couldn't even identify.

* * * *

When his cell sounded Jude sat straight up in bed and brought it to his ear in one smooth motion. "Bishop."

"We've got action in Deleon's place."

He was already on his feet, reaching for his jeans. "The safe house?"

"Nope." His operative sounded wide-awake. He was paid to be. "Her apartment."

With the cell caught between his shoulder and his ear, Jude pulled on pants, grabbed a shirt and his holstered weapon. "Video?" Shoving his feet into his tennis shoes, he bolted from his dark bedroom.

"Crystal clear picture. That camera you had us rig up is top of the line. Can't make out if the figure is male or female. The silent alarm went off as soon as the entrance opened. And Jude—whoever it is has a key."

"Have Hunter and Blake meet me there. I want one of them stationed at her entrances. Have them text me when they get there." He didn't wait to hear the other man's response before hanging up.

Taking a moment to shrug into his shirt and strap on his weapon, he was heading out the door as he got Caro on the line. "Check on Mia. Make sure she's still there."

The woman's voice was startled. "Of course she's here. Why wouldn't she…" He heard a sound from her end. Then Caro came on again. "Yes, she's asleep. What's going on?"

"Someone's in her apartment. I'll check in later."

Tucking the cell in his pocket he ran out the front door of his condo. And as his tennis shoes slapped down the stone steps, his operative's words reverberated in his head.

Whoever it is has a key…

* * * *

Jude's home in Georgetown was twenty minutes from the brownstone housing Mia's apartment in Old Alexandria. He made it there in fifteen and didn't wait for his operatives. He'd given them their orders on the way over. There were multiple exits from the building, but the location of each apartment gave its owner access to only two. He was familiar with the place. It was where they'd provided security to Mia five and a half years ago.

He had the keys she'd provided when they'd gotten back into the country. Jude hadn't expected to use them again so soon. Unlocking the front entrance to the brownstone building, he let himself into the common foyer.

Skirting the elevator, he used the stairs, taking them two at a time to her second floor apartment. Cracking the door of the exit, he scanned what he could see of the area. Two apartments took up the entire level, he recalled. There was no movement in front of either of them.

Crossing soundlessly to Mia's door, he pressed his ear to listen. Heard nothing. As quietly as possible he fit a key into the lock. The knob turned beneath his hand. The deadbolt hadn't been engaged.

Drawing his gun he pushed the door open. Swung inside, weapon ready. The place was dark, with an unoccupied air. Gleaming dark wood floors. Antiques whose price he wouldn't even try to guess. But it was the blueprint he was trying to recall now. He stepped out of the foyer to the living area. Large dining room, bath and kitchen to the right. Three bedrooms and two baths to the left.

He cleared the living, dining and kitchen spaces first. Saw no one. It wasn't until he was heading for the hall leading to the bedrooms that he saw it. The camera he'd had installed near the ceiling was hanging askew. Shards of something—probably a heavy vase, lay in pieces beneath it. Jude stepped carefully to avoid walking on one and giving his presence away.

Coat closet cleared, he moved down the hallway. Methodically he checked room by room. Two guest bedrooms across the hall from each other. The master bed and bath at the end of the hall. He took the one on the right first. Checked the closet.

He never made it to the other two.

There was a slight, nearly inaudible crunching sound. The shards in the living room. Jude ran back into the hall. "Hands in the air! Stop right there!"

A dark figure bolted around the corner into the foyer. He heard the door opening. It was closed as he rounded the corner. He pounded over to it. Yanked it open.

There was no one in the exterior hallway. The elevator had been activated. Had the intruder pushed the button to throw him off and then taken the stairs? He hesitated. If the stranger had managed to get into the elevator and chosen another floor, he or she would have access to different exits from the building.

Playing the odds, Jude took the stairs. Caught a flash of dark clothing at the bottom of them. Hopefully by now his men would be stationed outside. With a burst of speed, he took several steps at a time and raced to the bottom. To the front door of the building.

The landlord's door cracked open the length the safety chain would allow. "I called the police when I heard that racket," the older woman yelled shrilly. "They'll be here any minute!" He ran out of the building, heard the woman's door slam behind him.

He reholstered his weapon, scanning from right to left. It was an exclusive historic neighborhood. The area was well lit, and there were few hiding places. Nearby porches on adjoining buildings. Behind or between the cars parked bumper to bumper at the curb.

He bet on the street. Wondered where the hell his operatives were. Running to the driver's side of the vehicles he looked up and down the road. Saw someone jump out from a porch two doors down and speed in the opposite direction.

Shit. He took off after the figure, already hearing sirens coming toward him. The sound was followed by the appearance of two cruisers just as he got to the corner. Saw the person fleeing halfway down the block.

"Stay where you are! Hands up!"

Damning the fates all to hell, Jude halted and raised his hands, glad he'd had he foresight to put away his weapon. His eyes should have been on the officer who at this moment had him in his sights. But instead he watched the intruder run down the next block and turn the corner.

Far from where his man should be stationed at the back apartment entrance.

* * * *

Mia was still. Her blood was chilling from the inside out. "Who was it?" This wasn't a routine break in. She didn't need to see Jude's grim expression to realize it. When he raised a remote she followed the direction of his gaze to the laptop he'd set up.

The feed showed the interior of her home. The one left to her in a trust from her grandmother. She'd barely lived in it, but her happiest childhood memories were the times she spent there with the only person who'd truly loved her.

Her mouth flattened when she saw someone in dark clothes walking through the interior. "Since when do I have video surveillance in my home?"

"Since we got back from Vietnam." With one look Jude forestalled her objections. "I had someone monitoring the feed. If nothing showed up," he shrugged shifting his gaze back to the computer, "it would have been taken away eventually."

The chill transferred to her skin. She rubbed her arms bared by the sleeveless blouse she wore. "But you thought something would show up." A suspicion he hadn't shared with her.

He lifted a shoulder. "It was worth a shot. We had it alarmed so we'd get an alert when the door…" Leaning forward he said, "Here it is."

There wasn't much to see at first. The figure was trying to be stealthy. It went in the direction of the bedrooms. Was out of sight for several minutes. "And now…" Jude murmured.

"Damn you damn you damn fucking bitch!" The voice was low. Venomous. And indisputably female.

Mia swallowed hard. Her gut clenched as she watched the woman pacing the apartment, first hidden in shadows and then out again. Saw the exact moment she caught sight of the camera. She approached it. Stood still watching it for a moment.

Although her face was half in the interior's gloom, Mia recognized Four's vicious expression. "You fucking bitch. Are you watching me? I'm going to kill you, you cunt. When I find you I'm going to cut you into pieces. Look what you did to me. Look at it!" She turned and pulled up her sweatshirt. Two puckered fresh scars, stitches visible, marred the once flawless back. When she turned around again the woman was weeping. "He'll reject me now. I'm no longer perfect. He can't love me anymore. And it's…" she dodged to the side to pick something up. "…all…your…fault!"

Four heaved Gran's eighteenth century vase at the camera. There was a crashing sound. Then the screen went dark.

Stunned, Mia sat silently for a moment. She hadn't killed the woman. Obviously. From the signs of the wounds, the help she'd received for them hadn't been professional. How had she survived? How had she gotten out of the country?

"We deliberately didn't change the locks on the apartment. Had hoped to apprehend anyone who might break in. The police being summoned stopped that."

"How long did you spend in lock up?" Caro quipped. "I assume you got fingerprinted like the common crook you are."

Jude's tone was not amused. "Hunter and Blake got there just in time to get caught up in the whole mess. It never got as far as taking us downtown. Sorry to disappoint you."

"I should have been there." Mia shook her head, furious at the missed opportunity. "That's twice now I've missed the chance to question her." She arrowed a glare at Jude. "*I should have been there!*"

"No, you shouldn't have been," he countered calmly. He tapped the edge of the remote against the table, his only sign of impatience. "My services expressly revolve around keeping you safe. Your security interests demand you being kept somewhere far away from danger. Which is why you're here."

Frigid just a moment ago, Mia was boiling now. And all the frustrated emotion was aimed at the man surveying her much too calmly. "I can handle Four. I proved that in Vietnam. And it was my decision to make. Not yours."

"These decisions are best made by someone who can be rational about the risks." The inference was clear. "After I explained things to the officers, they questioned the gentleman in the neighboring apartment, and the elderly landlady. She admitted to supplying duplicate keys to someone she thought was you over three years ago. Said the woman had dark hair, and showed her your driver's license."

Mia was stupefied. "Mrs. Nelson has known me since I was a kid. And Four looks nothing like me."

"Yeah, well you once told me you hadn't spent much time there, especially after your grandmother went to the nursing home. Years later she sees a young pretty female, about your age. Similar color hair and style to the picture on the ID…she was probably easy to fool." He paused a beat. "I assume you had your purse with you when you were kidnapped."

She had. Of course she had. Her purse. Her ID. Credit cards. Keys. The keys wouldn't have helped him once Jude had changed the locks years back. So Four had been sent to acquire new ones.

Fury came on the heels of that realization. "She was in my home." Her fingers balled into fists and for a moment—for one scant second—she was tempted to take a swing at him. "She was our best chance to find him. Twice she's gotten away. Raiker won't be happy this opportunity slipped away again."

"Adam isn't foolish enough to use witnesses as bait." The note of finality in his voice said more clearly than words that for him the topic was closed. Aiming the remote at the computer screen again, he said, "Blake took a video of your possessions. Take a look and see if there's anything missing besides the vase she destroyed."

Sullenly, Mia folded her arms across her chest. Her eyes were on the screen, but her thoughts were elsewhere. She'd spent the last five years running. Never feeling safe. Never feeling secure. Haunted by memories of the past. Thoughts of the women she'd left behind were never far from her mind. If anything the last few days had shown her she'd been on a fool's errand. Safety was an impossibility. She'd never be out of danger while *he* was still free.

And every minute that he was allowed to operate in anonymity, nine other women suffered in her stead.

It was a self-defeating attitude. She watched the video clip of her Gran's things—she never thought of them as hers—in silence. Dr. Halston had chided her for it more than once. She wasn't the cause of the others' continued captivity. Logically she knew that. Emotionally though…

"Where's my laptop?" She leaned forward suddenly as the camera panned around the bedroom she used. "It should be on the desk across from the bed."

Jude backed up the film. Slowed it. "I've watched this once and didn't notice a computer anywhere." He glanced at Caro. "What about when you went to get some of Mia's things?"

The sturdy blonde woman shook her head. "There wasn't a computer in the room a few days ago."

"It was there when I left the country. I wiped the hard drive before leaving." Paranoia had ruled her life at that time. Comparatively speaking now she was a bastion of rational thought. "Nothing was left on it but the operating system." She saw Caro and Jude exchange a glance. "What?"

"We know last night wasn't the first time Four was in your place. She was likely looking for a lead to where you'd gone. A computer can be a wealth of information." Jude leaned back in his chair and stretched his legs, his voice deliberately neutral. "We did a thorough search of your place before supplying you with your first personal protection agent five years ago. We didn't find a laptop."

His words flayed, leaving a sting of guilt. "It was in a safe in my bedroom." He wouldn't understand that after three years of captivity she'd been both hungry for and terrified of freedom. The web had offered her a way of catching up on news and cultural events that had transpired in her absence. And it had given her an avenue to search for her own leads in an investigation that had never really gotten off the ground.

She surged from her seat. Paced. "I'm not an idiot. I was a freshman at MIT when he…when I…before. I had a better than average grasp on computer technology." She was even better at it now. The last five years had given her a lot of time to learn everything she could find on personal safety.

Jude shrugged. "She wouldn't know nothing was on it. Or maybe she figured the information could be recovered."

"She was alone in the video. She was alone in Vietnam." The realization swept over her, but it was still hard to fathom. Mia hadn't believed that The Collector would have trusted the woman so much…given her such freedom… A trust that was warranted, it seemed. Because she didn't doubt that the woman had gone back to him after the first time she'd been in Mia's apartment.

A traumatized homing pigeon, programmed to return to its abuser.

How long would it have taken, Mia wondered, a finger of fear tracing down her spine, before she had been turned into something similar? Every human spirit had a breaking point. A psyche could only tolerate so much abuse before becoming *other*. Sub-human. With every element of humanity in tatters.

Or perhaps something had already resided in Four that made her more malleable. Maybe for the woman evil hadn't been such a stretch.

"They've gone to pretty great lengths to find me." An eerie sense of calmness settled over her. The events of the last few days crystalized into a picture that was all too easy to read. She knew what she had to do. Perhaps on some level she'd always known. "Four won't stop trying." Her reasons would be personal now. Mia had done worse than kill her...she'd scarred the woman. Four had been right. She'd be rejected now by The Collector. Imperfection would never be tolerated.

Was that why Eight had died? Thoughts of the woman brought a violent pang. Had the woman sustained some outward injury that made her unworthy in his eyes? There was no way of knowing. The only people with answers were the woman who'd been in her apartment last night, and the master she served.

And despite Jude's argument otherwise, it was very clear to Mia that there was only one way to get the answers she sought.

* * * *

The young woman was nude. Spread-eagled on the mattress in the back of the van. Gagged. Bound. The bonds weren't needed right now though. The drugs he'd given her had done their job, and she was only barely conscious. Squirming and moaning as he completed his examination with the help of a handheld magnifying glass with light.

He tried to quell the excitement coursing through him. He'd been fooled before, in his earlier days. Sometimes the mind wanted something so much, the eyes passed right over slight flaws that were all too noticeable once the initial exhilaration was satiated.

But he'd conducted his analysis twice. Had first washed the makeup off her face. Natural beauties would glow without it. She had. Next he'd turned on the overhead light and used the glass. Peered at every inch of her body from her earlobes down to her soles. Back up again. Turned her over and repeated the process.

His breathing was coming faster. Okay, perhaps it was time to get a little bit excited. She may be…just may be… Putting down the glass he pressed his knee between her legs, opening her to him. He shoved one gloved finger inside her. Then two. Withdrew them to turn her over and probe her ass. Almost wept with the sheer joy of his find.

The most flawless beauty was marred if she'd been bored out by frequent fucking. It used to be if he chose them young enough he could guard against that. Not anymore. Even the youngest of women could be as indiscriminating as dogs. It was too much to hope for a virgin, but she was suitably tight.

Reluctantly, he withdrew his finger. He'd driven to a deserted road, pulled the van into a copse of trees. If she'd been less than suitable he'd have his fill of her now. He may be stringent on the requirements for his collection, but he wasn't above taking advantage of what was right in front of him.

But she *was* suitable. Perfect even. He'd take her to boot camp and begin her training. Condoms would have to be used until the results were back on the mail-in lab kit he'd use. A necessary evil. STDs were a nasty reality. But once she had a clean bill of health….

He sat back on his heels, peeling the latex glove off his hand and allowed the elation to take over. It was so long between true treasures. A less exacting collector would be more easily satisfied. But he thought his high standards yielded the most lasting gratification.

He had his Thirteen. Trembling with giddy joy, he ignored his straining cock and awkwardly climbed to the driver's seat. He wasn't superstitious enough to believe the number was unlucky. He started the van. Inched it out of his hiding place until he could be certain there were no nearby cars to see him. Thirteen wouldn't be jinxed, he knew it.

Because he'd already had his fill of misfortune with Eleven. The van bounced as he pulled onto the gravel road again. But his fortunes were about to change. He had a new piece for his collection.

And very soon Eleven would be back where she belonged. His fingers clenched on the wheel as he thought of her. It would be an exquisite pleasure to restart her training. He'd obviously been too soft before.

He wouldn't make that mistake again.

Mia pushed back from the computer Jude had sent to the apartment, stunned disbelief stirring through her. "You've looked at that screen all morning," Caro remarked walking up and handing her a cup of coffee. "My eyes go blurry when I'm on it that long."

She reached for the coffee and wrapped both hands around it, needing its warmth to counter the shiver working through her. Mia wanted to be wrong. She *needed* to be. The tremors were getting stronger, racking her body with enough strength to have the coffee splashing precariously close to the rim. "I need to talk to Jude."

Caro sipped from her cup, eyes watchful. "Jude texted while I was pouring the coffee. He's on his way up." Peering past Mia, she looked at the news story still on the screen. "Did you know this guy or..."

The alert on her phone sounded and the woman broke off to set her cup down, check the screen of her cell. Then she went to the door. Moments later Jude entered. His gaze went immediately to Mia where she sat grasping the coffee cup as if it were a lifeline. "What's wrong?"

There was a feeling of relief at his presence that was distantly alarming. He may have made it possible for her to disappear five years ago, but she'd spent the intervening time becoming completely independent. There were dangers in trusting someone else. Something that had just been brought home in the most brutal of ways.

She rose and stepped away from the computer. "I told you I'd been cautious overseas." She was incapable of preamble. Not with the fear and guilt clawing inside her chest. "I know how to disguise my IP address so my web location can't be traced. I'm skilled enough to cover my tracks online. And I was careful. Never used the same Internet café twice in a six-month period. I thought my precautions were good enough." Her voice cracked a little then. "But I didn't consider the risk to the person I contacted."

Without a word he strode over and sank down in the chair she'd vacated. Scrolled down the screen as he read the news story displayed there in silence. A long minute passed. Pushing the chair away from the desk he turned to look at her. "How do you know this Dr. Halston?"

She drew a breath, battled it through the knot in her throat. "I contacted him the first time while I was in Panama. He's a British forensic psychologist of some distinction. Although retired now he maintained a professional presence online. I…" Her gaze went past him to the computer screen again. "I knew I needed help. I researched. And in the end I reached out to him online. Assumed name. Just a few details at first. A couple questions. Then later…more. He was…kind." The word seemed artificially understated. Dr. Halston had saved her, emotionally speaking. And he'd died for doing so.

"The article said he was killed in a home invasion."

"I had just discovered that the last day in Da Nang. But this one also says although robbery was suspected, little was taken. His wallet. His computer."

Jude appeared to follow her line of thought immediately. And when he spoke there was a new softness to his tone. "You just said how careful you were. You can't know that this has anything at all to do with you."

She shook her head mutely. The fear had taken hold in her now and was wringing remorse with tight little talons. Getting up, she crossed to the desk and set her cup down beside the computer, leaning past Jude toward the touch pad. Brought up her browsing history. Finding a previous site she'd looked at, she clicked on it and straightened to let him read it. Mia looked away while he did so. Certainly she didn't want to see the words again.

Eventually Jude sat back. "So what is this, a blog or something?"

"Not Dr. Halston's. But it seems that he appeared as a guest on this forensic science blog, and answered questions put to him by professionals in the field."

He looked at her. "That example he used in his reply to a Dr. G about prolonged sexual abuse. You think he was referring to you."

There was no reason for it to feel like a betrayal. He hadn't identified Mia by name. Couldn't have, because she'd never provided it. But she saw herself in his answer. There were others who would, too.

"There are a few specifics there that The Collector would recognize. But he wouldn't have happened upon this blog by accident. It's too obscure. He would have had to be searching for Halston himself." She wrapped her arms around her waist. Wondered if it were possible for a person to be physically consumed by remorse. "I did my research before leaving the States. There would have been dozens of names in my search history. I didn't settle on Dr. Halston until I was in Panama." She shook her head, still unable to believe it was possible. "But I wiped the hard drive and did a seven pass erase over it before I left. I thought that would prevent anyone ever…" She stopped. Forced herself to take a deep breath.

"Seven pass erase writes a random seven character pattern to each free sector," Jude said for the benefit of Caro, who was looking completely lost. To Mia he said, "That was a decent effort. It would take a highly skilled technician to recover the files. Most likely your computer was useless to him."

She heard a 'but' in his words. "Most likely?"

He rolled his shoulders. Looked uncomfortable. "Do you have reason to believe that he has a great deal of knowledge about computers?"

She took a minute to think. Then slowly shook her head. "I don't remember him ever saying anything that would lead me to think so. But I really wouldn't know."

Jude leaned forward, hands clasped between his knees, his expression earnest. "Then I don't think he got shit off your computer. Is data retrieval possible? Depends. About the only thing that is safe from a skilled tech with the resources and time is taking a sledgehammer to the drive. But data retrieval can be dicey, and a lot of times it retrieves fragments of information, not entire blocks. So piecing together the results becomes another obstacle."

"I should have done a thirty-five pass, but it took too long," she murmured. She looked down, surprised by the slight sting in her palms. Found her fists curled so tightly that her nails were digging into the skin.

He blew out a breath, and she sensed his flagging patience. "Theoretically, a thirty-five pass isn't impossible either. But the skill level for retrieval is substantial. It requires taking out the metal platter and examining it with very specialized equipment. The fact is there are government agencies that dispose of hard drives only after they've been degaussed and incinerated. You have to weigh the possibility against the probability. And in all likelihood this guy doesn't have the talent, money, equipment and time necessary to recover your search history."

"But what if he does?" Jude was right about one thing; guilt was a useless emotion. It took more strength than she had to banish it, so she'd channel it to something more productive.

Because it helped her to think, she began to move. Nearly bumped into Caro as she paced. "That would be part of his profile, right? If he was a computer whiz of some sort?"

"Maybe." Jude's tone was cautious. "But could be he's not the one with the skill. Possibly a friend. Or someone he hired. Or…and most probable…there's no direct link between your computer and Dr. Halston's break in at all."

She arrowed a look at him. "If someone suspected I was in contact with the doctor, and took his computer to check, how difficult would it be to find the hundreds of emails we exchanged? Even if he'd deleted them…if the right person were looking, he'd recognize himself in the content. Are you saying that this same guy, if he's talented enough, couldn't trace where my emails were coming from, despite the efforts I took to disguise it?" She saw his answer in his expression and although she already had reached a similar conclusion, couldn't prevent her heart from sinking a bit.

"I can think of no other possible way for Four to have traced me to Vietnam." She paced around the small wooden table with its group of four matching chairs. "There was nothing on my computer about my new IDs. I didn't even make my own initial travel arrangements."

"If you're back to believing that I sold her that information…" Jude began.

"Bishop Enterprises would never sell out a client!" Caro put in indignantly.

"No." Her reply came so automatically it took Mia aback for an instant. The change had happened in increments, barely noticeable. She turned, met Jude's somber gaze. She'd moved past believing that he'd sold her ID information. The admission would have unnerved her even days earlier. "Before there seemed no other explanation for how Four could have gotten the information. I think we have a reasonable one now. The question is if my conclusion is valid, where does that leave us?"

He stood. Folded his arms across his chest. "Security-wise, it changes nothing. We keep the woman as far away from you as possible. You need to stay out of sight, because if Four knows you're back in DC, then so does he. And there's nothing to stop him from coming here to take over himself."

If he'd meant to frighten her, his words had the desired effect. Tiny tendrils of fear furled through her system. It took effort to battle back the paralysis that fear could bring. The kind that leached rational thought and elicited horrifying images from the past.

"He sent her here three years ago, rather than coming himself." At least, Mia thought as she angled past the counter to stride toward the door, it had been the other woman that had enacted the pretense with her landlady and the key. "The longest period of time he was ever gone was maybe a week. That happened several times. But usually it was far less. Too often he was there regularly." With no clocks or windows in captivity it had been impossible to guess whether it was night or day, which made it difficult to estimate his schedule.

But it was enough for her to guess he wouldn't leave the women for the length of time it would take to search for her. He'd wait until Four reported she had Mia, or had tracked her exact location before coming himself. Reaching the door she turned to stride in the opposite direction. It shamed her to admit how much that conclusion relieved her.

"I was in Nashville before I finally sought help from someone. I had no idea which direction I'd traveled. The two trucks I'd hidden in may even have gone in different directions." It had been made only too clear that her convoluted route had muddied the investigative waters immensely. "But I know the climate where we were kept had cold weather. It was heated a lot of the time, which suggests long winters."

"That eliminates only a handful of states."

Jude's words stung, although they were uttered dispassionately enough.

"Still." Stubbornly she clung to the point she was making. "Two long days traveling by truck. Likely I was moving south or east. Even if there was some backtracking by the second semi, that suggests I still ended up far from wherever I'd been kept. Wyoming— where they found the body—would fit that descriptor. Further west would not. Even if that mineshaft was a dumpsite, it at least narrows the possible map of where he kept the women. And how far would he have traveled with a dead body in his vehicle? Linking the body to The Collector gives Raiker's team a clue about where to find the others. A clue the first investigation didn't have."

"I think you're getting ahead of yourself." Jude rose. Propped a hip on the desk and folded his arms across his chest. "I came over to tell you that Raiker texted me earlier. He has a possible line on the ID of the remains found in Wyoming."

She stopped in her tracks, one hand rising unconsciously to her throat. "He has…a name?"

"Several actually." His tee shirt was green today, a shade darker than his eyes. "He got calls from four different law enforcement agencies so far. Now it's a matter of the families submitting DNA to see if there's a match. His lab will facilitate that, which will speed up the process."

Mia searched his expression. Saw nothing there to forestall her next question. "Were any of them from the area around Mackinac Island?"

"No." Her stomach plummeted. "But one was from Detroit. Same state."

She reached out a hand, suddenly unsteady. Clasped the edge of the nearby dining table. "Did he give you a name?"

"He won't until the ID is made. But from what he did tell me the investigation gets dicier once the victim is identified. The mining company who owned that abandoned shaft acquired his services. Bad PR for the corporation." The thread of sarcasm in his voice was unmistakable. "Especially when they're looking to expand drilling in the state. The scope of Raiker's involvement will be completed when a victim ID is complete. Generous mining CEO pays to reunite a grieving family with their long-lost daughter's remains."

She stared at him, easily reading between the lines. "But if Raiker suspects a link to my case it can't end there."

"The connection has to be pretty clear. And then it will be a matter of which law enforcement agencies will get involved and how well they work together."

Whichever one it is, Mia realized, there was no guarantee they'd hire Raiker. And even if she convinced the man to work for her, they still needed an approximate area in which to focus the search.

"I'm just telling you this so you'll realize it's all going to take time, Mia." She could feel his steady regard on her even before shifting her gaze toward him. He dropped his arms. "Raiker's involvement tends to speed things up because of the resources he brings to bear, but from here out things are going to grind along. I know you're impatient but that impatience can't get in the way of your security."

"You're telling me I have to settle in for the long haul?" she asked bleakly.

"I gave the DC police the name Four used on her passport and a picture. With the video surveillance from your apartment, they have cause to pick her up. But I don't kid myself that she'll be a high priority, especially since I didn't give them any information about what happened in Vietnam. Right now we have to start thinking about what your long-term security needs are and where you want to spend your time."

At her arched brow, he lifted a shoulder. "Nothing says you have to stay in DC. Or that you can't resume some online classes from MIT, using one of our secure computers. But you have to settle on a routine for yourself, or the waiting is going to drive you crazy."

If he only knew how close to that stage she already was. But Mia forced herself to nod. "I'll think about it." When his gaze sharpened at her easy agreement, she tried not to look away. It wouldn't do to underestimate his perceptiveness.

After all, he'd already realized how difficult it was for her to wait around for answers that might take weeks or months to come.

It wouldn't do to let him guess that she was already planning to accelerate that process.

* * * *

Caro looked at a price tag in the high-end boutique and then dropped it as if burned. "Wow. I guess the rich really *are* different."

Mia pretended to be engrossed in the racks of handmade jeans. "Everything in my wardrobe is dated. Eight, almost nine years is a lifetime in the fashion world." At nineteen the words would have perfectly personified her shallowness. Now it took supreme acting ability to feign an interest in clothes. But Caro had swallowed it and apparently so had Jude when the security specialist had relayed her concern to him about Mia's increasing disquiet. The barrage of requests she'd made had been carefully selected. Dinner at a favorite restaurant. A night out at a local dance club. Shopping at a recently opened mall.

Jude had nixed all of her appeals, just as she'd known he would. And he'd offered a compromise that suited her needs exactly. Shopping at one specific boutique of her choice that had first undergone a security clearance, followed by an hour in a public park, with Caro armed and at her side the entire time.

It was perfect.

Mia had engaged in a lengthy decision-making process with Caro, fretting and complaining about the difficulty of choosing only one store. The woman had been adamant that they follow Jude's orders exactly and with a show of petulance Mia had finally acquiesced.

It was a bit disconcerting to realize how closely her act had paralleled her teenage behavior. Her willfulness might have grown out of a pathetic textbook attempt at summoning her father's attention. But she'd topped it off with a casual sense of entitlement that had been a direct result of being allowed to do exactly as she pleased for much of her life. She liked to think that she would have changed; that it hadn't required three years at the mercy of a sexual sadist to acquire a hint of self-awareness.

"May I help you with those?"

"Yes, please."

She handed her selections to the clerk who smiled. "I'll start dressing room three for you."

Caro accompanied them to the corridor lined with four dressing rooms and startled the clerk by examining the area closely before indicating for Mia to proceed.

Once she entered the dressing room she wasted no time in swinging the door nearly shut and dropping to her knees next to it to examine the lock. The exclusive shop—which had been one of her favorites long ago—had updated their décor but the changing room doors remained the same. A simple push button lock on the inside of the room was deemed sufficient for privacy.

Mia pressed the button on the doorknob to lock it, then dug in her wallet for the stray staples she'd collected from the bottom of the drawer in the computer desk back at the apartment. Shoving the small bits of metal into the lock on the outside handle took a bit of fine motor maneuvering. But eventually she had four wedged inside and was unable to get the lock disengaged when she depressed the button.

Carefully she took an envelope out of her wallet and set it beneath her purse before rising. Mia stuck her head out the door. "Caro?" The woman pushed away from the wall she was leaning against. "Can you help me for a minute?"

At the other woman's instant alertness, Mia had a moment's misgiving. If this failed she wasn't going to get a second chance of perhaps slipping away in the park later. Caro would insist on taking her right back to the apartment.

"I guess I'm out of practice." The abashed tone wasn't totally feigned. She already had misgivings regarding what she was about to attempt. "Could you come in and pick out the ones I should try on first? The choices…"

The instant look of understanding on the other woman's face was a kick in the conscience. "Sure." She slipped into the dressing room and Mia picked up her purse and positioned herself behind the other woman, the door still open. "Let's see." Caro took a couple hangers from the hook on the wall and held them up critically, before starting to turn.

Mia was already out the door, quickly slamming it shut. "Mia!" The rattle of the knob sounded behind her, followed by a banging. "Mia! Don't do something you'll regret!"

Sailing by the puzzled clerk, she hurried from the shop, hoping with all her being that Caro's words wouldn't prove prophetic.

* * * *

There had been no money in the purse Caro had fetched from Mia's apartment, but there had been in the backpack she'd carried from Vietnam. She'd emptied it and much of the rest of its contents into her purse before going shopping.

The taxi driver she hailed was more than happy to take her to the bank and wait for her return before continuing on to Dulles where she'd rent a car. The long trip to the airport through the tangled DC traffic gave Mia ample opportunity to think. Plenty of time to send nerves scampering up her spine.

She turned in her seat, a vain attempt to search the line of traffic behind them for a tail. Then faced forward again, feeling immediately foolish. There had never been a time when she'd felt completely safe overseas, but in the States the paranoia was always worse.

Or perhaps what she was about to do was the cause.

To distract herself she mentally walked through the steps she'd rehearsed for the last couple days. One of her IDs, Isabella Ahlman had her as a resident of Arizona which meant her false driver's license from there was good for several more years. It—and a credit card in that name would help her rent a car. But every other purchase would be made under her own name. She didn't want to make it too difficult to follow her trail.

Mia looked out the window unseeingly. It was supremely clear to her that the quickest way to locate The Collector was through Four. She was betting everything on the woman finding her. And when she did, Mia would get the answers she needed, or die trying.

In the end, it really hadn't even seemed much of a choice.

* * * *

"I let my guard down." Shamed frustration radiated off Caro in waves. She sat in Jude's office, Kacee at her side.

"I kept my eyes peeled for the outside threat. It never occurred to me that she'd pull something like that. I mean, why would she? Days after the break in at her apartment. Does she have a death wish or something?"

"Apparently."

It was all Jude said but Kacee's quick glance at him was telling. After a few more moments of self-recriminations, she ushered Caro out of the office, murmuring to the woman placatingly.

Jude balled his fists and fought a temper he usually had tightly leashed. It took every ounce of strength he had not to heave something at the window. Because with the least bit of foresight this had all been preventable.

Kacee came back inside the office and shut the door behind her. Leaned on it. The diminutive redhead fixed him with a shrewd brown gaze. "This isn't all Caro's fault, you know."

"No." With conscious effort he uncurled his fists and strode to the decanters lining the carved table. "It's mine." He poured a finger of scotch into a glass, then, after a brief hesitation, added another one.

"Actually, I was thinking that the blame should land on Deleon's shoulders. She isn't exactly a model of predictability." Kacee pushed away from the door and came into the room, concern etched on her face. "Since when do you drink at this time of day?"

"Since I let myself get played like a violin." He took a gulp from his glass. Relished the burn down his throat. "I was getting to know her. I sure as hell should have seen this coming. She all but painted me a neon sign." The knowledge lodged fangs in his chest. Sank deep. "The restlessness, yeah that was real enough. So when she laid on the other, the wanting to get out of the apartment, I tried to pacify her with an outing when I should have seen it was nothing but a diversion. A smoke screen."

Kacee plopped down on his leather couch with a decided lack of grace. "The only thing you should have seen was that Deleon is a whack job. She was five years ago and obviously that hasn't changed."

"She's not crazy." He drank again, brooding over the amber liquid in the glass. "Damaged, yes. But she knew exactly what she was doing." Caro didn't get a pass on this. Personal protection duty was just as much about guarding the client from stupid choices they made as from physical threats. There were always the ones who wanted to hook up on the side, or slip in an unobserved business deal.

But he wasn't used to a client who was intent on using herself as bait.

"I still say good riddance." Denim-clad legs stretched out in front of her, Kacee clasped her hands over her stomach. "Caro said Deleon left an envelope with your name on it. Please tell me it was a check for services rendered."

The memory of the contents of that envelope wasn't guaranteed to settle Jude's temper. He took another pull from the glass and crossed to the woman and sank down next to her. Letting his head rest against the couch for a moment, he brought the cool glass to his forehead as if to cool the temper that still simmered.

"If you're not going to drink that, give it to me."

Faintly amused, he handed her the glass. "You don't drink scotch."

She took a deep swallow. Grimaced and shuddered. "And now I know why."

He took the glass back from her. Considered its contents unseeingly. "You remember Kuykendall? In Marja?" He and Kacee had met in the Marines. The woman had been part of a special female engagement team in the Helmand province whose role it had been to forge a bond with rural Afghan women. Cultural dictates prohibited the female natives from talking to male outsiders. The female team had no such obstacles. Their mission had been for both humanitarian reasons and intelligence gathering rather than actual combat. But the female Marines had unavoidably been caught up in daily firefights on foot patrol, causing a jittery Pentagon to pull them off their assignment weeks short of their ten-month deployment.

Her voice was flat. "I remember Ky. I recall trying to talk him out of volunteering for every damn suicide mission that came up." They were both silent for a moment. Because there had finally been a mission their friend hadn't returned from.

Jude brought the glass to his lips. "Mia's like that." He felt her look at him sharply. "I knew Ky before you did. Before he lost most of his battalion to an ambush. Something like that…it changes a person."

"So she *does* have a death wish."

"Not exactly." He took another sip and thought bleakly that times like this made him feel too damn old for his years. "People like them just don't feel like they have anything left to lose."

Jude sat there long after Kacee had left. Long after his glass was empty. He had a new client presentation to prepare for. Active op reports to go over. Specifications for a new anti-malware to run tests on. But instead of tending to any of them he stared at the letter he'd pulled from his pocket. It had been in the envelope along with a check, the addition of which would make Kacee happy. But there was nothing in the words written on the paper in surprisingly feminine handwriting to soothe the tension that was growing inside him.

I know how angry you are right now. I understand it. But you're wrong if you think I'm blindly walking into danger like some stupid heroine from a gothic novel, who goes down to the dark cellar alone when she hears a noise. I know exactly what I'm doing. I've done what you would refer to as a risk assessment and realized I'm risking very little. You were in the military; you understand that saving one life isn't worth risking many. Finding Four isn't taking a crazy chance; it's the only *chance. It should be my choice and it's a gamble I'm willing to take.*

Slowly Jude crumpled the note in his fist. The check notation had made it clear Mia was severing their contract. His was a business. It was rare to lose clients, but it happened. Normal MO would be to shrug and move on. When all was said and done, clients were given his professional recommendations and then they were free to make their choice.

So there was no reason—none—for this overwhelming urge to go after her. To prevent her from setting in motion the exact events she was hoping to bring about. To stop her—God help him—from putting herself in the path of a monster.

His fingers tightened around the paper. It would help if he didn't completely understand where she was coming from. And it was that understanding that was holding him here, motionless, when he had a hundred other details to tend to. It was useless to sit here trying to weigh exactly when his concern for Mia Deleon had seeped from purely professional to the personal.

Because it was way past time to consider just what he was going to do about it.

* * * *

The clock struck seven as he slipped into the dining room, ignoring Mother's pursed lips and pointed look. Thirteen's training was coming along nicely. So nicely in fact that he'd nearly been late for dinner, and that had never been tolerated in this household.

"Good evening, Mother." He kissed her cheek, ignoring the irritated expression she wore. He'd always been able to get around her. Tonight would be no different. "Is that a Kapcsandy Cabernet Sauvignon? Excellent choice." He went to the Hepplewhite sideboard and poured himself a glass. He did feel like celebrating.

"Dinner is likely cold by now."

"It's only just seven." He sat down next to her and patted her hand. "And I lost track of time while tracing a lead on a French Louis XVI marble and bronze candelabra." Winking at her, he tipped the glass to his lips, surreptitiously loosening his tie. He despised wearing a suit in the summer.

"It just sold at Christie's last year for nearly twenty-three thousand, but I understand the owner is in a spot of trouble. I think we could pick it up for far less. And you know the Barclays would be interested if we did."

Talk of business had her annoyance fading, just as he'd known it would. "Is it neoclassical? Hannah Barclay would snap that up. Especially if we arrange a special showing. She always pays more if she thinks she's getting first crack at it."

The maid carried in a tray and set their lobster and black truffle salads in front of them. He waited until the woman had left the room before laying his napkin across his lap and picking up his fork. "I'm sure that can be arranged. I'll call the seller first thing tomorrow."

"For that kind of money, I'd prefer you make the trip in person and conduct the authentication yourself."

Mentally he damned himself for bringing up the topic. He'd been guilty of neglecting his collection lately; he had a habit of doing that when he acquired a new item. But then he gave a mental shrug. The seller was in Atlanta, a major airport hub. He should be able to get there and back in one day, with plenty of time afterwards to tend to his own needs. "Of course, Mother. I'll arrange it."

Completely over her earlier pique she beamed at him. "You're such a good son, Anthony. I don't know what I'd do without you."

He dug into the lobster, shot her a smile. "You'll never have to find out."

"It's selfish of me, I know. But sometimes I'm just so happy things didn't work out for you a few years back when you were dating Victoria. I know I was guilty of pushing her at you from the first, but she just never was your equal, dear." She paused to bring a bite of lobster to her lips. Chewed and swallowed. "It isn't finicky to be particular, and Victoria was a bit too common for my tastes. Certainly not good enough for you, regardless of her family's money."

Victoria had been a pretentious bitch, rather plain looking really, and not at all unconventional in the bedroom. Anthony had lost interest in a month, but had waited until his mother had started voicing disapproval before breaking things off. It was easier that way. "You were right about her, Mother. You're an excellent judge of character."

She paused in the act of bringing her wine glass to her lips and smiled at him. "You have plenty of time to find a wife. Your father was forty-four before we started dating. There's nothing wrong with having exacting taste. It's what puts you a cut above other men and someday you'll find a woman who's your equal. She's out there, I promise."

His mouth curled. He could have told his mother that no woman was worthy. Not without his precise schooling and tutoring. But a patient man was rewarded with the rarest of treasures.

And the beauties in his collection were rare indeed.

7

It had been nearly nine years since she'd driven a car, and Mia had forgotten the sheer joy of being behind the wheel. She'd had a love affair with speeding once upon a time, as well as an impressive array of tickets to show for it.

Mia drove only a few hours before stopping in Johnstown, Pennsylvania. At approximately twenty thousand, the town was the perfect size. She didn't want to make tracking her too difficult. To that end, she stopped twice for purchases at gas stations, using the instant approval credit card registered in her own name that she'd gotten through the bank.

That experience had been more than a little disconcerting. It seemed the height of irony that after traveling under several false IDs, it was only when she professed to be herself that she had to submit to a fingerprint exam to verify her identity. Being Russell Deleon's daughter and heiress to his mother-in-law's fortune invited a higher level of scrutiny than did plain old Samantha Simmons.

The drive had allowed time for her plan to coalesce. She didn't believe Four would have the ability to trail Mia on her own. She'd take her orders from the man who'd once enslaved them both. Mia had to believe The Collector was somehow behind Halston's murder. That he'd tracked her through the man's computer. Either he or someone he'd hired had the ability to trace her movements online. She just had to hope he was still looking.

Choosing a motel took an inordinate amount of time before she finally settled on a cheaper one on the outskirts of town. It featured a string of rooms directly accessed from the parking lot outside. She made sure the lot was well lit and the door locks were sturdy. Mia had no intention of losing a struggle if Four came for her, so the element of surprise had to be eliminated. Either Mia's questioning of the woman would garner a lead to where The Collector kept his captives, or she herself would be taken back to the monster.

A trail of icy little ants crept up her spine at the thought. It solidified her purpose. She wouldn't lose the skirmish with Four. She couldn't.

After a trip to a supercenter discount store, she returned to her room and laid her purchases out on the bed. Another knife—a smaller one to fit in a sheath around her ankle. An even tinier blade that would be hidden in the channel meant to house the underwire in her bra. Two vials of pepper spray. First aid supplies. An iPhone with a service plan that she still needed to sync with the iPad. A mini-tape recorder. And a baggy pair of cargo pants that would house her various purchases.

Mia surveyed the items with an assessing eye. They represented more than preparation for battle.

They were tools for survival.

* * * *

"What do you want?" The heavy mask off, he swiped a hand through his sweaty hair.

"I called a few minutes ago, but you said never to leave a message. What were you doing?"

He watched Thirteen on the camera feed from the computer in the outer area. The private room in the newer garage on the property had been his father's addition. Maybe the old man had arranged trysts with the help there. Perhaps he'd snuck hookers on the grounds right under everyone's nose.

Anthony smiled at the thought. He liked to think the old guy was capable of it. Certainly he'd been delighted when he'd discovered the place after Father's death. He couldn't pretend that the space had made his own collection possible. It had already been well under way by then. But it had been nice to have an area for a boot camp so close to home. Although well worth the labor involved, the training for each new item for his collection was time consuming.

"I was working," he answered shortly. Thirteen struggled against her bonds, writhed on the bed and shrieked. He didn't have the sound on, but her throat was arched, the cords in it standing out in sharp relief. The room was fully soundproofed, of course. Father had been quite thorough. Still, it was a clear violation of the rules, and she'd have to be punished. His hand drifted down his bare body, stroking his cock as he gave thought to her discipline. The chamber he'd constructed with Eleven in mind was finished and waiting in the corner of this room. But even as he considered it, he discarded the idea. The key to effective discipline was choosing a punishment that fit the crime. Thirteen's violation deserved no more than a simple beating. Or perhaps the enthusiastic use of the speculum that she seemed to despise so much.

"I've got some credit card activity in that name you've had me watching."

Thoughts of the woman screaming in the next room were wiped from his mind. "Which one?"

"Mia Deleon. I check both the names you gave me regularly for credit card activity. She activated a card this afternoon. Had purchases in Hagerston, Virginia and

Johnstown, Pennsylvania. Nothing since then, but she used it twice in Johnstown, as recently as a couple hours ago. At a gas station and again at a Walmart."

"Interesting." The word, and the nonchalant tone it was delivered in contrasted sharply with the excitement chugging through his veins. *What are you up to, Eleven?* She'd taken great pains to this point to cover her tracks, thereby causing him a great deal of time and expense. A thought occurred then, eroding his joy. "Maybe it's someone else using her name."

He could hear the other man's shrug in his voice. "Always possible. Want me to keep on it?"

"Yes." His response was automatic. He used the computer in front of him to Google the two towns the man had mentioned. They were on the 270/99 Interstate corridor north of DC. A sense of satisfaction filled him. So she *had* run home from Vietnam. After her miserable failure in Da Nang, Four had gotten no sighting of her in the States. Certainly she hadn't returned to her own apartment.

One had to wonder where she was off to now. And if she had surrounded herself with security the way she did years ago.

"Why wasn't I called earlier?"

"I got a life, you know?" The tone set Anthony's teeth on edge. "I don't sit in front of the computer *all* day."

"You do if you want to get paid. Alert me immediately if and when you see activity again." The call ended, and he set the cell down, still studying the map on the computer. It wouldn't hurt to send Four in that direction. That way, if it was indeed Eleven using the card, she could easily be picked up.

But the vicinity of the card use made him think it was her. There was a hum in his veins, the kind he got whenever one of his possessions required punishment. He was being offered yet another chance to bring his missing item back to his collection.

He'd been exceedingly patient. But he'd tolerate no more screw-ups.

* * * *

It hadn't occurred to Mia that she'd be exchanging one cage for another, but by the time darkness fell she'd worn the carpet in the room a great deal thinner with her pacing. There was little to be done to pass the time. Having Caro to talk to had at least defused the boredom.

Thoughts of the woman brought a pang. She hoped she hadn't gotten the security agent in trouble with Jude. Mia doubted the man was particularly understanding about professional failures.

Although, she recalled suddenly, he'd been unexpectedly compassionate after they'd returned from Raiker's complex. The memory brought a wash of warmth. Events of the day had been trying, and her tolerance level had been at low ebb. She hadn't known what to expect when he'd knocked at her door. It was the first time he'd entered her personal space. But whatever she would have guessed would have missed the mark by several miles.

There had been pain there layered far below the dispassionate revelation about his childhood. She'd recognized the pain and understood the disconnection needed for the retelling. She still didn't know what had compelled Jude Bishop to offer her that slice of his personal history. Was half glad he'd never realize how touched she'd been by his words.

I hate that it happened to you.

She stuck a finger between the slats of the blind and looked out at the parking lot for the dozenth time. Likely any softer fleeting feelings he'd once harbored had vanished when he learned of how she'd slipped away from Caro. That, too, was understandable. Mia knew what she'd experienced would forever set her apart from most people. She didn't expect him to understand why she'd had to take this chance. Pulling her hand back, she turned toward the bed. With most of every waking hour for the last eight and a half years spent encased in misery or a quest for survival, she didn't process the world the way others did. She likely never would.

Using the bathroom, she then readied for bed by donning a fresh set of clothes. She transferred her purchases from the bed to the table next to it. Then she pulled the coverlet back and climbed onto the mattress. Arranged the pillows against the headboard and reached for the pepper spray. Clicking off the lamp, she settled into a more comfortable upright position. As an afterthought, she drew her knife from beneath her tee shirt. Set it on the mattress beside her.

Sleep wouldn't be easily summoned. It never was. Her subconscious was constantly on guard against the dreams that picked the twilight hours to haunt. Expecting Four to appear was just another sort of nightmare.

But it was one she was mentally and physically prepared for. She was doing the only thing she could to give the women she'd left a chance for freedom. There was comfort in that.

* * * *

Her eyes came open, took a moment to adjust before sorting shadows in the gloom. Instantly alert, she glanced at the clock on the table beside her. Nearly two.

She hadn't slept. Maybe dozed a bit. Her fingers searched for her weapon on the bed next to her. Closed around its hilt. Her other hand still clutched the vial of spray. Straightening in bed, Mia listened carefully for whatever had awakened her.

There were the usual unfamiliar noises from a strange place. The slight whooshing sound came from the bathroom, she thought. Pipes echoing the labor of ancient plumbing. Nothing moved in the bedroom. All was in place.

Her nape prickled. There had been something. Some *thing* that had brought all her senses awake and hyper-vigilant. Eyes burning, she stared at the covered window.

Skinny pale fingers of light spilled from the security lamps on the walkway and probed the edges of the blind. They did little to dispel the darkness in the room. She listened, ears straining, but heard no sound.

The glow at the left of the blind darkened. Staring hard she watched as a shadow fell across the right side of the window.

Someone was outside. Mia slipped out of bed, padded silently across to the door. Looked out through the peephole. Saw no one.

Soft amber pools beneath the scattered security lamps interrupted the darkness in the parking lot. She could see nothing amiss there, but her line of vision was restricted. Still, the flesh rose on her arms. From a well-developed primitive instinct or rampant paranoia, she couldn't tell.

She stepped away from the door. Someone had passed by the window. The motel had capacity for sixty someones, and any one of them could have been going to their room a moment ago. That was the reasonable explanation. One she almost accepted until the pale glow bordering the right of her shade abruptly went black.

Her heart tripped once. Paused. Then set up a steady canter inside her chest. The security lamps. The lights in the parking lot were too far away, but the ones on the walkway in front of the rooms were not. She'd specifically looked at them when she was deciding on a room. Had made sure they were in working order as night began to fall. Her room was two doors down from one on the right and another on the left.

And now neither of them worked.

She strode back to the bedside table. Secured the smaller knife sheath around her ankle. Started the mini-recorder and set it behind the cheap alarm, out of sight. She slipped the extra pepper spray canister in one of the pockets of the cargo pants she wore. The only entrances to the room were the door and the window. Mia surveyed both for a moment. Made a decision.

Crossing the room, she removed the safety lock. Opened the door far enough to flip the latch forward, which kept the door from fully closing again. Pulling the lone chair away from the desk, she set it in the bathroom doorway. Sat. The position gave her an unimpeded line of vision to the entrance. If Four was out there Mia was issuing an unmistakable invitation. If anyone else took her up on it…she smiled grimly. Tightened her grip on the knife. Then he—or she—would soon be having a very bad night.

Minutes crawled by. Adrenaline was coursing through her body, increasing her heart rate. Tensing her muscles. Shrouded in the darkness Mia felt herself reverting to a more primal version of herself. She welcomed a final showdown with Four. Whatever the outcome she was ready to end the period of suspended animation she'd been caught in for too long.

Twenty minutes passed. Thirty. Then there was a slight sound. A shoe on cement. Her muscles bunched. Poised to spring. Unblinkingly she kept her eyes on the door. Watched it slowly swing inward. Forced herself to wait until a figure darkened the doorway. Took a step inside.

Then she lunged. Mia was halfway across the room when a primitive area of her brain raised an alarm. The figure was bigger than Four would be. Taller than *he* would be. Simultaneously the stranger held up a pinpoint of light. Uttered one word.

"Mia."

She halted with a suddenness that had her body swaying in place. And was swamped with a tangle of conflicting emotion when she recognized the voice.

Jude Bishop.

* * * *

He flipped on the light. Took in everything in the space of a few seconds. Her sentry chair. Her weapons. And with an exaggerated glance behind him, the open door. "You did everything but leave a trail of gumdrops."

Adrenaline…at fever pitch moments ago was ebbing with an abruptness that left her muscles weak. "Why are you here?" Whatever she'd felt upon recognizing him, it was frustrated temper that was uppermost now. She reached out and gripped a handful of his shirt to pull him further inside the room and shut the door. "You're going to ruin everything."

"If by everything you mean your possible death and or kidnapping, that was sort of the point."

She shook her head, partly because she was unable to believe they were having this conversation yet again. And partly because she had to be a complete cretin to have felt, even for a moment, an unexpected burst of joy at seeing him again.

"I realize I left somewhat abruptly. If I neglected to fill out a customer satisfaction survey you can email it to me." She tucked the pepper spray into a pocket and placed her hand against his arm in an effort to nudge him on his way. He didn't move.

"I didn't come because I have a problem with client rejection," he muttered irritably. His expression matched his tone. He hadn't shaved that day, and his jaw was shadowed with whiskers. Though she'd often found his moss green eyes enigmatic, it was all too easy to read the annoyance in his gaze now. He turned and went to the door, opening it far enough to swing the latch back inside and shut it.

"Then why are you here?" She went to the window and cracked the blinds to look outside. Nothing was moving. The lights on the walkway were still dark, leaving the stretch of rooms on either side of her in shadows. If Four was out there somewhere watching, Jude's arrival would make her pull back. Or leave completely.

"Because I'm ignoring every ounce of professional business sense I have for a client with self-destructive urges."

Dropping the blind, she turned to face him. "Ex-client. We've had this conversation before. Nothing has changed. You can't talk me out of this. Not when you have no better alternative for getting a line on where he keeps those women. They've waited over *five years*. Did they think my escape would mean they'd be rescued? Have they spent every day since then, hope evaporating because I wasn't observant enough when I left? I didn't give a thought to how I'd lead the police back to them. I wasn't thinking at all." She drew a breath, half surprised at the ferocity of the words. They were true. Every one of them. And every day of her freedom she'd lived with the accompanying guilt.

He was still, watching her. His presence shrank the room somehow, made him seem closer, bigger than he really was. Mia drew a breath. He was just a man. It had been years since she'd gotten jittery being in contact with males. But this particular one elicited responses that were unfamiliar. Maybe it wasn't him who made her uneasy at all. Perhaps it was her reaction to him that set those inner alarms shrilling. Pushing her hair back from her face, she grappled for reason.

"You didn't erase your history on the computer at the apartment." The non sequitur caught her off guard. "Kacee found it when it was brought back to the offices. She's convinced that the fact you left evidence of your location was an open invitation for one of us to follow you. Called it a Rapunzel complex."

Now she was completely stupefied. "You mean because I signed up for a data plan and turned on location services for my iPad? Of course I didn't erase it. It's my fall back. I bought an iPhone and enabled it, too. If by some chance things don't go my way with Four, someone could locate us if I have either of the devices with me. At least they could find the last point we were before they were discovered. That way even my death wouldn't necessarily end the chances of finding the other women. I've thought this through, Jude. I'm not stupid."

"Not stupid at all. Just unbelievably fatalistic." He tucked something in his jeans pocket. His cell phone, she realized. He must have a flashlight app on it. "I suspected as much. I can't figure out if I'm more disturbed when I can predict what you're thinking or when I misread you completely." His meaning was clear.

Heat warmed her cheeks. She couldn't meet his gaze. But if anything this scene was a reminder of why she had to leave the way she did. "I hope you weren't too hard on Caro."

"I blamed myself more." He went to the bathroom and carried the chair she had set there back into the room. Sat in it and rolled his shoulders tiredly.

Foreboding filled her. "Did you get a room?"

Giving an exaggerated look around, he said, "Looks like you have plenty of space."

"No. You can't stay here."

His brow cocked sardonically. "How do you propose to get rid of me?"

Urgency settled in her chest. "She won't come if you're in here. I have to be alone."

"We have time." He toed his shoes off. Stretched. "You left a trail a child could follow with credit cards alone. But you've convinced me that Four is a tool and she doesn't move without being activated. I doubt it will be immediate."

"She may already be here." Explaining about the lights going out earlier, she ended with, "That's why I left the door open. Being fully prepared gives me an advantage."

"As much advantage as anyone has when they're inviting violence." But he rose and went to the door, unlocked it and stepped outside. It was several minutes before he returned. "Both bulbs are missing. You're sure the lights were on earlier?"

The question had her setting her teeth. If she were even half as security unconscious as he tried to make her feel, she wouldn't have lasted a week living alone abroad. "Quite sure."

"They would have been too tall for her to reach without standing on something. Did you hear anything before they went out?"

"No. Something woke me, though. And I saw a shadow move across the window around two." A sudden thought occurred. "How long were you out there?"

"About fifteen minutes before I came in. I was checking license plates on cars." He locked the door behind him and returned to the chair he'd vacated earlier. "None had Virginia plates, so it didn't tell me much."

That surprised her. "Mine is out there. Navy Ford compact."

"A rental?"

"From Dulles."

He shifted to get more comfortable in the chair. "If it's an open-ended rental they often give you a car with out-of-state plates in the hopes of getting them returned closer to the car's home."

Silence stretched then. Nerves scampered through her system. "Jude." His name tasted foreign on her tongue. She realized with a degree of surprise she'd never used it before. At least out loud. "What are you really doing here?"

He didn't respond for a minute. Then, "Short of convincing you to give this whole thing up?"

"That isn't going to happen."

"Then I'm here to keep you from getting yourself killed. Call it a professional courtesy. I realize—and believe me, this isn't easy to admit—that I can't force you to listen to reason. If you're set on using yourself as bait, there are methods to consider. You don't want the showdown to occur in a motel room, for instance. There are too many weapons here you'd be putting at her disposal. The lamp or its cord. The chair. The room confines her actions, but they restrict you, too. And that pepper spray you had in your hand? Bad idea in an enclosed space. Most likely it'd drift back and you'd be cross-contaminated. It should be used in an open area, outdoors, to be most effective."

Because his suggestions had merit she considered them seriously. "So where do I want to stage the meeting with her?"

"Outside, but in a place of your choosing. The more familiar you are with the area the more advantage you have. First you map escape routes, both yours and those she might take to evade you. You check for potential weapons. The likelihood of witnesses. Choosing the location gives you the upper hand." He slouched further down in the chair in an obvious quest to get more comfortable. Considering its back hit him mid-spine, comfort was going to be difficult to achieve.

"Is that what you learned in the military? How to stage an ambush?" Her attempt at humor fell flat. There was no answering flicker of amusement in his expression. His voice when he spoke was flat.

"I was a Marine. Recon. So yeah, I know a thing or two about that. I also learned not to send someone into battle alone." She was left with no doubt about his feelings. Jude was no happier about this idea than he'd been in the safe house. He couldn't very well toss her over his shoulder and haul her back to DC against her will. But he had a myriad of other options. She wasn't his responsibility anymore. He had nothing to gain from coming after her, at least that she could figure out. And yet here he was.

I learned not to send someone into battle alone. The words evoked an odd sense of relief. He wasn't here for her; it was some dated noble calling inside him that had compelled him to come. Mia wouldn't have known what to do with someone else's sense of obligation, and she certainly didn't want to be responsible for him. People who strayed into her path of personal misfortune had a habit of winding up dead.

Thoughts of Hoa and Dr. Halston brought a knot to her throat. Two people had died because of their association with her. Despite the doubts he'd expressed, Jude couldn't convince her otherwise. It would be better for her to be alone. Cleaner. She'd had everything mapped out specifically so that no one else would get caught up in this mess. Mia didn't think she could handle it if someone else ended up hurt—or dead— because of a connection to her.

It was only then that she realized she was still holding the knife. Feeling foolish, she put it back in the sheath. Lowered the hem of her shirt.

He didn't owe her anything. Not like she owed those women left with The Collector. But she hadn't reckoned on his misguided sense of duty to a woman he barely knew. She crossed finally to the bed. Sat down on the edge. There was nothing to do about his presence now. Mia couldn't get rid of him if she wanted to. She had even less chance of extricating Jude from her plan as he did at talking her out of it.

She sent a troubled gaze toward him. He was half lying in the chair, his long legs crossed at the ankle in a pose that would likely have his back screaming for a week. "You're not going to be able to sleep."

"I will. If you stop talking."

Mia gave a mental sigh. Wished the words didn't feel like surrender. "You can have the bed." Saying it out loud was as good as admitting what she'd already recognized. He was here to stay, regardless of how she felt about it.

"There's room for both of us." His words brought a spurt of panic, but he was already on his feet and approaching her. She rolled to the other side. Would have slipped off the mattress had he not laid his hand on her arm.

"We both need sleep, Mia." His voice was a low rumble in the darkness. "And call me suspicious, but I don't trust you across the room close to a door."

Ignoring the apprehension filtering through her system, she set a pillow against the headboard. Propped herself against it. She hadn't slept with someone else in the room since—her mind skirted the end of that thought. Not since her escape. Already her palms were damp. Her breathing quickening.

Stupid, she chided herself. Jude Bishop wasn't a threat to her. Logically she knew that. It was a simple matter of control. Mind over reflex. She focused on releasing tension from each muscle at a time. Toes. Foot. Calf.

"Why Vietnam?"

She froze. "What do you mean?"

He wasn't having the same problem she was relaxing. He was sprawled on the bed, taking up more than his share of space. "I mean why go there? How did you pick the countries you lived in? You were in Panama first, right?"

Shifting lower in the bed, she considered. She wasn't used to explaining her decisions. Had no one close to talk to in nearly a decade. Wouldn't have allowed anyone near enough if they'd tried. "Well…cost of living was one consideration. It was possible I'd spend the rest of my life abroad so I wasn't looking for someplace with extravagant prices. I weighed things like ex-pat population. Climate. Safety for women." That had ruled out several countries out of hand. "Distance away from the states. I…felt safer the further away I moved."

"Good things to consider. Is that why you left Panama?"

Under the blanket of darkness the conversation took on an intimacy she was unused to. But it was also easier to speak when she couldn't see his face. Watch for his reactions. She'd become a world-class observer and she couldn't seem to turn the trait off. "I wasn't crazy about the rainy season, but it was nice there. Pretty. But it was difficult for me to settle down. If I stayed in one place for too long I began feeling…"

"…trapped."

"Exactly." She brought up a hand to stifle a yawn. "Paranoia was my driving force and I hadn't learned to control it then. I moved around. Then eventually decided to try another country."

"And landed in Bermuda." His voice sounded sleepy. She knew for a fact that he was capable of instant slumber. And realized in a flash that the conversation was for her benefit. Like when he'd recognized the beginning of a panic attack in Raiker's lab.

Knowing that he could read her so well should have been disconcerting. And it was on some level. It also suffused her with an odd warmth. "Someone I met in Panama City talked about its beauty all the time. And it was. Gorgeous." She'd meant to stay as long as she had in Panama. At least a couple years. Had only made it one before nerves had propelled her to run further. Hide deeper.

"I was planning on Thailand next. Certainly it's easier to get into. But when I compared it with Vietnam online I got sucked in by the scenery. When you have no job to go to, no set routine, it helps to have mountains and beautiful beaches to explore." Her voice was wry. "Of course, the monsoon season was something of a downside."

"And after this is over?" He rolled to his side, shortening the distance between them. She was intensely aware of that fact. And the expected anxiety was there. Her heart rate sped up. Her muscles tensed. But the responses were more muted than before. Sheer exhaustion, perhaps. "What will you do when there's no longer any reason to run? When you can do exactly as you please without looking over your shoulder?"

"I don't know." Better to ignore the question than to admit she hadn't let herself think about it. What-ifs belonged to people with a future. People who could afford to dream and hope. Those who actually remembered *how* to hope. After eight and a half years she finally had a purpose. Something that drove her besides fear and pain, nightmares and rampant paranoia. It could be enough. If in some small way she could help free those women she'd ask for nothing else.

"Start thinking about it, Mia." His voice was barely audible, as if he were fighting sleep. "The guys I wanted at my side in a fire fight? They weren't the ones who had nothing to lose. They were the ones who had something to live for."

She considered his words long after he slept. Long after she should have followed suit. He was still turned toward her, and she watched him in the darkness. His position was likely to ensure that she didn't sneak off. His ruined cheek was pressed against the mattress and only a perfect profile was visible. Jude was the embodiment of his own words. He'd survived. More probably, than she could know. Even more, he'd thrived. And that was a condition she was still striving for.

She could be satisfied with less. A sense of contentment. Life without fear. It was more than she'd once dared ask for.

But optimism about the future was something she wouldn't even try to resurrect. Because there was no pain quite like that of hope dying, a fraction at a time.

Ironically enough, for a woman who could buy just about anything she desired, hope was the one luxury she couldn't afford.

* * * *

Mia woke up to find herself alone in the bed and more than a little shocked to discover she'd slept. No dreams, unless she counted that constant buzz of nerves that she blamed more on Jude's presence than the possibility of Four being nearby.

The bathroom door opened and he stood framed in the center of it, clad only in unbuttoned jeans. There was an open duffel bag sitting on the chair by the desk. Shock filtered through her. She'd not only slept, she'd done so soundly enough that she hadn't heard him go out to retrieve the bag. Hadn't even heard the shower running. Stunned, she shoved her hand through her hair and watched him mutely.

"Sorry." He crossed to his luggage and dug around in it, straightening with socks and a navy tee in his hand. "It's still pretty early. I didn't want to wake you."

Glancing at the clock she saw that it read six-thirty. So they'd only slept a few hours. Nothing unusual about that. But the fact that she'd slept like the dead next to him *was* unusual.

"I'll be done in here in a minute. Need to shave." He rubbed his free hand over his jaw. "Unless…" He cocked his head toward the room he'd just vacated. "If you need it first…"

"No. I'm fine."

He disappeared into the bathroom, shutting the door behind him. Mia let out a long stream of pent-up breath. Bounced from the bed and headed to her backpack. She was used to traveling light, and his bag held more than her pack did. At least…she snuck a peek. It had more space. It looked as though he only had another change of clothes and some sort of gadget enclosed in a black case.

Gawking at his things made her feel a bit like a voyeur so she hastily averted her eyes. She had to go far back to her late teens to remember the experience of waking up with another person. Sharing a room with him. A bathroom. The memory had a name. Kevin Burnett. A guy she'd met at MIT and had—for the briefest of time—fancied herself wildly in love with.

The recollection was tangible but fuzzy at the edges, made so not just by the passage of years but of a lifetime. Mia shook her head as she rooted around in her pack for a different shirt. She could no longer imagine ever being that comfortable with someone. That emotionally intimate. Giving the bathroom door a quick visual check she replaced her shirt and briefly considered switching pants. Decided the pockets in the ones she wore were as handy as an extra purse.

"Okay, all yours."

She swung around to face him. Noted the clean-shaven jaw. His short brown hair was already dry. "While you're getting ready I'm going to go take another look around the parking lot and the surrounding area. Lock up after I go out." He strode to the door then turned to laser a look at her. "And Mia. I expect you here when I come back."

The return of his distrust might have been earned, but she still felt vaguely insulted. "I'll be here." Subterfuge was useless at this point anyway. He went out and she followed him to the door. Secured it behind him. Then hurried to use the bathroom before he came back. It had already been a morning of firsts. She didn't think she was up to adding another.

Fifteen minutes later Mia unlocked the door again to let him in. He raised a brow. "I didn't knock."

"I was watching through the window." He'd walked the parking lot like a grid, looking the cars over, subjecting anyone who happened by to a thorough visual examination. "What are we going to do about my car?" It was parked almost directly outside her front door.

"I'll have to send a couple people after it." He'd parked his vehicle at a perpendicular angle to hers headed toward the exit of the lot. "Give me the keys and wait here." Jude unlocked it with the fob, pulled open the door and dropped the keys to the floor mat before manually engaging the lock again.

When he returned she inquired, "How do you expect them to get the keys out of a locked vehicle?"

"If they can't figure that out, they shouldn't be working for me." A door next to hers opened then, and he crowded her back inside as a man in a suit walked briskly out to the middle of the lot. They waited until he pulled away before he seemed satisfied. "Okay."

Mia walked close to him, her gaze darting from right and left. Last night she'd been convinced Four had followed her to this motel. In the light of day her suspicions had faded slightly. Maybe the woman had seen Jude and been scared off. Perhaps not enough time had passed for her to have trailed Mia in the first place.

The element of danger had felt all too real just a few hours earlier. It hadn't completely subsided. "She could be here," she murmured. "Waiting. Watching. Maybe intending to get in her car and follow us when we leave."

"That would save us some time." He rounded the hood to open the front passenger door. "Get in. We'll discuss it while I drive."

At a sound behind her she turned to see a man with a ball cap pulled low come out of a room and head across the lot. He had his head down, appearing more interested in the fast food bag he was carrying than in them. She slipped into the seat. Noticed in the next instant that the man had halted at their car. Looked up and raised something in the air.

"Get down! Get down!"

"Gun!" Mia's voice mingled with Jude's simultaneously a split instant before there was a loud report and he crumpled to the pavement, his body spasming uncontrollably.

Reaction was instantaneous and automatic. Mia rolled out of the car, digging in her pocket for the pepper spray. Pulling out the knife in a swift practiced movement. Her focus was fractured by the sight of him jerking uncontrollably on the ground—*not dead not dead not dead*—and the figure who was approaching, hand trembling as he ejected a cartridge from the gun he carried and replaced it with a different one from the sack.

Comprehension slammed into her. Not a man at all she saw now, but Four. No blond hair in sight, her bald head was covered by a Phillies hat. Mia brought her hand up, finger on the button of the vial.

"If you try it I give him another jolt." The woman pointed the TASER at Jude's heart. Mia hesitated. Jude's muscles were still contracting and releasing violently. Two probes were buried in his shoulder. She could see the wires leading from each one. "Who knows, at this range it might be lethal." The woman smiled gleefully. "It'd be sort of fun to find out, wouldn't it?"

"All right." Mia straightened, hoping to take the woman's attention off Jude. She held out the vial with two fingers. Dropped it. It rolled a few feet away. She visually measured the distance between her and Four. Her muscles tensed. There were at least six feet separating them. If she could get closer…

"And the knife. Now!"

Mia made a show of holding it away from her side as she inched toward the woman. "He isn't involved in this. It's just you and me. Let's go before anyone else comes along. Let's go."

The woman's finger tightened on the trigger. "Stay where you are and drop that knife or I'm going to do my damnedest to stop his heart."

She halted, her gaze scanning the parking lot for someone, anyone who might happen by. It remained maddeningly empty, their little tableau playing out for an audience of three.

Four's finger tightened on the trigger. "Or maybe you don't care."

The knife clattered when it hit the pavement. "Kick it under the car." After Mia did so, the other woman's lip curled. "Maybe you obey a bit better for me than you did our Master." She raised her hand to reveal a key fob. As she pressed a button, the trunk of a nearby sedan raised. Four rose. "We're going to go over and you'll get in the trunk. Then the two of us will be on our way."

Mia cast a glance at Jude. How long did the effects of the TASER last? Already the spasming had lessened. His gaze met hers and she knew that all she had to do was buy them both some time. But it would help to get Four as far away from him as possible. "All right." After she'd put several feet between them and Jude she deliberately slowed. Four violently shoved her forward. "He's due for another jolt and this thing is effective up to fifteen feet."

She put one foot in the trunk, using her bent position to grip the knife hidden at her ankle. Heard the telltale sound of Four's weapon being fired again and the noise released something dangerous and primitive inside her. "No!" She straightened and whirled, knife in hand. Mia swung the blade in a vicious arc at the same time Four reached to give her a push. Sliced the woman across the arm.

With a high-pitched howl Four snatched her hand back and ejected the cartridge. Evading the next slash of the knife, she pressed the weapon against Mia's back. The jolts of electricity had her arching, her body going numb from the stunner.

"More trouble than you're worth. I always told Master so." The pain, fierce and brutal at first, faded when the device was removed. But her muscles were jerking and unresponsive. Four folded her into the trunk and Mia couldn't summon a physical response to stop her. Something pricked her arm and a wild shriek emanated from her. In her mind she was fighting the injection. Screaming and struggling and battling like a wild thing. In reality she was motionless, the world already spinning away in a dizzying spiral.

She felt the backpack being torn away. Two hands shoved her further into the trunk. Mia saw the lid closing and ordered her muscles to come to life. They didn't respond. The car started. Began to move. Consciousness fading, she willed her body to respond. There had to be some way to get out the trunk of a car. A lever or cable… The thought was hard to hold on to. Her thinking was muddled. Mia felt like she was being sucked into a turbulent vortex. She had one last guilt-ridden thought about Jude's fate before everything went black.

8

Jude opened his eyes. Stared at the overhead lights before closing them again. Fluorescent dots danced beneath his eyelids. Forcing them open once more he grasped a metal bar next to him. Hauled himself upright. Stared hard.

A hospital bed? What the hell? Snippets of memory swirled in his head but his mind was muzzy and he had a bastard of a headache. Four had tased him. He shook his head, bit back an oath when the movement threatened to jar something vital loose in his brain. Shit. He didn't need a hospital after being tased a couple times.

Because he didn't have the strength to climb over the bars, he started to scoot down in the bed to where they ended. Was brought up short by tubes attached to his hand. An IV. Wincing, he yanked off the tape holding the needle in place and removed it. The action summoned another flicker of memory. He'd managed to get to his feet when Four had come flying across the parking lot. Someone had been there to help him. But she'd shouted at them to leave him alone. He frowned. Struggled to remember. A heart attack. She'd said he was having a heart attack. And then there had been a needle.

She'd drugged him. Which meant she'd likely drugged Mia. Recalling her panic attack at the mere suggestion of a narcotic, his mouth flattened. He had to get to her. Before the whacked-out robot of a woman did her real harm.

At the edge of the bed now, he tried standing, wobbled a bit and then spied his clothes in a plastic bag on a chair. Stumbled toward them. Dressing was going to have to wait a couple minutes. Right now he needed the support of a chair to keep from sliding to the floor.

Whatever Four had injected him with packed a helluva wallop, and he had at least seventy pounds on Mia.

An image of her as he'd found her last night swam across his mind. Armed to the teeth. A look of ferocity that had been jarringly out of place on that beautiful face. As much good as he'd done her today, she would have been better off facing Four on her own last night.

He dug in his pants pocket to bring out his phone, his gut clenching. If he dwelled on what she might be going through right now he'd be no good to either of them. Jude speed dialed a familiar number. Waited impatiently for Kacee to answer. When she did he spoke with all the urgency he was feeling. "Things went south in Pennsylvania. Four has Mia."

"Four? That woman from the security video? Gone south how?"

He clenched his jaw, throttled down impatience. "Top priority, Kace. Code red. Activate the location features on Mia's electronic devices. I need to alert the police to find the car she's in. Put a call into Raiker." He might end up needing the law enforcement doors the man's name could open. "Tell him she's been kidnapped by a woman who'll deliver her back to The Collector." Speaking the words aloud made it impossible to contain his nerves. He surged to his feet. Reached for his bag of clothes. Mentally cursed when a wave of dizziness hit him.

Pulling out his shirt he frowned as colored bits of paper drifted to the floor. Comprehension filtered in sluggishly. "Evidence. There will be confetti at the scene where I was tased." He ignored the concerned exclamations from Kacee as he removed the rest of his clothes from the sack, careful to preserve the brightly colored snippets of paper. The TASER would have released dozens of the tiny pieces each time it was discharged. They acted as personal identification features. If a crime was determined to have been committed, the corporation would match the information on those pieces and release the identification of the owner from their AFID database to law enforcement. A process that no doubt would take far longer than Jude was willing to wait.

"Send two operatives up here. No, send one and have him accompanied by Logan. Tell him to bring whatever he needs to work on the road." Logan Spirrow had orchestrated the infiltration of necessary databases in Vietnam. Jude would be much too busy to take care of that end of things himself. "Have you got a location yet?"

"Let me get to the computer. I'm half a building away." But from the sounds of her breathing Kacee was running. "You took your mini laptop with you. Can't you use it?"

"It's still at the scene." Jude had no idea where his car or belongings were. But on his priority list that hit squarely at zero. Mia's welfare was number one. And he was reminded of the reason it was imperative to maintain a distance with clients. To keep anything that hinted at emotion locked away. It clouded logic like nothing else could. And damned if he wasn't feeling emotion right now. An overwhelming tangle of anxiety and guilt that threatened to choke him.

He elbowed that aside to focus on Kacee's next words. "Okay, I'm bringing the location up now. I feel short on details here. What else aren't you telling me?"

"That I'm standing here in a girly hospital gown with my ass hanging out," he snapped. "The location, Kace."

"O-okay. This map is a more appealing image than the one you're painting anyway. The Friend's Inn. Looks like a mile or so outside Johnstown, Pennsylvania."

Disappointed hissed out of him like steam from a kettle. "Are you sure? That's where this all went down. In the parking lot."

"I'm certain."

Somewhere down the hall a cart creaked. A distant voice sounded on a loudspeaker. "Are you looking at the iPad location feature?"

"That's what's on the computer."

"Because she bought an iPhone. The devices should be synced."

"Did she set up iCloud? Why yes, she did. And here's a doc with her Apple ID." Now Kacee appeared to be talking to herself more than him. "Very convenient the way she left all this information for us to find. I still think my guess about her…"

"Was wrong." Dead wrong, Jude thought bleakly. Mia hadn't let the information because she wanted a white knight chasing after her. She'd expected to meet the danger alone. And the way things had transpired she might have been better off doing so.

He looked around the sterile room. Two beds, the other neatly made and vacant. Logically he knew that had Mia faced Four alone, the end result might have been the same. But today the woman had successfully used Mia's concern for him against her. He'd become a liability, in a way he never would have foreseen.

"Okay, here it is. Find my iPhone…it's just outside Pennsylvania, barely. Near Morgantown, West Virginia on Interstate 79. On the move, it looks like."

"Good. Text me updates every five minutes along with her iCloud password. I'll take over the monitoring when I get back to my computer. And get that call into Raiker. I have a feeling I'll be needing him."

"Got it."

He disconnected, a familiar sense of calm settling over him. Barring the possibility the phone had been ditched in another vehicle, the location app was a powerful tool in locating Mia. If Four's car was still moving, she was as safe as she could be at this point. It was when it stopped that the danger for her increased exponentially.

He set his phone down on a table next to the bed and pulled on his clothes, shooting a look around the room as he did so. One other bed, which was empty and neatly made.

There was no clock in the room, but the one on his phone indicated that Four had over a three-hour head start.

If Mia still had the phone on her, the lead wouldn't matter. Shoving his feet into his shoes, he grabbed his cell and headed for the door. Had to duck out of the way when it swung inward just as he was reaching for the handle.

A stout middle-aged woman in a bright pink smock looked at him in shock. She held a water pitcher. "What in heaven's name are you doing?" She took him by the arm with her free hand. "You need to get back to…you took out your IV! Mr. Bishop, the doctor is not going to be very happy with you."

He pulled away from her grasp. "Get the doctor in here and call the police. It's urgent."

She eyed him shrewdly. "There's an officer right outside who accompanied your ambulance. Sit back down on the bed and I'll get her for you."

Because it seemed more expedient, he did as requested. And was rewarded a couple minutes later when a female officer and a doctor entered the room. The man was tall and spare, with wide framed glasses that slid down the bridge of his long thin nose. He pulled out a small computer from the pocket of his lab coat and typed something into it.

Ignoring the man, Jude focused on the cop. "There was a kidnapping at the site where the ambulance found me. The Friend's Inn parking lot. Happened at about seven-oh-five. The suspect is female, bald, wearing a baseball cap. Five foot five, one hundred ten pounds. She's driving a black Honda. 2012 maybe." He stopped when he noticed the officer wasn't writing anything down. His gaze narrowed. "Do I need to speak slower or is your memory that good?"

She took a notebook from her back pocket but didn't open it. "Let's start with the part of who tased you."

"We removed the prongs from your skin, Mr. Bishop." The doctor looked up from the file he was reading on the screen. "There can be problems with infection from them, but I think with the antiseptic..."

"I've got a location on the kidnapper's car." He stood, still directing his words to the officer. "From a find my iPhone app loaded by Mia Deleon, the victim." The last word knotted in his throat. He knew how much Mia would hate having the descriptor applied to her. "It shows her just over the state line. You need to alert the West Virginia state police. They can find the car and..."

"Deleon?" He finally had the officer's attention. "Isn't that the name of the gal who sent police agencies all over the country on a wild goose chase for a fictional kidnapper years ago?"

Swiftly he considered his options and focused on the one most certain to garner cooperation. "She's one of the richest women in the country and you need to consider what would happen to your career if you didn't act with the expediency this situation deserves." Jude had no idea what Mia was worth, but if the inside of her apartment was any indication, it was more than he could fathom. Money talked. He needed something that did.

The officer, whose nameplate identified her as Megan Ryan, looked uncertain. "I have to talk to my chief."

Jude bared his teeth. "Then do it. Because if this thing goes very bad I'm going to be the guy speaking to CNN about the price of your inaction."

Without another word she left the room, taking her cell out of her pocket as she went. As she left, Jude switched his attention to the doctor. "Did you run labs on my blood work?" The bandage on the inside of his elbow told him the answer better than words.

"Yes." The man looked at the screen of his tablet again, scrolled down the page. "It doesn't appear that the results are back, however. Most likely it will be tonight or tomorrow morning."

"Did you run a tox screen?" Jude was pretty sure they would have. He'd definitely been altered when they'd brought him in. He didn't even have a memory of the trip to the hospital.

"You were unable to answer any questions about what you might have taken," the man began.

Jude smiled grimly. "I didn't take anything. I was injected. Likely a sedative of some sort, but fast acting."

"We can test for the most common types of recreational drugs found, but if this is one of those exotic blends that crop up now and then, it's going to take a forensic level screen to decipher it. That kind of testing will be beyond the capabilities of this hospital."

"But you'll have plenty of blood for them to run the extra screen?"

The man smiled drolly as the officer came back into the room. "Why do you think we fill so many vials?"

Raiker's lab could run the test, Jude thought. The results would be quicker, and the man employed a team of forensic scientists with the expertise to identify the ingredients used. He turned to Ryan as his cell alerted of an incoming text. He needed to talk to Raiker, find out the current state of the investigation. Maybe he'd discovered a connection between his case and Mia's that law enforcement entities would find convincing.

"West Virginia State Patrol has been alerted. It will be up to them to issue a BOLO for the vehicle you described," the officer announced.

"I've got an updated location, as of a minute ago." Jude pulled out his cell screen and showed her the recent text. Watched as she took out her own phone and copied it. It was gratifying at least that she was finally taking him seriously. "Write down the information above, too." He scrolled up to Mia's iCloud information that Kacee had passed on. "You can log in to her device from a computer in your office and communicate the phone's whereabouts to the state police down there." Every time the vehicle crossed state lines, a new law enforcement entity would have to be brought on board, further muddying the waters.

Jude pulled out his wallet and sorted through the business cards to hand one to Ryan. "This has my personal number on it. You can call me with updates." Stuffing the wallet back in his pocket he casually picked up the bag his clothes had been placed in, folding it to keep the tiny bits of confetti at the bottom of it secure.

"That's not exactly the way these things work, Mr. Bishop." The woman's gaze dropped to his card. "We're not in the habit of keeping civilians in the loop regarding ongoing investigations."

Inclining his head he started for the door. "That's okay. I plan to stay updated on my own."

"You haven't been discharged, Mr. Bishop." The doctor's voice was stern. "You really shouldn't leave until we've identified the drug you were given. We won't know the possible long-term effects until we do."

"If you go anywhere, it will be to headquarters with me." Officer Ryan stepped in his path, halting his progress toward the door. "There are details we need for the report."

"Get the security cameras from the motel, if they have them. You have witnesses that saw at least part of what went down there." Deliberately, he stepped around her. "I've given you all the information I have." At least every detail that would aid in Four's apprehension. "You can get in touch with me if you need to, but I *am* leaving."

"What's so urgent that you have to go right now?" the officer's voice demanded behind him.

He opened the door and walked through it. "I'm going to find Mia Deleon."

* * * *

Anthony was halfway to the airport when his phone rang. Lost in thought, he drew out his smartphone first, before realizing the call was on his other cell. Excitement thrummed in his veins as he answered. "Yes."

"I have Eleven."

He closed his eyes for a moment, letting the sheer pleasure of the words wash over him. "Where?"

"In the trunk of my car." The explanation tumbled out of her in a torrent, and it took some careful questioning to piece together the events of the morning. "I gave her the drug you sent. And I used the TASER in the package on the bodyguard. Twice."

He laughed, delight filling him. Eleven was *back*. Had any words sounded sweeter? And soon she'd be exactly where she belonged. "My trust in you wasn't misguided. I admit, Four, when you bungled things in Da Nang…I had my doubts." All the woman had needed to do was track Eleven in the city and hold her in the room he'd rented for them. The private flight he'd planned to charter to fetch them back would have been quite expensive, but well worth it. Difficult to hide from Mother. She pored over the business's books like a miser counting her gold. But he'd stockpiled some of his own money by using cards taken from the women he selected. It was, he thought fancifully, a dowry of sorts. And useful. Taking care of his collection appropriately could get expensive.

He flipped off a driver who cut him off on the exit ramp. Punctuated his displeasure with a blast of his horn. A female. Of course. He shuddered to think of Four's driving skills these days. She hadn't been behind the wheel of a car in more than fifteen years.

"Tell me exactly where you are." He listened to her description, thinking the whole while. "Did anyone see you take her, besides the bodyguard? Any chance you're being followed?"

"There were people in the parking lot before I could get away. I pretended I was a doctor, helping the man I zapped. I remembered everything you told me. Everything."

Was that a note of pride in her voice? That was a quality he didn't tolerate in his possessions. He gave a mental sigh. Eleven might not be the only one in need of retraining when they were all settled again. "Stay off main highways. County roads will be better. You may go east into Ohio, or south into West Virginia. No further. At this point, you just need to put as much distance between you and Johnstown as possible. I'll call back after I make arrangements with further instruction."

"And Four," his tone turned caressing. "You did quite well. I'm very pleased." He ended the call. Drummed his fingers on the wheel in a moment's indecision. He could cancel the trip to Atlanta. Send someone in his stead.

But in the next moment he discarded the idea. An alternate would never be able to make the scheduled meeting with the seller. This could work. There was time to arrange a place for Four to go and await his arrival. From Atlanta he could rent a van and drive to fetch them. Satisfied with the plan, he turned on the radio. Selected a classical station. There'd be a story to spin for Mother, but she was easily handled. And his possessions always had ample food for three days, for emergencies just like these.

He raised one finger off the wheel in an imaginary conduction of the song's orchestra. Any extraordinary collection carried with it the burden of responsibility for proper care. Climate control for rare works of art. A regimen of polish for admirers of antique armor. And careful security for anything of value. He accepted that responsibility for his collection willingly.

The rewards were more than worth it.

* * * *

By the time Raiker got back to him and Jude finished filling him in on Mia's kidnapping, he was close to the Pennsylvania border. The man was silent for a long moment. "The device appears to still be moving?"

"The location app says it is." He glanced at the mini computer he had set up on the seat beside him. He'd bummed a ride from an elderly man in the hospital parking lot and had been dropped back off at the motel to collect his car before heading out. "The route has gotten sort of random. They've crossed back and forth between Ohio and West Virginia several times. I can't figure out why they haven't been picked up yet."

"Communication lags. Change of jurisdictions. Finding cruisers in the right area. Multiple cars fitting the same description…" The man's voice was dry. "Welcome to my world. Right now they present a moving target. They'll be scooped up quick enough when they stop."

Thinking about what happened when they stopped was exactly Jude's concern. Four couldn't hurt Mia while she was driving. But once she wasn't… He glanced in his mirrors, pulled in the next lane to pass a bright red semi. Accelerated. He'd directed his operatives to head straight to West Virginia and once they were in position he'd relay the coordinates to them so they could join the search. At least *they* wouldn't suffer from jurisdictional issues.

"What are the chances Four could be taking Mia directly to the Collector?" Voicing the fear out loud gave it more credence. Filled his gut with lead. "If he's housed somewhere on the east coast, Mia would be in his hands by nightfall."

"I can't answer that. I can definitely say that the victim we found wasn't killed east of the Mississippi, however."

There was a flicker of relief. "And you know that how?"

"Caitlin found a small section of a plant in the tarp around the body. The forensic botanist has identified it as coming from a western prairie fringed orchid. They're found only west of the Mississippi, in Iowa, Kansas, Minnesota, Nebraska, North Dakota and in Manitoba, Canada."

Jude mulled that over. "Mia thought that the trucks she rode in after her escape may have come from the west or the north. She ended up in Nashville over a possible two-day period. She also said the winters where she was kept were cold. That would square with any of the states you named."

"I know. But Jude..." the man's voice held a hint of warning "we're nowhere near being able to link the body pulled out of the mineshaft with Mia's case. *I* believe they are connected. More so after speaking with her. But what I think and what I can prove are two different things. So far."

"Yeah." His eyes burned as he stared at the ribbon of road ahead of him. He'd said as much to Mia before she'd bolted. The twist in his belly was likely close to what she'd felt hearing the words.

"That doesn't mean I won't offer any assistance I can."

The screen next to him showed Four's car moving steadily east into West Virginia now, nowhere near the Ohio border. At this rate he'd find Mia himself before the cops were any damn use at all. "As a matter of fact..." He told the man about the tox screen he wanted run. "Maybe the drug is one he uses on the women. Could be we'll get a link that way."

"We can test it at my lab facility," the man said immediately. "I'll arrange for the transport personally."

"Your name will carry weight with the local police department." Jude's gaze dropped to his gas gauge, estimated how much time he had before he needed to refill. That thought led to another—wondering when Four's car would require refueling.

"Keep me posted. I'll let you know when we find something solid connecting Mia's case to the one I'm working."

After the call ended Jude updated Hunter and Logan. Given the meandering route Four had taken, he was within a couple hours of the car's location according to the app. "How sure are we that the phone is still in that car with Mia?" Hunter voiced the fear that had been nagging at the back of Jude's mind for hours.

"There's no way to be certain." He hugged the outside lane as a convertible came up beside him, weaving erratically. Like him, the driver was on the phone. Unlike him, the other man didn't seem capable of multi-tasking. "Mia's backpack and purse were at the motel, and her iPad was in the pack. I know she's got her phone on her. She specifically bought it for this purpose, just in case…" Just in case what was happening actually occurred, he finished silently. Just in case her plan backfired and she landed in the hands of a madman again.

It wouldn't happen, he vowed, unconsciously pressing down harder on the accelerator. He'd be damned if he'd allow it to.

"Things went down fast. I don't think Four had a chance to search Mia before forcing her into the trunk." That fact had given him the tenuous thread of hope he'd clung to all day. "I know she'll do whatever she can to hang on to the cell. She knows it's our best shot at finding her." He disconnected the call without mentioning that Mia was even more concerned with getting information from Four about the man who had kidnapped them both.

Jude couldn't imagine the other woman giving it up freely.

He drove another hour following the roundabout route Four's car seemed to be taking. The next time he looked at the screen, it took a moment to realize what it was showing.

The car had finally stopped.

* * * *

The darkness consumed her. Mia moaned. Brightly colored shapes wheeled beneath her eyelids to explode in her skull. Her gut was churning, her mouth watering. She tried to drag herself out of the morass of gloom. Couldn't manage to open her eyes.

Then light sliced the shadows like a knife splitting a shroud. She threw up a hand to cover her eyes. Groaned again. Long moments passed before comprehension made a belated appearance. Light. How was there light?

Her eyelids cracked open. Giant specters of green loomed over her, rays of sunlight bouncing off them to blind her. It took another minute before her brain made sense of the visual imagery it was receiving. Trees. Sky. Sun.

Where was she? And more importantly, where was Four?

The hair on her arms rose. Instinct had her doing a quick search of the trunk. Found it completely empty. But her pockets weren't empty, she recalled finally. Squinting, she shaded her eyes with her hands and surreptitiously checked her pockets while straining to see beyond the raised lid above her. It hampered her vision but there was no one in sight. Nothing but rows and rows of trees.

She found the extra pepper spray canister. Palmed it. Discovered her phone in the other pocket and hesitated. For the first time she noticed there was no road beneath the vehicle. Hard packed dirt littered with dead vegetation was directly beneath the car.

The other woman would never have opened its lid if she hadn't planned to remain in the vicinity.

The realization had Mia taking out the phone and stretching her hand behind her blindly to tuck it in the farthest corner of the trunk. She could always retrieve it to call for help if she was truly alone.

If she wasn't, she didn't want to alert Four of its presence.

Scooting to the edge of the trunk, she put her knees over the side. Then leaped out, pepper spray ready. At least that was the plan. Her knees failed to hold her up, and she fell to the ground, dizzy and stunned.

There was a crunching sound. Something whizzed through the air and she rolled reflexively as Four swung a tree branch at the exact place where Mia would have been standing, had her legs been capable of it. The woman was on her in two quick strides with the branch raised again. Mia stretched out an arm and pressed the button on the vial, covering her eyes with her free hand.

She got her legs beneath her and did an awkward crab walk, trying to get out of the line of the descending branch and the spray.

Four gave a gratifying screech at the same time the branch came down across Mia's right hip. Pain radiated in agonizing waves, stealing her breath, drawing a high-pitched moan. She tried to rise. Could do no more than crawl, half dragging one leg behind her. She had to put as much distance as she could between her and the car.

The other woman was sobbing, hands searching along the vehicle blindly until she found the front door handle. Mia struggled to her feet, her injured hip sending up a howl of protest as she tried a stumbling sort of run.

She had no idea how far they'd come, or even what state they were in. Nothing was familiar, with the canopy of trees stretching overhead, blocking out all but snippets of sky. It occurred to her then that the trees were growing denser as she ran. The ground began to slope upward. She stumbled on, dodging low hanging branches, once tripping and sprawling over a rotting log.

The woods were shadowy, allowing only occasional slants of sunlight to penetrate the forest floor. Mia's breathing sounded loud in her own ears. She tried to quiet it. Stumbling to a halt behind a fat tree, she attempted to listen for someone following her.

A rustle sounded behind her. She whirled, the canister of spray ready and winced when the movement sent a zing of pain through her hip. A rabbit sat frozen for a moment before zipping into some brush.

She released a shaky breath. Continued on, slowing to a walk. Her hip was singing a chorus of pain. But Jude had been right about using the pepper spray outside. The other woman had been affected while she'd been unscathed.

The underbrush was getting thicker, slowing her progress. With every step the ground beneath her feet seemed steeper. Maybe the woman hadn't followed her at all. The last sign Mia had had of her, Four had been trying to get in the car.

But on the heels of that thought came the certainty that whatever she'd been doing, the woman hadn't been intent on leaving Mia here alone. She'd had a reason for stopping at this particular place, in these isolated woods. To kill her? Skirting a thicket that looked impassable, she rejected the idea. Maybe *he* was here somewhere. The thought had her jerking around again, half expecting to see a naked man with a heavily adorned mask, eyes glittering with the promise of depravity to come.

She gave herself a mental shake. Turned and continued on, but the specter from the memory had left a chill in its wake. Sometimes when she dreamed she wouldn't see the full man at all. Only a mask and those eyes behind it. They'd been a different color each time she'd seen him. Brown, green, blue... His use of colored lenses had even denied her that one small descriptor of him.

With that memory lodged in the back of her brain, every tree and boulder took on a sinister appearance. She shook her head to eject the feeling. When she'd escaped she hadn't run through forest. The copse of trees where she'd taken shelter had been surrounded by open area. There had been fences, and she thought she'd traveled through both pasture and cropland of some sort. But the terrain had been nothing like this. She could be certain that wherever she was right now, it wasn't near the place she'd been kept captive.

Her mouth was dry, both from exertion and the after effects of the drug. She chose a tree, relieved herself near it and then found another several yards away. She sat down with her back against it, hidden from view by a thick tangle of brush. Her hip protested the position. She rested long enough for her breathing to return to normal. Long enough to examine the tree line head of her and realize she was still climbing upward. Her gaze landed on a bush a half dozen feet away. Made out the shape of a deer lying within its branches. Mia realized she'd blend in to her surroundings as well with the dark tee shirt and black cargo pants she was wearing.

She still had the canister of pepper spray gripped in one sweaty fist. She slipped it in a pocket. Remembering the small blade she'd hidden in her bra, she twisted around to unsnap the garment, then, after careful maneuvering, removed it through one sleeve. That had been a trick learned in high school, one she never would have considered having to use deep in a forest with a deranged woman after her.

The blade was smaller, folded in half but sharp enough to do some damage in close proximity. That went into a pocket, as well. The act of re-donning the bra was accomplished as surreptitiously as it had come off. She didn't want to leave anything behind that would hint at her presence here.

It appeared that she'd outrun Four. Successively hidden from her, at least for the time being. But remaining in the forest once night fell wasn't something Mia was looking forward to.

Neither was avoiding Four indefinitely. The woman had the answers she was seeking. Mia wasn't leaving these woods without getting them.

Outside, but in a place of your choosing. Jude's words echoed in her mind. The thought of him brought a clutch to her chest. A well of emotion that she didn't feel, not ever. Guilt, yes. God she was familiar with that. Carried it within her for Hoa, Halston and all the women she'd left behind. But it wasn't only guilt she was feeling right now.

What were the physical implications of being tased twice in a short amount of time? She didn't know. And she couldn't understand how a man could sneak beneath her personal guard so easily and lodge there with a singular tenacity. It couldn't be allowed. Personal relationships were a quicksand of emotional entanglements, and emotion equaled vulnerability. There was no place in her life for that kind of weakness.

But the thought lacked her usual resolve. If Jude was able he'd have followed her phone. Whether or not anyone else was looking for her, she knew he would be. And Mia would have to be made of stone to not be affected by that realization.

Rising, she brushed off the seat of her pants, a plan forming. She needed to backtrack until she found Four. And then they'd have the conversation Mia had been wanting. Under her terms. On her grounds.

* * * *

There was a navy and gold West Virginia state police SUV parked near a small wooden building just inside the entrance of Cooper's Rock State Forest. A feeling of urgency riding him, Jude parked nearby, and grabbing the mini-laptop, strode toward the building. The sign identified it as belonging to the Division of Forestry services.

He walked up to the counter where the state policeman was standing in front of a large map listening to a uniformed forester.

"...over twelve thousand acres in this forest alone. And that's not counting private nearby forested property. That's a lot of area to cover."

"Do you have a search and rescue unit?"

"We can put one together." The forester, a freckled young man in his late twenties, cast a quick glance at Jude before returning his attention to the trooper. "It would help to have a place to start looking."

Walking up beside the officer, Jude set the laptop down, turned it toward the other man. "Jude Bishop. I reported the kidnapping in Pennsylvania." He stabbed an index finger at the highlighted dot on the screen. "You found the device in this car?"

The officer had the tired eyes and creased visage of a veteran. "Got some ID, son?" He took the driver's license Jude handed him and studied it carefully before handing it back. "Got word you might be showing up. But this is a police matter, and as such we're not at liberty..."

"Meaning you don't have jack."

The two other men exchanged a look. "I just arrived myself," the officer admitted. "I haven't had time to assess the situation."

"Have you found the car?"

It took an inordinate amount of time for the officer to answer. "What did you say you did?"

Jude wasn't fooled. They would have checked for ID at the hospital, if the Officer Ryan hadn't done so first. And there would have been a complete background check run on him before the Johnstown Chief of Police ever issued alerted state police. "Personal and professional security."

"Uh-huh." The trooper took a moment, seemed to come to a decision. "I'm Sergeant Fenton. Why don't you follow me and I'll show you what I have discovered."

Jude tucked the ID back in his wallet and picked up the mini-laptop. He trailed the man out of the building and across a cleared lot meant for parking. They walked beyond it. Far beyond. They strode silently through a mile of heavily wooded land until they came to a hard packed path that wouldn't qualify as a road. Followed it another half mile.

The trooper stopped but Jude moved past him. Toward the black Honda parked askew, surrounded by tall oaks, its trunk lid open.

He peered inside. At first he thought it was empty until he saw the glint of something in the furthest corner. He picked it up with two fingers. Mia's phone. A deep shuddering breath worked out of him. There was nothing else in the trunk but the driver's door was open. An empty bottle of water and two caps were on the ground next to a brown tee shirt, turned inside out.

Gingerly he rubbed the inside neckline of the shirt with one finger. Felt the faintest burn on his skin. The empty water bottle took on new meaning. "Good girl, Mia," he murmured.

"You make any sense of this?" Fenton had come to stand over him.

"The woman in the trunk. Mia Deleon. She was armed with pepper spray. A knife. There was a struggle before she was forced into the trunk." He recalled that much at least. Just like he recalled the sensation of watching Four stride back over to him when he was helpless to move away. "Even if she was disarmed of the knife, the kidnapper didn't get the pepper spray." He gestured to the tee shirt Four had been wearing earlier that day. "There's remnants on the shirt."

"So the water was to wash it from her skin. Her eyes maybe." Fenton nodded thoughtfully. "There wasn't luggage in the car. Did the victim have anything with her? A purse or bag?"

Jude shook his head. "Both were found at the site where she was taken." Spying something on the ground he backtracked and bent down to look at the smooth limb lying near the trunk. A hiker might have chosen it for a walking stick. It was free of bark. It was fairly stout, although perhaps partially hollow. There was a crack in it, slightly below half way.

He looked from it to the yawning trunk, thinking out loud. "So you have someone in the trunk of your car. Drugged. Quiet. But you don't know if she's still out cold or just waiting for you to open that lid. Victim was armed before and you didn't disarm her before shutting her in there, did you? The injection would knock her out for hours. But you couldn't be exactly sure when it'd wear off. So you pick up a branch. Open the trunk lid remotely and hide behind it, out of sight. Wait for her to make the first move. And she does. But her reflexes are slow from the injection and she doesn't get clear before you swing…"

The officer looked at him with a glint in his eyes. "That's how you think it went down?"

"I was at the site when it happened. I saw enough to guess the rest." Jude turned in a slow circle, surveying the area.

"Maybe you have a guess about why they parked here."

For answer, he went to examine the inside of the trunk lid. Lowered it to look at the top. "Mia was unrestrained. If she were kicking and pounding, the racket may have frightened her kidnapper. Could have stopped to bind her." But he didn't think so. There were no visible signs of violent kicking inside the trunk lid. And she would have been weak with the after effects of the drug. So why else would Four stop at this exact location?

"What's in the area?"

"Right on this property? Campsites, some with electrical hookups. The forester says they get a lot of illegal camping. Hikers wanting to rough it around the lower Cheat Canyon or on their way to the Coopers Rock Overlook. Neither is close to here, though."

"They aren't here to hike or camp." Again Jude peered into the dense trees around them. "The driver could have stopped to subdue Mia…maybe thought to tie her up her before the drugs wore off. Or…she was told to come here."

"Told by who?"

The shadowy forest seemed to hold secrets in its depths that it was unwilling to reveal. Jude thought of Mia somewhere in their confines and a trickle of fear traced down his spine. "By the man who ordered the kidnapping."

9

Mia doubted she'd come more than three miles. Her flagging energy level shouted five, but the most wearisome part of her journey had been trying to make her way through the underbrush when no animal path had been available. Her hip was on fire. Her shoelaces and socks were filled with small cockleburs she'd picked up fighting through the thickets. She'd found a few in her hair, as well. The headache she'd awakened with in the trunk had settled to a dull throb.

But at least the fresh air had cleared her mind. She knew exactly what she had to do and had spent an hour making preparations. She'd filled a pocket with small pebbles she picked up and another held a fist-sized rock. It had taken longer than it should have to search for a stout stick much like the one Four had hit her with. Then she'd been ready for battle.

Mia tried to retrace her steps toward the car. There was no way to be sure how accurate she was. She'd run with the sole purpose of getting away from the woman, weaving from a straight line to take advantage of the small trails that appeared through the area. Backtracking took longer, because now she spent as much time looking at the ground as she did ahead of her. At first glance the area seemed undisturbed. But a closer look revealed a broken twig here. A heel mark in a mossy area there.

Dark humor filled her. She'd never been outdoorsy. Hadn't gone to summer camps, at least the variety that involved nature. But if her escape that night from The Collector had taught her anything it was to be aware of her surroundings.

She walked for what seemed like forever, her pace slowed by her attention to her own trail and for any signs of Four. The woman would likely have entered the forest at approximately the same point Mia had. Traveled in as straight a line as possible. But traversing around rocks and thickets could have taken her far enough afield that she'd be unseen in the dense growth of trees even if Mia were parallel to her. With that in mind she started walking in more of a grid pattern the way she'd seen Jude do in the parking lot. Covering more ground side to side but moving back to the center each time to look for signs that she'd passed that way before.

Mia heard Four before she saw her. The woman had quite an imaginative vocabulary and she was using it now as she trudged along. She moved into Mia's view on the right, close enough to hit with one of the rocks she'd collected earlier, about ten yards away. Her shirt now was white. She carried a bag slung over one shoulder and held a water bottle in one hand. Instead of drinking it she dribbled it over her arms and then splashed some in her face. Apparently she was still suffering the effects of the pepper spray. The woman wasn't moving especially fast, but all things considered, she hadn't been all that far behind.

As silently as she could, Mia widened the distance between by cutting to the left while continuing to move parallel to her. The trees had thinned the further they climbed, she recalled. Even more so beyond the point where she'd rested earlier. Her best chance for an ambush was soon, where the thicker forest provided more shield.

Taking care to keep out of sight Mia ran ahead of the other woman, staying low. She circled around and positioned herself well ahead of the path Four was taking. Then waited, crouched behind an outcropping of rock. The woman bent and fiddled with her shoe, the bill of her cap pulled low, muttering inaudibly. The distance between them was too wide, Mia realized. Reaching for a pebble from her pocket she tossed it over the woman's head. Saw her jerk up to look around her.

"Mia?" She crooned the word with a note of relish. Straightening, she looked all around, otherwise unmoving. Mia waited until she finally started forward again. This time the pebble she threw wasn't nearly as close to Four, landing only a few yards away from where Mia waited.

The first sound had heightened the woman's senses. Now she froze again, before creeping toward Mia's hiding place. Past it.

She took the stick in both hands and swung it low as she was coming out behind the rocks, taking the woman's feet out from under her. Four hit the ground and Mia jumped on top of her. They rolled, Four grappling to get her bag open. Mia dug the tiny knife from her pocket, all the while battling to keep her seat as the woman heaved beneath her. She sliced the strap so the bag fell off Four's arm. The woman reached up to wrap her hands around Mia's throat. Squeezed.

Mia pressed the edge of the small knife against the woman's left eye. Both were red and puffy from the pepper spray. "Forget those knife wounds in your back. The one you bandaged on your arm. Will your master still want you if I cut your eye out?"

Four stilled. "I'm following his orders. He'll be here soon. We must go to the cabin he rented for us to wait."

Icebergs formed in her veins at the thought. "Where is the cabin?"

"Come with me. I'll show…" The woman's blue eyes widened in fear when Mia increased the pressure on the blade.

"Where…is…the…cabin?"

Four swallowed. "Near here. Cardinal Cabin Rentals. He said…hide the car. Walk to the cabin he has waiting for us. He described the directions exactly. It's about a mile from where we left the car."

"I'm guessing he also told you to secure me first." Keeping her gaze fixed on the other woman she yanked the bag over and unzipped it. Four picked that moment to reach up, try to pry the knife from the Mia's hand, while bucking and lunging beneath her. Deliberately Mia nicked the other woman's face with the tip, drawing blood and a frustrated scream from Four. "Now we know how sharp it is, don't we?"

"You fucking bitch." Her voice was venomous. "I've always hated you. Always. From the minute you joined us. I am perfect! Obedient and focused on giving him every pleasure. You…constantly fighting him. Breaking rules. You did it to draw his attention! He always had to be focused on you!"

Mia gaped at her. The line of reasoning was so warped it was stunning. The damage from the woman's prolonged captivity bordered on mental illness. "No." She rummaged in the bag until she found what she was looking for. A pair of plastic zip cuffs. The TASER, without a cartridge now, was tossed into the brush. "I'm not like you. I never could be."

The hat sat askew on the woman's head. Mia could see the bottom of the numbered tattoo on her scalp. She must have worn a wig in Da Nang. And she'd shaved her head recently. The realization brought mingled shock and pity. Nothing revealed more clearly how completely enslaved the woman was than the fact that she carried out The Collector's wishes even when he wouldn't have known otherwise.

"You could have run." She lowered the knife to keep it pressed against the woman's cheek as she flipped her over. Slipped the loops of the cuffs over each of her wrists one-handedly and tightened them. "You were free. You could have gone home. To the police."

Four was weeping now, a trickle of tears running down her beautiful cheek. "My master *is* home. And I can't get back until he takes me. There are masks…in the bag, see?" Mia reached over and pulled out two cotton sacks with a drawstring at the bottom. "Just like the first time. We can't see his face or where he takes us. Our home is with him."

Mia felt a dart of pity, in spite of the cruelties the woman had been capable of when they were imprisoned. Her brainwashing had been total. Four would never be able to function in the normal world even if the women could be freed. Her prison went much deeper than the physical.

But as she pulled Four to her feet, the woman's words took on a different meaning. "You know what state you were held in." Four shook her head. "You have to," Mia insisted. She pressed the knife against her cheek threateningly. "He trusts you. He would have let his guard down with you. You know something! Where he gets the women. How he chooses them. His name."

"I know only what you knew. That we must obey and he will care for us forever."

The crushing weight of disappointment was like a boulder on her chest. Was it possible that even with the latitude he'd allowed the woman, Four had no more information on their captor than Mia did? She didn't believe it. Refused to.

Deliberately she tried a different tack. "He'll care for you forever? You're *scarred.*" She pressed a hand to

Four's back directly over the place where those marks would be. Gave her a push to start her back to the car, before bending quickly to retrieve the woman's bag. "Who sewed your wounds up, a blind man? They look hideous."

The look the woman sent her over her shoulder was venomous. "A fisherman…he found me in his boat and took me to his wife early the next morning. She got me to another city. To an airport." Mia wondered what sort of story Four had spun to make that happen. "And our master will still love me because I got the scars serving him. I know it."

"If you say so." Mia let the doubt drip from her words as she steered the other woman to a faint trail through the brush. "But you're not perfect anymore, are you? Even if he's grateful—and he should be grateful for all you've done—he'll always choose one of the others over you. How many are there now?"

"We are twelve with the new girl at boot camp. She will join us soon." Four tripped over a tree root and would have fallen flat if Mia hadn't reached out to grab her shirt. Twelve. Her blood ran cold. There had been nine when she'd escaped. Counting Eight's death, he had to have selected five more victims in the nearly five and a half years of her freedom. He'd never acted so fast while she'd been held, which meant he was escalating.

A weary sort of hopelessness filled her. Five more women had entered hell because Mia had been unable to lead police to the monster.

"Why did he kill Eight?" How much further was it to the car? The woman ahead of her trudged along, her pace deliberately slow. Mia couldn't tell what time it was, but the light filtering through the leaves seemed dimmer.

They'd seen no one since they'd left the vehicle. Somewhere in the distance she could hear a dog bay.

"He did not. She killed herself."

Mia ground her teeth. Four was so completely indoctrinated, she was unable to ascribe any blame to the man who enslaved her. "How did she die?"

The woman looked over her shoulder, her expression sly. "She killed herself. When Master was gone she wrapped a sheet around her head until she couldn't breathe. Now none of us can have bedding, even if we earned it with good behavior."

The desolation that coursed through her then was nearly debilitating. Somehow she believed the words. The Collector prized his possessions much too highly to kill one of them. She had said as much to Raiker. But she thought one might have gotten ill, despite the vitamins and antibiotics that had been pressed on them. She had hoped, for Eight's sake, that the woman had died a natural death.

But instead Eight had chosen her own kind of escape. And Mia was left to wonder, if she hadn't managed to get away, how long it might have taken for her to choose that end, too.

Four stumbled. "My shoe always falls off."

Mia looked down. The woman was wearing an old sneaker. Where did the clothes come from? Did the monster keep the things they'd worn when they'd been kidnapped? The shoes looked as though they'd been found at a thrift shop.

She paused while she waited for the woman to try and get it on again, bending the heel down in the process. "I need help. I can't use my hands."

Warily Mia crouched down to straighten the shoe, holding the knife against the other woman's calf in case she tried to kick her. A crashing sound had her raising her gaze. An animal was running at them. A large animal. Mia jumped up, realizing in the next moment that it was a dog.

Taking advantage of her distraction, Four lowered her shoulder and knocked her off balance. The dog was circling them in short little arcs, barking furiously. She fell and Four took the opportunity to run. Mia was on her feet in the next moment. Turned and started after her. The dog held her in place, blocking her every attempt to follow the woman.

Mia eyed it anxiously. Dogs had not been allowed on the Deleon estates, or in Gran's brownstone. Her experience with the animals was nil, but this one was big and black and ferocious looking. Taking a deep breath, she reached for the large rock she'd gathered in case she needed it and then ran, leaping over the animal when it tried to block her path. Her hip howled in pain, in tune with the frenetic barking of the beast behind her.

She chased after Four with adrenaline-fueled speed, leaping tree roots that would have tangled her feet and battling through underbrush. Unlike the woman's pace earlier, she was fleet-footed now, and had a head start.

The dog ran beside her, barking incessantly and kept trying to cut her off. The din almost masked the sound of a distant voice yelling her name from behind her. "Mia! Mia, stop."

Disbelieving, she swung around, scanned the area. Saw nothing. The dog took the opportunity to start running those crazy arcs around her again, trying to keep her in place. She caught a flash of fabric between the trees, and then saw a strange man in a bright orange vest step through it. A moment later Jude joined him.

The leap in her heart was an uncontrollable response, one she couldn't have controlled if she wanted to. He broke into a run when he saw her and if he'd suffered any ill effects from being tased this morning, they weren't in evidence.

"Four's on the run!" She pointed in the direction the woman had headed. "I've got zip cuffs on her, but that animal…" The dog seemed to be standing on guard in case she tried following the other woman again. "It keeps getting in the way."

Jude gave her a visual once over that was as complete as it was swift. Warmth bloomed in the wake of his gaze. "You okay?"

The urgency of the situation faded for a moment. She nodded. "I pepper sprayed her when I got out of the trunk."

His mouth curled. "Remind me to stay on your good side."

The bearded man next to Jude knelt next to the animal, feeding it a treat from his pocket. "This is Emma. Her methods are a bit unconventional for a SAR dog, but she gets the job done."

"Search and rescue," Jude explained when she looked at him. "Al came immediately when the state police made a request and we gave the dog your phone to scent, and it picked up your trail." He took out his cell and sent a text. "I'll let the trooper know you've been found. He's coordinating things with a couple of my operatives and a group of search volunteers."

The man was vigorously rubbing the dog's ears. "Don't need 'em now, do we Emma? You're one of a kind."

"Can she follow a trail from smelling someone's bag?"

Al rose, cocked his head at her. The dog seemed to follow suit. "Depends. If the person handled it a lot, the bag would work. The handle especially. Does it belong to the woman on the run?"

"Yes." Mia started over toward the bag she'd dropped when Four had shoved her. The man brushed by her.

"If it's okay with you, I'll do it." He pulled a latex glove out of his jeans pocket. "We try to be careful with the scent articles so we don't get too many different scents on it." He peered into the bag before reaching into it. "There's a phone in here. That might be a better scent article than the bag." He withdrew it and held it up.

Mia backed away involuntarily. The phone was black. Nondescript. But she knew without being told that Four had used it to communicate with The Collector. It was ridiculous to feel as though by touching it she was somehow touching *him*. But she was helpless to control the feeling.

The handler held it out for the dog to sniff for several moments. "Go find, Emma. Go find." The animal turned and trotted off a few feet, nose in the air, before lowering it to smell the ground. "She's a tracker, but she'll use air and ground scents."

Her earlier wariness around the creature forgotten, Mia trotted after it. Jude fell into step beside her. "Can the phone be traced?" she asked him. "Maybe back to the caller?" Could it be as easy as that? With all the hoopla about the NSA collecting cellphone data, how difficult could it be to track the man who had been giving directions to Four via this cell?

Jude shot her a glance. Let it linger. "Depends. If it's a TracFone or other disposable, or if it uses prepaid minutes without a contract…probably not."

The tiny hope faded before it could completely unfurl. "Not even by Raiker's lab?"

"His guys are good, but they can't be better than the technology at hand." The ground began the incline she'd noted earlier. And with adrenaline fading, she was starting to feel the effects of the last several hours.

Jude's hand brushed hers. "You gave me a few bad moments today. Actually the whole day sucked."

Heat from his touch transferred to hers. She curled her fingers into her palm, trapping it there. "Things didn't go according to plan. But once I had her under control I questioned her…" She looked away then, her jaw working. "Maybe a trained interrogator would get more. Probably would."

"She doesn't know anything?"

"Just where he's supposed to meet us tonight. At Cardinal Cabin Rentals. She said it was near here. That he had given her explicit instructions. But she was supposed to dump the car and then the two of us walk. She said it was close." Mia stopped in her tracks, unable to believe she hadn't thought of it before. "We know where he'll be!" Earlier Mia had focused on the horror of being close to him again without even considering what that proximity could mean. The prospect of the man being caught—perhaps in the next few hours—was too dizzying to contemplate.

Jude took his phone out of one pocket and a card out of another. He unfolded a small attached antennae on the cell, saying, "That's a detail we can use." She listened as he called someone named Fenton and relayed the formation to him. After listening for a moment he looked at her. "Any idea what time he's to arrive or the name of the actual cabin?" When she shook her head, he pressed, "Did Four make the arrangements or did he?"

"He did." Of that she could be sure. The woman had said as much and their captor controlled everything from afar, while sending the woman to carry out his wishes.

But it could be over soon. The thought of it quickened her step. Made the increasingly steeper grade easier to traverse. The possibility of his capture seemed surreal. The Collector had been loose for years, snatching women away from their families and leaving little evidence behind. It still seemed amazing to her that the crimes had never been linked. The last thing she remembered was slipping out of a crowded DC club with friends for a smoke. The others had later gone back inside, while Mia had stayed for a second cigarette. She'd awakened in an unimaginable hell.

The trees began thinning. When Mia looked behind her she was shocked at how far they had climbed. The ground grew rockier beneath their feet. And when she heard the excited baying ahead, she reached out to clutch Jude's arm.

"Tell him to keep the dog back. I want to try to approach her."

"Not a chance in hell." Quickening his stride, Jude's tone brooked no opposition. "You've been through enough."

She stayed his progress with a hand on his arm. "There's no danger. You'll be right behind me. I want her to see you here. The dog and the handler, too. She'll realize she has no choice but to come with us. But your presence might scare her into running again, too, and at some point it's going to get dark. I'd rather put an end to this sooner than later, wouldn't you?"

He stared at her then, a familiar glint in his eyes. "I'm getting to know you well enough to realize that when you sound the most reasonable all hell is about to break loose."

"Relax." She gave him a small smile. "I still have some pepper spray in my pocket."

"Duly warned. Still…"

The adrenaline that had faded earlier was making a comeback. Excitement was beginning to thrum in her veins. This could all be over before the end of the day. She didn't dare believe it. But there was something deep within her that longed to. Surely it was time. No evil could run unchecked forever. "Maybe the police can use Four in some way to prepare for later tonight. Or the phone she has could be used to contact him. We need to bring this to a conclusion. One way or another."

His expression softened infinitesimally. "Yeah, we do. You get within ten feet of her and the cavalry is coming in, got it?" She nodded, impatient, and he blew out a breath. "Okay."

When Mia broke from the cluster of trees to where Emma was prancing and barking, the first thing she noticed was the spectacular view. They had indeed climbed some distance. The ground was almost all rock ahead, with a jagged ledge running twenty feet from left to right that jutted out over the forested valley below.

And in the center of that ledge, close enough to the edge to weaken Mia's knees even from where she stood was Four. She looked the worse for wear. Running through the forest and up an angled slope would have been difficult with her hands bound behind her. There was a scrape on that exquisite cheek. A bruise forming on one arm.

"Emma. Come." With a visible show of reluctance the animal stopped its cavorting and returned to its owner, who was waiting next to Jude well behind Mia.

"It's pretty, isn't it?" The woman's voice was held a thread of wistfulness. "It's easy to forget there are spots like this. Where you can see the world all laid out beneath you."

Mia approached her, being careful to keep her promise to Jude. But she had to be near enough to the woman to have a conversation. "There are more places like this. All over the world. You could see them. Anytime you want. All you have to do is come with me."

"I'd like that, I think." The woman turned to face her and Mia's heart jumped a little. She was way too close to the edge. "We could go together, you and me. See every lovely site nature has to offer."

"We could." She took a step closer. Heard Jude's warning growl behind her. "Let's start now. Walk toward me and we'll talk about what we want to see first."

"Come and get me," the woman invited. "At least meet me halfway. Otherwise how will I ever trust you?"

"You don't have to trust me." Mia was getting desperate. There was a look in the woman's eye that she'd seen all too often. "You're free to leave here. Now. Go anywhere. Do anything. All you have to do is take a step this way. And then another."

Four sighed prettily. "It would be so much more satisfying to take that step together. I'm afraid. Come take my arm. Lead me back with you."

She wasn't even aware that she'd taken another step toward the woman. Not until she saw Jude coming after her from the corner of her eye.

"You're a fool and you never deserved to be chosen." The dreamy quality was gone from the other woman's voice to be replaced by a familiar acrimony. "You can't see that life without our master is no life at all."

"You're wrong." She didn't move another inch. She knew she didn't. But Jude's hand was clamped around her arm just in case. "You have to give it time to realize what freedom feels like." It had been an adjustment all those years ago, regardless of how much she'd coveted it. There had been no warm homecoming. No credibility. No feeling of safety. But it was millions of times better than being subjugated and abused nearly every day.

"I'm going to be free. I just wish I could take you with me." Four smiled a horrible smile. Backed up.

Jude leaped forward as a strangled cry broke from Mia's lips. But it was already too late. Poised on the edge of the ledge the woman leaped backwards. The moment slowed as if she hung suspended in the air. Then a moment later Four was gone from sight.

In a few quick strides Jude was at the edge, looking down. Mia didn't move. Couldn't. When he turned back to caught his gaze with hers, an unspoken plea on her lips. The expression on his face said it all.

"Oh my God." The dog handler came bounding up to them. "Did you see that? She just let herself fall!"

When Jude would have led her way, Mia's feet remained rooted in place, her eyes glued to the spot where Four had been just a moment ago. And when he folded her into his arms, pressed her face to his chest, she let herself lean, just a little, against his strength. She'd known how emotionally traumatized the woman was. How impaired. But it was still hard to fathom that given a choice, Four had chosen death rather than the thought of being parted from a monster.

* * * *

He waited impatiently miles away from the cabin, the van tucked into a gravel road with trees overarching it, branches mingling like interlocked fingers. Four was supposed to text him every hour on the hour. He hadn't heard from her since this afternoon when she and Eleven had arrived in the area.

Something was terribly wrong.

Rationally he knew that, but his mind kept reeling out several plausible options. The phone could be lost. It could have been stolen. The battery may have gone dead and the charger was misplaced. It was two hours past the time that Four was to have contacted him and still no word. The phone lay in his lap. All he had to do was reach for it. Make a call that would put an end to his wondering.

And yet he didn't reach for it. Because then it would be all too final. All too real.

The local news channels were worthless. Either they didn't know anything—likely didn't—or they were keeping it under wraps.

Twenty more minutes crawled by. Mother had called twice on the other phone and he'd fobbed her off with a story about not feeling well and flying out later. The candelabra was safely packaged, insured and on its way to their business, because he'd intended on taking a couple days to get home.

Finally unable to stand it any longer, he snatched up the phone and brought up the voice alteration app. Dialed the familiar number. After three rings he heard it picked up. But Four didn't answer.

"We're waiting for you." That voice. So familiar. So *dear*. "Why haven't you come to get us?"

"Eleven." He breathed the word, his cock stirring in interest at the sound of it. "Where's Four?"

"She got hurt walking to the cabin. She needs help. When will you be here?"

And then he knew the truth. The horrible final truth. The knowledge had been inside him for hours but there was no longer any denying it. "I have something picked out just for you." The fury washed over him, and he struggled to rein it in. "You will be brought back to where you belong. And you will pay dearly for what you've done."

"I want to come." His eyes closed as a terrible pleasure pain shook him. The loss…he knew he'd suffered one. Four would have called had she been able. At the same time the sweetest of all his items was likely very close by. "Please come get us. It's not too late."

The lies the woman could tell without blinking an eyelash. He'd never broken her of it, though he'd been harsher with her than with any of the rest. But he would, he vowed. There were other ways. "Soon."

He disconnected. Methodically took off the back of the phone and removed the battery. Like an automaton he started the van. Executed a three point turn and drove back the way he'd come.

When he got to the bridge he stopped and got out, hurling the phone and battery into the water below. Then he gripped the railing with both hands and let loose the scream of grief and rage that would no longer be contained.

10

Jude looked at Mia with grim concern. She was huddled in the passenger seat, her arms clasped tightly around her middle as if to keep herself from flying to pieces. Although likely he was underestimating her. He had a habit of doing that.

When the state police investigators had come up with the farce they'd wanted her to take part in, he'd been vehemently opposed. After taking their sweet time tracking Mia's location, they'd picked a bad time to play Super Cop. But Mia had agreed. Of course she had. And now she was paying the price for it.

"You cold?"

She shook her head, the way she had the last two times he'd asked her. He'd never been drawn to emotional females, but a little falling apart right now would be preferable to her rigid control.

"He won't come."

Headlights approached in the oncoming lane, spearing through the darkness. Jude took his gaze off them to look at her. "The police think it's possible…"

"…that he'll wait until he thinks it's safe and then appear. He won't." Her brittle tone told him how tightly she was holding her emotions in check. "He knew. That's why he didn't call, because he already sensed the danger to him. He's got animal instincts. Maybe that's how he's survived all these years. Flourished. Free to pick and choose victims at whim."

"Think about this." The lights of Morgantown winked in the distance. "No one has ever heard his voice before except for his victims. Now they have it recorded."

"Right. And it sounds like Eeyore."

The man they were seeking was cautious. He'd turned on an electronic alteration app before calling. "The recording can still be examined by a forensic linguist. You'd be surprised by what they can discover about word use, vowel patterns, and intonation."

Finally he'd sparked some interest. She turned toward him. "Even if the voice is altered?"

"An aural spectrograph can be used for voice analysis. I know they can match voices even if someone deliberately tries to change their accent, pitch or tone. What they can do with an electronic alteration is a question for Raiker."

She digested that for a few minutes. "So now all we have to do is find them the subject to match it to."

He gave a mental headshake. They should be talking about something else—anything else—to avoid her reliving the events of the day. Yet here she was, still on point. "We may have picked up a lead. I've got Logan, one of my techs, running an identification on the TASER confetti." Sensing her confusion he explained about the AFID process, without going in to the need for a breach of the database. Some people were high-minded about such things. "With any luck he'll soon have the name of the person the weapon was registered to. Owners have to go through background checks. It's highly unlikely Four would have done so."

"As careful as The Collector has been, I doubt he'd chance having his name registered either." Interest had sparked her voice and the sound of it was satisfying, despite the topic. Anything to jar her out of the cocoon of misery she'd seemed encased in earlier.

"It's possible." He slowed down as he entered town, watching for a hotel with a restaurant. He hadn't eaten all day. She wouldn't have either. "Weapons represent power and if there's one thing this guy seems to be into, it's power and control. He has to make a mistake sometime. Everyone slips up eventually."

She said nothing to that. Her silence lasted the whole time he spent choosing a hotel. Continued while he gathered their bags that he'd retrieved from the parking lot this morning and while she accompanied him inside to get a room. She hadn't blinked when he'd gotten only one double, citing concern for her protection. But when he ordered food, she finally roused to life. "A ham sandwich. Lots of cheese. And fries with a caffeine free Diet Coke."

"Double it," Jude told the front desk clerk. "Except bring me a Coors Light."

"The restaurant and bar are right down the hall, sir," the young man started.

"But you'll place our order for us." It hadn't escaped Jude's notice that Mia was swaying slightly on her feet. "And have it delivered for us."

A moment's hesitation. Then, "Yes, of course."

"Thanks." He led Mia to their second floor room. Ushered her inside it. It was a medium priced motel, but the room was luxurious compared to the one she'd chosen last night. She'd looked out of place in the slightly shabby room he'd found her in. Even if he hadn't known about her privileged upbringing, she had an air of refinement that was difficult to miss. Coupled with her gut-wrenching looks and kiss-my-ass cheekbones, she'd looked right at home in some fancy lunchroom eating rabbit food and sipping expensive tea.

But he'd made the mistake of judging her based on her looks and background on more than one occasion. Jude would never make that mistake again.

He caught the longing look she threw toward the bathroom. "You've got plenty of time for a shower before the food arrives." He set his duffel bag and her backpack next to the wardrobe. She carried her purse. Was worrying the strap with nervous fingers.

"Maybe later." The cause of her reluctance was clear.

"I'm going to step outside." He made the decision without forethought. "I want to get a look at the set up of the floor. Exits. Windows." He had a pretty good blueprint in mind just from observation on the way up, but it was a decent idea anyway. And would remove him from the room for as long as she needed.

The relief in her expression would be hard to miss. "I'll lock and latch the door."

Jude lingered in the task, giving her nearly a half hour. When he saw the server arrive with their food he returned, and waited for Mia to unlock the door so he could bring it inside.

She was barefoot, but otherwise fully dressed in a tee shirt and jeans, her hair dried. Following him to the table in the corner of the room, she snatched the cover off one of the plates on the tray. "I haven't thought about food all day but you mentioning it triggered my appetite. I'm starved."

They ate in companionable silence for a while. When he'd finished his fries and attempted a stealth attack on hers, she slapped his fingers away. "I'm territorial about my food." But there was a smile on her lips when she said it. "Too used to having to ration it, maybe. We were never sure how long it would be before he came back. Occasionally it was a few days or more."

The identity of the *he* she referred to was all too clear. "How did he store it?"

"We had places for it in our cells." She ate quickly and efficiently. "He called them that, but there weren't bars. The back of each was stone, the sides, front and top charged wire. You got a heck of a jolt if you touched one. Although not as bad as the stunner Four used today. Anyway there was always bottled water. The food was packaged in plastic bags. There used to be a plastic trough bolted to the stone wall to hold the food in each cell. I broke it once. Thought I could use a jagged piece as a weapon." She chewed reflectively. "That cost me an extra week at boot camp for retraining."

The reference to what she'd endured made it suddenly difficult to swallow. Jude reached for his beer. Took a gulp. It did nothing to alleviate the sudden burn in his chest. "Did others fight him the way you did?"

"Some. At least at first." Her voice turned pensive. "In time, enough abuse will cow anyone. Others turned vicious, although none were as bad as Four. Most would immediately rat you out for the slightest transgression as soon as he reappeared. Which was unnecessary, since the cameras caught a lot of it. But Eight never did. Not even when we were both allowed to paint once and I used my time to figure out how to pick the lock on the door of the room where he kept the discipline tools. The paintbrush had this little wooden piece down by the bristles. It was held on by bits of wire and I'd pried one off. After I discovered I could get the discipline room door open, I hid the wire in my cell. In case I ever got a chance to try again on the main door."

"Hard to believe he ever let his captives out of the cells when he couldn't control their movements."

"He didn't. Not during showers, exercise time or any earned free time. We wore shackles on our wrists and ankles. Fur lined of course." A note of bitterness tinged the words. "No marks to mar the items of his collection.

200

The only time we weren't chained was when we were in our spaces…"

…or when he was sexually assaulting them in a group. She didn't need to finish the thought. She'd already revealed once how she'd happened to be free to attempt her escape. Talons of fury for what she'd experienced raked through his system. And a half acknowledged realization actualized in his mind. He wasn't law enforcement. He'd never been above operating slightly outside legal boundaries when he needed to acquire information.

And he sure as hell wasn't going to waste any time worrying about legal niceties while he searched for the evidence needed to bring her former captor to justice.

The fully formed thought had him freezing in the act of bringing the beer to his lips. He wasn't sure when it had occurred, but there it was, along with a map of the steps he was going to take toward that end. Raiker kept talking about the connections they needed between the corpse in the mineshaft and Mia's case. Jude could find them. He wasn't an investigator, but he had skills of his own.

What he was considering was far afield from the services his business offered. But this was no longer about a job. He flicked Mia a glance over the top of the bottle he held. She caught his gaze, smiling as she deliberately bit into the last French fry.

And if he hadn't realized it before, he finally recognized just how much trouble he was in here. His famed objectivity was shot to hell when it came to her. And he wasn't exactly sure what to do about it.

Brooding over the rest of the beer, he considered the problem. Decided how to broach it. "I'm going to track down the owner of the TASER myself," he finally stated baldly. "I'll give the information to law enforcement. At some point." Right now the cops would be interested in the detail only as it pertained to Mia's kidnapping today. They had nothing on which to base a broader scope of investigation. So he'd get it for them. "But first I'm going to take a run at him, after doing a background check to discover exactly what I'm dealing with."

Her smoke gray eyes widened a little. "Good. I'll come with you."

He set the bottle down with more force than necessary. "No. You won't."

"Okay." She picked up the remainder of the sandwich and nibbled on it. "I'll follow you then."

"Mia."

"Jude."

A part of him was distracted by the sound of his name on her lips. He could count on one hand the number of times she'd said it. But he wasn't a hormone-driven teenager panting over the prom queen. It wouldn't deter him. "We have to keep you safe. That's more important now than ever. You heard what that scumbag said to you on the phone tonight. He's still coming after you."

Watching the way her creamy complexion paled was a kick in the gut. But he wasn't above using whatever tool necessary for her security. "I have to know you're protected in order to do my job. I'll personally update you daily so you're kept abreast of developments. You can even pick your own protection detail. You already know most of them."

"Okay." She piled her plate back on the tray. "I pick you."

"That isn't an option."

Leaning forward, her gaze caught his. Battled with it. "Here's the thing. I'm no longer your client. My check effectively ended our arrangement. You can't keep me from doing anything I want, and I am not going to be kept a silent bystander while others fight this battle on my behalf." Her mouth twisted. "That hasn't exactly worked out in the past. I can hire another investigator. One who can track your movements if I'm unable to. One who will be paid well enough not to care if I accompany her. But I won't be updated every day. I'll *be* there."

A thread of pleading entered her tone. "Believe me, I don't want to get anywhere near him on my own. This isn't like confronting Four. I wasn't terrified of her. But I'm no longer going to be a spectator in my own life. If we get close…there might be something familiar. Something that triggers a memory. A landmark, a sound that points us toward the location where those women are being kept. You need me there."

Everything inside him rejected her assertion. He *needed* her safe. And given the events of the day he'd already failed her once. "I can't follow leads and tend to your protection at the same time." When faced with a losing argument, use reason. "Neither of us can afford for me to splinter my focus."

She appeared to give his words serious consideration. "You're right. So you'll have to bring along another operative to stay with me while you're following those leads. I'm fine with whoever you choose."

Getting up from the table, she walked over to one of the beds. Arranged the pillows and sat down to prop herself against it. As if the discussion was closed. As if she'd left him with no alternative.

Temper simmering, he went to grab his duffel and took it in the bathroom. Shut the door. There was always an alternative. He'd had recalcitrant clients before, although as she'd pointed out earlier she wasn't technically a client anymore. He stripped, started the shower and stepped in. His first choice when faced with a lack of cooperation had always been logic. But he'd resorted to using fear tactics with some to keep them in line. There had been one or two so impossible that he'd been driven to terminate the contract.

And none of those options applied here. Mia was plenty logical; he just didn't agree with her line of reasoning. And she didn't scare. Or she did, he corrected himself, rinsing the shampoo from his hair. But the woman had more guts than most people he'd met. Fear wasn't a deterrent. The hell of it was he even respected that on some level. When the worst has already happened, a person could curl up or fight. They were both fighters. But it wouldn't do him any good at all to focus on the similarities between them.

He turned the issue over in his mind while he turned the shower off. Stepped out to drag a towel over his dripping body. There had to be a way for both of them to get what they wanted. But in the time it took to brush his teeth, pull on jeans and stalk out of the bathroom, nothing had occurred.

She was still sitting in the same position, hands locked in her lap. At some point she'd gotten up to plug in her phone. It sat on the table between the two beds. The TV was on but she didn't seem to be paying attention to it. "I'm sorry." They were the last words he'd expected. The last that he wanted, short of a total capitulation of their earlier argument. "Not for insisting on going with you tomorrow. But because I didn't thank you for coming after me today. For finding us. I knew you

would, if you were able to after her attack. It helped…
knowing that. I'm not used to depending on others." A
smile flitted across her lips. Was gone in the next
moment. "Guess I'm not very good at it."

How was it possible to be angry with a woman and
be disarmed by her at the same time? It was like a sneaky
one-two punch. It was impossible to be unaffected when
he recognized the utter earnestness in the sentiment. He
continued past her, then closed his eyes a brief moment.
Struggled to find an even keel. "You're welcome."

Sitting down on his bed, he plugged in his own
phone, after first checking for messages. As a distraction
it was only partially successful. Jude was too aware of her
presence behind him. Could feel her gaze arrowing into
his back.

"I think when you talk to the owner of the TASER
you should take my mini-tape recorder along and record
his voice. It could be sent to Raiker. Maybe his scientists
will be able to match it to the recording from the call
tonight."

It was maddening to discover her thoughts ran so
exactly parallel to his. "I don't need the recorder. There's
a recording app you can get for your phone." He put his
cell down and yanked the covers back on his bed. Got in
it.

"There is? Then why did that clerk sell me both
without telling me that? Jerk."

Any other time her annoyance would have amused
him. Now, however, it would be a lot easier to regain his
equilibrium if he could forget she was there in the room
with him. He turned his back toward her. Tried to get
comfortable for what he already knew was going to be a
very long night.

"Before you send the recording, I want to listen to it first." Every muscle in his body tensed. Because of course he knew what she had in mind. She stated her intent a moment later. "I won't need a spectrograph. I'll recognize his voice, I'm sure of it."

This time her name was gritted from between clenched teeth. "Mia." He didn't continue. He couldn't. The tangle in his chest made it impossible to articulate his conflicting emotions. If it were just frustration he felt, there wouldn't be an issue. But he needed time and distance to regain his usual control. She gave him neither.

"What? You don't have to hold back whatever you're feeling. I know you're angry."

He propped himself up on one elbow and turned to look at her. She was kick-in-the-gut lovely. Completely exasperating. And he'd never found that combination irresistible before. She ignited something in him that was usually carefully guarded.

Without conscious volition he rolled from the bed and strode toward her. Her expression showed no fear. But her eyes widened a little when he placed a knee on her bed. Propped his hands on either side of the pillow she was resting against and lowered his face close to hers. She looked up at him, with thickly lashed eyes that had gone the color of fog. And he knew his earlier battle for restraint had fragmented. "I'm not just angry."

A flicker of unease in her expression would have had him regaining his senses. Or any visible sign of distrust. But instead her hand came up to cup his damaged cheek. Her lips parted, eyelids drooping.

And he was lost. He leaned in, brushed her mouth with his, eyes slitted to observe her expression for any indication of distress. She was hesitant, but not anxious.

So when her lips moved beneath his he sank into the moment.

There were all kinds of kisses, and Jude wasn't a saint; he'd experienced them all. But this was more than an initial contact between two semi-strangers. He didn't know Mia time wise, but he *knew* her in a way he thought few others did. Partly because of what she'd revealed and partly because he recognized in her elements that he still battled in himself.

Her flavor was foreign, forbidden and he couldn't prevent himself from pressing closer, using his tongue to open her mouth so it could sweep inside. He touched her nowhere else. He didn't dare. Her tongue met his in a tentative glide and his breath stopped in his throat. Just a moment more. Then he'd call a stop to the madness. But the rollicking in his pulse called him a liar.

Already he was craving another taste, and therein lay her danger. He wanted to steep his senses in her, and realized even now that he wouldn't be readily satiated. This wasn't a woman a man could easily walk away from. She was a knot of complications. An endless source of fascination. But when her teeth closed over his bottom lip to score it lightly he knew he wouldn't be satisfied until he'd unlocked all her secrets.

He flicked the delicate roof of her mouth with his tongue, pleased when he felt her shiver. It ignited a hunger that tantalized him to take a little more. Their breathing mingled. Teeth clashed. The muscles in his arms were rigid with the willpower it took to not settle himself against her. To stretch out beside her and see how well they matched. Chest to chest. Hips to hips. Thigh to thigh.

The dim thought elicited a hard fought flicker of reason. It was more difficult than it should have been to tear away from her. Nearly impossible when he dragged his eyes open and saw the dazed expression she wore. Swearing mentally, he managed to speak. Was dismayed at how ragged the words sounded. "This," he whispered against her mouth, "is exactly why I'm not going to be worth a damn protecting you."

Her hand moved to his hair, rubbing it delicately between two fingers as if to test the texture. Her words did nothing to soothe the emotion churning inside him. "Then I guess," she brushed her lips against his, "that it's a good thing you'll have help in that area."

* * * *

"The owner of the TASER is a man named Raymond Tuttle." Logan sat at the desk of the motel room, reading from the screen of a computer he'd brought in with him. "AFID's a nifty little system. I would have liked to have had time to poke around a bit more."

Jude narrowed his gaze at the man. "But you didn't." The mark of a good hacker wasn't the act of infiltrating the online security of others; it was in leaving no trace of having done so.

"Of course not." There was indignation in the lanky blond man's tone. But there was a trace of wistfulness too that Jude could empathize with. "I checked and he's still at the address listed on his registration. 1105 Coral Drive, apartment forty-seven, Tucson, Arizona."

Jude saw the disappointed slump in Mia's shoulders. Tucson didn't have hard winters. They didn't have winters at all, compared to DC. Wherever she had been held when she'd been kidnapped, it hadn't been Arizona.

Still. According to Raiker's forensic anthropologist's discovery, the woman in the mineshaft hadn't been killed in Wyoming, either, yet she'd been found there. She hadn't been killed in West Virginia, but the kidnapper had planned to go there yesterday to retrieve Four and Mia. He exhibited a willingness to travel to accomplish his goals. Maybe they'd discover he'd been to Tucson.

"Ran a background check on him on the way over." His other operative, Hunter Mason was sitting at the table with Mia. At six-six and two hundred fifty pounds, he was the agent Jude used most often with skittish businessmen in need of protection. Something about his girth and booming voice inspired confidence. "Busy guy. Long arrest record, no convictions. He must have a talented defense attorney. He's wiggled out of a couple drug charges that could have brought some stiff sentencing. Got community service for an aggravated assault and an attempted rape charge was dropped when the witness declined to testify."

"So he's a model citizen." Jude wasn't totally unhappy about the man's unsavory past. Criminals—even those who hadn't been convicted yet—usually had more to hide, which gave him a potential bargaining chip.

He looked at Mia. "Which passports did you bring?"

"All of them." She tried to hide the satisfaction from her expression but was unsuccessful. It didn't matter. He'd realized last night he was royally screwed where she was concerned. "They're hidden in the lining of my backpack."

"Use the third one." He didn't want anyone with an interest discovering the names Mia Deleon or Samantha Simmons on a flight manifest. And just to be safe, may as well not use the passport she'd entered the country with either.

"All right. Should I dye my hair red before we leave?"

The picture had been taken with her as a redhead, he recalled now. They'd used a wig at the time. "No.

Women dye their hair all the time. You should pass scrutiny." His focus shifted to Logan. "I've got Blake and Caro on the way to Johnstown to return Mia's car. You can drive the one back that you and Hunter arrived in. We'll take my vehicle and fly out of Dulles."

"Once you buy three tickets," Hunter drawled, hooking one ankle over his knee. Jude had already discussed options with the man on the phone this morning when he'd sent him out for coffee. The operative had drawn a blank when it had come to thinking of another alternative regarding Mia.

Jude's gaze settled on her again. The early arrival of his operatives this morning had made it easy to avoid any awkward conversations about last night. Not that she'd seemed inclined to start any. His usual ability to fall asleep in a matter of minutes had deserted him after the kiss. He'd known by her breathing for hours afterward that she wasn't sleeping either. And the awareness had done nothing to beckon slumber.

"Yeah," he answered finally with a tone of resignation. "Once I buy three tickets."

* * * *

1105 Coral Drive, apartment forty-seven, Tucson, Arizona was a shithole masquerading as middle class digs. Considered generously, forty years ago it might have been decent. But Jude wasn't in the mood to be generous. The complex was a set of three two-story buildings with ten apartments doors lining top and bottom, all facing the parking lot. If someone had stacked two Friend's Inns, the motel he'd found Mia in, on top of each other, Tuttle's building could pass as its twin. The communal pool was neglected and looked unused. At least no one had entered the sagging gate that surrounded it in the eight hours or so that Jude had been parked on the street beside the lot.

He tried to find a relaxing position in the rental. The sedan was mid-sized, but still not comfortable for hours on end for someone his height. And there hadn't been much to see until after nightfall. He wouldn't even have known Tuttle was inside if he hadn't gotten the man's plate and vehicle model from Arizona's Motor Vehicle Services. Tuttle was home. Maybe he'd slept all day.

He wasn't sleeping now, however. The man had started getting visitors about seven-thirty, a few at first, arriving alone or as a couple. When it had gotten dark the trickle had turned to a steady stream. Jude recognized the short swarthy man who let each in from the driver's license photo. He knew even from this distance that the buttoned loose-fitting vintage shirt the man wore was meant to hide a weapon beneath it.

Tuttle's frequency of guests obviously wasn't due to his hospitality. The average stay was twelve minutes. It would take a semi-astute observer all of an hour to figure out what was going on in apartment forty-seven. Raymond Tuttle was a dealer.

The realization wasn't totally surprising, but it was going to come in handy. Jude looked up the number for the Tucson police department and added it to the contacts list on his cellphone. Then he started the car and pulled into the parking lot, picking a spot where he had an unfettered view of Tuttle's place. Taking out his phone again, he began filming the activity at the man's door.

It was after two AM and the procession to apartment forty-seven was starting to wane. When Jude saw the last guest leave the apartment and head back to his car, he got out and ambled toward him. "Hey."

The kid—and he was no more than that, Jude estimated when he got closer—startled. Shoved whatever he was carrying down the front of his pants. "What?"

Jerking his head toward the apartment, Jude said, "Does he have good stuff up there?"

"I don't know what you're talking about." The boy wiped his nose with the back of his free hand, and began to sidle away.

"What's your name?"

"Mind your own business, man." His hand on the car door, he pulled a fob out of his pocket.

Jude held out the video he'd just shot. "I just want to make sure you get credit on this film."

The boy peered closely, releasing a groan when he recognized himself. "Aw, shit. Are you a cop or something?"

"Or something. Show me your ID."

With a low moan the kid reached into his back pocket, his fingers trembling so hard he could barely get his wallet out. Jude took it from him and used the flashlight app on his cell to read the name. Aiden Barclay.

"Okay, Aiden." He handed the wallet back. "Answer the question. If I go up there, does he have good shit?"

"Yeah." The kid's head bobbed nervously. "I mean, I don't get anything fancy, but my friends get some pretty sweet blends from him. Ray can mix *anything*. You just tell him what you want it for and in a couple days he'll have something whipped up. Or maybe he gets it from someone else. Guess I don't know." There was a click as he unlocked his car.

"Don't come back here," Jude advised, giving the boy a hard look. "I'm going to use your name and he probably isn't going to be happy with you after I leave. But if I find out you called him and told him about me, I'm coming after you. And then none of us will be happy."

"Oh fuck," the boy moaned. "All I wanted was some Oxy."

"Remember what I said."

The kid fumbled with the door handle, finally yanking it open and sliding inside. Jude waited until he'd squealed out of the lot before heading to the metal stairway, taking the short wooden sap from his back waistband and moving it to the front, beneath his shirt.

He knocked at the door like he'd seen the stream of other customers do.

"Name."

He knew he was being surveyed through the peephole on the door. The man would be suspicious of a strange face. "Wallace Prescott. Aiden told me about you."

"Don't know an Aiden." Still the door didn't open.

"Maybe you'll recognize him in this." Taking out his cell, Jude pressed play and held the video he'd recorded up for the man to examine through the hole.

"Fuck that shit. Get the hell out of here. Don't come back without a warrant."

"I'm not a cop so I can't get a warrant. But I'm guessing when I take this down to the police station and show them the last few hours of film—I made several of these, because you're a very popular guy—they'll be here shortly with one in hand."

There was the sound of a deadbolt unlocking and then the door opened a few inches, held in place with a security chain. One baleful red-rimmed eye stared out at him. "What the fuck do you want with me?"

"To trade information for information."

The man surveyed him for a few moments. Jude had the feeling he wasn't unused to the concept. There had to be some way Tuttle had managed to avoid any charges sticking. Sometimes the police would trade a smaller fish for one further up the food chain.

"Okay." The door shut again and there was a rattling sound as he unhooked the chain. Jude exploded into action, grabbing the knob and pushing the door open in a short violent motion that would knock the man off balance, before drawing the sap as he entered low. He brought it down hard on the man's wrist, and Tuttle cursed, his fingers loosening around the handgun he held. Jude hit him again, one foot going to the door and kicking it shut behind him. Tuttle dropped the gun. Jude drove the end of the sap into his gut, and the man folded over, wheezing.

Picking up the weapon, Jude never took his gaze from him as he resecured the chain on the door. "Sit down." Tuttle started to stumble in the direction of the couch. "Not there." He probably had another gun stashed in the cushions. "On the folding chair."

"Robbery is a very bad idea." The man's words came between gasps. He was still struggling for breath. "Everyone has bosses, you know? And you do not want to steal from these people. Your head will wind up on a stake."

"Or yours will. Chances are they'll never catch me." Jude watched the guy's florid expression go ashen. "Lucky for you, I'm not here to rob you. I just want to talk to you about your TASER."

Tuttle's eyes went shifty. He definitely lacked a poker face. "I don't have a TASER."

"Not now." Jude's voice was silky. "But you have one registered in your name that's not in your possession. Who'd you give it to?"

"I didn't give it to anyone."

Jude blew out a breath of frustration and pointed the man's gun at him. "Buddy, sitting outside for the last several hours did nothing to improve my patience. Who did you sell the gun to?"

"No one. It was stolen."

Temper frayed, he glared at the man for a long minute. "Fuck this." He stood up, went to the couch and started tearing off the cushions.

"What the hell are you doing?"

"Taking your place apart. You can keep the drugs. I'm guessing it's the money your bosses are going to be most upset about missing. Well, damn." He saw the barrel of a sub-compact pistol almost buried beneath the attached back cushion of the couch. Jude pulled it out, stuck it in his waistband. "You are not a trusting guy. Not particularly smart either, willing to take a bath for someone who left you hanging after he committed a crime with a TASER you gave him."

Jude continued tossing the place, turning over furniture before moving toward the big screen TV. "Okay, wait a minute," Tuttle said hastily. "Yeah, maybe I mailed one out a few days ago to a friend. I had no idea what he'd do with it."

Stopping to stare at him, Jude said, "Mailed where? What friend?"

"Some DC motel. I can't remember which one. It went to a lady. Shelby something."

"Shelby Kronberg." It'd been the name on the passport that Four had used to get into Vietnam.

"Yeah. Shelby something. I don't know what happened to it after that. I sent it along with two cartridges and a cocktail I'd mixed for this friend before."

Tuttle cringed when Jude crossed the room toward him, fist clenched. "A drug cocktail?"

"Party drug, you know. K-Sleep I call it. A ketamine base, blended with a couple of sedatives…seriously this stuff is better than what they give you in the hospital. Had a hernia repaired last year. Woke up in the middle of surgery, for crissakes." When he got going, Tuttle was quite the talker. "You stick a girl with this stuff, she isn't going to wake up until long after the party's over, know what I mean?"

A red wash of anger flooded Jude. He knew exactly what the man meant, having just experienced the effects himself yesterday. "And people say chivalry is dead."

The man shrugged. "Hey, I don't create the demand, just the supply."

He battled for control. There wasn't a doubt in his mind that this was the guy who supplied The Collector with the drugs he used for kidnapping the women. No sedative on the market was as fast acting as what he and Mia had been injected with. And from what she'd said, a similar drug had been used the night she'd been taken five and a half years ago.

"I want the name of the man you supply."

Tuttle looked unhappy. "Hey, this guy's a good customer. I do a steady business with him."

"He's such a good customer he's going to let you take the fall for the crime committed with the TASER you sold him."

11

"Fucker's going to pay double next time," the man said furiously, raking his hand through his slicked back hair. "But I'll tell the cops it was stolen. They can't prove different."

Jude rubbed his forehead, as if in pain. "The stupid. It burns." With exaggerated slowness, he enunciated, "I am still here. I will still rob you and spit in your face after your bosses impale your head on a stake in the parking lot. What. Is. His. Name?"

The man took a minute to consider his choices and it was apparent that the brain activity was agonizing. Finally he shrugged. "He's a black hat. Know what they are?"

Interest stirring, Jude nodded. Hackers often referred to themselves in those terms. White hats were those computer security experts who operated within the law. Black hats had criminal intent. Jude and his crew would be most appropriately referred to as gray hats, since they'd been known to operate on both sides of the law, with no criminal intention. A yearly expenditure at his business was sending his computer techs to the annual Black Hat convention. But maintaining a presence in the underground computer world was the best way to keep a finger on the pulse of current hacker issues.

"Danny Munson. His black hat name is SpidyDance."

Neither name was familiar. "Where do you send the merchandise?"

"It's a Denver mail drop. I have a standing order for a few mixtures monthly, but sometimes he contacts me to ask for more."

"Or to ask for favors. Like with the TASER."

"Oh, yeah." Tuttle was obviously unfamiliar with the concept. "Well, he's getting billed for it, so…"

The plant particle found on the corpse dumped in Wyoming hadn't come from Colorado. The trail was going to be more convoluted than he'd thought. Which was to be expected. The Collector would want to be insulated in as many layers as possible. That was likely how he'd avoided detection as long as he had.

"I need the address for the mail drop." Tuttle recited it and he keyed it into his phone. Then he looked it up on the web for verification. Figured the man was probably telling the truth. The address was indeed for a mail drop service.

Having gotten what he came for, he stood. "I don't need to tell you how very unhappy I'll be if I discover you lied about the name. Or tipped Munson off."

"Yeah, whatever."

"It wouldn't be hard to find out who you work for. Only takes an anonymous tip to the right person that you've been bragging about skimming profits. From my experience those guys are overly suspicious. Of course, maybe your books can stand up to increased scrutiny, right?"

Tuttle glared stonily back at him, but the muscle jumping in his jaw was evidence enough that Jude had struck a nerve. He backed slowly toward the door, the first gun he'd taken from the man still in his hand. He checked the judas hole before undoing the security chain.

"Hey, I want my weapons back."

"That's not going to happen. I'll be watching your door. If I see it open in the next fifteen minutes I'm going to use it for target practice." He let himself out quickly.

"Asshole."

The man had no idea. Jude smiled grimly as he made his way back to his car, opening the trunk to place both weapons inside. When he got done with Tuttle, his lucky streak of avoiding conviction was going to come to an abrupt halt. And once he had a clear link between The Collector and the drug Tuttle had supplied, there was a very good chance Tuttle would be in jail for decades.

He got into the car, started the ignition. Tuttle had earned a far worse fate. And so did The Collector. Jude was going to make certain they both got the end they deserved.

11

Mia listened to a portion of the recorded conversation with Tuttle. "It's not him."

Jude was sitting at the desk of the motel room, using on his mini-laptop. "After talking to him it was clear the man doesn't have the brains. We knew it was a long shot anyway. No harsh winters here."

"I know." But she still had a feeling of letdown. The hours had dragged by in his absence, despite the improved surroundings. Jude had wanted a better hotel because of the increased security. But four walls were four walls, no matter what color they were painted.

"How soon before we hear anything from Logan?" Hunter yawned and scratched his bare chest. Mia and he had been asleep when Jude had come in.

"Depends how long it takes him to get the information we're looking for, and to get inside the CMRA's files. This computer doesn't have the tools I need to do it myself." Jude shot a glance at Mia. "CMRA is the mail drop office. They'll have an address for Munson. Either he picks things up there or they deliver on for him. But he'll have had to fill out some sort of registration. Come look at these."

Curious, she got up to join him, handing him his phone before looking over his shoulder. He had three photos on the screen that he scrolled through slowly. "Recognize any of these men?"

Peering closely, she finally shook her head. "They're all named Danny Munson?"

"They all have Colorado driver's licenses in that name. Once Logan gets back to me with an address, we might be able to match it with one of these."

She reared back to look at him. "You're in the Colorado DMV database? Is that legal?" His green gaze was amused. "You have an intriguing fixation on legalities for someone who has traveled with false identification for the last five years."

Because he had a point, she returned her focus to the pictures. "The Collector is five foot nine or ten, one hundred sixty or seventy pounds. None of these guys are close." One was a balding man with graying gingery hair in his fifties. From the weight stated on the driver's license he had at least a hundred pounds on the kidnapper. Another man was Hispanic and the third would barely be out of his teens.

"Okay." To her surprise he powered off the computer. Pushed his chair back. "I've got a call in to Raiker, but there's nothing more to do tonight—or this morning—until I hear from him or Logan."

"My thought exactly." The room was a suite, with Hunter sleeping on the fold out in the outer room, and Mia and Jude occupying the double beds in the bedroom. Hunter padded back to the sofabed. "You're going to pay the chiropractor bills after this," he warned. "The springs on this thing are brutal."

"There's always the floor," Jude said unsympathetically as he headed into the bedroom.

Mia was left with little choice but to follow him. Jude disappeared into the bathroom and she got in bed, now wide-awake. The entire day had been spent in alternating boredom and a now familiar restlessness while she awaited word about what Jude would discover. But now that he was back, the jitter in her pulse came from another source.

He hadn't mentioned the kiss this morning. Neither had she. Perhaps regret was the reason he'd barely looked at her today during the drive to Virginia and the flight to Tucson. He took his security duties seriously. That was one of the first things she'd learned about him.

And after last night she'd learned something new about herself.

Unconsciously she brought two fingers to her lips. She'd forgotten the exquisite intimacy a kiss could represent. She'd still been in her teens when last she'd experienced it. The intervening years of abuse—and her battle for recovery afterwards—had superimposed on her memory, hazing recollections that were sweeter. Gentler. And therein lay the risk. She'd already known Jude was adept at slipping through defenses she once thought stalwart. But their kiss had beckoned something inside her that would be better locked away. It summoned softness when it was critical to remain strong.

He was right about one thing…they both needed to retain focus. She knew how to guard herself: her security, her privacy, her thoughts. It had become not just a way of life, but a defense mechanism so deeply embedded that she was helpless to reverse course now. She couldn't pretend to be other than she was. Flawless on the outside. A patchwork of semi-healed scars within. But despite realizing how little she had to offer, last night she'd been very close to offering more.

In a day laced with regrets, she could at least be grateful she hadn't added another to the mix.

* * * *

Mia entered the outer room of the suite the next morning to discover Hunter and Jude grouped around the small laptop. The sight was familiar. So was the voice coming from the computer. Curious, she walked closer and saw Logan Spirrow's face filling the screen.

"Long night, but fruitful." The man was speaking animatedly. "I was able to infiltrate the system for the Denver mail drop Tuttle used. The CMRA server wasn't too sophisticated. The Danny Munson associated with the registration had this address listed." He read it off.

Jude looked up as she joined them, giving her that swift assessing gaze she was becoming to equate with his version of a visual wellness check. "That address matches the first photo I showed you last night."

She remembered the one. A big middle-aged man with fading reddish hair, he was too large to be The Collector.

"Not only do they keep track of their clients, obviously, but they track the packages in and out of the service. This is where it gets a bit complicated. Munson never actually picks up the package from Tuttle. His mail drop is little more than a conduit to the next one, in Binton, South Dakota. That's in the southwest corner of the state. The South Dakota drop is registered to Eldon Weales, from Custer, South Dakota. And from there things get real interesting."

Interesting was one word for it, Mia thought as she pulled up a chair in view of the screen. The information so far had her eyes glazing. "Weales does a ton of shipping from that CMRA in South Dakota," Logan continued, "but not only to other mail drops. Frequently he mails to residential and business addresses all over the United States. A few are sent to mail drops, most recently in Iowa and Missouri."

"But Weales actually picks up the package sent through Munson's mail drop in Denver?" Hunter asked.

"He does." Logan looked down at something in front of him. "Of course, there's no way to tell if he later sends it on, but his drop isn't a sail through. Packages are held there to be collected."

"Maybe some illicit activity going on," Jude murmured.

"My thought exactly." Hunter rubbed a spot at the base of his spine. Mia made a mental note to make sure Jude got the man his own room with a more comfortable bed at the next stop. She was coming to like the big operative. He'd spent most of the day yesterday teaching her more than she'd ever thought to know about the intricacies of blackjack betting. "Lots of drug dealers make shipments that way."

"Raymond Tuttle included." Jude looked back toward the Skyped image of Logan. "Okay, I think I've got it. We need to check out Eldon Weales. What'd you find out about the black hat, Munson in Denver?"

Logan's expression turned gleeful. "I recognized his nickname right away from the black hat forums. SpidyDance is a piece of work. Better than average skills, from what I gather. Not as stellar as he'd like to believe. Claims to have infiltrated the FBI and White House servers, but who knows how far he got. There was some pretty convincing talk that he was behind the breach of Belways customer payment information, though. Compromised more than a million credit cards. He definitely has the skills to have been the guy to track Mia."

The blood in her veins congealed. She'd mistakenly considered the man harmless since it was clear he couldn't be The Collector. But that didn't mean he didn't work for the other man. She'd have been no more than a name to him, representing an online game of hide and seek. "So you think my laptop was sent to him after it was stolen? And Dr. Halston's?"

"We won't know that until we get a look at his files."
Jude's tone was cautious.

He'd tried to dissuade her from believing just that those only days ago, she recalled grimly. To assuage the guilt she was feeling for possibly being the link to Halston. They'd had no evidence of it then. But she was betting they could find it through Munson.

"With the K-Sleep drug going through his mail drop, the possible connection between him and The Collector definitely bears checking out."

"Can't hack a hacker," Logan offered. "We're too savvy. He's not going to leave his system open to possible breaches."

"So don't breach it." The three men looked at Mia. "He probably received two stolen computers to pry through, mine and Halston's. Steal his and do the same thing."

Hunter sent her an amused glance. "I'm beginning to like you more by the minute."

"We'll figure something out," Jude told Logan. "In the meantime, put a dossier together on Munson. I'll need details I can use when I confront him."

Mia's earlier resolve wilted a bit at the reminder. Jude would meet with the man alone, the way he had the drug dealer last night. He actually seemed to relish the possibility. But she knew she was in for more excruciatingly long hours waiting to hear that he was all right. She wouldn't be allowed anywhere close to the encounter. So she'd have to start thinking of a plan that would minimize his risk.

Logan signed off and she went to the other room to pack, a feeling of foreboding tightening in her belly. People with a connection to her continued to die. And she knew she'd never be able to live with herself if Jude was next.

* * * *

"What happened with the Tucson police?" Hunter wanted to know as they fastened their seatbelts. They sat three abreast on the plane, Mia in the middle.

"Raiker made a call to smooth the way." The plane began its taxi down the runway. "I met with a vice cop by the name of Sanchez who seemed pretty interested in the video I took of Tuttle's apartment. And he was more than happy to take the guy's guns off my hands."

"How did you explain discovering Tuttle's ownership of the TASER?" Mia asked. Seeing Hunter's fingers grip the armrests, she gave the man a sympathetic smile. She'd noticed yesterday that he was a nervous flyer.

"Said I had a tip. He seemed satisfied with that." His legs fit the small space only slightly better than Hunter's. "He'll get in contact with the investigation out east and law enforcement can take it from there."

"Good." There were more drug dealers on the streets than would ever be brought to justice, but she desperately needed to believe that eventually Tuttle would pay for arming criminals with exotic drugs specifically blended to assault women. The man was just as responsible for the misery caused as the ones who executed the abuse.

There had been other drugs in The Collector's arsenal. Her inner defenses rose, but too late to keep the memory from surging. Ointments to apply after a beating that kept the pain inflamed. Hallucinogens during the abuse to turn the nightmare experience into a fiery pocket of hell.

"Raiker thought his people might be able to do something with the recording the state police took of the conversation you had with The Collector. It's on its way to his lab right now. And he had a message for you," Jude told her.

Mia welcomed the distraction from her thoughts. "Did he get a DNA match?"

"He did."

Unconsciously, her hand crept to touch his where it lay atop his denim-clad thigh. "And?"

His fingers linked with hers. "Her name is Jody Wilcox. She's from Detroit, Michigan."

Jody Wilcox. In death at least, thanks to Raiker, the woman had resumed her identity. Perhaps the most dehumanizing part of their captivity had been to be stripped of their name. To be denied the very integral sense of self that accompanied the personal label affixed at birth. Tattooed with a number, the meaning of which they'd never known.

Tears were a human function she was no longer capable of. But deep inside her something wept for the woman she'd known only as Eight.

Jude's voice softened. And he didn't let go of her hand. "The Detroit detective who had her case said she'd disappeared at a concert. He'll be looking into her disappearance with a new eye, especially since Raiker informed him of the details surrounding your kidnapping."

When her gaze flew to his, he cautioned, "Long road there. Lots of law enforcement entities to get on board before we get a national manhunt for this bastard. But the pieces are falling into place."

She took a deep breath. Released it. "Then we'll get them more pieces." Jody Wilcox and her family had closure now, finally. But there were eleven more women waiting for someone to release them from never-ending torment.

"Next step is figuring out how to approach Munson. I'll want a clone of his hard drives, because he almost certainly has several computers."

"We wait for him to leave the house and stage a break in." Hunter had been listening.

"There's no we," Jude reminded him drily, as he sent a thumb skating over the top of Mia's hand still clasped in his. "You and Mia will be in a secured hotel."

"These hackers…they're paranoid sorts, right?" The last time Mia had held hands was when her Gran helped her cross the street. She might have been five. Her pulse was jumping from the sustained contact. But there was no underlying sense of panic. Perhaps she'd come further than she'd given herself credit for.

Hunter and Jude smiled broadly at her statement. After a puzzled moment she understood why. "Present company excluded, of course."

"Don't look at me," the operative said. "I'm not on the techy side of things. I was hired for my brawn and my movie star good looks."

"You do bear a striking resemblance to Homer Simpson," Jude told him consideringly.

Mia wouldn't be distracted. "I mean these black hat guys. Distrust of the government is part of it, right? So he'd likely have some pretty good home security. Both for his house and his computers. I'm guessing it would take some effort to get into them."

"I'm not without my own skillset." Jude's voice was dry. "But yeah, there's a few details to work out yet." He rolled his shoulders tiredly, brushing against hers with the movement.

"Perhaps Munson could be, uh, persuaded to let you make the clones," Hunter suggested delicately.

"You need to approach him when he's in the house." Mia broke off when the attendant stopped a cart next to their seats and proceeded to hand out beverages. She drank thirstily from her soda. She hadn't had near enough caffeine before they'd left the hotel this morning. "Likely if he's home, the computers would be running. He'd be logged in and save you a lot of trouble."

When she leaned forward to pull the tray down for her drink, she caught both men's gaze on her. "What?"

"There's a kernel there we can massage," Jude said slowly. "Go up to the door? He's a suspicious type, remember? He'll never let a stranger in."

"Getting the door open at least gives you an opportunity," Hunter inserted.

Mia thought more about it for a moment. "He has to want you inside. If you can do something for him...have something for him..."

"Pretty sure the Publishers Clearinghouse scam isn't going to work."

Ignoring Hunter's humor, she considered. "It has to be an opportunity he can't pass up. You offer to share hacking information with him. No." She dismissed the thought as soon as it occurred. "What would he want that you have? It came to her in the next moment. "Money."

Jude's expression was intrigued. "You have a devious side that's very appealing. Why do I want to give him money?"

"I can't do all the heavy lifting. There's your nugget. Massage it." And she sat back in her seat, more than a little fascinated as the two men proceeded to do exactly that.

* * * *

There was no way to determine if Munson was even home. Jude parked on a residential Denver street well down the block from the man's small white clapboard house. Its attached garage was closed, and the blinds were drawn. It wasn't yet seven PM. Too early for lights to go on in an occupied house. With a sense of déjà vu he settled in.

His wait was rewarded far more quickly than it had been in Tucson the night before. After only thirty-five minutes the garage door at the house raised. A decades old black Jeep Cherokee backed down the drive as the door lowered again.

Jude fired up the engine of his rental. They'd taken out extra insurance precisely because of what he was going to do next.

Accelerating, he caught up with the Jeep quickly, because Munson was already slowing for the stop sign ahead. Jude did not. He hit the Jeep's bumper with enough force to jolt it forward several yards, before screeching to a halt.

He was out of the vehicle before the other man exited his, kneeling down to survey the damage. "Oh man, oh man, oh man," he moaned rocking a bit in his position. "I'm really sorry. It's my wife. She calls me every damn time I get behind the wheel and distracts me."

Munson was a hulk of a man whose stated weight on his driver's license had been a result of wishful thinking. And he was a seething hulk of a man right now. "You idiot! Are you blind? Stop signs are red for a reason!"

"I know, I know." Jude got to his feet, staggered just a little. "It's my fault, totally. I'll pay to have the dent removed from your bumper."

With a cagey expression Munson said, "You'll do more than that. The whole damn bumper will have to be replaced. Not to mention where you scraped the paint."

Lowering his voice, Jude pulled out his wallet. "Listen. We can take care of this, just the two of us, can't we? I'll make it right. No one says the police have to be involved." He swayed a bit. Visibly fumbled to open the wallet he'd prepared earlier in the day.

The big man stepped closer when Jude started pulling out bills. "You maybe trying to avoid a drunk driving conviction, is that it, pal?"

"No, no." A hundred dollar bill fluttered to the ground and Jude made a grab for it. Fell to one knee in the attempt. "Couple of beers, that's all."

"Yeah, right. How many DUIs do you have already? I oughta let them haul your ass to jail right now."

"Look, I got five hundred on me." Jude pulled the cash out and folded it in one motion, tried to stuff it in the other man's hand. "I'll get more."

"Uh-huh." Munson wasn't having it. He wiped his perspiring forehead on the edge of his shirt. "You know, now that I think about it, my neck is killing me. Whiplash is a bitch."

"How much? How much to make this whole thing go away?"

Munson sent an appraising look toward the white Impala Jude had rented. Thought for a moment. "Three thousand."

"Three thous--," Jude threw up his hands. "C'mon, you're killing me here. That's a month's wages."

"Then you can afford it," Munson said unsympathetically. The outcome of the evening wouldn't have altered either way, but Jude was sort of glad the man was a complete prick. It made what was to come halfway enjoyable.

He studied the pavement for several moments before letting his shoulders slump a little. "Okay. I gotta go home. Try to sneak in without the wife seeing... She's going to miss the money, man. I'm gonna have to take it out of her stash."

"Do I care about your problems? Give me your ID."

With a show of reluctance, Jude removed his false license from his wallet and handed it to the man. Munson studied it. "Sam Fielding. What the hell are you doing here from New Mexico?"

"Moved six months ago." Jude manufactured a morose tone as he pretended to study the damage again. "Fresh start and all that. Like hell."

"You've got an hour to bring me the rest of the money or I call the cops." The big man waved the ID Jude had given him.

"Okay. All right." His tone sounded properly defeated. "Where's your place?"

"We can meet at a bar I know. It's not that far from here."

"Are you kidding me? I swear to God my wife is on speaking terms with every bartender in a ten mile radius.

They'll rat me out. Plus I gotta go to work in an hour. If we're going to do this thing, it has to be quick."

Munson thought better of the idea. It was clear from his expression. But the cash clenched in his fist was a powerful motivator. "Okay. See that shit yellow house down the street? 11876. It's mine. If you're not there in an hour, I'll make sure your ass is in jail."

"Your wife gonna be home? Because if she is, you don't want her to know you've got this kind of money, believe me."

Curling his lip, Munson said, "I was never dumb enough to get married."

Jude returned to his car, satisfied that the man would be alone later. He waited for Munson to pull away. There really was a good-sized dent in the man's bumper. A matching one in his rental's. If he were feeling generous at the end of this, maybe he'd let the man keep the five hundred.

He timed it almost to the minute. He wanted Munson sweating his return. Pulling up in the driveway, he switched off the ignition and reached for a sack on the seat beside him. Running up the front walk to the porch, he pounded on the front door. It was opened immediately.

"Almost thought you weren't going to show." Munson held the knob with one hand to leave only a small crack in the door. He stuck a sneaker-clad foot in the narrow opening. "What's in the bag? Give me the money."

Jude made a show of looking over his shoulder uneasily. "Fuck that, I'm not waving around this kind of cash on the street. All I need is to get mugged before my wife can kill me first. The cash is in the bag." He opened it briefly to show a stack of money. Closed it again.

"Let's do this inside." There was a long silence. "C'mon man, we gonna do this or not? I gotta get to work."

Finally Munson opened the door wide enough for Jude to slip through. He dug in his front pocket and brought out a fat wad of cash. "I need my license back."

Munson took the thick stack of bills and smiled. "License is going to cost you another hundred."

"Shit!" He reached toward his back pocket, but took the sap out of the waistband of his jeans. He slammed it upwards to make contact with the man's chin, before rapping it smartly above his ear.

Munson staggered back, shook his head. Then, letting out a roar he rushed toward Jude, fists flying. He managed to duck the first one. The second roundhouse caught him in the left temple and had him seeing stars. He grabbed the man's wrist and pulled him around, using his momentum against him. Yanking his arm toward the center of his back, Jude ran him toward the doorjamb and rammed his head against it with as much force as he could muster. Once. Twice. Again.

Munson still didn't crumple. But he was dazed enough that Jude could get the zip locks out of his pocket and tighten them over his wrists. Because he didn't think that would keep the man down, he shoved him onto the floor and used Munson's belt to wrap around the man's feet.

By the time he rose, Jude was breathing hard and had a bitch of a headache. He scanned the front room. Was gratified to see three computers taking up an entire side of it. "Well, this is convenient." He locked the front door before going to the adjoining kitchen and rummaged in the drawers for a dishtowel. Behind him, Munson was yelling at an ear-splitting decibel. Returning, Jude wadded up the towel and shoved it in the man's mouth.

"By the way," he said casually, gathering up the bag and prying the money out of the man's fist. "TopCat says hey."

According to Logan's report, TopCat was the name of the man's nemesis with which he had a long-running feud. Munson would be looking for a reason for Jude's interest in his hard drives. The name of the other black hat would give him one.

Stepping over his body, Jude dropped the bills back into the top bag and pulled the entire sack away from the one hidden beneath it. The bottom bag held four stand-alone hard drives that he'd bought when they'd gone shopping after landing in Denver. He'd need only three, one for each of the computers on the long table in front of him.

Jude took a moment to look at each screen and grinned. Mia had been right. The man was home, so he was wired. Maybe he should put her on the payroll.

He took a few minutes taking the hardware out of the boxes and hooking them up to the computers to clone Munson's hard drives. Realizing what he was up to, the big man fought to his feet and hopped toward him, fury in his eyes.

Sighing, Jude got up and grabbed the man's shoulder, tripping him and shoving him down ungently at the same time. The floor shook when his weight hit it. "This is going to be very tiresome if we have to do this over and over, so stay down. I'll be out of your way soon enough."

Munson stayed down. Crossing to the computers again, Jude began looking at what the man had. Most of the files were encrypted, which wouldn't be a problem when he got the cloned drives back to the other purchased equipment at the hotel. He'd spent a good deal of money duplicating hardware he already had at headquarters, plus he'd likely have the expense of shipping it all back east. Tossing the man a look, he saw he'd rolled to his back, all the better to glare at him. "Hope this is worth my time. I heard you were behind that breach at Belways. Am I gonna find all those customers' credit card info on here?"

Munson gave a muffled roar and Jude smiled. "TopCat will be pleased. Have to wonder why you're living in this shithole if you struck the big time, but maybe you've got your money stashed somewhere, huh? If so, I'm sure we'll find it when we have time to go through the drives later."

It was hard to tell if the man was buying the farce, but Jude figured he'd installed plenty of doubt. He spent the remainder of the time looking through the web search history on each machine. Found nothing of interest. There might be more hidden deeper, but it was likely the history was securely wiped at regular intervals.

It was Munson's email that would be the most valuable, of course. It would save them a lot of time if they could find verification of Eldon Weale's location. Or damning proof that Weale was the man they were hunting.

The copying was finished in less than half an hour. Whistling tunelessly, Jude unhooked his drives and piled them in the bag again. "You can keep the five hundred," he said, skirting the man's body as he lifted the blind of the front window an inch to peer outside. Getting close enough to go through his pockets wasn't worth the possible trouble. "It won't buy you a new bumper, but I have a feeling you weren't going to fix your car anyway."

* * * *

In addition to the new computer equipment, the three of them had bought some clothes. But it was the hardware that took up most of the available surfaces in the outer room. Jude had ordered another suite, but because Mia had suggested it he'd gotten Hunter a separate room for use when Jude was here. Likely the man's whining about his back had eventually gotten to her. After updating his operative, he'd dismissed him hours earlier. The man had a lot of qualities that made him a valuable employee, but his computer skills weren't among them.

Not for the first time in the last few hours, Jude glanced at the bedroom door. Resisted the urge to check on Mia. It took more self-control than it should have. He didn't want to take the chance of disturbing her. She needed the rest and he couldn't afford the distraction. Already thoughts of her were lodged in the back of his skull, difficult to banish.

Rubbing his eyes with the heels of his palm, he stared blearily at the computer screen. He'd gone through two drives already and it had taken him most of the night to crack the encrypted files. There was plenty there to intrigue. Munson kept logs of his successful breaches, proving once again that ego could trump self-preservation. He also apparently did freelance work for anyone with the money to pay. The spreadsheet of labor and payment was coded. Jude ignored it for the time being. If they found nothing else Logan could tackle it. So far Jude hadn't found a link to Mia.

He discovered it on the third cloned drive. He stared, half stunned as he recognized the contents of the file he'd cracked. There were screen shots of blocks of jumbled computer gibberish. Beneath each were typed snippets of information that the man had obviously pieced together from them. Names were highlighted. A note in all caps was at the bottom of the document.

Dr. Joan Young 16 Dr. Erich Halston 21 Frederick Paulus 14

Jude sat back. Studied the comment. Realized that Munson had likely counted the names of psychologists Mia had researched most frequently. The man who'd hired him would need to narrow his focus in his search for a link to Mia. This recovery of her computer information would have helped him do so.

A primitive fury flooded his system, lacing his muscles with tension. The hacker had painstakingly pieced together that mess of numbers that Mia's wipe of her hard drive would have left in its wake. It would have been tedious work, and the price for it wouldn't have come cheap. His fingers curled into fists at the visual image of the man laboring over Mia's laptop. He wouldn't have cared why his employer who'd hired him wanted the information. Or what he planned to do with it. Like Tuttle, Munson just cared about being paid.

Had the man also examined Halston's computer? It seemed logical. It would have been child's play compared to restoring the wiped information on Mia's. That a man had died in the process of its theft wouldn't have been a factor to Munson. Jude had met the man. If he'd ever possessed scruples they'd been ground out long ago.

So. He took a deep breath to dissipate the anger that could cloud reason. The chain was starting to make sense. Tuttle with the drugs and eventually the TASER. Which linked to Munson with the computer know-how and the pass through mail drop for the drugs. Then the trail to Eldon Weale, who collected the drugs in South Dakota.

With renewed determination he began narrowing his focus to finding clues that would lead them to Weale. Email seemed the most likely place to start. The password on Munson's account was better than decent and had Jude swearing under his breath for most of an hour before he finally cracked it. The man used a proxy web service, of course, to disguise where his emails originated. But many of his correspondents did not. Jude was able to look up most of the geographical locations of the IP addresses utilized by the sender of the messages.

It didn't take long to discover several cryptic emails from Eldon Weales. They revealed no useful information, Jude realized, scrolling through them. Codes for a drug order for Munson to pass on, maybe? He had more luck when he dug into the IP address on Weales' messages. It wasn't a South Dakota address to match the one listed on the registration for the mail drop the man used. It listed the man as residing in Davison, Nebraska.

He tapped the table in front of the keyboard as he thought swiftly. IP addresses could be spoofed to make it appear as though they came from somewhere else. Knowing this, he swiftly readjusted his plans. Binton, South Dakota wasn't going to be his next stop, after all.

They were heading to Davison, Nebraska.

* * * *

"Anthony!"

The sharp tone snapped him out of his reverie. "I'm sorry, Mother. I was lost in thought." He couldn't concentrate on the mindless details for the upcoming customer appreciation party. Who could blame him? He was drowning in a well of depression and anger. The story of the woman falling to her death in Coopers Rock State Forest had been easy to find in the forty-eight hours since he'd spoken to Eleven.

The name of the victim hadn't been released. Without checking his records, Anthony couldn't be certain of Four's given name himself. Because it was meaningless. He'd tagged her, much as they marked the priceless pieces for sale on the floor of their antiquities showroom. She hadn't had a value until her selection and he'd taught her the true meaning of her existence.

And now she was gone in the most final way possible. The way Eight had been. He'd thought he'd known true grief then. But Eight's replacement had eventually healed his loss. Four's death left a void that wouldn't be as easily filled. She'd been the first item he'd collected and thought of nothing but pleasing him. None of his other possessions came close to her slavish devotion.

"You've drifted away again." With a no-nonsense click of spiked heels on the marble floor, Mother approached to lay a hand on his forehead, a look of concern on her elegant features. "You don't seem to have a temperature, but I'm not convinced you're fully recovered from that bug you had a couple days ago when you went to Atlanta."

"I'm fine." He tried to work up a smile for her. "Maybe just a little blue."

"Well, you certainly have nothing to be depressed about darling. Those candelabra were a marvelous find. I'm half inclined to keep it for myself."

He knew she wouldn't. The antique, while exquisite, wasn't the type of thing she was drawn to. And the money it would fetch was too attractive. "Maybe I am still a little under the weather," he lied. He returned his attention to the spreadsheet of guest names, accommodation details, and menu. They'd kept in mind the tastes of their most valued clients when they'd finalized it. Frankly he found the incessant fussing over trivialities exasperating at the best of times.

He was hardly in the mood for a big celebration in a couple days. But bringing in some of their most valued customers every summer gave them a chance to preview the Davis Antiquities fall catalog and whet interest for the annual auction. The business his grandfather had started would never be on the level of a Christies. But what they lacked in volume they made up for with meticulous client care and an eye toward the rare and unusual.

He'd turned that same eye toward selecting items for his own collection.

"Maybe you shouldn't go in to work today." A frown marred Mother's face, the only line that dared to settle there. "Stay home and go over the details with me."

He'd rather take a knife to the chest. Forcing a smile, he reminded her, "Everything on the showroom floor has to be perfect. You know many of our guests will want to tour it the day after the party."

"You're right. Of course, you're right." He turned and headed toward the front door. "But an afternoon nap would do you wonders, dear. You push yourself much too hard."

Mother was correct, as usual. He jogged down the steps to his car, which had been brought around for him this morning. Maybe he'd leave work early, spend several hours tending to his collection. He'd neglected it recently. Thirteen wasn't going to train herself, and the others required regular tending, to prevent a return of bad habits.

Getting into the car, he felt a trifle better at the thought. But as he drove down the curved drive he knew that resuming his daily routine wouldn't be enough to shake off this unusual lethargy. Perhaps only one thing would do that.

Eleven's return to her rightful place.

12

"Davison, Nebraska." Mia read from her iPhone as Hunter drove. "Population nine thousand four hundred thirty-two, as of the 2010 census. Home to the Fox County seat, and situated…" she squinted, stretching the image so she could read it better. "…second county over from the Wyoming border, and bordering South Dakota to the north." There was a buzz of excitement in her veins, mingled with trepidation. Jude had filled them in on what he'd discovered so far on Munson's computer, and the reason for switching their focus from Binton, South Dakota. The picture he'd shown her of Eldon Weale, from his foray into the Nebraska DMV showed a man who was startlingly ordinary. An inch shorter than she'd described for the police. Ten pounds lighter. Brown hair. Brown eyes.

Were they the eyes of a soulless monster? Mia had spent a long time looking at the picture, her flesh prickling all the while. Because of course she couldn't be sure.

Wasn't that always what the neighbors said when they discovered a nearby resident had committed an atrocity? *He seemed so ordinary. Just a regular guy.* Eldon Weale was someone she could pass on the street and never even notice. Which would be a handy quality for a serial kidnapper to possess.

Jude had told her about a piece of an endangered plant found with Jody Wilcox's body. Iowa, Kansas, Minnesota, Nebraska and North Dakota. Mia had the states memorized. They were the only ones where the plant was found, so one of them must be the state where she died. And Eldon Weale was in Nebraska.

Jude turned away from his laptop then to look at her in the back seat. She met his gaze blandly. It wouldn't do for him to realize how jumpy she was feeling. Not after the conversation they'd had this morning. "I'm going to hold you to the promise you made earlier." Mia nodded. The moment Jude had reason to suspect that Weale was more than just another conduit to the drugs Tuttle shipped, she and Hunter would head back to Denver and take the next plane to DC. In return she'd extracted a concession from him; if they left, Jude would have another operative fly out to join him.

The fear she was beginning to feel for his safety wasn't logical. If ever there was a man who exuded a reassuring capable toughness, it was Jude Bishop. But the fear was there, an insidious growing weight that had lodged in her chest and showed no signs of lessening.

"Weale has no criminal record, according to what I'm finding online. Not even a traffic ticket. But I've got an address that matches the one on his license." He'd also gotten the exact location the man's emails had originated from through a discreet probe of the ISP provider's server. He was certain it would come in handy locating the man.

Mia set the phone down to focus on the scenery flashing by her window at a significantly faster pace than what was posted on the speed limit signs. Lots of plains, which she'd expected, interrupted by occasional large rock formations, which she had not. The reading she'd done earlier had mentioned cattle ranching and farming, with the most frequently grown agricultural products being forage crops and wheat. Could she have been running across fields of either crop when she'd escaped? Racing over pastureland? It seemed possible.

But the other possible states would not be so different from Nebraska. With a tinge of frustration, Mia recognized that she wasn't going to be able to narrow the The Collector's location through geography alone.

"You figured out yet how you're going to handle the approach?" Hunter had volunteered to drive to free up Jude to do research. Mia suspected the man really just enjoyed being behind the wheel.

"I want to get a feel for the place first." Jude straightened in his seat, facing forward again. "Every small town has its own unique social system in place. I'm guessing I can learn a lot just by asking the right questions. I'll determine my approach from there. I'm most worried about the security at the hotel you booked."

"Only three to choose from. One is surprisingly decent for a town that size. Built five years ago, the webpage said. It was our best bet." The operative fiddled with the radio controls on the steering wheel. Settled on a country station that had Mia smiling.

"My ears are already bleeding," Jude said in a pained voice. "Is that the only station that comes in?"

"I would never have figured you for a country fan, Hunter."

The operative caught Mia's eye in the rearview mirror and winked. "Guess people are always full of surprises."

They were, she thought bleakly. Which was what made it so difficult to figure out which ones harbored evil.

* * * *

Hunter was right. The Davison, as the hotel was called would suit their needs well enough. Apparently it suited the needs of a great many people because the rooms were completely booked.

"It's for an event in town, sir," the girl behind the counter offered sympathetically. "A local business is having its annual customer appreciation gala tomorrow, and the majority of the guests come from out of state."

"What about a suite with a fold out?" Hunter would bitch, but it would be better than nothing.

"I'm sorry. All I have is the VIP suite, which offers a large sitting or conference area with two bedrooms, one on each side of it. Double beds in both. It's quite nice." When she quoted the price, Jude stared hard at her, certain she was joking. "How is it you can charge DC prices in a town of nine thousand?"

With a fixed smile she turned back to her computer. "Let me see what I can do." In the end she lowered the price from the stratospheric range to the merely ridiculous. Shaking his head, Jude offered a credit card issued for the ID he'd used in Denver and went back to the car to accompany Hunter and Mia to the room.

"Nice digs." Hunter took a quick look in both bedrooms before dropping his bag in one. "Lots of room in the sitting area to resume Mia's poker lessons."

"Lots of room for the computer equipment," she corrected. "Before Jude leaves he's going to teach me the rudiments for cracking the encryption on Munson's files."

Amused, he started toward the other bedroom carrying both their bags. "I am?"

"It makes sense." She followed closely on his heels. "I can be doing something useful while you're out. We can kill two birds with one stone."

He set their luggage on the low dresser. Her idea had merit. He'd figured out Munson's encryption methods. It would just be a matter of demonstrating them and letting her try her hand at the files. If successful, it would save him work when he got back. "Okay. Hunter can go unload the computer equipment and bring it up."

"That's one of the burdens of being so incredibly brawny," the operative said as he passed by the door. "I get to do all the heavy lifting."

There was the sound of the door closing. Mia's face was troubled. "If I promise to chain myself to the couch would you consider taking Hunter with you today?"

Jude's mouth curled. "You sick of him already?"

She jerked her shoulders and wandered through the room, trailing a hand over the dresser where he'd set their bags. Since their shopping trip she'd ditched the jeans and tee shirts and was in a pair of white capris that hugged her legs and butt, and a green filmy top. With a purely male's sense of appreciation he applauded the change. "It seems a waste is all. The two of you could cover more ground together."

"There's not all that much ground to cover in a town of less than ten thousand people."

"You know what I mean."

He sat down on the corner of one of the beds. Something was on her mind. Something far different from an argument about her security detail. "What's this about?"

She turned, arrowed a look at him. "This will be the third day in a row that you've tackled a suspect on your own. I've been learning a lot about the law of averages from Hunter's gambling lessons. At some point your luck is going to run out."

"I don't know. I've always considered myself a pretty lucky guy."

Her expression was somber. "I'm serious. It's been a long time since I worried about someone's well being. It's as if…" She searched for words for a moment. "All the feelings most people have…they've been locked away. Like in a vault. Fear, hunger, pain, boredom. Those are my normal. The others take some getting used to. I don't want to worry about you. Don't give me reason to."

Heat bloomed in the pit of his belly. "Ditto."

She pursed her lips. Narrowed her eyes. "It's not the same. I've got a protective detail. A very brawny operative, to use his own words. You go out there alone each time."

He waggled his fingers in a c'mere motion. Her hesitation was visible before she slowly walked over to him. Spreading his knees, he hooked an arm around her hips. Pulled her closer. "The correct response in this pose is for you to put your arms around my neck. Not my throat," he added, only half-jokingly.

There was a playfulness in her expression he'd never seen. Her hands slid around his shoulders. Her fingers clasped there. "We'll make a pact. Neither of us will do anything stupidly dangerous for at least the next twelve hours."

Cocking her head, Mia finally nodded. "Not a terribly difficult promise for me, but okay."

"All right." When she went to move away, he held her in place. "It's customary to seal a bargain after it's been struck."

Her eyes glinting, she lowered her head toward his. "I think I know what you mean," she breathed against his lips. A moment later she stuck out her little finger. "Pinky swear?"

Humor filled him. Just when he thought he was getting to know her on some level, she showed him facets he hadn't seen previously. He wondered if she just kept them closely guarded, or if her rigid reserve was finally thawing. Whichever it was, the results were fascinating.

He hooked her finger with his. "Pinky swear."

* * * *

The more Jude drove around the burg that was Davison, Nebraska, the more he was reminded of the place where he'd grown up. Not with his grandfather. That stay had lasted less than two years and carried no pleasant memories. But the foster home he'd landed in had been all right. More than all right. Decent people who had seen him through the long months of surgeries and the pain of recovery. Burnsville, Maine, was half a continent away, but it had enough in common with Davison to give him a sense of déjà vu.

The town's main street was long and wide, perhaps designed back in the day when they'd needed to accommodate horses and buggies. There were a handful of empty storefronts, an affliction of many small rural towns in America, but most of the shops were occupied and painted in cheerful colors. An old-fashioned movie theater marquis quoted a cover price of two dollars for the nightly show. An ice cream shop was squeezed next to it, flanked by a large hardware store on the other side.

A few blocks away were a public library, fire station and police department, all looking relatively new. A chain convenience gas station sat directly across the street from one that appeared privately owned. A man was standing in front of the price sign holding a long pole, a pile of plastic numbers at his feet. Without much thought, Jude pulled into an empty space in front of a pump and got out to gas up, despite the rental being half full.

With the nozzle in the gas tank and switched on, he shoved his hands into the pockets of his jeans and ambled over to the man. "Prices set to go up or down?"

"Down. That seems to be the way things are going around here these days." He lowered his pole. Short, with a scruffy beard and a shirt emblazoned with 'Steve' in unraveling red embroidery above the left pocket, he seemed friendly enough, if a bit resigned.

"You the owner?"

"For now. Until this price war puts me out of business."

Jude's gaze traveled beyond him to the convenience store across the street. "No way you can meet their prices when you don't get the bulk discount."

"Tell me about it." He'd obviously touched on a sore subject. "We've got another one like it out by the Interstate but this one is killing me. If it weren't for the repair part of my business, I'd have gone under months after this one opened." He scratched the back of his head. "You from town or just passing through?"

"I was in the area. Thought I'd stop by and look up an old friend. Eldon Weale. You know him?"

Steve hooked another number with his pole and reached up to affix it to the sign. Price was about to drop ten cents, Jude noted. "Yeah, I know Eldon. I've done some work for him. Decent guy. How'd you say you know him?"

"Grew up together."

"Yeah? Well, you're not far from his place. He lives on Spruce." The man lowered the pole again for another number and repeated the maneuver. "Won't be home now, of course. He'll still be at work."

Jude cast a glance over his shoulder. His rental would be done filling now, but he had a feeling that Steve wasn't done talking. "Where's that?"

"Only place he's ever worked, far as I know. He's a buyer at Davis." At Jude's expression the man said, "Sorry. I'm talking about Davis Fine Antiquities. Used to be on Main Street when I was a kid, but now they've got a big fancy place south of town. Their ancestors settled this area and they don't let anyone forget it."

Finished with his task, he obviously thought better of his verbiage and shot Jude a glance. "Sorry. They're the ones who put up that bastard across the street." He nodded to the convenience station. "Built the new hotel too, to house the customers that travel from who knows where to Nowhere, Nebraska. Along with driving the fundraisers for the fire department, police station, library and ball diamonds. Eldon's done well for himself working for them." He headed back toward the station. "Heard tell he bought himself a place in Jackson Hole. He's quite a fisherman. 'Course you probably know that."

"I remember," Jude lied. It wouldn't hurt to take a look at the property records for Jackson, Wyoming. He was familiar enough with the area to know that it housed some extremely expensive real estate. He wondered for the first time where in Wyoming that mineshaft was located.

After leaving the gas station he drove to the address he'd gotten for Weale from the DMV. Spruce Street was a nice residential neighborhood. Not ostentatious, but definitely upper class. There didn't seem to be anyone home, but there was really no way to be sure.

He pulled over at the next block and called Mia. "What are you doing?"

"Hunter and I are running away to Las Vegas." The smile in her voice evoked an answering one from him. "I'll introduce him to the best clubs, and he'll help me clean up at the blackjack tables."

"You should probably know that he loses more than he wins."

"In that case we'll just stick to the clubs."

An elderly lady walked by on the sidewalk with a tiny fur ball on a leash. She gave Jude's car a long suspicious stare. "I want you to see what you can find on Eldon Weale." After the woman passed his vehicle, she turned a few times to look back at him. "Marital status, family…try the archives in the local paper."

"I can do that after finishing decoding the emails from Weale to Danny Munson."

That snagged his attention. "You decoded them?"

Her tone turned somber. "It took me a couple hours, but I figured out the pattern he was using. It helped that most of the messages were similar. They were orders for K-Sleep, LSD and Ecstasy, in varying quantities. I'm not done yet, but so far I've found orders dating back for the last eight years."

Jude absorbed that information. He didn't have to ask what had gone through her mind when she had made that discovery. He knew the trauma of being drugged by The Collector still lingered.

"There's nothing in the orders except for street drugs. But he had more. We all took birth control pills daily. They were with our food. He had to have used sexual performance drugs, and he forced us to take pregnancy tests each month. Twice he gave one of the other women an abortifacient. So if he wasn't getting those medications from Tuttle through Munson, maybe there's a pharmacist in the area he was dealing with on the side."

He hated to douse that hopeful tone in her voice. "I doubt it. It would be risky, and there are enough illegal online pharmacies he could order from anonymously."

"Well, at least we'll get enough information from these files to bury Munson for his part in this scheme." Mia was silent a moment. "I'm not sure how you can use the cloned hard drives for evidence, though."

"Leave that to me." When the time came there were plenty of ways to get the information in the right hands, no matter how it was arrived at. "Let me know when you have more information on Weale. I'll see you soon."

"Jude?"

He heard her voice an instant before he disconnected. "Yes?"

"You've got ten more hours. Keep being smart."

That drew a laugh from him. "I think I've got ten more hours in me." He ended the call and started the car, noticing that down the street the older lady was making a return trip with her dog. He needed to move on or she'd likely contact the police to report a strange vehicle. As he drove by her, however, his thoughts weren't on the woman.

He was wondering whether Mia would consider his next move smart.

* * * *

Anthony hissed out a breath as one of his sales attendants knocked on his half-open door. "I'm sorry, Mr. Davis. But there's a customer on the floor asking for Eldon, and I haven't been able to locate him."

Pursing his lips, he pushed away from the inventory spreadsheet he'd been perusing. "Perhaps I can assist." Weale couldn't be found because Anthony had sent him to South Dakota to take care of some shipments. "Is it one of our regulars?" Many of the guests for tomorrow's party had arrived. The hotel management had informed him earlier that day that it was booked. Although he and Mother always opened the showroom for any interested guests the day after the party, it wouldn't be unusual for someone to want a sneak peek at the merchandise.

"I don't recognize him, sir, but perhaps he's an online client."

Highly likely. Anthony rose from his desk, smoothing his tie. The bulk of their business took place over the Internet. "I'll see to him." He followed the woman out onto the showroom floor and took a moment to study the profile of the man half turned away studying the floor to ceiling glassed-in showcase of antique masks. "Hello." His voice imbued with genial charm, he approached the stranger. "I'm Anthony Davis. I'm afraid Mr. Weale is not in the office at the moment. Perhaps I can help you."

The man spoke as he turned to face him. Anthony completely missed his words. The sight of that scarred visage froze his mind.

The bodyguard. He gave himself a mental shake. Or at least the owner of the agency that had provided services for Eleven after she'd slipped away from him. Jude Bishop. He had never known how she'd managed to make her way back home, but she'd been easy enough to keep tabs on for several months after she did. He'd learned the name of the security agency she'd used at the time. When she'd disappeared from DC Anthony had been desperate for information. But even Munson hadn't been able to break into the Bishop Enterprises' computer network.

And now the man was here, in his showroom, just days after Eleven had evaded him yet again. Anthony didn't believe in coincidences.

"I'm sorry, I didn't get that."

Bishop gestured toward the case of masks. "Interesting display. Are they for sale?"

"No, I'm afraid not." His tone was droll. "It's quite a rare collection, started by my father." But utilized by Anthony. The thought brought a secret flicker of amusement. "We would, however, be glad to take your name and conduct a search for an item of your specification."

The man nodded thoughtfully. Moved a few steps to examine a fourteenth century jewel encrusted chalice. "Maybe I'll talk to Mr. Weale about doing so when he gets back. When do you expect him?"

Making an instant decision, Anthony lied smoothly, "I'm afraid I'm not quite sure. Eldon has taken a few days off to go fishing. He wasn't clear about when he would return." Because he'd text the man the moment Bishop left and make sure he didn't show up until he was given the word.

"I'm sorry to hear that." Bishop's flat green stare gave away nothing. "Maybe you can help me. If I were to buy this." Anthony winced as he picked up the chalice carelessly. "Could I get it shipped to my home?"

"Yes, of course." He reached out and took the item from the other man. Set it back on the shelf. "You could get overnight door-to-door delivery. We see to the shipping arrangements ourselves."

"What shipping company do you use?"

Unease shot down Anthony's spine. What was the man up to? Why was he here? "We're willing to use whatever method the client prefers, as long as it comes with insurance and delivery guarantees. Is there something here that you're interested in, Mr...?"

With a humorless smile the man said, "Sam Fielding. And I'd want to be certain my purchase arrived in one piece. I've heard some unsavory things about outfits like yours using mail drop services to cut down on expenses."

The incredulous laugh he gave wasn't totally forced. "We deal with priceless treasures, Mr. Fielding. I can assure you we treat them with the respect they deserve. We would never handle them so carelessly."

"Good to know." Bishop moved away, pausing to study an original Faberge egg. "My contact was certain that Weale uses a mail drop. Perhaps he has a business on the side."

"I couldn't say." Forcing the words around the knot in his throat took effort. "Our employees' private lives are their own. Please feel free to browse." He moved away. "And let us know if you're interested in something."

Without undue haste Anthony returned to his office. Closed the door. But once inside the façade was dropped. He took out his cell. Noticed distantly that his fingers were trembling. He sent a text to Weale. *No pickup. Don't come back until further notice.* Then he made a call. "I need you here immediately."

Bishop had left long before Sully appeared. But Anthony showed the man the security footage from the time he'd been in the store. "This man," he tapped the screen, "has some information that could be quite valuable to me." His stomach quivered in excitement. It would be quite valuable indeed if Bishop could be forced to reveal what he knew about Eleven's location. And Anthony had an arsenal of tools at his disposal that would be quite persuasive. "I need him picked up, *discreetly,* and brought to my property. I'll tell you where to meet me. Take Eppley and Donaldson. You can get his vehicle information from the exterior cameras." He thought for a long moment. "Listen carefully. This is how you'll do it."

* * * *

After a couple more hours spent poking around—both in the town and on the web—Jude headed back to the hotel. The lot had gotten even fuller in his absence and he cruised the area around the building before finally pulling in to an empty slot.

Locking the vehicle, he crossed the blacktopped expanse toward the side entrance. A man was hurrying down the sidewalk outside the building. "Hey, Weale!" He appeared to be hailing a second man who was disappearing around the corner of the building.

Jude changed direction. Followed the duo to the back. His research had located only one Weale in town. If the man had a family, they hadn't shown up on any search he'd done. Intrigued, he rounded the corner to see the two strangers, heads together, ducking behind a line of Dumpsters. He couldn't make out their conversation from this distance, but from the pitch of their voices it was animated.

He got as close as the back entrance using the sidewalk. But the men were another hundred feet beyond him. Sometimes a direct approach was best. Spying a fast food cup on the ground, he bent down to scoop it up, and ambled for the nearest Dumpster as if to dispose of it.

"…telling you…out of sight." Far from the lively pitch of their conversation earlier, now the men's voices were barely a whisper. Jude took only a moment to consider. He knew what Weale looked like. It would just take a few seconds to discover if he was here. He moved around the trash container far enough to glance behind it. Heard the scrape of a shoe behind him and immediately realized his mistake.

A body hit him hard, propelling him the rest of the way around the Dumpster to land with bone-jarring force against the bricked exterior of the hotel. He aimed a vicious kick at his attacker's groin, peripherally aware of the presence of the other two he'd been following. Ambush. His brain had time to register the fact before instinct took over. He ducked a roundhouse punch from one of the men, but wasn't quick enough to dodge a fist in the gut from another. The three spread in an arc in front of him, their intent silent but unmistakable. Warily, Jude kept the wall at his back. It would be a mistake to let one of them get behind him. He took a good look at the three. None were Eldon Weale. Of course they weren't. A quick visual assessment told him all he needed to know from there. They all had the bulked up physique of hired muscle. He watched their eyes, for their nonverbal communication with each other. The biggest one was a punk. The shortest a follower. It was the one on the left that Jude was going to have to watch the closest. Take him out, and the other two would be clean up.

There were false starts. Testing practice swings. Jude easily ducked the first blow. Landed a right hook to the punk. Absorbed a kick to his thigh that sent shockwaves of pain eddying down it. Then the three spread out. He recognized their intent even as they all rushed forward as one.

He hoped like hell he was still standing to perform that clean up.

* * * *

A heavy weight crashed against the door. With a cautionary glance Mia's way, Hunter surged to his feet. Crossed to the door to peer out the peephole. Swiftly unlocking it, he pulled the door open.

A body fell inside the room. "Jude!" Mia launched herself from her chair in front of the computer and rushed to his side. Hunter took a careful glance up and down the hallway before shutting and resecuring the door. "My God! What happened to you?"

"I'm okay." He rose as far as his knees. Seemed to lack the strength to stand. "Probably...looks...worse... than it is."

Blood was seeping from his mouth, making the words sound garbled. Leaving him to Hunter for the moment, Mia dashed to a bathroom. Hurried back with several wet washcloths, anxiety twisting in her stomach. "Here you go, buddy." Hunter was helping him to his feet. Leading him over to a couch. "You coughing blood? Puking?"

Jude collapsed on the sofa. It was a measure of his injuries that he didn't even protest when Mia began wiping the blood from his face. There was so much of it. A shudder worked through her at the thought of the abuse that had caused that kind of damage. "You need stitches." The cut on his forehead, and another on his chin gaped open and were oozing sullenly even with the wet cloths pressed against them. She looked at Hunter. "We have to get him to a doctor."

The operative's expression was properly concerned. But he didn't rush to agreement. "How's your vision?" There was an ugly raw abrasion at Jude's left temple. "How bad is the headache?"

Jude took one of the wet rags from her and held it to his mouth. Spit blood into it. "No double vision or blurriness." He spoke slowly, but Mia was relieved he seemed coherent. "Losing vision in the left one, though."

"Yeah, it's swelling shut." Hunter reached for a wet cloth from the pile Mia had brought and crossed to the ice bucket the staff refilled daily. Wrapping several cubes in it, he returned and pressed it to Jude's eye. "Keep ice on it. It'll go black regardless, but you can reduce the swelling."

"This does not meet the definition of being smart." Mia's voice shook violently as she dabbed at the cuts on his face. "Who did this to you?" Efficiently Hunter shoved Jude's bloodstained shirt up to examine his torso. Gave a low whistle when he did.

"Someone really worked you over. Hope you got in at least a few good shots before you lay down and let him use you for a punching bag."

"Bite me." Jude's body jerked as the operative probed his ribs.

"None broken." A note of empathy entered the other man's voice. "Doesn't mean they won't hurt like a bitch for a couple weeks though." With a hand to Jude's shoulder, he leaned him forward so he could examine his back. Pushed him straight again. "Any teeth feel loose?"

"Mine don't." One hand was still holding the ice to his eye. He brought up the other rag he held and wiped more blood from inside his mouth. "Two of the other guys might have lost some, though. At least my hands sure feel like it."

So concerned had she been about his appearance, Mia hadn't even thought to look at his hands. The knuckles were scraped and raw. "They look like you held them in a meat grinder."

He slumped back on the couch. "The way I feel right now, that'd be an improvement."

"How many were there?" Hunter took his phone from his pocket and peeled Jude's hand from his eye for a moment. Turned on a light on the cell and pried open the eyelid to peer closely at it.

"Three. But one was a pussy, so once he went down there were only a couple to focus on."

He'd been jumped by three men. Her skin went glacial. There wasn't a logical reason he'd still been standing, much less able to make it back to the room on his own volition. "Who were they?"

His good eye glinted. "We didn't exchange names, but I'm guessing they were sent because someone didn't like me asking questions about Weale." Hunter moved Mia aside so he could get a closer look at the cuts. Jude bore his ministrations stoically. "I figured I had nothing to lose with a direct approach. Town this size, looking like I do it was only a matter of time until someone got interested. I took a look at Weale's place. A break-in there would be risky. Too many nosy neighbors. And his address didn't match the location I got when I took a peek into his ISP service provider's server."

"So you tried the place the emails originated from?" Irritation was shoving aside her anxiety on his behalf. "Because that's a smooth investigative move, just waltzing into the lion's den and poking it with a sharp stick."

He surveyed her cautiously. "It can be effective in some situations. Shake people up, take them unaware. But Weale wasn't there." He paused a moment. "At least I was told he wasn't. The IP address was from his place of work. Some fancy business that deals in antiquities. I went there, asked a couple questions. I think I might have stirred something up when I mentioned the mail drop service Weale used."

Hunter gave a low whistle between his teeth. "You didn't just use a sharp stick, you used a club."

"Yeah. A couple hours later someone returned the favor. But that means I got a reaction to my questions. A pretty strong one. It remains to be seen if Weale is the one providing that response or whether I spooked someone else. These guys…they weren't just there for a random beating. I heard one tell the others a couple times to get me to the truck. Either they wanted to finish the job in a more secluded place, or…"

"…or maybe someone else had a few questions he wanted to pose to you." Hunter straightened. "I think a few butterfly bandages will be as good as stitches. You okay here? Because if so I'm going to go out and buy some first aid supplies." When Mia didn't resume her aid, the operative gave her an odd look before holding a hand out to Jude. "Keys."

Digging into his pocket, he handed them to the other man. "Where did this happen? I'll take a look and see if anyone's still around."

"In the back. Behind the Dumpsters. But they'll be gone by now." He paused to consider. "Although one might have had trouble standing for a while."

"Keep fresh ice on his eye," Hunter told Mia as he passed her to go out. She secured the door behind him. Leaned against it. She didn't recognize this tidal wave of tangled emotion engulfing her. It rocked her system, frothing and pounding inside until she felt hammered from an interior assault. The strength of the storm left her knees weak, and as always weakness infuriated her. She seized on the anger. Held it close. That at least was familiar.

"Your word means nothing." Her accusation hung there, sharp little barbs meant to sink deep. "This wasn't a random attack. You may as well have sent engraved invitations out to come try to kill you." She gave a brittle little smile. "I'm not the security expert, of course, but your approach seemed to lack your usual finesse."

He was watching her as if she were a bomb about to detonate. "I thought the risk was one worth taking. I seem to recall a conversation where you said much the same thing, so I know you understand the reasoning, even if you don't agree with it in this instance."

She shoved away from the door, stalked toward him, her fingers closing into tight fists. Having her words paraphrased and thrown back at her did nothing to defuse her fury. Because surely it was only fury that was pulsing and churning inside her. "I don't want another death on my conscience, do you get that? Let's leave. All of us. Tonight. You can do your investigating from afar. Better yet, dump everything you have so far in Raiker's lap and let him piece it together."

"I need more before I can turn it over to him."

She drew a breath, battled for a control that seemed beyond her. Her defenses were in chaotic disarray and the reason for that was sitting right before her. Without another word she whirled and retrieved the laptop she'd been sitting at when he'd come in. Yanked the power cord loose and carried the computer over to him. She set it ungently in his lap. "You want more? Here's more."

Without being urged he brushed the touch screen with a finger, bringing the monitor to life. A newspaper article, topped with a photo, filled the screen.

"Here's something his driver's license didn't reveal." She watched as he swiftly scanned the picture. Saw the moment comprehension flashed across his expression.

Eldon Weale could have matched what little description she'd been able to give to the police after her escape. Just a shade shorter. His weight a bit lighter. He was shown in the picture holding one side of a large placard check denoting a sizable donation to a new fire department. He grasped it with only one hand. The other arm was six inches shorter and hung uselessly at his side, likely the result of a birth defect.

"Eldon Weale is not The Collector. He's likely just another small link in the chain." The tension welled up, threatening to choke her. Turning on her heel, she strode to the other room where she wouldn't have to look at his bruised and battered face. Wouldn't have to deal with the feelings it elicited. "And you can get your own damn ice."

* * * *

"Three of you." Anthony closed his eyes briefly. Struggled to harness the seething rage bubbling inside him. "And you couldn't manage to subdue one man?"

Sully's beat up face looked uneasy. He'd changed clothes and now wore his hotel security uniform. "He's got some skills. Donaldson's not much of a fighter, so that only left two…" His words trailed off when Anthony stared at him. The man took a cautious step backwards. "We can try again. Grab him up the next time he leaves the hotel."

He was a man used to being surrounded by the finer things in life. Unfortunately that didn't extend to the intellect of those around him. "You already failed at that, remember?"

"Here." With visible eagerness Sully pulled some folded pictures from his pocket, smoothed them out and handed one to him. "I pulled some still images off the security feed. He came in with two others." He held the second picture out. Anthony made no move to take it. "This is a shot of the second man with him. He went out later this afternoon, after the…after we were gone. Wherever he went, he was back in half an hour. We have no visual of the woman ever leaving the hotel, though."

The words were little more than meaningless buzzing in his ears. Anthony smoothed his finger over one of the faces in the first photo, the gesture as light as a caress.

Eleven. A wave of exultation crashed through him. She was here. In his town. In his hotel. Oh dear lord, did it get any more delicious? Any more *fitting* than this? He'd wondered if Bishop would have information about her whereabouts when the whole time she'd been with him.

Anthony had long known that he was special. Some men rose to a level above others, their rightful place because of their own smarts and the blessing of a benevolent god. Never had that seemed more evident than this minute.

He didn't speak until certain he could suppress the emotion in his voice. "I believe in second chances. If you can manage to complete one other task successfully, you'll be rewarded appropriately. I'll need some input with the actual planning, as well as the execution."

The gleam of avarice in Sully's eyes was unmistakable. "I can guarantee I won't let you down again."

His gaze drifting down to the image of Eleven, Anthony said, "See that you don't. You won't get a third opportunity."

13

Mia stood shrouded in darkness, her arms wrapped around her waist. The tumult that had racked her earlier had calmed, leaving her empty. Aching. She'd heard a low murmur of voices in the sitting room, indicating that Hunter had returned. But there'd been no sound now for a couple hours.

The door opened nearly silently and she turned to see Jude enter the bedroom. She hadn't expected him. Had thought instead that he'd give in to a male's natural reluctance to face a woman's ire. She should have known better. When had he ever shirked difficult situations?

"You're awake." He paused in the doorway for a moment before swinging the door shut behind him.

"There's a flight leaving Dulles for Lincoln at eight tomorrow morning." Mia had her phone in the room with her. She'd looked up the information. "I'll agree to leave tomorrow night, or the next day if that works better. As long as you have at least two agents join you here before Hunter and I leave."

He didn't seize on the offer as quickly as she thought he would. A long minute stretched. "Okay."

Something about his tone, his acquiescence had intuition stirring. "You were going to suggest the same thing."

"Not tonight." He crossed to sit down on his bed. "And probably not the part about the two operatives instead of one, but yeah. It's time." Despite the shadows she could feel his gaze on her. "Weale may not be the man who held you captive, but he's a crucial link. I said earlier that I got into the server for the ISP service provider to determine the exact origin of the emails to Munson."

She remembered. "You said it came from his employer's business."

"Davis Fine Antiquities." He stretched out on the bed, flat on his back. "But when I went inside I talked to a saleswoman first. She tried to find Weale and couldn't. That's when she summoned the owner who said the man was gone indefinitely. "After leaving there I did another dive into the ISP server."

"What happens if one of these places ever realizes you're breaching them at will?" she wondered.

His teeth flashed in the darkness. "Discretion is key. My point is, less than forty minutes after I was in there, a message was sent to Munson in Colorado, wanting to know if anyone had been around to ask about the mail drops. The only person I mentioned that to was Anthony Davis, the owner."

Intrigued in spite of herself, Mia moved across the room to sit on the edge of her bed facing him. "So either they lied about Weale not being at work..."

"...or someone else at the business sent the email. And maybe the same person has been sending them all along."

Her flesh prickled. The news muddied the waters instead of clearing them. Were they looking for one person or two? During her long years in captivity she'd begun to think of her kidnapper as omnipotent. Certainly he'd done everything he could to encourage that belief. But now they were discovering that he didn't act in isolation. Couldn't. Others assisted, even from afar with threads of the operation. Someone to provide drugs. Computer expertise to track her.

She rubbed her arms briskly at the thought. The threads were tenuous perhaps, but each tied directly to the monster. What other links might there be? Did someone else prepare the food he brought them, buy the cases of water or supply the props he used during the sexual torture? So much could be attained through the anonymity of the Web. But not everything.

Weale's importance suddenly crystalized for her. He was a thread, too, and sometimes when a string was pulled, everything unraveled. "How many work at this place? Which employees were there yesterday? Who had access to the computer?" She was thinking aloud, but she knew he would have already considered the questions.

"A Chamber of Commerce blurb about businesses in town lists Davis' with a dozen employees." He propped himself up on his elbows. "I had a feeling that the saleslady was surprised when her boss told me Weale would be gone for a few days. I'll take a run at her tomorrow, see if she reveals more in private."

And by doing so he'd invite more violence. Her muscles tightened. By now he had a target on his back. Whoever was behind his attack would only be more determined the next time.

"I hate that you're putting yourself in danger." Her voice was a near whisper. "I hate that it's because of me. It's selfish, really. I'd rather go back to feeling little at all than to experience this crippling fear on your behalf." Perhaps the newfound emotion seemed sharper, because it was so fresh. She'd prefer that to the other explanation —that the cause was the man sitting across from her.

Because for a woman who'd spent the last several years avoiding weakness, Jude Bishop represented the most powerful vulnerability she'd ever imagined.

He rose and crossed to her, reaching for her hand to tug her toward him. She was very much afraid that leaning against his strength would sap her own. But her arms lifted of their own volition, her palm going unerringly to his face. And when his mouth found hers, she returned his kiss with just a hint of the wildness that was suddenly chugging through her.

The softness of his lips was an intriguing contrast to his muscled strength. It would have been easy to suspect he was all hard angles and steely resolve. Certainly she would have believed it in Da Nang. Unfortunately she'd learned he was far more than he'd seemed. The realization had led to the first tiny chink in her emotional armor.

Too late she remembered his injuries. The pressure of her mouth against his softened, and the tip of her tongue soothed his lip where it was split and swollen. But Jude clearly wasn't seeking tenderness from her. He pulled her closer, his mouth eating at hers with thinly veiled hunger. She gave a little sigh and sank into the kiss.

Last time only their lips had touched. She could appreciate now what that must have cost him. A long inert need was rising, whipping her pulse with demand. Giving into it she pressed nearer. Felt her heart give a bump of pleasure at the contact. He was shirtless, and her breasts beneath the thin fabric of her blouse were flattened against the muscled wall of his torso. She brought a hand down to trace the spot where his pecs bisected his chest. Stayed to explore the angles and hollows where bone met sinew.

Jude nipped at the corner of her mouth before strewing a line of stinging kisses down the cord of her neck. He found the pulse that beat madly at the base of her throat and bathed the area with his tongue. She understood hunger, but not the type a woman felt for a man. The longing to immerse herself in the taste and feel of him was foreign, but deliciously tempting.

He slid a hand under her shirt, trailed it down her spine. Heat bloomed in its wake. Mia had the tantalizing mental image of bare flesh against bare flesh. His hair roughened chest against her smooth skin. And the vision lingered. Beckoned. Until she reached down and dragged the hem of her shirt over her head. Let it drop forgotten to pool around her feet.

His hand went to her back and released the clasp of her bra in one smooth motion. His fingers spread across her skin, each an individual brand. Dragging the garment down her arms, he tossed it aside. Then held her a little away so he could visually feast on the flesh he'd bared.

Despite the bruises blooming on his face, the scrapes and lacerations, she could still recognize the stamp of desire in his expression. It ignited an answering fever in her blood.

Mia swayed toward him, brushing her nipples against his skin in the lightest of touches. His hands settled on her hips, fingers clenching at the exquisite contact. The air sizzled with sexual tension, the energy humming and sparking between them. Every sensation seemed new. Exhilarating. But when his arm banded around her back to bring her closer, the evidence of his impatience was even headier.

Her hands mapped his chest, skirting the areas she knew would be tender. When her fingers moved lower to brush across his belly, she felt his muscles jump, a signal that he was as affected as she. Her touch slowed. Grew teasing. His reaction stoked hers. And summoned a long slumbering sensual power that could be utilized to heighten pleasure for both of them.

He drew a crooked knuckle over the curve of her breast and her breath hitched once, before holding in bated anticipation. She released it in a delighted gasp when he caught one nipple in his fingers, rolled it gently. Her back arched in an invitation as old as time. It was one he didn't refuse.

Cupping his hands beneath her breasts, he leaned in to take a nipple in his mouth, batting at it lazily with his tongue. His fingers stroked its twin as he teased and tempted before giving in to his appetite for flesh and sucking strongly from her. Sensation arrowed a path straight to her womb. Reason receded. The world abruptly spiraled away until there was only this man. This moment.

Her fingers clung to his shoulders, battered by sensation. The effect was alien. He made her feel too deeply. The danger there would be wanting too much. Mia had learned to live without expectations. Life seemed less cruel that way. But somehow she knew missing this night with Jude would have left a nagging void she never would have been able to fill.

When he lifted his head she stared at him with heavy eyes. The intensity in his gaze should have brought an answering skitter of nerves. They were absent. The frankly carnal passion between them wasn't so much frightening as it was intoxicating. One hand slid to his biceps, flexing as she moved closer, pressing her mouth to his chest before testing a hard muscle lightly with her teeth. She brushed her fingers over his back, feeling the skin punctuated by vertebrae. The muscles beneath her touch quivered like an impatient stallion's.

The pleasure he brought her was addicting, igniting a craving in her blood. But knowing she could bring him pleasure in return, could make him shake and want, held a tantalizing allure.

They were wrapped in a cocoon of shadows, which heightened the sense of intimacy. Her hands went on a quest of discovery of all the places that made him shudder. The soft velvety skin beneath his arm. A light scrape of a fingernail across his nipple. Her fingers meandered lower to trace the silky line of hair that descended from his navel.

His hands were still on her breasts, his thumbs making lazy circles designed to draw the nipples into taut sensitive buds. She trailed a finger along the skin of his belly where it met denim, and smiled when she felt the muscles bunch beneath her touch. As if realizing something between them had shifted, he stilled in what Mia recognized as tacit male approval.

Her hands went to the button of her pants, lingered. His gaze narrowed. Heated. She slipped the button out of its hole, and moved with excruciating slowness to the tab of her zipper. Released it a fraction at a time, revealing a wedge of flesh above a scrap of lace. She would have denied choosing them with him in mind. It had been a very long time since she'd given consideration to lingerie. But right now, with his gaze fixed on her movements, she could believe that ever-constant thoughts of him had guided the selection.

Hooking her thumbs in her waistband she shimmied out of her pants, peeling them down her legs an inch at a time. She balanced herself with a hand on his arm as she pulled first one leg and then another over her ankle. Was pleased to feel the rigid muscle beneath her fingers, signaling better than words the effect she was having on him. Kicking the slacks aside, Mia felt a sudden sliver of unease. She banished it by closing the distance between them, and pressing her lips to his.

At first he was still. Doubt bloomed, and there was a moment when she almost pulled away. Then a violent shudder quaked through him and his arms snaked around her waist to bring her tightly against him. His mouth moved over hers. Hot. Wet. Rawly carnal. The tight leash on his control had slipped. One hand explored the curve of her butt, the dip of her waist, before sliding lower.

The taste of him whispered of promised pleasure, a devastating dive into sensation. His finger traced the crease of her thigh before cupping her where she was damp and heated.

Heat, a quick stabbing spear of it, arrowed up her spine. Her bones went to water. She clutched his muscled shoulders in a sudden need for balance. And when he parted her folds and slipped one finger inside her, her senses fragmented. Colors wheeled beneath her eyelids. A tight fist of need knotted in her belly.

She tore her mouth away, her breath coming in short ragged little pants. She wasn't used to this rollicking in her pulse. The fierce compulsion to strip him bare and explore every inch of him. Mia jerked in his arms when his thumb circled her clitoris, rubbing it rhythmically. Her hand slipped between them, fighting to unzip his jeans and release his heavy penis. She had time to encircle him with her fingers. Stroke once before she felt herself being lifted.

Disoriented, it took a moment to realize he'd bypassed the bed. Her feet touched the floor and she was grateful to have the wall at her back for support. He was yanking the denim down his legs with a violent movement that spoke of fraying restraint. Then he was against her and the kiss of flesh to flesh had her head lolling.

He lifted her with both hands beneath her butt, urging her legs around his hips. Fitting his straining erection to her moist heat, he gave a surge that had them both groaning. He buried his face in her neck and began to thrust. Mia opened her eyes. Tried to focus. She couldn't breathe. Couldn't think. Sensation layered over sensation. Every surge brought her a little bit closer to a release just out of her reach.

A hazy snippet from the past rose from the recesses of her mind. The shadows in the room began to form then reshape in sly mental images that were usually locked tightly away. Wings of panic fluttered. "I need to see you. Your face." The words were edged in desperation.

Jude lifted his head, looked into her eyes as he rocked his pelvis against hers. "I'm here, Mia. Look at me. See me."

She shivered at the sound of his voice, raw and guttural. And felt herself being sucked into that vortex of desire again. Nerve endings spiraled to concentrate where they were fused so intimately. The rhythm quickened. Her blood began to pulse, molten rivers of pleasure beneath her skin.

And when the climax shattered her, it was Jude she saw. Jude she clung to as she was swept into a pool of tumultuous pleasure.

Somehow they'd made it to his bed. She didn't remember getting there. Mia stared at the ceiling, waiting for her breathing to recover, with him pressed against her side. Even as her body still quivered and her senses remained steeped in him, whispers of unease were creeping along nerve endings recently satiated.

Wanting something was a stepping-stone to wanting more. That truth hammered inside her. To pretend otherwise was a lie and Mia made it a point not to lie to herself.

He turned toward her, seeming half asleep, the picture of a lazy satisfied male and hooked one leg over both of hers.

She froze. Her reaction wasn't logical. They'd just been shatteringly intimate. But nothing about her most visceral responses was rational. The unease bloomed to distress, and it took every ounce of strength she had to battle it back, shove it aside, her muscles tense with the struggle.

As if he recognized her sudden agitation, he moved away, leaving several inches between them on the bed. Only their hands touched. A silent breath of relief streamed out of her.

"Just so you know." His voice was a husky rumble in the darkness. "When we're back in DC…when this is all ended…you and I will just be beginning."

His words elicited a tiny quiver of joy that was quickly doused by a bitter dose of realism. "That can't work."

"I know why you don't think so. You're wrong."

She turned her head to face him. That calm certainty, so reassuring at times now had nerves scampering up her spine. "I'm not like other people." Acceptance of that fact followed her every day since her escape. "My thinking, my responses. I'm broken. And that isn't going to change."

"Here's the thing." He rolled to his side, careful not to move too close. "A man who would ask you to change isn't someone who deserves you in his life. You've got more guts than anyone I know, Mia. You've got the courage to reach for something good, too."

He could have been reading her mind earlier. She shook her head. Sought for a way to convince him. "I can't bathe with you near." Her words were a shamed whisper. "Twice a week we were allowed to shower. All under his observance. No privacy. Sometimes…he assaulted us there. And it's stupid that I can't shake the fear. The bathroom door…has a lock. Sometimes reason is no match against the flashbacks."

"Logic is just the shiny wrapping around our most primal instincts. Sometimes those instincts win. It doesn't change who you are. It just is."

And he would know, she recalled swiftly. The trauma he'd endured as a child would have had to leave inner scars as well as exterior ones.

He spoke again, in what had to be a deliberate attempt to lift her spirits. "I know how you feel. That filleting knife? I still can't eat fish."

A breath of a laugh escaped her. "That's awful."

"It is." His fingers laced with hers. "Makes Lent tough."

She was lying in the same bed with a man that she'd just made love with. Maybe he was right. It would have been unimaginable even a week ago. "I didn't know you were Catholic."

"My foster family was. Some of it stuck."

"You went into foster care…after?"

"My father was killed in prison. I landed with good people. Small town, a lot like this one. Big dopey dog. Brothers and a sister. The Gilberts were there for every surgery. Every recovery. And after my dad was gone they wanted to adopt me. I couldn't do it."

She gave his fingers a squeeze. "Why not?"

"Maybe I was like you." His speech was beginning to slow, as if succumbing to sleep. "Afraid to reach for something in case it didn't work out. I didn't know then that if we don't make a grab for happiness when we can, we might never get another chance."

Mia lay awake long after he slept. She waited for the gradual skittering of nerves that would force her from the bed. They never quite appeared. She was aware of him, in a heightened sense that made sleep difficult, but not unpleasant.

She wanted to embrace his words, but the past had a way of rubbing sooty fingers over the future. It was easier to be alone. Safer to have no hopes.

But far lonelier.

And as night turned into the first pale light of day, she still hadn't figured out which was worse.

* * * *

"Try not to get the shit kicked out of you today."

"Hunter!" Mia admonished the operative. Then her mouth curled. "I can concur with the sentiment while objecting to the phrasing."

"Yeah, you two are hilarious." Jude closed down his mini-laptop. "The next time I have a vein open, I definitely want you both at my side." He knew what he looked like this morning. His face was a lot worse than it had been last night. The bruises were darkening and his eye, despite the application of ice, was swollen half-closed.

"What'd you figure out from the property records searches?" Mia asked. She'd kept her distance this morning, sitting on the sofa with Hunter drinking coffee.

Jude recognized she was attempting to rebuild her guard after last night. He even understood it. She could have her space. He just wasn't going to let her use it as a wedge to lever him out of her life.

"Weale's home in Davison lists for three hundred thousand and change, which is well above average for houses in this town." He started to lean back in the chair. Stopped at the warning pull in his ribs. "The Jackson Hole property is assessed for about the same, which isn't extravagant at all considering the market there. It's not on water, which would have upped the value appreciably."

"So there's no evidence that he's fallen into a big pot of money." The disappointment in her tone would be difficult to miss.

"Without knowing what his paycheck is, it's hard to guess whether he's living within his means. But there are no red flags at this point, no." According to what Mia had found online yesterday they could be certain he wasn't The Collector. But it was still a mystery as to who had sent the email to Munson yesterday and that was one of the answers Jude hoped to get today.

He rose, the small laptop in his hand. "After nosing around a bit more, I'm going to drive to Jackson Hole."

There was a flash of something in Mia's eyes before she disguised it. "That's a seven hour trip."

"About that."

"Blake and Paulo will be here this evening," Hunter pointed out. "Why not wait for them?"

"By the time they arrive I'll already know if there's a reason for them to meet me there. Otherwise it'd be a wasted trip for all of us." But he was willing to bet if Weale was laying low it wouldn't be here in town with overly interested neighbors and friends who might check up on him. Jackson Hole was close enough to arrange to

send three thugs after Jude. And there was still the link
to the South Dakota mail drop to look into. "Don't
worry." He set Mia a half smile. "I won't use the direct
approach this time."

"Stealth would be good," she agreed faintly. "So
would keeping your head down until your backup
arrives."

"We'll make arrangements to fly out tomorrow
morning," Hunter said.

Jude's gaze lingered on Mia, but she refused to meet
it. Something inside him twisted. He wouldn't push, no
matter how much he wanted to. No one knew better
than he did how long it took to reverse defenses years in
the making. "I checked online. Carlson Motors is a local
car dealership and their site says they rent vehicles."

Hunter nodded. "I'll call them. You be careful out
there. You can't afford another day like you had
yesterday."

He opened the door. "Any fight you can walk away
from is a win."

"Or crawl," Hunter muttered.

It was too early in the morning for dark humor,
especially at his expense, Jude decided. He was well
aware of the wide berth the people in the hallway of the
hotel gave him when they passed. He'd just been lucky
not to run into someone yesterday when he was
returning to his room looking like a prizefighter after
going ten rounds.

He kept an eye out for the men who'd jumped him,
but not surprisingly didn't see any of them. Jude would
have liked to get some answers about whom they were
working for. He may still get a chance. Whoever had
sicced the trio on him likely wasn't going to give up
easily.

He swung by Weale's house. It didn't look any more occupied than it had yesterday, but there really was no way to be certain. The same elderly woman was walking her dog, and it was clear from her stare that she recognized his car.

He got out of the vehicle and approached her, being careful to keep his hands in the open and not to get too close. His face would be threatening enough.

Sure enough her eyes widened, and she bent down to snatch up the fur ball she'd been walking. "Good morning, ma'am. Wondering if you could answer a question for me." He stopped several feet from the curb. But looking harmless was a feat that was beyond him.

"What happened to your face?" She hugged the small creature she was holding to her sagging chest.

"I got mugged on my way back to the hotel." Mugging was an understatement given the intent of the crew sent after him, but she'd understand the term. "I'm an old school friend of Eldon's. We haven't seen each other for years. I was traveling nearby and thought I'd detour to surprise him." He gestured to his swollen eye. "Got this for my troubles. Not a friendly town, apparently."

She seized on the words, as he'd hoped she would. "Davison is a very friendly place. No one from here would do something like that. But we do sometimes get a large group of strangers who come for some showing or other at Davis Antiquities. I believe they have something going on now, in fact."

"Well, I'll probably be on my way. Hate that I didn't get to see Eldon, but I stopped in where he worked yesterday and they told me he'd gone fishing."

"Oh." The news seemed to take her by surprise. "He usually mentions his trips to us. No wonder we didn't see him come home last night."

That information was really all Jude had been looking for. "When you see him, tell him Sam Fielding stopped by." He started to head back to his vehicle.

"I'll be sure to do that. And I hope you'll come back sometime. Things like muggings don't happen in Davison. We're a quiet little place."

Next Jude drove by the Davis Fine Antiquities building, surprised when the parking lot was almost completely empty. There was only one car there and the lights were off inside. A sign on the front door said it was closed for the day for a Customer Appreciation party. No indication of where the party was to be held or the time. Apparently if people were invited, they already knew.

He pulled next to the lone car outside the building and proceeded to wait. His patience was rewarded twenty minutes later when the willowy saleslady he'd seen yesterday came out the side door and carefully locked it before hurrying toward her car. Her steps faltered when Jude got out of his vehicle.

"I was in your building yesterday. Do you remember me?"

She glanced around, saw they were alone and halted. "I do. Hello. You seem to have had an accident since then."

"Ran into a door," Jude said laconically.

The woman blinked. "That must have been some door. I'm sorry, as you can see we're closed for the day. We'll open again tomorrow."

"The sign said some big shindig was going on." The lady kept her purse clutched to her chest as if it contained something valuable. Or held a canister of Mace.

"Yes, at the Davis estate. It's an annual event." She gave a slight smile. "Invitation only, I'm afraid."

"Will Eldon Weale be there?"

She looked surprised at the question. "I don't know. I was surprised to learn he wasn't working yesterday. Mr. Davis indicated to you that he was on vacation, so perhaps not."

"Seems odd, doesn't it?" Jude walked toward the hood of his car. Stopped when she took a nervous step back. Propping himself against his vehicle, he continued, "I'd assume all the employees would be needed to help. Lots of details to tend to while putting something like that on."

"There are, yes. The event runs all day and evening, and tomorrow we'll have a crowd at the business. But Mrs. Davis, Anthony's mother, takes care of much of the planning." She made a move toward her car. "I really need to be getting back. I just stopped to pick up something for Mrs. Davis."

But Jude wasn't done with her yet. "How many employees were working yesterday?"

"Ah…well, three in the morning, I think." She resumed walking toward her car. "I'm sorry, I don't mean to be rude but I'm impossibly late. The others were attending to details at the estate. And in the afternoon it was just Mr. Davis and myself." She got in her vehicle. Started it and back out of the space.

Jude doubted very much whether the woman had been the one to send the email. Which left her boss, Anthony Davis.

Mia had thought her captor might be law enforcement, he recalled. But maybe he was just someone who thought of himself as above the law. Wealth could do that to a person. So could getting away with kidnapping and raping women for more than a decade without having anyone link the crimes.

He pulled out his cell to call Hunter. "I want you and Mia gone, today, as soon as you can arrange it." A new urgency had risen in him, one that was impossible to ignore. He told him what he'd just discovered. "Do what you have to in order to get a rental delivered now. Pack and head out. Mia can make the flight arrangements on the drive."

"She made them right after you left, using the same ID as the last couple flights. We fly out of Omaha at five o'clock tomorrow night. We'll book a hotel."

Jude thought again of the trio who'd jumped him yesterday. "Watch for anyone who might be following you."

"I know how to spot a tail. We'll be careful. What are you planning to do? Still going to Jackson Hole?"

"Yeah." He got back in his car. "Sounds like Davis is going to be tied up until later tonight. Which means it would be an excellent opportunity to catch up with Weale and have a little chat." Jude started the car. Drove out of the lot. The man would talk to him, because Jude wasn't going to give him a choice. And by the end of the conversation, he hoped to be a helluva lot closer to discovering the identity of The Collector. At least close enough to provide Raiker with all the connections he needed to prod law enforcement into launching a large-scale investigation.

He needed proof. Because he already suspected the man known as The Collector was Anthony Davis.

* * * *

Tension laced Mia's muscles as she sat on the couch, her bag next to her feet. Hunter hadn't given her details for their sudden departure, citing only a change of plans. But she knew better. Jude hadn't been gone an hour before he'd called the operative. Whatever he'd discovered, he'd considered it a threat.

And the only threat she could imagine was if he thought The Collector was close.

A hot tangle of nausea roiled in her belly at the thought. The possibility had her anxious to be gone already. If she'd had the power she would have jet-propelled herself across the state and already be on an airplane, putting hundreds of miles between her and her predator. And even that might not be far enough.

But even when she was gone, Jude would still be here. Possibly facing the monster alone in the hours it took his operatives to arrive. And the fear that arose for his safety eclipsed what she felt for her own. A knock sounded at the hotel door and Hunter frowned, rising.

"Is that our rental delivery already?"

"They'll call when they arrive. They don't have our room information." He went to the door and looked through the peephole. "Cops."

Her unease intensified. "Maybe they're here about the men who assaulted Jude." A report hadn't been filed but perhaps exterior security cameras had caught something.

Keeping the safety latch on, Hunter pulled open the door. "Officers." Craning her head Mia could see two men, both wearing a navy uniform. "What can I help you with?"

"Could we see some ID, sir?" one of them asked.

"Why?"

"Just the ID, please."

With growing concern Mia watched Hunter take his license from his wallet and pass it through the door. "Sir, please step out of the room."

"Not until I know what this is about." It didn't escape her that the operative's ID hadn't been returned.

"Mr. Mason, where were you last night between five and six PM?"

Hunter's answer was slow to come. "Here. Except for a quick trip at about five-thirty to pick up a few supplies."

"We had a complaint filed against you last night by a young woman accusing you of attempted sexual assault. She was able to reveal that you were staying here, and identified you from hotel security photos. We'd like you to come with us to answer a few questions."

Stunned, Mia rose from the couch and approached the door. "Mr. Mason was gone only a short time. I was here when he left and returned."

"What's your name, ma'am?" Hunter gave her a warning look, preventing her from answering. It wasn't necessary. She was well aware of the ramifications of providing a false identity to law enforcement. She'd lived with the risk for the last five years.

The second officer, the one with Hunter's ID, spoke for the first time. "The name on your license does not match the one given to rent this room. Nor was it indicated on the hotel registration that there would be more than one person occupying this room. Is Mr. Fielding here?"

"He stepped out." Mia knew Hunter wasn't about to the reveal the information that Jude had used a different ID to rent the room.

"Please come with us, sir." The second officer spoke again. "We'll get this sorted out downtown."

"I'm on a security detail here. Personal protection." Hunter withdrew a card from his wallet and handed it through the door. "I'm not leaving my client."

The policemen peered at Mia. Then one said, "She'll be safe enough if she stays inside. The Davison has excellent security. But if you agree to come with us now, we'll call another officer to come sit with her until we're finished."

"I'd like to see your badges first."

"Sir?"

"Your credentials. I want to see them." Hunter studied each and then handed them back, before taking out his cell. He called information for the Davison Police Department and when someone came on the line he said, "I have two men at my door claiming to be police officers." He was silent a moment. "At the Davison Hotel." A longer silence as he glanced at the men again. "Describe them, please." Apparently satisfied, he hung up. "Okay. Call for that other officer." He turned to Mia. "You know the drill. Door closed and locked. Don't let anyone in."

Swallowing, she nodded. When the men had left, she resecured the door after them. The episode had done nothing to calm her jittery nerves. She went to her cell. Called Jude and relayed what had just transpired. "Where are you?"

"An hour away, but I'm turning around." His voice was grim.

"This can't be genuine, can it?" Tiny tendrils of fear were uncurling in her veins, spreading through her system. "It seems too coincidental after your ambush last night."

"It's possible," he said cautiously and she felt a flash of irritation. He wouldn't say anything he thought would alarm her. "I'll be there in an hour. Call me in fifteen minutes if that officer hasn't arrived." The policemen at least had had their identities verified. The knowledge soothed a measure of her anxiety. "Get ID from the officer before..."

"I will. I'll make a call to verify it, too."

His voice softened. "Good girl. It's all going to be okay, Mia. I'll be there soon."

She disconnected. Oddly enough, just talking to him was enough to allay some of her stress. There had been plenty of anxious moments traveling and living alone in foreign countries. With Dr. Halston's help she'd learned methods to ease it. But as she sat and watched the door, Mia realized that none of those methods was going to completely diminish the strain she felt right now.

That thought was underscored ten minutes later when the fire alarm sounded.

14

Mia sat, frozen. Then she went to the door. Peered out into the hallway. Doors were opening, people piling out. Smoke was thick in the air. She put a hand to the door. It didn't feel warm to the touch.

She went to the hotel phone and called the front desk. "I'm on the fourth floor and an alarm has gone off…"

"Yes, ma'am," a harried voice responded to her question. "The fire alarm is sounding throughout the hotel. We're in the process of notifying all rooms now requesting that people evacuate the premises. Hotel security has been dispatched to every floor to help with the process. The fire department is on its way."

There was a pounding on her door. "Hotel security. Please evacuate the hotel using a stairwell exit." Hanging up, she went to the door again and saw a man in dark pants and white shirt walking away. He was difficult to see through the smoke, which seemed to have thickened. It was curling beneath her door now.

She took off the safety latch, collected her purse and phone and stepped into the hallway. Immediately her eyes started to sting.

"Is there anyone else in that room, ma'am?" The security officer was still nearby, his back to her.

"No."

"Come with me. I'll show you the exit they want us to use."

Her eyes watering, Mia began to cough as she followed the man. "You can use these stairs." He pushed open a door at the end of the hall. "When you reach the bottom floor, please go directly outside."

She stopped, peered through the doorway. Then above it. "There's no exit sign." She looked over her shoulder at him. Froze when she realized the significance of the cuts and bruises on his face. Mia drove her elbow into his gut and tried to run, but he clamped an arm around her throat, forcing her through the door, one hard hand over her mouth. Panic sprinted through her system. She struggled like a mad woman, biting at his hand, stomping on his foot while reaching back to rake his cheek with her nails.

"Fuck this!" He whirled her around and she balled her fist, swung. She had a brief moment of satisfaction when she connected before he gave her a violent shove on the landing of the stairs. In two quick steps he reached her side, taking her head in both hands and slamming it against the wall. A brilliant display of light exploded in her head before darkness descended.

* * * *

He'd told her to call in fifteen minutes. Accelerating, Jude called Mia's phone at minute sixteen. After six rings it went to her voice mail. A cold knife of dread lodged in his belly. He tried it again before calling the hotel.

"Connect me with room 419, please."

"Sir, all rooms have been evacuated due to a fire in the hotel. All of our guests are outside as the matter is being investigated."

Trepidation surged. "Can you ring the room?" Jude was helpless to curb the desperation sounding in his voice.

"Security has cleared all the rooms using a master key, sir. No one is left inside."

The call ended. Jude wished he felt reassured. But the fire, coming so close on the heels of the trumped up charges against Hunter was too convenient to ignore. He brought the phone up again. Used information to connect to the Davis Police Department. They'd promised to send an officer to Mia's room. Maybe he could get them to comb the crowd in the parking lot for her.

But the fear clogging his throat now labeled the hope as fantasy. Panic was clawing in his chest. Mia was gone. And if The Collector didn't have her now, it was only a matter of time until he did.

* * * *

Reading Sully's text message sent a giddy wash of euphoria spreading through his system. *I got your cargo.* Anthony closed his eyes, feeling light-headed.

Eleven was back. Or would be, only minutes from now. He turned, brushing by the throng of people mingling by the pool and outside bar. Elation filled him, even as he tried to temper the response. There had been disappointments before. He'd been close to retrieving his possession other times, only to be thwarted. Add in the fact that he seemed to be surrounded by incompetents and he didn't quite dare—not yet—to believe it.

But the exquisite possibility was sweet indeed.

"Where are you rushing off to, dear?" His mother hooked her arm in his, slowing his progress to the house.

"Oh, a delivery got screwed up." He smiled at her, the fingers on his free hand curled tightly around the flute of his wine glass. "Don't worry, I'll steer it away from our guests' cars to the detached garage. It'll be safe enough there until tomorrow."

A frown marring her face, she sipped from a tall glass of lemonade. "That's odd. We've never gotten deliveries at home before."

"Probably a new driver. Or a new dispatcher. It doesn't matter. I can unpack it and take it to work tomorrow."

"Well, don't misplace the invoice dear." Seeing someone she wanted to talk to, she patted his arm and headed away. "And don't fuss with it too long. There are clients here that require your attention."

Don't fuss with it. Gloatingly, he savored the words. If Sully had been successful, Anthony was going to fuss a great deal.

He could already see the security guard's car at the end of the driveway and he jogged to his own. He drove down the drive carefully to avoid the crowd of cars parked there and the grass adjacent to it. The structure that he led Sully to sat well away from the house. His father had built the home after tearing down the century-old ranch house five miles out of town. Much of the land was rented out. The Davis's hadn't been cattle ranchers for a generation.

He pressed the button on the opener and a garage door ascended. Waving Sully's vehicle inside, Anthony parked and strolled in after him, closing the door behind them.

"Where do you want her?" The security guard rounded the car, a broad smile on his face. He popped the lid of the trunk, and Anthony peered inside at the large wiggling garbage bag, secured at one end with a twisty tie. Hardly daring to breathe, he unfastened the tie and with one finger pulled the bag aside to reveal the face of Eleven. Her eyes were murderous and shooting sparks, but she was unmistakably the missing item of his collection.

He stroked her cheek with his finger, chuckled when she jerked away. "I've been waiting so long, Eleven."

Defiance faded from her eyes, to be replaced with fear. Satisfied, he turned to Sully. "Just set her down in the corner." The man hoisted her out of the trunk, the bag falling away as he carried her. She was gagged and bound with duct tape. Wise. Anthony recalled what a fighter she'd been when he'd first selected her. Her retraining wouldn't be easy, but this time he'd take a firmer hand.

Something caught his eye then and he frowned. Crossing swiftly to where Sully was lowering her to the cement floor, he placed one hand under her chin and turned her head to better inspect the bloody abrasion marring her forehead. Rage and revulsion worked through him and it took a moment to speak. "She's *damaged.*"

"Yeah, I had to give her a tap. She's a wildcat." The man was too stupid to notice Anthony's anger. "The whole thing we planned…it all went off without a hitch. I even managed to make it look like Quimby's fault that the security cameras failed. When the cops find the smoke canisters on all the hotel floors, he'll be the first one they'll suspect."

Tucking the fury away, he forced a smile. "You've done well, except for forgetting that she needed to be blindfolded. Come over to the workbench. I've got your money."

"You doing some painting out here?" Sully asked as he stepped onto the twenty mil tarp spread on the floor near the bench.

"Just some clean up. The cash is in that toolbox. Reach down and get it, will you?"

"Sure." The man squatted.

Anthony reached for the crow bar hanging above the bench and brought it down on Sully's head. The first blow knocked him flat, but didn't kill him. The man was struggling to rise, as Anthony picked up the folded bath towel laid out for this purpose. Dropping it over Sully's head he hit him a second time. And then again.

Panting from the exertion, he stopped and watched the still form for signs of life. From the amount of blood and matter soaked into the towel, even if the man wasn't dead yet, he would be soon. Briskly, Anthony walked over to the work sink tucked in the corner of the space and washed off the crowbar, then wiped his shoes in case a stray droplet of blood might have sprayed on them.

He took a wet paper towel with him to wipe off the toolbox and put it away before hanging the crowbar back up above the bench. Searching through the drawers he found a pair of work gloves to don and grabbed some bungee cords. A memory flashed through his mind, of him standing in the field, wrapping Eight's body in a similar way. Sully was much bulkier and by the time Anthony was done he'd worked up a sweat. He dragged the tarp to the man's still open trunk and with a great deal of difficulty managed to dump it inside. Close the lid.

Later that night he'd dispose of the car in the Buffalo Point Reservoir. No need to drive clear to Wyoming. Right now, though…his gaze went to the woman. He closed his eyes for a moment to savor the delicious sweetness. He went to the wall of shelving and pressed the lever that had the sheetrock and attached shelves sliding silently to the right. Then he picked up Eleven and carried her inside, the familiar pride and excitement bouncing and spiking inside him. He smiled down at her, relishing the panic in her expression. "Welcome back."

* * * *

"So you're saying this woman was kidnapped eight and a half years ago. Again a couple days ago. And you think it just happened again today." The expression of doubt on the face of the Davison Police Department investigator was matched in his voice.

Jude was prepared for the skepticism. He took a sheet he'd prepared beforehand from his pocket and slapped it on the man's desk. "All I'm asking is that you check this out. Call the Chief of Police in Johnstown, Pennsylvania. Sergeant Fenton of the West Virginia State Police. Or better yet call Adam Raiker of The Mindhunters." He caught the glimmer of surprise in the man's eyes and smiled grimly. Somehow Raiker's name seemed to have that effect on cops, no matter where in the country they were located.

"Raiker? He's involved in this?" The investigator, a Sergeant Carter, picked up the sheet to study it.

"Yes." Jude had spent the better part of the frantic drive back to Davison on the phone with the man. "Two of his investigators will be here this evening to help with the search." And Raiker had promised to start rattling the cages of the feds to get Mia's investigation restarted. But Jude knew that she didn't have that kind of time.

What had she suffered in the time since she was taken? The question hammered brutally in his skull. If he dwelled on it, the welling guilt and panic would suffocate him. Make it impossible to think. To construct a rescue plan.

"We can talk to people at the hotel. She should have been out there in the parking lot where most of them were gathered until the fire department cleared the premises. Maybe someone saw something."

Jude tamped down frustration. What the man was offering wasn't enough. "I'm guessing she never made it to the parking lot. And that the fire was staged. Just like the phony charge against my operative this morning. First the kidnapper made sure Mia was alone. Then he constructed a way to get her out of her room."

The sergeant shot him a hard look. "That's a lot of supposition, Mr. Bishop."

Jude pointed to his face. "Does this look like supposition? Yesterday three guys assaulted me, intent on getting me in a truck. I declined. We've been targeted since we got to town and started asking questions. And apparently we're making someone nervous."

Sergeant Carter picked up a pen on his desk. Twirled it in his fingers. "Maybe if you tell me what questions you were asking and to whom, it'd give me a place to start."

"Eldon Weale. Anthony Davis."

The man's jaw dropped a bit. "What could Davis possibly have to do with Deleon's…"? He stopped as Jude's meaning struck. Grinned broadly. "I'm sorry, Mr. Bishop, but you're barking up the wrong tree. I can't think of anyone less likely to be involved in this. The Davis family is…"

"Rich. Influential. I get it." Jude pushed away from the man's desk forcefully. "Helped build this police station, didn't they?"

Carter's faced darkened. "That doesn't mean they bought the force. I know how to do my job. But it doesn't include throwing around wild accusations without evidence."

"Really." His voice dripping derision, Jude said, "I'm sure Hunter Mason would disagree."

"Mason is free to go. For now. He was brought in for questioning. Standard procedure when someone files a complaint." When Jude just looked at him, the man clenched his jaw. "If the contacts you listed verify your story, I'll ask Davis some questions." Clearly the man thought Jude would have to be satisfied with that.

"And you'll question Weale. He's not in town. He might be at his place in Jackson Hole."

The sergeant slammed the pen down on his desk. It rolled to the edge. Teetered there.

"We'll do our job, Bishop. Just stay out of the way. And do not—I repeat—do not attempt to approach either of the men on your own. Because if they have cause to lodge a complaint against you, I will personally haul you in myself."

* * * *

Violent shudders worked through Mia in great heaving waves. Her skin was clammy, her mind numb with disbelief. All the fears that had haunted for years coalesced into this moment. The monster from her past had clawed through the fabric of her memory and lunged into her present. And this time the monster wore a face. Somehow that was even more terrifying.

"There." Sounding pleased with himself, the man working above her set down the metal scissors. "It wasn't easy to cut those clothes off without nicking you, especially with the way you're shaking." He'd managed to do so without releasing her from her bonds. Now he loosened the tape over her mouth with surprising gentleness. "Say thank you, Eleven."

Her lips parted. "Go…to hell."

His slap was sharp and vicious. It rocked her head to the side and for a moment stars danced beneath her eyelids. "Ungrateful. You always were. It's to be expected, I suppose. Does a slab of marble thank its sculptor? A canvas its artist? And I'm rushing." He stood and picked up the scraps of fabric and the scissors. Busied himself for a few moments disposing of the material in a wastebasket. Taking the scissors back to the cupboard he'd gotten them from.

The cupboard was above a short counter and were loaded with boxes. Supplies he used with the women he enslaved? He took a box off the shelf, opened it with the scissors and then disposed of the wrapping. When he approached her again she rolled away. Didn't get far before he caught up with her. "First things first." She struggled mightily as he shoved his knee between her legs to open them and took swab samples. Then he rose, carefully placed the swabs inside the case provided and carried it back to the counter. "Safety is critical. Who knows what you've been doing and with whom while you were roaming around lost for the last few years."

Lost. A hysterical laugh welled up in her chest. As if she'd merely been off course. When in reality she'd spent the last five years running as far and fast as she could away from him.

"You killed that man." The horror of watching the swift brutal attack was emblazoned on her mind.

"Think, Eleven." He thumped her forehead with his index finger. "I could hardly let him live after what he'd done for me." He must have read her thoughts in her expression. "Ah. I see the mental processes are waking up. Too much information can be a dangerous thing. You're the first to have seen my face, given that cretin's ineptitude. That will require some careful consideration. Not that you'll be slipping away from me again."

He got up and went over to the wall opposite the cupboard where a long Plexiglas container with an attached cradle of sorts was tucked in the corner. It was about six feet long. Two feet high. It had a lid that latched on to the body at several junctures. The man released each fastener. Struggled to lift the lid off and lean it against the nearby wall. Her heart scrambled inside her chest like a wild thing, sensing the horror to come.

He looked at her and his smile sent hot balls of dread spreading through her veins. He was an average looking man. His nose a little too short for his face. His mouth a bit petulant. A non-threatening façade to hide the evil within. "I've given this a great deal of thought."

Striding over to her he picked her up easily and carried her over to place her in the clear box. Her weight had the container swaying on the attached cradle. "Your boot camp training was quite thorough. One can't expect a second round of training to be successful given the apparent failure of the first. At least not without adjustments." Leaning forward, he fiddled with a faucet mounted above the receptacle. For the first time she noticed the hose connected to the front. A thin trickle of tepid water began dribbling from it.

He reached up for another twist of the knob and the trickle turned to a slow stream. "You can get anything off the Internet. Even made it to spec for me. But you haven't seen the most ingenious part." The heavy lid was lifted and fitted into place. Observing the tiny pinholes that perforated the inside of it had despair crashing over her with the force of a riptide. Mia battled to withhold a low moan of despair. Because it wasn't difficult to imagine the function of the container.

He took another hose that was hanging loose on the wall and fitted it to the lid above her. Within moments a fine mist began spraying through the small holes at the top. "I know you'll be tempted to fight. To struggle. Let me show you what will happen if you do." He rocked the box violently and her eyes widened as the trickle at the front turned into a gush. The light mist became a heavy spray.

In the short bout of activity, at least three times as much water entered the chamber. "Stop!"

He laughed delightedly, giving the side of the container an affectionate pat. "It's motion activated. The hoses begin the flow, but the slightest movement of the box increases it substantially. There's a drain, of course, but it can only be operated from the outside. Struggle or not, it will take a bit to fill and I have to get back to my guests." He straightened. "Probably should change my clothes first. I'll be back in a bit. It's when the chamber is nice and full that the fun really starts." She heard a repeated clicking sound. Realized in a wash of despair that he was latching the lid.

And the tiny sound of each lock being secured just punctuated the bout of misery she knew was just beginning.

* * * *

Hunter gave him a hard look as they walked out of the police station together. "Why are you here? Where's Mia?"

"That's the question of the day." Jude filled him about about the hotel fire and Mia's subsequent disappearance.

The operative slowed his pace as he listened, eventually coming to a complete halt.

"Fuck me. This is all my fault. I should have let the cops rot out there until the other officer was on site. Goddamn it!"

With a nudge of his elbow Jude got the other man moving again. He felt as though he were standing in place already; as if time was rushing by while he was on a treadmill trying to catch up. "Unfortunately, I don't think that would have made a difference. There's no way the cop would have kept her in there while the fire alarm was having the building cleared?"

"Yeah, but the cop would be armed," Hunter said darkly.

"Paulo and Blake will be here in a matter of hours. Raiker's is sending a couple investigators tonight." Jude lifted the fob and unlocked the door. As they both slid into the vehicle, he continued. "I want you to go Jackson Hole. Someone has to keep an eye on Weale. We can't afford to overlook the possibility that taking her to his place there would be a quick way to get her out of town."

"No." Hunter correctly interpreted Jude's narrowed look. "We aren't splitting up. Not with the way things are going. You can send two of the other ops there when they get in. And in the meantime I can hire a PI to track down Weale and keep tabs on him. But I know you well enough to figure you're hedging your bets. You don't expect her to be in Jackson Hole. You think she's here where Weale's employer is." When the seatbelt alarm dinged Hunter belatedly secured his.

The problem with hiring your friends, Jude thought as he started the car and drove out of the lot, is that they knew you too damn well. "We've got a direct line to Weale. I don't have proof that Davis is involved, other than the email that was sent to Munson yesterday when Weale wasn't here. But nothing the cops would find convincing."

"Then what are we waiting for?" There was a grimness in Hunter's voice to match Jude's. "Let's go get some."

* * * *

If she gave in to the stark hopelessness filling her, Mia knew she wouldn't have a chance. There had to be a way out. The monster said he'd had the chamber made to order. But, she reasoned, shivering as the water lapped under her shoulders, the manufacturer couldn't have known how it would be used. Surely the weight of a full size adult would put a strain on it, wouldn't it? Even aquariums, built to withstand the pressure of the water they would hold, might give if something within applied even more force.

The constant mist collected inside, minuscule drops melding and merging to form crooked pathways tracing down the interior the glass. Her bound wrists were behind her. Useless. Her best chance was to explore with her secured feet. She drew her knees up, alarmed when even that movement had the container swaying. The mist instantly grew heavier. The hose gurgled and sent a violent gush of water from the front opening. A ball of dread lodged in her throat, Mia went very still until the flow slowed again.

A long breath shuddered out of her. She looked around the room frantically, seeking inspiration. It was a fairly small space, only a few feet longer than the box she was in, but there was a door next to the cupboard. Another room? A closet? Recalling his mention of boot camp earlier, she stared at the space with new eyes.

When she'd managed to escape she'd run out a stout wooden door. Up stone stairs, through an unlocked door, then suddenly she was outside. She'd traveled down no steps today. This was a garage, with what looked like a false wall concealing this space from the outer area. Her gaze traveled slowly around it. The walls and ceiling were covered with a thick white padding. Though she'd never seen anything like it before, it suddenly occurred to Mia that it was there for soundproofing.

A frigid shiver crawled up her spine, one vertebra at a time. Deliberately she tried to send herself back to the days when she'd first been captured. Everything inside her shrank from the memory. The drugs. The beatings and repeated rapes. But the place she'd been in had been small, hadn't it? Concrete walls. She'd been hooded when she arrived at 'training' both times and again when she'd left. She'd been alone there.

The building where she'd been imprisoned with the others had stone walls. Stone floors that were so chilly in the winter he'd allowed them to earn rugs for their cells. Mia's behavior had never merited one.

There had to be a reason this room was soundproofed when their prison hadn't been. Perhaps in their cells there'd been no chance of anyone hearing them, even if they'd dared make a sound. When she'd escaped Mia couldn't be sure how far she'd traveled before seeing a house because she'd tried to avoid roads. Move only at night. Because their prison had been isolated?

And this place must hold the risk that someone might hear a woman screaming in agony.

The realization solidified her resolve. Tamping down the dread at what she was about to do, she lifted her feet from the floor of the Plexiglas container. The water pressure increased slightly. It was lapping above her shoulders now. How long to fill it? She tried not to consider the answer. She raised her feet, one fraction of an inch at a time, consciously aware that the action had the mist turning more to spray. The trickle from the front opening increased to an even flow. By the time her feet were pressed against the lid of the container, every pulse in her body pounded with a frantic intensity.

Taking a deep breath, she kicked at the lid with all her might, shutting her eyes to the instantaneous spurt of water. It ran down the sides of the vessel and she felt it creeping into her ears and the sensation was almost enough to have her hesitating. Until her gaze landed on the door to the next room. Four's words blazed across her mind.

We are twelve with the new girl at boot camp.

If there was another woman locked inside the next soundproofed space, Mia was going to do whatever she could to get them both out of here.

She drew her knees back and kicked her feet hard at the top. The water spilled down the sides of the container. Jetted through the front hose. But she didn't stop. Couldn't. The lid was heavy. She'd see him struggle to even lift it. Changing tactics, her next kick was aimed at the front panel of the enclosure. With all her might Mia slammed her feet against it over and over again, the answering incoming surge of water keeping time with the force of her kicks.

* * * *

"These binoculars suck."

Jude could heartily agree with Hunter's muttered assessment. The equipment at headquarters far outpaced what they could find at the local department store. The narrower vision view consistent with high magnification glasses was worse than expected and they were far more difficult to keep focused. But they allowed him to keep an eye on Anthony Davis, so they served their purpose.

They'd had to approach the house two miles out, creeping as close as they dared to the party that was being hosted in the back yard of the Davis home. As a house it was impressive, a three-story structure featuring multiple porch lines and soaring peaks, acres of plate glass hemmed in by gleaming diagonal wood siding.

"The sale of old crap must pay a helluva lot better than Bishop Enterprises," Hunter muttered over the cell.

Each of them had taken a different angle of the house. Jude had a center view of the back yard, where at least one hundred people were gathered. Hunter was on the side of the crowd, well beyond the detached structure that must be another garage. Given of the size of the holdings he'd found online for the family, he could be fairly certain they were still on Davis property. But they were nearly three hundred yards out from the house, where the manicured grass had been allowed to revert to a natural prairie state. The tall grass would hide them from view for as long as they wanted to watch.

Jude was just interested in observing as long as Davis was there. His binoculars were trained on him now. Despite the fact that the temperature hovered in the mid-eighties, Davis wore a button down shirt with sleeves rolled up to mid arm and dark slacks.

A three-piece band had started playing about an hour ago. Some of the group was eating at long covered tables inside a voluminous white tent. Others were clustered in small groups enjoying cocktails and conversation. Two couples were dancing to the music, perilously close to the pool.

They were no closer to discovering where Mia was being held. Or even what part Davis had played in her disappearance. And that knowledge was a torch to the patience he tried to summon. As long as he had Davis in his sights, Jude could be certain the man wasn't near Mia. The PI that Hunter had found in Jackson Hole who was currently camped outside Weale's place was fairly certain the man was alone.

Which still left whoever had snatched her in the first place. Someone hired by Davis, maybe.

"Doubtful she'd be in the house."

"Agreed." Jude looked at it again. It was huge. From what he'd discovered mother and son lived there together.

"And somehow I don't see him keeping enslaved women in the basement of his business."

Jude watched Davis throw his head back and laugh at something said by a gray bearded gentleman before clapping the man on the shoulder. The picture of the genial host.

"What else do they have for property?"

"From what I could gather online, among their other holdings they have about ten thousand acres of land, mostly rented to neighbors."

Hunter gave a low whistle. "If this doesn't pan out we should determine what they don't rent and take a closer look."

The muscles clenched in Jude's belly. Not because it wasn't a good thought, but because if this surveillance didn't elicit any further information, then that would mean they'd wasted valuable hours finding Mia. He couldn't let himself think about what might be happening to her in the meantime, because then this hot wall of panic would turn into an inferno. A man could be crippled in the grip of it. No good to Mia at all.

Instead he forced himself to think of her mental toughness. Her ability to face trouble head on. He needed to believe she could do that now, at least until they found her. Needed to believe that she had a bit more time.

His focus sharpened as Davis started moving toward the throng of people. At first he just looked as though he were mingling, but after several minutes it was clear that he was making slow progress toward the corner of the house. "He's moving your way. You see him?"

"I've got a view of something even more interesting," the operative said. "There's a Davison City police car coming up the lane."

* * * *

Escaping from their guests was like trying to extricate himself from the tentacles of an octopus, Anthony thought when he was finally able to slip around the corner of the house. He checked his Rolex. It wouldn't do to leave Eleven alone too long. Until she realized the very serious consequences of struggling inside the chamber, he couldn't be sure just how quickly it would fill.

Her first retraining lesson would begin when it did.

He walked toward the front of the house until he could be certain he was out of view of the guests then started across the drive toward the garage. And was shocked to see a police car making its way toward him.

His first thought was the business. They'd had break-ins before, despite a top of the line security system.

There were several special items purchased for just this occasion, which might be a temptation to someone in the know. Anthony veered toward the cruiser, anxiety welling.

"Dale." He greeted Dale Carter with a fixed smile. "Something wrong downtown?"

The investigator got out of the car. Shut the door behind him. "Nope. All looked quiet when I drove by."

At the man's answer Anthony felt the pressure in his lungs release a bit. It returned in the next moment at the man's next words. "We had a missing persons report filed in town today, and your name was mentioned as a person who might know something about it."

He didn't have to feign astonishment. Sully was dead, his body safely locked away in the garage. And no one else knew a thing. In the next moment, indignation bloomed. Who would *dare*?

"A child?"

"No, no." The man was visibly uncomfortable. "A woman by the name of Mia Deleon. Your name and Eldon's came up in the report. I'm sorry, Anthony we have to check it out."

This bite of anxiety was a new experience. Years ago the investigation into Eleven's story had gotten nowhere near him. As far as he could tell it had collapsed under a complete lack of leads. As it should. How could mention of him come up now? "I'm afraid the name doesn't ring a bell."

"Here's a picture." Dale handed him a newspaper clipping that must have been taken several years ago. "Not recent, but best I could do."

Anthony pretended to study it. "Pretty girl." He manufactured a grin as he handed it back. "Wish I could say I had seen her. Somehow the women I meet don't look like that, and if Eldon's having different luck he sure hasn't bragged about it to me. Where was she last seen?"

There was no answering humor on Carter's face. "Your hotel. Everyone was evacuated, but I can't find anyone who recalled seeing her. I'm trying to track down Bruce Sullivan, one of the security team. I was told he cleared the floor her room was on. No one has seen him for several hours."

And here was his opening. Folding his arms over his chest, Anthony lowered his voice confidentially. "I don't know what you may have heard from the fire chief, but he reported to me directly. There was no fire at all. Smoke grenade canisters were found on every floor. I think they're chalking it up to a very expensive prank."

"I'd call it something more serious than that, if the false alarm was instigated to cover up a kidnapping. If you see either the woman or Bruce Sullivan, I'd appreciate a call." Dale got in the car. Slowly backed it down the crowded drive.

Anthony watched it go, and then walked swiftly toward the garage again, a plan already forming. Sully would make a perfect patsy. Dale already suspected the man might have been the last to see Eleven. When it became clear that both Sully and the woman were gone, they'd be chasing after the guard, diverting attention from Anthony.

In death Sullivan might prove to be more useful than he'd been alive.

15

The glass had held despite the assault Mia had waged on it. The water had risen fast. So fast. It parted and closed around her, eddying around her chin. Her hair spread in the water, encircling her head like a feathery wreath. She was still now, crouched on her knees with her face pressed as close to the lid as she could manage. She wondered if she could count how many more pulses of liquid would be pumped in before even the small space devoid of it would be gone.

There had been many times in her captivity that she'd thought she would die. Especially in those first brutal weeks. Even more times later when she'd longed for death. But here, now, she could feel the imminence of her demise hovering with an almost physical tangibility.

Water lapped into her nose and she shook her head, causing the container to rock. She closed her eyes as she heard the hose feed the liquid in faster and tried to wipe her mind of everything else. But regret was one thing that refused to be dislodged.

She'd failed, miserably. She wouldn't be part of rescuing the women she'd left behind. Nor could she assist the one in the next room escape. And she would no longer need to anguish over a possible future with Jude. She had no future now. In the end the decision had been made for her.

Jude. His name shrieked across her mind, a silent howl of desolation. For a woman who had taught herself to expect so little, he represented the ultimate overreach. It'd been paralyzing to have everything she thought she knew about herself be so easily swept aside. Crippling for a woman who'd never wanted to discover that she could long for something until it was a physical ache.

He'd made her want, even when she knew how dangerous yearning was. He'd almost made her believe that there could be something more.

But she'd been right all along. Having something to lose was the worst kind of pain.

There was a slight sound. The quick stride of footsteps. Then a shadow fell over her. "Willful." That hated voice had her skin chilling in the warm water. The next moment there was a gurgle and the drain in the corner of the container opened, greedily gulping the contents of the vessel. "See how dangerous your stubbornness can be? Obedience can save your life, Eleven. I'm going to make sure that's a lesson you never forget."

The level of the liquid lowered to below her chin. Her muscles slackened in involuntary relief, the bunched tension easing as her body relaxed. She hauled in a deep gulp of air. Then the drain snapped closed again. "This is what disobedience feels like." He went to the foot of the container, grasped it in both hands and rocked it back and forth violently.

Mia had been on her knees, but they slipped out from beneath her now and she submerged under water. Her feet scrambled beneath her, tried to get purchase. She pushed against the bottom with her bound arms, attempting to arch her body out of the water. She broke the surface, sputtering and gasping. The tiny taste of oxygen was all she got before he repeated the action, the movement sending the water sloshing over her head.

The container began to fill rapidly as he swung it back and forth on the cradle. She choked and gagged, water up her nose, down her throat, and burning a path to her lungs. Mia tried to get her feet set against the glass so she could rise to a half sitting position, but the constant motion made it impossible. Each time he swung the Plexiglas box she was knocked off balance and slipped under the liquid again.

She was drowning. Panic surged. Water surrounded her, filling her sinuses. Trachea. Chest. Her lungs expanded, swelling with the need for oxygen. Then burst, as she coughed and inhaled more liquid, her body flailing as she gagged repeatedly, each time swallowing more water.

Mia wasn't sure how long it was before she was aware the container had stilled. She was resting on the bottom of it, stomach cramping as she retched violently. The last few inches of liquid seeped slowly down the drain. The sound of the trap closing again made her stomach lurch. "No," she croaked, too weak to push herself up. "Not again."

"Yes again and often. Until you've learned complete submission."

The sound of his voice ignited a quick and steady flare of hate. Mia felt the mist starting. The trickle from the hose streamed down the wall and began to pool around her body. "I'll be back soon to help you again. And afterwards you can join Thirteen in boot camp for a group lesson. I'll show you just how much I missed you."

She squeezed her eyes shut, revulsion washing through her. And wondered just how long it would take her to forget what it had ever felt like to be free.

* * * *

A band of tension was squeezing him, making it impossible to remain still. Jude crawled up beside Hunter who looked unsurprised at his presence. "Still no sign of him."

Frustrated, Jude raised his binoculars. There'd been no point in watching guests mingling at the party. The man he was interested in was no longer present, and hadn't been for the last twenty minutes.

"What the hell is he doing in there?" The question scraped at Jude's nerves. "He's got a yard full of guests and according to the showroom saleslady I talked to, this is a pretty big deal for the business." At first he'd thought the man had meant to get in a car and leave, but Hunter had reported differently. "I need a look inside that garage."

At that moment Davis exited a side door on the structure, carefully locking it behind him. He adjusted something on the doorjamb and then turned and strolled back toward the party, his stance jaunty. Rejoining his guests, Davis snatched a drink off a tray held by a waiter and turned to a group of people who were conversing.

"Cocky little prick," Hunter muttered. He and Jude were lying side by side on their bellies a hundred yards out in the tall prairie grass, which, after several hours was beginning to feel like lying on a bed of needles.

Jude was studying the garage. "No windows. And no question that the doors are alarmed." He looked at his operative. "So if we can't get through the window or door, how do we get in?"

They answered in unison. "Through the wall."

Twenty-five minutes later Jude was crouched behind the detached garage, with a cordless Sawzall, two twelve-inch blades and an extra battery. After fetching the purchases in town, Hunter had resumed his previous position. The vantage point would give him a view of Jude and anyone who might approach from either side of the structure. Behind Hunter were acres of tall grass riddled with wildflowers. As long as he stayed flat, he had some cover from anyone going by on the road out front. Jude would be more visible.

Wearing the gloves Hunter had bought, Jude stuffed the packaging he'd removed from the products back into the bag. He fit the blade into the saw and turned it on. The product was labeled as low noise output, but it seemed ridiculously loud to him. He turned it off again. Called Hunter. "Did you hear that?"

"Hear what?"

Relief filled Jude as he disconnected. If the operative couldn't hear the sound of the saw, there was no chance that someone at the party could, especially with a band playing. Restarting the instrument, he cut through the exterior siding, put it aside. Then he set the saw to the drywall. Didn't get far before striking something unforgiving. Thinking he'd hit a beam, Jude moved the blade to the left six inches and tried again with the same result.

He stopped to look at the blade. It was already bent in one place. What the hell? This time he cut away just a piece of dry wall large enough that he could use the light on his cell to peer inside it. Cement.

"I'm going to the east side." Picking up the tools, but not the debris, Jude went to the corner of the structure and peered around it.

"What?" Hunter's voice on the cell was apprehensive. "Why? You're in full view of the road from there."

"I hit concrete block. I'm going to try closer to the front."

"Not exactly stealthy, but I'll shift over. Try to keep both sides in view."

Jude moved halfway down the east wall of the garage. Hunter was right. The house was set deeply back from the road, but the detached structure was far closer to it. Four hundred feet maybe. And he'd be clearly visible to any vehicle going by or to a late arriving guest. It was still light. He could only hope that anyone catching sight of him would think he was working for the owners.

He had better luck with the Sawzall at the new location and it wasn't long before he had cut away a big enough piece of drywall. He removed it. The wall studs were set sixteen inches apart, but that gave him ample room to wiggle inside.

Turning, he reached out a hand and gripped the piece of drywall he'd cut away and pull it over the hole. The result likely wasn't going to stand up to close scrutiny, but it was better than leaving the hole there for someone to see. Satisfied, Jude stood up and looked around.

It was a roomy area, with easily enough space for four cars. The attached garage at the house was similar in size. But there was only one vehicle in this one. A functional workbench stood on one wall with a sink tucked into the adjacent corner. Next to the sink were four floor-to-ceiling shelving units. Assorted lawn equipment hung neatly on hooks across the garage.

"Tell me what you see."

Jude gave a grim smile. It was always far worse being the guy on the outside. The not knowing was nerve-wracking. "Not much. Just a garage with a piece of shit vehicle in it." He started toward the car. "Why would the Davises have a piece of shit car?"

"For slumming? Is it locked?"

Jude was in the process of discovering that for himself. "Nope." He leaned in the passenger door he'd opened and checked the glove box. Found the registration. "Bruce Sullivan. See what you can find out about him." He shut the glove box. Backed out of the vehicle and straightened to look around. There was a large garbage bag, the kind that lined big trash bins, lying on the floor about six feet from the car's back bumper. Jude looked into it. Empty. He looked back at the car, swamped by a feeling of foreboding. "You got anything for me yet?"

"He's on some social media sites. Here. I'm going to send you a pic from his LinkedIn page." The man broke off for a moment. "Jude, it lists him as working security at the Davison."

A moment later he was looking at the photo Hunter had sent him. He swore an oath. "This is one of the guys that jumped me the other day." Adrenaline, mingled with a singular dread, was pumping through him. "He snatched her. And then he brought her directly to Davis."

"That's enough then. Let's get the cops in here."

"It's enough for me. Maybe not for a warrant. The Davis family has a lot of influence." And it wasn't enough for Mia. Anxiously he scanned the interior again. Where the hell had Davis taken her? "Give me more time." Mia had said there were stairs where she'd been kept, he recalled and checked the walls carefully for any sign of a concealed passageway. That could be the answer. Perhaps she was even now being held below this structure with the other victims. But if that were the case, there would still need to be a staircase to access the basement.

Jude looked around the interior with new interest. "What would you guess were the dimensions of this structure?"

"Fifty by fifty, maybe."

Almost square. Jude walked the area, making a mental estimation. "I wouldn't guess the inside as more than fifty by forty." The cement he'd hit on the back wall. The connection finally hit him. "He's got a hidden room." One that ran the width of the building and perhaps housed a stairwell that would take him to Mia.

He went to the back wall and began to examine it inch by inch. Then looked at the shelving. Reaching out a hand, he gave one of the shelves a tug. It held fast. Bolted to the wall. He started shoving items aside to better inspect the sheetrock. And finally found the switch cleverly concealed nearly behind the side of the metal shelf closest to the sink. When he pushed it the expanse of sheetrock and shelving swung open. "I'm going in," he said to Hunter. "I'll keep you posted." He tucked the phone away in his jeans pocket and stepped inside the shadowy interior.

Dim recessed lighting punctuated the ceiling. Jude had expected to find himself at the top of a staircase. Instead he walked through the passageway into an image from hell. "Mia!" She was lying still, so still in a large glass case that almost looked like a coffin. Water was dribbling into it. The liquid swirled beneath her, around her, high enough to reach her elegant cheekbones. When he rushed to her side she turned her face to look at him, eyes wide and frightened, and the tidal wave of relief was nearly debilitating. She was alive.

"What the hell?"

He ran his hands over the clear box she was in. Saw the latches attaching the top to the body of the vessel.

"There are locks on the lid."

"I see them." His fingers felt fat and clumsy as he undid each one, but he couldn't remove it without dealing with the hose attaching to the lid. Rounding the case, he shut off the faucet mounted on the wall. Then went back to unscrew the hose from the top. The lid was surprisingly heavy. As he lifted it off, Mia lurched upward, water streaming from her hair. She half leaped into his arms as he reached for her. "Oh, God, baby." He held her tight, the feel of her an exquisite pleasure he'd feared he'd never experience again. His shirt was saturated from holding her soaked body, but it didn't account for the moisture in his eyes. "What the hell did he do to you?" He reared back, took her face in his hands, anxiety riding him. "What is that thing?"

She shuddered against him and burrowed more closely in his arms. "A chamber he had made to teach me obedience. It fills up…" She swallowed hard. "It's like drowning. I thought I was dying. Then he emptied it but he's coming back to do it again. We have to get out of here…"

Spying a towel in the corner he led her over to it, bent to snatch it up. He wrapped it around her and tried to beat back the rage that threatened to engulf him. Drowning. The strange box in the corner took on a newly sinister appearance. And if Jude had his way, Davis would be the next one to feel its effects.

"Did you see a staircase in here anywhere?" When she looked confused, he added, "I thought maybe he might have the women kept under this place."

Doubtfully, she looked around. I don't think so. When I escaped and ran up those stone steps I was outside. I think…" Her gaze fixed on the enclosure next to them with its padded walls. "I think that might be his boot camp. And I know someone is in there. Thirteen, he called her. He said…tonight. We'd all be together tonight."

Jude went to the door of the space. Instead of a doorknob it had a keyless entry. He drew a quick mental blueprint. The section of space they were standing in was L-shaped but small, the area taken up mostly by the cupboards, counter and the vessel he'd found Mia in. The way the next room jutted out it almost seemed as though it was barely an alcove. But there had to be an additional space inside it that was at least forty feet by ten.

"Can you get her out?"

"I don't know." He went over and scrutinized the padding on the wall. Slid his hand beneath it. "Concrete. The whole back wall is, so I imagine that these interior ones back here are, too." He pulled out his phone to call Hunter. Noticed he'd missed a text a couple minutes ago. Likely when he was lifting Mia out of that sick bastard's torture chamber. He read the message. Froze.

He's coming.

Springing into action he hurried her out of the room with one arm clamped across her back. "Quick. He's on his way." He felt the sudden violent shudder that went through her as he rushed her across the garage floor to the gap he'd cut in the wall. Davis would pay. Dearly. But not until Jude was sure Mia was safe.

They heard a slight noise. A shoe on gravel, just outside the side door. "Get down and crawl through there. Head north, left, and run like hell. Hunter's in the tall grass beyond the yard. Hurry!"

She crouched down to crawl through it. Hesitated. Turning, she rose to grab his arm, her voice insistent. "You'll come right after me?"

"I will. Go!"

But she was barely through the hole when the side door pushed open. Jude had a split second to make a decision. And turned to face the man that was entering.

Anthony Davis took several steps inside before he stopped. Caught sight of the opening to his hidden room and his jaw dropped. "No!" His voice was anguished. Enraged. He started toward it. Noticed Jude.

"Yes." He stepped away from the wall, saw Davis' gaze go to the area he'd cut out of it. "You do have the damnedest time hanging on to her."

"What have you done with Eleven?" The anguish was gone, leaving pure fury in the man's tone.

"Mia." Jude gritted the word as he stalked toward him. "Her name is Mia, you sick fuck. The only time you'll see her again is when she's testifying against you. But before things get that far, you answer to me."

"You think I'm afraid of you? You? With your chewed up face, scuttling around stealing other people's possessions?" Davis took two quick steps to the workbench. Grabbed a crowbar that was hanging above it. "I'll smash your skull and go back to my party. Tell everyone I walked in on you as you killed Sullivan after he kidnapped the girl for you, then turned on me."

Jude glanced at the car, realization blooming. "He's in the trunk?"

Davis smiled. Came closer, hefting the instrument threateningly. "Where you put him. The two of you planned to frame me. You broke in to allow him inside."

"Nice try." He scanned the area for a weapon. Davis held the most lethal one. He went to the opposite wall and took down a spade. Cocked it like a bat and stepped toward the other man. "How do you expect to counter Mia's version of events?" The rage drumming through him turned to ice. "The way you tried to drown her." While Jude watched from afar wondering what the hell the man had been doing in the garage. A fist of guilt clenched in his chest.

"No one will listen to Eleven." He came near enough for a practice swing, dancing away when Jude stabbed at him with the shovel. "The didn't believe her last time. She has no credibility." Davis swung the crowbar and connected with the handle that Jude held horizontally to take the blow. The vibration from the connection thrummed through the wood. He switched positions to swing it at the other man and caught him in the shoulder with the metal blade. Smiled at his exclamation of pain. "You've got a heavier weapon, but shorter reach." They circled, each looking for an opening. Parrying. "You're going to have to get closer than that."

"Am I?" Davis swung again then backed up a few steps. "I like my odds."

Jude's gaze went to the opening in the wall behind him. The other man was positioning himself to make a run for it, he realized. "Maybe you've got another weapon inside there. In case you need to protect yourself from the women you've tortured for years."

"Taught." The man punctuated the word with a swing that Jude warded off. "Perfected. They are thankful for being selected. There's not one who will say otherwise." Unexpectedly he launched the crowbar at Jude and he ducked. It missed his head and slammed into his shoulder. Shockwaves of pain eddied down his arm. He launched himself at Davis, still carrying the shovel. The man scrambled for something in a box on the shelf. Then turned, a gun aimed at Jude's midsection.

He skidded to a halt. Backed up.

"I think you'll agree the odds are in my favor." Davis stalked toward him.

Time slowed. Jude's training in close combat situations clicked in. There were handgun disarm techniques, but the timing was crucial. The move dangerous. "The question is, do you know how to use it?" He inched closer as he said the words.

"Want to find out? Get on your knees. Now. Now!"

"Okay, take it easy." Slowly he started to a kneeling position. Davis was following his movement closely. "Don't sho—" Jude lunged forward, grabbing for the man's wrist at the same time Davis pulled the trigger.

* * * *

The shot echoed across the grass. Some of the party guests turned. Others fled behind the house. Mia and Hunter had been running across the tall grass beyond the garage, away from the property. The sound halted her in her tracks. She jerked around. "Jude."

Hunter stopped, too. He was bare-chested, having given his shirt to Mia, and his jaw clenched as he looked behind him. Then after a fraction of a moment, he put his arm around her and propelled her forward. "He's fine." She heard the lie in his words. "My job is to get you out of here."

Twisting away she spun and sped back the direction they'd come. He hadn't followed her. Hadn't gotten away and now… Panic fueled her feet, gave them wings. He had to be all right. Had to be had to be had to be…

A force nearly knocked her off her feet before two hard hands gripped her. "You're not going back there." Distant sirens sounded. Moments later they were followed by the flash of strobes. The lights were visible before the police cars could be seen coming fast down the ribbon of road in front of the property. "You have to go back for him," she told Hunter beseechingly. "He's you friend! He could be…" Her brain reared away from completing the thought.

"You're my job right now." But the man's face was grim as he changed position and led her toward the ditch where they could hail one of the cruisers. And nothing Mia saw in his expression countered the sick twist of dread that was welling inside her.

...you and I will just be beginning...

There was an insidious fear spreading through her system that his promised beginning was never going to materialize.

* * * *

The scene at the Davis house was chaos. Mia stared out the window of the cruiser at the mob of people clogging the drive. Some were attempting to get in their cars, but two police cars strategically blocked the end of the drive. Mia searched in vain for some sign of Jude. Didn't see him.

She opened the door and got out. "Mia." Hunter was one pace behind her, his hand on her arm.

"No!" She whirled on him then, her tone fierce. "The police are on scene and you don't get to try and stop me. I'm warning you, Hunter. I will hurt you."

His gaze went beyond her. He raised his hands in surrender. "You win." He smiled. "I guess he can handle you from here."

Spinning, she looked in the direction of his gaze and her heart flipped. This time when she took off running, Hunter didn't try to stop her.

The police did. She dodged one who was securing the outer perimeter. Didn't make it past the next. She struggled in the man's grasp, drinking in the sheer joy that was Jude. On his feet. Unscathed. His expression was sober as he talked to a policeman.

Until he saw her. His gaze went intense. He strode away from the officer, who called after him, his strides eating up the distance across the lawn. He broke into a trot. Mia calmed in the officer's grasp until the man loosened his grip. Then she pulled away to race across the grass toward Jude.

The tears running down her face felt foreign. But his arms were familiar. And when they closed around her to hold her close, it felt like coming home.

* * * *

The victim Davis had held in the room he'd used as boot camp had been rescued right away. But it had taken another day to find the spot where the other women were imprisoned, because The Collector wasn't talking. And right now, three days after the arrest, watching the video of that scene was enough to have nausea churning.

The property had been in the Davis family for generations. The original ranch house had once graced the acres. The local history archives described what a showplace the property had been, with one of the few underground barns in the country. It had once been attached by tunnel to the house so the family didn't have to go outside for chores in the harsh Nebraska winters. Nearly one hundred years later the house was gone. And the buried barn had become a playground for a madman.

"He's a sick son-of-a-bitch, but ingenious." Police investigator Dale Carter watched the video with them. "See this structure directly over it? It houses the water and electrical connections. Mrs. Davis claimed Anthony built the place as a hunting cabin, but there's barely space for the utility hookups inside." He sent a quick glance to Mia. "If this is too difficult…"

Jude's hand reached for hers under the table. Interlaced their fingers. "No." She'd watch it through, squelching the memories the scene evoked. "If it was once a barn, how did the animals get in and out?"

The man fast-forwarded to shots of the exits. One had two big double doors that looked like an entrance into the back side of the hill. There had been no sign of them in the barn. Davis must have sheet rocked over them when he'd built the shower and the discipline storeroom.

"Here's the exit you would have escaped from." She squeezed Jude's hand as the next part of the film showed a large door fitted at a slant into the front of the slope. "That isn't the original door or frame. You can see that this was custom made." Another shot showed it lying next to the yawning stairway. "He put in deep panels that would hold soil and used them for planters. So when it's closed it looks just like the rest of the pasture. You can't tell that the door is even there until you're right on top of it."

It'd been unsecured but heavy when she'd run up those steps. He hadn't gone back to lock it. Why bother when the interior door was secured? She could watch all of the footage on the computer with an almost clinical detachment until they got to the part where the women were being led up those stairs. Traveling the same path Mia had taken five and a half years ago.

A sob caught in her chest, and she swallowed hard, beating back emotion. She watched them ascend that stairway one at a time, each wrapped in a blanket. Mia saw familiar faces. Some she didn't know. All shielded their eyes when they reached the bright sunlight they hadn't seen for years.

"Is Davis talking yet?" she asked.

Carter's mouth twisted. "That's not going to happen. He's got some fancy LA defense attorney burying us in paperwork. Doesn't matter. Thanks to you two we had a good idea of where to start looking. There's enough to convict the guy."

"Explain the Eldon Weale connection to me." Jude's question gave her an excuse to take her gaze off that video, even while she felt like a coward for doing so.

Carter leaned back in his chair. "Had the Jackson Hole police pick him up but when we served the warrant on his two houses, we didn't find anything that led us to believe he knew anything about these women being held."

"He received the shipments for the drugs used on them," Jude interjected. "Had a mail drop in another state to do so."

"Yes, and we found a shipment still waiting for pick up when we went to check it out. We found plenty of other stuff, too." The sergeant shook his head in wonder. "I mean, here we have these two guys living in town and we have no indication of what's going on beneath our noses. Davis was using the credit cards he took from some of his victims and buying items online before they were cancelled. Then Weale repackaged them to sell on eBay. Eldon admits he thought Davis was possibly using client information to run a scam, but I guess as long as he got the extra cut he didn't ask questions." Jude snorted and the man gave a wry grin. "Yeah, it's weak but that's his attorney's problem. We'll keep poking at him, especially once we get the records from his mail drop."

"The card use would have muddied the waters for investigators looking for the missing women." At least it had for hers, she'd been told. "I think he might have tipped off paparazzi in my case, claimed to have partied with me in Vegas or LA." And the tabloids had aired the stories with their usual lack of compunction for facts.

He leaned forward to open a file folder and push it toward Mia. "This is a photo of a map we found in Anthony's office."

She picked the picture up and stared at it. And knew without being told what the numbers on it meant. When Jude saw it he glanced at her, concern in his expression. She gave him a tiny shake of her head. She was all right. Finally.

"You can see how the map of the US in the picture is divided into sections and numbered one through thirteen. Employees at the business say the numbers represent districts, each consisting of multiple states. Different salespeople are loosely in charge of clients in the districts assigned to them." The numbers started on the northern west coast and were numbered one through three in descending order. The pattern continued until it ended on the eastern seaboard, which was numbered ten through thirteen.

"He selected an item for his collection from each district," she whispered. There was a small cluster of states labeled eleven, representing millions of people. And somehow, somewhere she'd been the one to come to his attention. Where had he seen her? She knew they hadn't met. Mia hadn't recognized him when she'd first seen him in that garage.

The Collector had told them over and over how carefully he'd chosen them. And it had just been their miserable misfortune to have matched some impossible idea of perfection he'd had that set the wheels in motion.

"I think you're right," Carter agreed. "The map matches up with the home areas of most of the women, although a couple were snatched while they were on vacation."

"Raiker can give you a couple more nails for this guy's coffin." Jude reached to flip the folder closed, shoving it over to the other man. "His lab was able to analyze Davis' voice even though it was electronically altered when he talked to Mia on the phone in West Virginia. Get a sample of his voice and Raiker will run the tests to match them."

"Not to mention the tox screen." When the investigator looked puzzled, Mia explained. "When I was kidnapped in Pennsylvania Jude and I were injected with something. Raiker had his labs do a tox screen on Jude's blood samples. I think you'll find it has the same components as one of the drugs discovered on Davis' property." Perhaps found in those cupboards in the room where she'd been kept.

That made her remember the container she'd been locked in and she wasn't able to conceal a shudder. Seeing it, Jude stood, his chair scraping the floor. "I think we're good for now. I appreciate you keeping us in the loop."

Carter stood as well. "It's the least I could do. Any other detail you can think of that will help us tighten the noose around Davis, make sure you let me know."

They crossed to the door, then Jude stopped. Turned. "Am I safe in assuming the complaint against Hunter Mason have been dropped?"

The man had the grace to redden. "Uh…the complainant rescinded her story. Finally admitted that Bruce Sullivan had put her up to it. Given his part in this thing, it's pretty easy to see it was a ploy to get Ms. Deleon's bodyguard away from her side."

They walked through the station and out the front doors. The realization hit Mia like a physical force. "It's really over." She looked at Jude. "I mean, forever."

"Forever," he echoed. But his voice imbued the word with a totally different meaning. And the look on his face had her heart stuttering. Her hand still in his, he pulled her to a stop before they got to the car. "This is the end of you running, Mia. The end of you never feeling safe. But it can be a beginning, too. For us."

He seemed to be waiting for her to speak. To say something. Anything. But the familiar fear was fluttering, preventing the words she'd most like to give him.

His gaze was intent. "You said once you were broken. We both are. But together we make something whole. Something damn well worth hanging onto. I've never said the words before myself, so believe me I know how scary they are. But I love you, Mia. I don't expect you to be whole. I don't expect you to be anyone other than who you are. I just want you to be as brave about this decision as you've been about every other damn thing that has happened in your life."

Feeling like a fraud, she shook her head. "I haven't been brave. Trying not to feel—at all—is really a sort of cowardice." One that had served her well, she thought wistfully, until she'd met him. "When I heard that gunshot, I realized my days of feeling nothing were over. Because the fear of losing you was…" She searched for the words to describe the terror that had locked up her lungs. Frozen her veins. The memory made her voice shaky. "I can't promise this is going to be quick or easy. But for the first time in my life I'm going to reach for something more. I can promise to love you with everything I have inside me."

He tugged her into his arms in a quick sneaky move, and his embrace was nearly fierce. Reaching up a hand he brushed her hair back from her face with a touch as soft as gossamer. "That's more than I could hope for." His mouth came down on hers, and their kiss helped banish the old anxiety before it could rise.

Hope. With this man at her side it was no longer something to be feared.

39110772R00190

Made in the USA
Lexington, KY
06 February 2015